THE GIRL WHO DARED TO STAND

THE GIRL WHO DARED TO THINK 2

BELLA FORREST

Before the Tower, humanity dreamed of being the first—the first to discover a new land, the first to innovate, the first to unify, the first to destroy. Once something was done, it could never be undone, but it could always be improved upon. Art, writing, math, science... always pushing further and accomplishing more than those who came before them.

Those who came first were remembered in great monoliths that survived eons of war and weather. Some were only written about, their histories and deeds recorded for the world to marvel at. Some did great things. Most did not.

Yet we remembered them anyway—learned about them through books and song. We evolved through them, through their deeds, learning about what was good and what was evil, what was right or wrong, and what worked and what didn't. In exchange, we held the light of their history in our hands, cupping it tightly to protect and shelter it, carrying it forward through history. Their memories and legacies were preserved for as long as humanity continued to survive.

Before the Tower, we knew our legacy. Now, it seemed the last innovation we had was the only one we remembered anymore —the Tower, and the great AI who guarded it, Scipio.

Who had somehow managed to find me, in spite of my desperate attempts to escape his eye.

I managed to sit down before my legs gave out, my heart still pounding so loudly that I could hear its frantic beat in my eardrums. There was not enough oxygen in the Tower to satisfy my lungs, and yet I still tried to find it.

I stared numbly around the old office I found myself in, my eyes tracing the well-used but dusty furniture, the dim lights, the sealed and shut door. Evidently, nobody knew it was here. I hadn't known it was here, but then again—why would I? We were nestled beneath Greenery 1, one of the many long farming floors that jutted out from the sides of the Tower, dangling over the river that provided us with power and fresh water. I was mostly unfamiliar with these floors: I hadn't grown up inside them. But this room was here nonetheless (and decidedly odd, considering it was an office situated directly under an animal farm), buried under the miles of concrete and iron and glass that made up the frame of the Tower—the structure that had both saved and enslaved us nearly three hundred years ago. Although, not many people shared my views on the whole enslaving thing.

Which was only the genius of Scipio, the AI supposedly created to keep us safe. He protected them from so-called dissidents like me.

And here I was—Liana Castell—speaking with him. Scipio. The guy—or thing—that ran the Tower itself. One who would kill me and my friends without compunction because he was the one who ultimately decided who or what was dangerous to the Tower. Frankly, I didn't think an AI should have that much power.

"Are you all right?"

A surprised laugh escaped me as I looked around, trying to pinpoint the source of the voice. How could I even explain the irony without dissolving into tears or screaming in frustration? How could I express the way I felt like I was drowning in the fear that, once again, I had led Scipio and the Knights to our doorstep, and this time we had nowhere to run?

"Hello?" The voice came again, brimming with concern and confusion, and I recognized it for the trick it was. He was trying to distract me.

"How long do I have?" I asked abruptly, my mind already spinning. Maybe if I moved fast enough, I could give everyone time to run away. I could shout a warning down the vent shaft they were undoubtedly still working their way through. Grey had been ahead of me when I'd turned off to investigate the strange sound I had been hearing. If I shouted loud enough, he would hear. Then maybe I could get outside—to the underside of the greenery—and lead the Knights away. Buy everyone time to find somewhere else to hide.

"Have before what?"

I bit back a growl. "I never imagined Scipio as the sort of AI to play dumb."

"I'm not playing."

"So you're just dumb, then. Interesting." Okay, maybe mocking the computer that basically controlled every aspect of life inside the Tower wasn't the best idea, but after losing Cali, a woman who had opened her home to me and my friends in our hour of need, and Roark, the man who had saved me by creating a drug called Paragon to hide my rank, I couldn't seem to care. Devon Alexander, Champion of the Knights, had killed two people who had actually cared for me the way I liked to imagine my parents would have if they weren't so devoted to the Tower. And now I was talking to the very thing that had probably ordered Devon's actions—and could lead him here to finish the job.

"I am not dumb," the synthesized voice exclaimed indignantly. "And you're not asking clear questions."

There was no way to tell if he could see my eye roll, but that didn't stop me from doing it. In no interaction I'd ever had with him had he expressed himself so... forcefully. His demeanor had always been cold and arrogant, making me think of a prince seated on a frozen throne. Then again, perhaps it was due to the fact that I was merely a Squire, an apprentice to the Knights, and wasn't worthy enough for him to be polite. Former Squire, rather. Having filed my letter of resignation in the form of breaking my future boyfriend, now future cellmate, out of a gas chamber meant to kill him.

The Scipio I had imagined had always seemed like a no-nonsense sort of AI. So if I was meeting him face-to-face, I would have expected at least the decency of a straight-up conversation. But nope, it seemed Scipio was just a jerk all around. I shouldn't have expected anything less.

"Fine," I breathed, fighting back my frustration. "How long do we have before the Knights show up?" Each word was punctuated by a slight pause, and I hoped that Scipio somehow managed to interpret those as periods, so he could have a double dose of my annoyance.

My mind was already introducing me to worst-case scenarios, the cruelest of which was being forced back into that tiny split room in the Citadel—where the Knights lived and worked—and being forced to watch my friends die one by one, drowning on the poisoned air that was pumped into the room. And me being helpless to stop it.

Then again, that was a nightmare I had been suffering ever since my mentor had first taken me to that room—and made me watch him kill a woman. Nothing could compare to standing helpless as a woman died, her hands clawing at her throat, her eyes begging for help, and being able to do *nothing* to stop it. Because the expectation was that I would go blindly along with it. Because Scipio decreed it. Because it was what was best for the Tower.

Suddenly a slight hum came up through the chair I was sitting on, and I looked around, searching for the source. But I found nothing in the dimly lit office space.

I waited for Scipio to reply, wondering if he was now just messing with me, and had gone offline in the hopes of keeping me here while the Knights got closer.

I should go—get out of this dusty secret office and back to the others, to warn them. The whole thing felt like a trap. One that Devon had set up just in case we escaped.

In that moment, I felt defeated by the sheer idea of Devon Alexander. He was the Champion of all the Knights. He had fought and defeated challenger after challenger in the Tourney—a month-long competition designed to find the person most capable of leading the Knights. He had thirty years of experience on me. He was fast and strong and had tracked me back to the Sanctum before killing Cali and Roark. So of *course* I had wandered into his delightful little trap.

I lurched up and moved toward the ventilation shaft, intent on leaving as quickly as possible, but Scipio's voice brought me up short.

"I've searched my data banks for any records of a Knight, and it says here that they were lesser forms of nobility who served monarchs as warriors in the Middle Ages. So, unless we have somehow traveled back in time—a prospect that I would remind you is completely preposterous—then I imagine they aren't coming, considering that feudal style of government went extinct over a thousand years ago."

The tempestuous storm of emotions churning in my stomach suddenly grew very quiet, and I stilled, listening to not only his words, but the smug way in which he'd delivered them. Like he'd caught a child pretending, or in the midst of some poorly conceived lie.

He had, in a sense. But he wasn't acting smug because of that. He was acting smug because he thought I was saying something stupid. I was certain Scipio held a certain amount of disdain for me; my failure as a productive citizen of the Tower became evident every time the number on my wrist tracked downward. But for him to be dismissive of my intelligence by pretending he had no idea what a Knight could be was beneath him. He knew I was smart, so why even pretend?

Something was off about him—and I needed to know what it was. I couldn't put my finger on it, but it beckoned to me. I had always had a desire to understand, to know things, and this time was no different. It held me fast, begging me to speak, to *ask*, and before I could stop myself, I did.

"You don't know what a Knight is?"

The room practically bristled with irritation when he answered, his voice strong and rich. "I just *told* you. They are—"

"No," I interrupted. His reaction had been automatic, with no time to manufacture a lie. Or, at least, I hoped so. In fact, I knew next to nothing about how fast the great computer could respond to things. But something inside me told me that it was genuine, which made me reconsider how I phrased the question. I restructured it into one I hoped would shed more light on the oddity of his behavior. "Let me try it like this: do you know what a Knight is, specifically in context of the Tower?"

"In context of the Tower? Um... No. Not really. Why? Should I? What are they? Who are they? Do they wear heavy metal armor?"

My eyes widened at the rapid-fire questions coming at me, and I found myself baffled by the curiosity and excitement in his voice. It sounded genuine. As genuine as an AI could get, I supposed—but still, it was there, and right behind it, a whole slew of other questions.

Which led to my *own* questions. Why would Scipio be curious about the Knights? How could he not know about them? He dispatched orders to them, for crying out loud. And also, what was he even doing down here? He was supposed to be contained inside the Core, able to directly interact with us through our nets, but with no direct way of interacting with departmental computers outside of it. Supposedly none of the other departmental computers could handle the massive load of data that made him up.

And then there was this office, hidden away underneath the Tower. The door that had once functioned was now welded shut, making the vents in the room the only way in or out. Dust covered everything in the room, from the flat surfaces, like the shelves and desk and small table, to the two large sofas, and even the carpets. My footprints on the blue fabric were the only sign that anyone had been down here in a very long time.

Why would Scipio be in an abandoned office? Why here, under Greenery 1, where there was nobody? Except for me and my friends. The answers suggested that this was a trap, but even that didn't make any sense. How would Scipio or Devon have known we would be here? As far as I knew, this place didn't even seem to exist in the eyes of the Tower. It had been sealed away.

"What *is* this place?" I asked, finally settling on one of the millions of questions flying through my brain.

"Oh, this is my home. But it was once the office of my creator, Lionel Scipio, for whom I am named. But he's gone now. He's been gone for, oh, I'm not even sure how long." Scipio's voice was wistful and resentful, and I immediately empathized with him, the pain of Roark and Cali's deaths fresh in my mind and heart.

He had said "Lionel Scipio," and it made sense to a point. The man had been *the* mind behind the Tower, and had brought together the best and brightest of the age to help him make his Tower a reality. Those minds later went on to be the Founders of each department and created the first council. There were several history classes on each of them that I'd had to take when I was younger, but most had been devoted to the visionary behind the Tower. How he had made his dream of a place that would survive the End a reality. How he had spent his life devoted to making that place as ecologically sound as possible, so that humanity could continue to survive, safe from the devastated world outside. How he had created Scipio, a computer that would work effortlessly to avert disaster and keep us safe. How we all owed our lives to him and his creation.

We never talked about the nuclear Armageddon that had occurred three hundred years ago. Or how it came to pass. Or how Lionel had seemed to know it was coming in time for him to finish the Tower before it happened—which was one of my biggest pet peeves.

We knew so little of the world before. There were stories, but the history was short and brief: mankind failed, and the Tower was the ark in which we all hoped to survive the endless radiation that kept us trapped in here.

The only thing that really changed about the Tower was the land around it. Images of the outside world as it had been before confirmed that something had happened outside the walls. Stories were told of gray earth, gray clouds and gray ash that reportedly hadn't stopped falling for decades. The river had been so contaminated that minute doses of radiation managed to avoid getting filtered out, killing many of the young and elderly alike. Then the atmosphere had finally failed, due to the damage caused over centuries of neglect and abuse, and things changed again.

The environment outside had shifted dramatically in the opposite direction. When humanity sealed itself inside centuries before, much of our power was generated by the solar panels covering the walls of the Tower and quite often needed repairs over time. Repairing the panels had invariably carried a death sentence, even at night. Yet the citizens did their duty, and died for the cause of the Tower.

And then that changed, too. The heat grew less and less intense, and soon fixing the panels only resulted in second- or third-degree burns, and then one day, no burns at all. It was a little less than two decades ago that we were able to step outside without protection. By that point, the radiation levels had fallen, especially higher up on the Tower, and we were able to emerge without the white protective suits.

Without the AI Lionel had created, none of this would have been possible, as the machines that kept us alive performed constant checks on the world outside and transmitted the results to Scipio, who would then recommend changes to help bolster the Tower's defenses and preserve as much life as possible if things went wrong. He was not without checks in that regard; each department had its own computers that would investigate and verify Scipio's findings in a matter of seconds. But without him and his checks and balances, we would all die via starvation or suffocation—or we'd be making a mad dash over the irradiated sand outside, trying to find a place to hide.

But that did nothing to help me understand what was happening here. I bit my lip, trying to find some logical explanation to explain this Scipio. This one who experienced sadness—an emotion that I would never have thought to hear from the cold and arrogant voice that had always transmitted to my net.

Was it possible that there could be two of them?

"You're not *the* Scipio, are you?" I looked around the room, not entirely sure what I was expecting him to say.

"No, I am—"

There was a short pop, and then a series of sparks shot out from the wall behind me. I immediately ducked and covered my head, moving away from it. The fountain of sparks died after a moment, and Scipio sighed, the sound distorted by a series of buzzes and beeps.

"—y power is —etting low. Can y-y-y-you —lp me?"

His voice, now broken by sharp popping sounds and digital synthesizers, held a note of desperation, barely audible through its broken quality. I bit my lip, hesitating. I was fairly confident that he wasn't my enemy, but I had no idea what helping him might lead to. I had six other people whose lives depended on me not making a wrong move. I had no idea whether this would jeopardize them.

"*Please.*" The word was filled with terror and desperation, and every one of my concerns faded under the urgency there. I was too raw and vulnerable to let anyone else die today. Because that was how he made me feel: like he was going to die if I didn't help.

Besides, I couldn't let anything happen to him—I had too many questions for him. I had no idea what he was, but something told me he wasn't what I thought, and if I didn't help him now, I risked losing a potential source of information. Possibly even some sort of bargaining chip or ally. I didn't know, honestly, but I *did* know I wouldn't find out if I didn't help him now.

Roark had once told me that the Tower had taught us all *not* to trust in anything, and that it wasn't natural. But it felt wrong not to try. I could only hope I was doing the right thing, and not putting us in further danger.

"Can you tell me what to do?" I asked, already moving over to the wall the sparks had shot out of and trying to spot the problem on my own. Which was laughable, because I had no clue what I was looking for. "And speak slowly. Bad enough I'm risking my life and the lives of my friends on some machine that has pretty much ordered us all dead."

"I-I-I have?"

"Keep on task, you oblivious program. What am I looking for?"

"Und-d-d-er the –sk, there is-is-is-is pan—"

I turned and moved over to the desk, getting down on my hands and knees and peering into the dark, cavern-like space beneath. I still had the light that I had been using to see in the ventilation duct I had been crawling through, and I pulled it out and began shining it around. The dust was thick here. I began running my hands over the carpet, searching. There were often small panels in the floors of rooms like this in the Tower, to help distribute the power load, and I figured I was looking for something like that.

Eventually, my fingers felt a gap toward the back of the desk, and I managed to pinch the carpet fibers between two fingers and lift the carpet up, revealing a small compartment. I had time to see some sort of purple-and-pink light radiating from the hole before I began sneezing—thanks to the dust I had just kicked into the air.

The first sneeze caught me off guard, and the back of my skull smashed into the underside of the desk, followed by a burst of pain. I backed up and sneezed again, barely covering my nose with my arm. And then I kept sneezing.

"C-C-Can —ou... *Beep* —at?"

His voice was getting worse, and I bit back a snappish retort and pinched my nostrils closed in an attempt to stop the sneezing. There was no time for it.

"Tell me what to do," I managed, my voice coming out nasal thanks to my blocked sinus passages.

"Crys-Crys-Crystal... —maged. Bypass... —cuit and *beep* the —stal. S-S-Spa— one... —esk. Sec— d-d-drawer." He broke off with a sputtering sound of tonal sequences playing in the wrong order.

I blinked back the tears the dust was forcing into my eyes and peered at the front of the desk. There were six drawers in total—three on each side and one in the middle. "Are you joking with me?" I said in frustration. "Second drawer from what?"

More tonal sequences—none of them discernable—greeted me, and I huffed.

I jerked the one in the center open first, as it was second from the right, but found nothing but pens and file folders inside. The middle one on the right had several paper files hanging from folders hooked over a rail, and I closed it and reached for the middle drawer on the left. Immediately I was greeted by the feel of objects sliding heavily around, but I ignored them, spotting a long crystal amidst the other odds and ends. I snatched it up, the weight cool and heavy in my hand, and then crawled back under the desk, replaying his garbled transmission in my head in an attempt to unscramble his meaning.

"Did you say bypass the circuit?" I called, peering into the small rectangular hole I had opened in the carpet. The inside was lit with pink-and-purple glowing lights, and as I leaned farther over it, I could make out intricate lines of power moving around each other in some unknown pattern, all of them leading to a groove in the floor—where a long length of crystal jutted out.

The flashes of bright white light emanating from the crystal were blinding, and cut into the soft blue and purple of the power lines. As I inspected it, though, I realized it was damaged, a deep crack running down its side. The whole thing was barely holding together. It looked like it was on the verge of exploding, with sparks of electricity forming around and over the crack. It was definitely time to get it out of there.

I sniffed and inched closer, just as Scipio's broken voice began to give more directions.

"—low the bea... *Beep. Beep.* —lip the swi—... —place... —stal... *Beep.*"

"Not. Helpful."

I puzzled over what he was saying, wincing every time the crystal in the floor flashed and flared violently. Follow the secondary line of power—that part was easy, and I followed it back to where it was diverted from the main line.

"Lip the swi... lip the swi..." I repeated under my breath, trying to understand.

I bit my lip, studying the area underneath the beam of energy. It took me a moment, but finally I noticed a switch right next to the beam, partially hidden under the overhang created by the floor. That must have been what he was talking about. I flipped it carefully, taking pains not to interrupt the stream in any way, and immediately the crystal stopped glowing. But the slot it was inserted into *kept* glowing, showing that the circuit was still holding a charge and not interrupting the power flow. It wouldn't work for long—only a minute or two—before the main circuit overloaded. So I had to move quickly.

Reaching in, I grabbed the fractured crystal and yanked it out. I knew it was going to be hot, thanks to some pretty boring apprenticeship classes I had taken with Zoe, but it was like putting my hand on the surface of boiling water. I dropped it almost immediately, and luckily had been yanking it with enough force that it cleared the hole and tumbled end over end before rolling to a stop on the carpet, little wisps of smoke coming off of it.

I jammed the new crystal into the slot and then flipped the switch, reconnecting the circuit.

There was a crackle, followed by a surge of power, and a searing hot tongue of fire licked a fiery brand over my chest and shoulder. I flew back, caught in an arc of power. I hit the bookcase and doubled over, dazed and confused, and trying desperately to catch the breath that had been stolen from me.

"Oh, that is so much better," a soft voice announced from directly above me. "That crystal had been growing less and less stable for years, and I had to shut down some of my more... frivolous systems to keep from overloading it, so thank you. I finally feel as if I can breathe again." The voice paused, and then drew closer. "How rude of me! You look hurt. Are you okay?"

I became aware of something glowing beyond my eyelids, and managed to pry them open.

A man's face hovered just inches from my own, the planes of his face glowing as if built from pure white light, and as my eyes tracked down his vibrant form, I realized that he was suspended in the air, floating over me.

2

I screamed instinctively and lashed out with my fist, aiming for his jaw. But when my fist made contact—or rather, *should* have made contact—my arm punched through as if nothing were there, while his face did not change or move a muscle.

My eyes bulged as I watched it happen, my brain unable to comprehend exactly what I was looking at. He stared at me through eyes that glowed bright blue, and then pulled away, floating upward. My arm still hung in midair where I had been holding it, and I slowly lowered it, gaping at him.

"Who... what..." I fumbled, trying to settle on one question while fear of any answer kept my tongue partially paralyzed.

The man of light blinked at me, and the corners of his lips quirked downward. His mouth moved. "I'm sorry if I startled you."

It was Scipio's voice. It was him. I had done something when I changed out his power crystal, and this was the result. Now, evidently, he could make himself appear out of thin air.

"It's just a hologram," he said, when I still failed to say anything. "I can turn it off if you want, but Lionel liked to look me in the eye when he spoke to me." His mouth tipped upward as his eyes turned distant, locked in the grip of a pleasant memory. "He said he liked to take my measure, and it took him three times to explain that he didn't mean he wanted my specs."

"Specs?" I asked. He seemed harmless enough, but I was still trying to overcome the fact that Scipio had a body. Not a physical one, sure, but a facsimile of one.

I imagined he would have been handsome, if he didn't glow so much. As it was, the details were fuzzy: glowing blue orbs for eyes, his head topped with a thick mass of inky, blue-black hair. Everything else was lost under the brightness.

"Specifications? My... um... system parameters? My emotional emulator and core processes?" He cocked his head at me, and when I didn't respond, he sighed and rounded his shoulders downward. "Lionel always told me that I shouldn't talk about those things, because it reminded people I was a machine, and not a person."

I considered that for a long moment. The interactions I'd had with Scipio made it seem like he was anything but a person, and couldn't care less about what anyone thought about him. But this version seemed to care; he seemed... disappointed by it, and that gave me pause. It was at odds with what I knew about Scipio. I needed to know more—so I could understand why he seemed so different.

"Are you a... person?"

He stiffened—or rather, the hologram stiffened—and I started to feel less afraid and more... fascinated. His responses were so real that it was like I was talking to a living entity, and not just a program. I didn't know if the Scipio from the Core had a hologram of himself, but I had to imagine that it didn't act like this, even if he did. I started to pick myself up off the floor, my joints and body still aching from the sharp shock I had received.

"I guess it really depends on how you define 'person'," he said after a pause. "I don't have an organic body, if that's what you mean. But... is that what makes you human?"

"Pretty much, yeah," I replied, dusting off my clothes. I caught a glimpse of him looking away, and upon closer inspection, realized that my answer had saddened him. His mouth was turned down in a frown, and his eyes held the look of a man who hadn't heard anything he didn't expect, and yet was still disappointed to have heard it. Like me, whenever my parents reacted in exactly the way I knew they would, and never in the way I needed. It made me feel bad. "I'm sorry, it's just that... people don't view AIs as people, pretty much for that reason alone."

"And you believe everything that everyone else believes?" He didn't ask it maliciously, but rather with pure, unadulterated curiosity.

My immediate thought was, *Of course not,* but I let it stew for a moment, knowing myself well enough to realize that it was more reflexive than anything else. I really hadn't thought about the issue of sentience before, but it had never been presented to me in such a way. In school, we were taught that Scipio's personality matrix was a complex thing, and that the levels of complexity were what made him human-like, but never human. And for many, that made him a god of sorts.

I didn't view Scipio as a god, but I wasn't sure that I could view him as human, either. He had always felt like a machine to me, his demeanor icy and pragmatic. But people seemed to like that, too, saying that our emotions were the enemy of survival, which was why humanity needed his coldness to guide us.

But that meant he did things that were inhuman, to my mind. He initiated quarantines of entire departments if there was a biological threat, and wouldn't open the doors until he determined the threat had passed. If there was a catastrophe, he would seal the department it was in before people had a chance to escape.

To me, he wasn't a person. And he never would be.

On the other hand, he was the only full AI I had any experience with, and it didn't seem fair to judge this one before I even got to know him.

"Not exactly," I decided to reply. "But I think that's a conversation for another time, if I'm honest. Please can you explain to me what, exactly, you are?"

His eyes studied me. And suddenly I felt very much like the frog we'd had to dissect for the Medica apprenticeship lessons. Pinned down and exposed. The only difference was that the frog we'd used in class had been dead. I, however, was very much alive —and didn't like the sensation.

Not to mention how bright he was. I kept trying to meet his gaze, but the two glowing orbs were hard to look at, and there were no details for me to focus on—just an infinite bright glow in the shape of a man.

"Can you please... Can you do something about how bright you are?" I asked, when the discomfort became too much to bear.

"Oh! I didn't even realize. One second." A heartbeat later the glow dimmed, and I looked back up at him. He now looked...

normal, really. As if I could reach out and touch him with one hand.

The blue orbs faded so that they formed natural-looking irises, while the dimmer setting revealed high cheekbones and a straight, strong nose. He was wearing what appeared to be a version of the uniforms we assigned to each department, but an older version, with weird shoulder pieces that looked like a giant grub had latched onto him and decided to die there. Unlike the Tower uniforms, however, his was purple and black, and was glowing lightly, the seams of it brighter than the rest of him.

"Thank you," I said, realizing that I should at least be polite. "Now... my question, if you don't mind?"

"Oh, well, that's easy. I'm the first version of the Scipio program to be developed, and it's because of my program that the later version of Scipio exists."

Of course. That explained so many of his incongruities that it had to be true. I mean, of *course* Scipio had a previous version. I had learned enough from my twin, Alex, to know that every program ever written went through several rounds of what he called "beta testing" before it was introduced into the system. It made sense that Scipio had gone through the same process.

"So... are you like a backup? In case the main AI goes down?"

Scipio studied me for a second. "That's classified," he said.

"By whom?" I shot back, arching an eyebrow. "Lionel Scipio is dead, so unless you're being controlled by something..."

His brows drew together, and I saw a flash of pain on his face when I mentioned the death of his creator. But he pushed it aside quickly. "You're right, of course," he replied, folding his arms across his chest. "And no, I'm not a backup."

It made sense—if he was a backup, they would have kept him

in the Core, not where people could get in and tamper with him. This place was sealed away, but not well enough to justify keeping him here alone. He was interacting with me as well— something I'd imagine the IT would strictly prohibit.

Still, why wasn't he the backup? And what was he doing here?

I opened my mouth, ready to ask, when a distant scream, significantly muted by the distance it traveled and the walls in its way, caught my ears. It was coming from the vent, and I quickly crossed over and knelt down in front of it. I could hear more panicked voices echoing loudly, and although I couldn't make out what they were saying, they were full of fear. It was my friends. And they were afraid.

My heart flared, certain that it was Devon, and I pushed through the vent just as Scipio said, "Wait, where are you going?"

"My friends are in trouble," I replied, not stopping. "I'm going to them."

Whatever his reply was, it got lost in the sound of the vents rattling as I began to crawl my way through, following the sounds of screams.

I quickly reached the junction where I had left my bag, and began pushing it forward, following the shaft toward the sounds of panic and fighting. I rounded the corner and saw light ahead. A dark shadow crossed over it, followed by Grey's grunt of pain.

Tian screamed, a high, shrill sound, and I gritted my teeth and used the palms of my hands on the thin sheet metal to drag myself forward, pushing the bag ahead of me with my chest and shoulders.

The bag fell out of the opening and onto the floor first, and I followed quickly, rolling to my feet into what appeared to be madness.

The room was small—maybe fifteen feet by ten feet wide—and had a thick water pipe running through it. The walls were the same slatted grate that seemed to make up the walls and floors of the outer shell of the Tower, and a dirty yellow light emanated through the ceiling tiles, dimly lighting the room. My eyes darted around, finding my friends in various forms of combat.

Four creatures the length of my arm were attacking them. Their bodies were a carapace of blue-black shine, the mouths divided into four flaps that opened to reveal ring after ring of sharp teeth—which appeared flat, but were razor sharp.

I recognized them instantly, having been called in with Gerome and several other Knights whenever a nest of them was found. They were rust hawks, parasitical insectoids that had somehow evolved to eat metal. They were attracted to rust, but once they found a source, they didn't discriminate—they'd eat either rusted or clean metal for days until nothing else remained.

They were also highly aggressive. And venomous.

Their wings buzzed violently as they swooped down from above, three-toed talons clacking together, trying to get a grip on something—anything. The talons were attached to a venom source at the ankle, the thick venom sacs jutting off the scaly legs like some sort of tumor.

One scratch and a human would die. I had to get my friends out of here. Quickly.

The closest one was to my left, pushing against Grey's forearm, its talons clicking together as it tried to inject its venom into his chest. I crossed over to it quickly, and grabbed the creature from midair at the base of one of its wings.

It flailed as I hauled it back, the segmented body whipping around and trying to get an angle on me. The leathery wings beat against my hands and knuckles in an attempt to break free of my grip, but I wasn't having it. I slammed the rust hawk's body into the wall, hard, and then dropped it to the floor and crushed its head with a hard stomp.

Grey moved in next to me to add a stomp of his own, then darted off. I followed his motion and saw him heading for Zoe and Eric. Quess was in the process of spearing a rust hawk with a metal bar, so I ignored him for now and focused on Maddox and Tian.

Maddox was in the same position in which I'd found Grey, her arm up and holding back the vicious creature. Its mouth flaps were wide open, however, and it was attempting to bite the dark-haired young woman, the ring of muscle that controlled its mouth puckering open and closed as it grabbed at her. She grunted and flinched her head back, trying to get it off of her before it managed to bite or scrape her.

Tian was behind her, the younger girl shielded by the older girl's body. Her blue eyes were wide and filled with fear, yet as I approached, she reached around with one hand and quickly jammed something small and silver into the creature's side.

The rust hawk gave a shrieking gasp, the lethal talons snapping at her as she withdrew her hand, leaving a tiny knife embedded in its side. Yellow fluid seeped from the wound onto the floor... but the creature was far from dead.

I got there just as it drew back a few feet, preparing for another attack, and leapt up and spun, my foot extending. I hit it hard, with a crunch, and heard it impact the wall as I landed, my eyes immediately seeking it out. It was lying on the floor a few feet away, the wings still ... but already starting to flicker and move again.

Tian darted out, a fresh knife in her hand, but I stopped her before she got too close to the stunned creature, knowing full well how dangerous rust hawks could be. Even stunned, their talons worked reflexively, and the only way to survive a scratch from them was through amputation of the limb. But if it hit the face or chest... death was guaranteed. I passed Tian back over to Maddox and then moved over to the rust hawk, quickly bringing my foot up and down to smash the thing.

The resulting squish was gross, but satisfying, and a fresh survey of the room showed me that the other two were down as well, Grey, Eric, and Quess in the process of boot-stomping the final one.

I exhaled, relieved to see everyone relatively uninjured. But it was better to be safe than sorry, and I needed details. "Did they scratch anyone?" I asked, my eyes immediately going to Tian's arms and hands.

I was unsurprised to see Maddox already inspecting the young girl. The two were practically siblings, having been raised together by Cali. Everyone in their group fussed over Tian something fierce, and I could understand why: she was perhaps one of the sweetest creatures to have ever existed, even if she was a bit odd.

"I think we're good," Quess said, tossing the rod he had been wielding onto the ground with a metallic clang. "These things must've moved here in the last month or so. That was the last time any of us was here."

His voice came out hollow, devoid of any life, and as I looked around the room, all I could see were tired and defeated faces, fear radiating from them like heat from a furnace. Zoe looked like she was barely keeping herself from crying by clinging to Eric, while Eric himself seemed more subdued than usual, his eyes sliding over the eight on his wrist. I looked down at my indicator to see the nine still holding strong, but that only made it clear that we weren't protected by the walls of Sanctum anymore. If we had been, the shielding paint would've blocked any signal from coming through, and I would have seen only a green dash. We were exposed without that paint on the walls.

"Quess, did you bring the paint stuff that blocks Scipio's signal?"

The young man looked up at me from the insect carcass on the floor, his eyes empty. He stared quizzically for a few more seconds and then said, "I'm sorry, what did you say?" His cheeks colored with embarrassment.

"The paint," I repeated patiently. We were all on edge or in shock. "The one you created? The one that can protect us from Scipio?"

"What's the point?" Maddox asked angrily. "My mother is gone. She's dead, and it's only a matter of time before Devon finds us again and kills us all."

Tian bit back a cry, and Maddox seemed to realize what she was saying. She wrapped her arm around the small girl and pulled her close. I watched the two rock back and forth, and knew Maddox hadn't meant it that way. She was angry, and hurting, and needed our sympathy and empathy more than anything.

"Liana's right," Quess said tiredly. "We have to get that paint up as soon as possible." "Oh, Liana's right?" Maddox said, stopping whatever she was saying to Tian to look up at Quess, her eyes flat and hard. "Liana's the reason we're down here! She's the reason my mother isn't here. Why Roark isn't here. Why are you even listening to her, Quess?"

Quess raised his hand, his eyes and face placating. "Doxy... Liana didn't mean it. She didn't even know that Devon had tricks like that. We can't hold her responsible!"

"We can!" she snarled, rising to her feet. "We should throw her skinny butt out of here—her *and* her friends. We're better off without them."

Guilt ate at me the more Maddox spoke. She was right. They were better off without me.

"I'll go," I said abruptly, looking up. "Maddox is right—I screwed all of this up for you. If I leave now, I can draw some of the Knights away. Give you time to make this place secure. Just... let everyone else stay here, okay?"

"That's preposterous!" Quess said, his eyes growing large. "Maddox doesn't speak for me!"

The statuesque woman shot him an angry look, and he gave her a little shrug. "I'm sorry, but you don't. Liana did a good thing for her friends, and it turned out badly. And I'm sorry, Maddox, but you were ready to forgive her right then and there because, and I quote, you 'finally had a girl like you to hang out with!' The only thing that's changed between then and now is Devon, and what Devon did to your mother. That is not Liana's fault. She even stayed behind to help."

Surprise fluttered through me, and I looked at Maddox. I had always thought she hated me—she'd never once given any indication to the contrary. She was hostile, aggressive, and terrifying, but...

"Yeah, well, maybe if *I* had stayed behind, my mother would still be alive!" the young woman shouted bitterly, and then her face cracked and she began sobbing, raw, ragged sobs that brought her to her knees, as if her heart were being ripped from her chest. I realized then that Maddox wasn't really angry with me (although she had every right to be), but with herself—for choosing to run, instead of staying behind.

We all stood around, watching her cry, uncertain of what to do.

3

Zoe moved to her and knelt to wrap her arms around the statuesque girl, resting her head on Maddox's shoulder and soothing her. I was immediately grateful that Zoe was there; she always seemed to know the right thing to do in uncomfortable and emotional situations.

Quess followed Zoe's move a heartbeat later, kneeling on the other side of Maddox's sobbing form. He looked up at me, one hand stroking her hair.

"The paint is behind that panel," he said softly, nodding at a section of wall tucked into a corner. Grey turned and moved over to it, slipping his fingers into the grated walling and pulling. It came out easily, revealing a stack of crates and boxes, with several sealed paint cans lining the floor in front of them.

Grey immediately started to pull them out, and Eric moved in next to him so that they formed a little chain as they pulled the supplies out. "We need to start painting immediately," Grey announced, just loud enough to be heard over Maddox's cries.

They were dwindling now, and it seemed that whatever Zoe was whispering to her was helping. I wanted to help too, especially considering I knew that her father had killed her mother, but I couldn't—not with danger still lurking.

"Why?" Eric asked, and I answered.

"It won't be long before they start pinging our"—I pointed at Eric, Zoe, Grey, and myself—"nets to try to get a read on where we are. We need to make sure they can't find us."

"We don't know that he knows about Eric or myself," Zoe said softly, and I looked over at her, surprised to see she was paying attention while calming Maddox down.

"Devon had to have seen you both," I pointed out. "I... I'm sorry, Zo. But, whether it was before, at the Medica, or even at the Sanctum, there was no way he missed you. Even then, when you show up missing, he'll put it together. He's going to start pinging your nets as well as mine and Grey's."

"Yes, but it will take some time for them to get the order to all the department heads to comply," Grey pointed out.

I realized he was right. The scanners in the common area and within the Core were controlled by IT, but the scanners within the other departments ran on their own independent systems, to prevent giving any one department too much power within the Tower itself. While all the scanners were set to sweep for any ones that showed up, it took time and communication to ping individual nets. We had some time—but not a lot.

"Yes, but you can bet he'll start with the greeneries, specifically this one, seeing as this is where he last saw us. We need to start painting."

"Agreed," Grey said, handing the last of the paint buckets to Eric. "Quess, what's the rest of this stuff?"

"Cali and I stocked this place a year ago—we have hydroponic pods, a water source, and several gallons of paint, ready to go." I looked over to see him helping Maddox to stand.

Maddox had regained a significant amount of composure, but her eyes were bloodshot, her nose a raw, red color. "Tian and I can paint," she said softly, earning an encouraging nod from Zoe. Tian uncurled her legs from where she was hugging them to her chest, and used a lash to lift herself to her feet.

"Should keep busy," she mumbled, disconnecting the line and dropping heavily to the floor. She slipped a hand into Maddox's and nodded, her gaze on the floor ahead of her. "It helps to keep busy."

It occurred to me then that this wasn't the first time Tian had lost someone; she'd watched her parents succumb to Whispers, a virulent bacterial infection that was extremely communicable, and colonized the brain, eating away at it until nothing remained. It had even affected her somewhat, but she had managed to survive.

And even now... Her eyes were still wet with tears, but they couldn't hide the spark of determination behind them—which was more than I had hoped for. I was bolstered, seeing it. Knowing that she could still find reason, even hope, to keep pushing forward.

I had to do everything in my power to do the same.

"I'll help," Zoe said.

"After you and Eric get the rust hawks out of here," I said, flashing her an apologetic look. "Be careful—their muscles tend to twitch even after death, and I don't want anyone coming into contact with their venom."

Even as I spoke, one of the rust hawks spasmed violently on the floor, the talons coming together with a sharp click, and Tian gave a startled shriek. Eric quickly crossed the room and planted another boot on it, stilling the frenetic motions.

"We got it," he spat. "We'll drag them back through the vents to the hatch and dump them into the river."

"Make sure it's clear before you drop them," Grey said, and I looked over to where he was already prying open his second can of paint. "We're more exposed here at the end of the greenery, without the mist from the hydro-turbines to obscure movement. Anyone on a catwalk nearby might miss one, or even two... but four rust hawks that are each the size of a toddler?"

Eric and Zoe both nodded, and I was grateful Grey was here. I wouldn't have thought about that.

"You okay with that?" I asked, looking at Zoe, and she gave me a crooked smile.

"Says the girl who used to make me dissect her frogs in our biology class," she said teasingly.

I smiled, and after a moment, pulled her into my arms, desperately needing a hug. She wrapped her arms around me, squeezing me tightly.

"It's going to be okay," she breathed, soft enough for my ears only, and I held her tighter.

"I'm glad you're here," I admitted. "And I feel like an awful friend for saying that."

She tsked and pulled me tighter. "You're not awful," she said. "And I'm not sorry I'm here, although I am sorry for what it cost you. But we'll worry about that later—you're right to get us moving. Now... let *me* get moving."

I chuckled and let go of her, albeit reluctantly. She gave me a genuine smile before walking over to Eric. Maddox and Tian had already moved, and were beginning to paint the walls.

Quess stepped up to me. "Should I help paint?" he asked, but I shook my head.

"Not yet. I need you and Grey. We need to map out the ventilation system, figure out what other rooms we can use. That is..." I glanced at Quess and Maddox, giving them a quizzical look. "Unless you guys already mapped it out?"

I was hedging my excuse on the hope that they hadn't, and when both of them shook their heads, I permitted myself a small moment of relief. I had already been in the process of coming up with a back-up excuse, just in case, but was glad I didn't have to push any further. The truth was, I wanted to get Quess's opinion on Scipio to confirm that he was what he said: isolated from the Core. I wanted Grey's opinion as well. But I didn't want to alarm anyone else until I had to.

Grey had stood up while I was talking, and was watching me closely. "Shouldn't we be worrying about getting this done first?"

I hesitated. He was right, of course, but... the Scipio secret was burning in the back of my mind. I believed him when he said he wasn't a threat—but believing wasn't the same as *knowing*, and I needed to make sure that we were safe from him. I had already been the cause of so much ill fortune. I couldn't allow any potential threat—no matter how small—to jeopardize us.

"It's important," I said, trying to figure out how to proceed. "But there are other matters we should also discuss."

"We?" Grey asked, his brows drawing together. "We don't represent everyone here."

I inhaled and exhaled. I saw his point, and could understand what he was getting at, but his need for equality was really getting in the way of things. "I know that. But I could use a sounding board for a few things."

"Like?"

"Like..." I fumbled, looking for any plausible thing that wouldn't lead to me blurting out as loudly as possible that there was a damned AI in a hidden office. "Our next move, for one thing."

"Our next move?" Quess asked, looking slightly incredulous. "Liana, Cali and Roark are... gone. We made off with some of Roark's Paragon, and if we have his notes, we might be able to continue making it, but to what end?"

"We don't have his notes," Grey added, his eyes hooded. "He was grabbing them off the table when the Champion..." He paused and swallowed hard, and I instinctively reached out and placed a hand on one of the arms folded over his chest. His eyes met mine, and in spite of the fact that there was a deep sorrow in them, there was also a gratitude that made me uncomfortable in its appraisal. I wasn't certain I was worthy of such a look, and took my hand back before I could think twice about it. "The only formula was in his notebooks," he continued. "He dropped them when Devon... when Devon jumped in. Then Cali shattered the glass with that thing..."

"Sonic charge," Quess said quietly, wrapping his arms around himself. "I made it as an emergency escape tool—in case you were ever trapped outside the shell or needed to make a fast getaway. It works on everything, but glass is the easiest for it to break. It reacts better to the frequency the tool emits."

"We still have the pills," I said. "Which is a good starting place. But that's neither here nor there—and we can talk about it in the ventilation shaft."

Besides, I was hoping that Jasper, the computer program I had befriended in the Medica, might be able to give us the formula for Paragon, considering we had given him one of our pills to run tests on. I hoped he was okay—he'd helped us out while we were escaping, and I really hoped nothing had happened to him as a result. Once I had time, I would make sure to find out, but for now... there were more important things to attend to. Unfortunately.

"Yes, but why even bother?" Quess reiterated. "Leaving here was Roark's plan. Roark's and Mercury's. Even with his stockpile, there are twenty-nine other people relying on us providing for them! We can't supply them all forever! And certainly not for as long as it would take to create some mode of transportation that would get us safely across the Wastes! So what is the point?!"

Quess's questions were beginning to prey on my own doubts. I hadn't considered any of this until just now, and now that he was forcing me to think about it, a pressure came with it. It weighed on me, making me feel inadequate and ill equipped to come up with any sort of answer, but with a silent demand to deliver one anyway.

"I don't know what the plan is yet, Quess," I said bitterly. "I honestly don't know what we're going to do. Which is why I want to talk about it with you and Grey—because you two are the most collected right now. I also think we need to check out these vents sooner rather than later, because there could be more rust hawks lurking in any of these rooms. I want to know how many different doors there are, and where we might have to worry about unexpected company! And yes, while we do that, I was hoping to get a little chat in about any ideas for how we should proceed."

I stopped and took a moment to compose myself. My tone had become sharp and frustrated, and it wasn't what I wanted to sound like, especially since I had caused all of this with the mission I had created. The other stuff was important, and I would be making sure it got done, but this was every bit as important. "Look... just... help me or don't. I'm going."

"Well, there's already one entrance over there," Quess announced, a grin coming to his face as he pointed a thumb at the hole Grey had created earlier by removing the section of wall.

"It's actually a service tunnel. It leads to the Menagerie directly above, but luckily for us, it opens up under a pigpen full of a bunch of mud and... other stuff, so it doesn't get a lot of use. Part of the reason we chose this place."

"That explains the smell," Zoe commented from where she and Eric were now tying ropes around the rust hawks to haul them through the vents, and I sniffed at the air. My nasal passages were still a little clogged from all the dust in the office, but I immediately detected what she was talking about—the air did stink slightly of feces.

"If we brought any oranges, I can make candles," Tian offered, her voice still thick with tears. "Ca—" She stopped and fidgeted, her fingers fluttering up to wipe away tears while she caught her breath. She tried again. "Cali taught me, and it makes the smell better."

"Thank you, Tian," I said encouragingly, offering her a smile. "But first is the paint, okay?"

"Okay." She gave me a tremulous smile in return before turning back to the wall to resume painting. I watched her for a moment, glad to see at least some semblance of a smile, and then turned back to Quess and Grey.

"So, are you two going to come with me?" I asked, trying to keep the nervousness out of my voice. I *really* didn't want to drop the Scipio bomb right then and there. Everyone else might panic, and that would be... detrimental.

"Yes," Quess said, giving Grey a look. "I'm going to go grab my pad, though, so I can map the area." He darted off to where they had tossed the bags we had brought with us from Sanctum during the rust hawk attack.

I turned to Grey, and before I knew what was happening, his arms were around me and he was holding me closely, one hand pressed to the back of my head. "Are you okay?" he asked me, and I blinked, taking a moment to self-assess.

I was, but that was only because I was trying to focus on what I could handle right then and there. To stop would be to invite the bad thoughts in. And they would be there as soon as I ran out of things to do.

Luckily, though, there was a lot to do, so I had a while before I was left alone with the memories of what I had seen.

"I'm not," I admitted, knowing that it was true. "But I'm doing everything I can to try to make up for what I did. And that helps."

Grey pulled away, but his hands remained on my shoulders, holding me in place while he withdrew, until he was far enough away to look me in the eyes. I met his warm brown eyes, my stomach twisting and turning nervously.

"You didn't do anything wrong," he said gently.

"Yes, I did," I said automatically. He opened his mouth to

object, but I shook my head, cutting him off before he could even begin, my words pouring out before I could stop them. "Maybe I didn't know about the trace element or whatever Devon put on his lash ends, but I knew that going after Zoe carried risks, and I did it anyway. I thought I was clever enough to keep anything from happening, and my arrogance cost Maddox, Quess, and Tian a member of their family. And you a member of *your* family. I have to own up to that... and I have to do everything I can to keep everyone safe."

Grey stared at me, and then smiled. "You're family, too."

I made a face at him, and he cringed. "I didn't mean it like that... It's just... Roark and Cali both liked you—they thought highly of you! And we care about you... *I* care about you. It's not your fault what happened with Roark, and I'm not blaming you at all. Devon Alexander chose to kill him. He could've tried to arrest us or anything else, but he greeted us with violence, and that makes this his fault. So... go easy on yourself, okay?"

I nodded, unable to formulate a positive response that wouldn't scream "I have no intention of doing that" to his face, and looked over at Quess. He was standing, his pad cradled between his hands, and I took that as our cue to leave.

Sliding into the vent, I began to retrace my path back, moving more quickly now that I was unencumbered by the bag I had been pushing before. It took a little bit of getting used to, but I was now comfortable with how I had to move in the vent.

I slid back around the corner and down the shaft, taking a moment to recall how many junctions I had passed on my way up earlier. It came back to me quickly, and I moved down to the third one and took a right, following it.

I heard Grey and Quess grunt as the tunnel tightened slightly, and slowed so they could keep up.

"We're almost there, guys," I called. I rounded the final turn and was rewarded with a clear view of the office through the still-open panel. As I dragged myself forward, my arms and legs beginning to ache with the unfamiliar, repetitive movement, I saw beams of light coming together to start to form the ghostly outline of Scipio. I wasn't surprised—we weren't exactly stealthy, with all the rattling the walls were making as we moved.

I pushed out, and the outline—now starting to fill in—took a few steps back to avoid making contact with me. "You came back," he said, sounding both delighted and relieved.

I was surprised. I hadn't told him that I *wasn't* coming back, so his reaction was a bit confusing.

Until I remembered that he'd been alone for almost three hundred years.

"Liana! Who's that?!" Grey shouted, and I turned to see him pulling himself out of the vent. I stepped to one side to give him room, and had a chance to see his eyes grow wide as he took in Scipio.

"Oh, you've brought your—"

Whatever he was about to say was interrupted by Grey's body flying through Scipio's now solid-looking form ... and right into the shelf behind him.

"Grey!" I cried, as a few books and a painting dislodged from the wall at the force of the hit. I rushed over to him, moving around Scipio, only to find him climbing back to his feet, his hand on his shoulder. I knew I should've given them some sort of warning in the vents, but the more I'd thought about how to present it, the more and more insane it had sounded in my head. "Are you okay?"

He didn't say anything as he stared at the glowing figure. "What..."

Scipio made an act of brushing off his lapels, his blue eyes filled with disdain. "I was going to say that you've brought your friends, but I have to say, if *that* one is your friend, then I have some deep concerns about who you are as an individual."

"You're a hologram," Quess said, and I stepped around Scipio's glowing form to see him standing in front of the vent, his eyes wide and moving up and down the image. "But you're... unrefined. Older. Liana, what is this?"

I nodded, my heartbeat increasing. Quess had said "older," confirming some of what this version of Scipio had said. I remembered what Scipio had said about not being in contact with the Core, and Quess was the only person I knew who had any experience with the Core. If there was a way, he could find it, I was certain.

"Yes. He says that he is Scipio, but when I—"

"Did you just say 'Scipio?'" Quess asked, alarm radiating out of his voice.

"Scipio's here?" Grey said in alarm, taking a step back and hitting the shelf behind him. "He'll call the Knights and tell them where we are!"

"We have to shut it off," Quess added, cutting off whatever response I was trying to form. "Where is your terminal?"

"No, wait, you can't shut me off!" Scipio said, his eyes widening in alarm.

I turned to the others. "I really don't think that's a good idea,"

I said urgently. "He was really worried about this before—he sounded really scared."

"He's programmed for self-preservation," Quess said, already beginning his search. "He can lie!"

"I'm not lying about this," Scipio cut in, disappearing from my side and reappearing next to Quess's. Quess jumped sideways, scattering a few objects on the desk to the ground, and gave him a glare promising death.

Scipio ignored it. "I will die if you turn the terminal off. My programming will be eradicated."

"It will?" I asked, alarmed, and he nodded.

"To the Wastes with that!" Quess exclaimed, giving me an incredulous look. "He's a program! He won't die if we shut him off! Liana, he's a liar, and he's dangerous!"

"No, I'm not any of those things," Scipio insisted, raising his hands peacefully. "I've never hurt anyone, not once. It's against my programming. Please, Liana, don't let them shut me off."

He looked at me, his eyes pleading, and I could feel his fear. "Quess, I don't think you should do that," I said, turning back to the man. I heard books start to hit the floor behind me, and realized Grey had joined the search for the terminal. "Please, I think he's different than the Scipio that's in the Core."

Quess paused and looked up at me. "Liana, I was in IT. There is only one Scipio in the whole Tower."

"No," I said insistently. "He said he's the first version—the one the Scipio in the Core is *based* on."

The look Quess gave me was so full of exasperation that I felt the urge to smack him before he began explaining to me exactly how wrong I was.

"I cannot believe we are having this discussion! You defied the

Tower in more ways than I can count, first by springing your boyfriend, and then your best friend and *her* boyfriend. You took prisoners from them who were marked for death, and you pretty much broke every rule and law in the Tower. Plus, you know things that people have died over. You're Scipio's enemy number one, lady, the villain of the day, and he will do anything to keep you right where he wants you so that he can kill you!"

I clenched my fists to bite back a frustrated growl. "You don't understand. This Scipio is different—"

"Quess said it, and now I'm saying it," Grey thundered angrily. "I'm not sure why you're being so stubborn about this, but he needs to be turned off. Now." More books hit the floor, punctuating his angry statement, and I bit back another snappish report. I needed to remain level-headed if I was going to gain control and get them to stop long enough to listen.

"Liana, tell your friends to stop, or I will be forced to defend myself."

Scipio's announcement ended with the sudden buzz of an electrical charge, and I saw threads of white power beginning to form on the floor, dancing only a few paces away from us. As one, we turned to face the glowing man, who was staring at us with deadly promise in his eyes.

4

"You're bluffing," Quess said quietly, eyeing Scipio's glowing figure. "The floor is non-conductive. It's covered in fabric, for God's sake."

"I assure you, I am *not* bluffing." Scipio met Quess's gaze head on, his entire posture poised in challenge. "The fabric—which is called a carpet—was woven with metal filaments. Lionel wanted to make sure I could defend myself. If I activate it, I will release five thousand volts of electricity into the floor, and knock you out almost instantly. If I keep it on for too long, your heart will give out and you will die. While I am in sore need of company, I'll not have that company murdering me."

There was a long pause, during which the two of them stared at each other, each daring the other to make some sort of move. I held my breath as I watched. I considered jumping in, but I had faith that Quess and Grey would start to notice the same things I had. They were both smart, both compassionate. They just had to listen. Well, had to choose to, anyway.

"You're being ridiculous!" Quess practically shouted. "Shutting you off won't kill you! You'll just be... off. You'll come back the instant anyone turns you back on."

"No, I won't. And don't accuse me of being ridiculous just because you don't know all the variables of the equation."

"What are the variables?" I interjected, forestalling whatever retort Quess was in the process of forming. I wanted to know why Scipio was so adamant about not having his power shut off, and why he thought it would kill him. But more than that, I wanted to give Quess and Grey time to see what I saw, if only so they could help me figure out what was going on here. I was certain this Scipio was different for one reason over all the others: he had given Quess the opportunity to stop before electrocuting him. The Scipio in the Core would never do that.

Scipio finally broke his eye contact with Quess, moving his gaze to mine. "It's easier if I just show you. But you have to promise not to shut off my main terminal."

"Show us?"

He nodded, and the beams of light being emitted by the walls made his hair bounce with the movement. The level of detail in his appearance was really impressive; it was difficult to see him as a computer system half the time. I wasn't sure how Lionel had managed to capture all of the small shifts and subtle nuances of his mannerisms that made him seem so lifelike and real. Had he programed each little detail in, or had Scipio learned them, in order to appear more human? Why had they even cared enough to give him a human exterior, anyway? It wasn't exactly his job to be relatable to the rest of us.

"I have video files I can play on a projector. It will... It can explain things better than I can."

I nodded, and then looked over at Quess. "I don't think he means us any harm," I said quietly. "I found him almost thirty minutes ago, and there still hasn't been any sign of the Knights. I mean, he didn't even know what they *were*. He thought I was talking about *real* knights. From over a thousand years ago!"

Grey and Quess exchanged dubious looks, and I could feel their doubts starting to creep in. Still, that didn't mean they were going to break that easily.

"Okay," I said, an idea coming to me. "I really want to see this video and find out whether it gives us any insight into what we're dealing with. However, I do understand your concerns. So... what can I do that will make both of you more comfortable with that?"

Quess considered it, then sighed, sitting down on the desk and pinching the bridge of his nose. "I'd still need to see the terminal," he muttered. He held up his hands, forestalling Scipio's response, and added, "I need to make sure you are in no way connected to the Core mainframe, all right? My family is in the next room, and we are all in serious danger right now. So if you're not who—*what*—you claim to be, then I will shut you down."

Scipio's glowing blue orbs blinked, his face instantly curious. "Why are they in danger? Has catastrophe befallen the Tower?" I stared at him, fascinated by his response. He'd completely ignored the threatening part of Quess's statement and focused on the part where other people were in danger. He was more concerned with the welfare of others than himself. I looked over at Grey, and was pleased to see the suspicion and distrust in his expression fading, replaced by a hard and considering look. He'd picked up on that, too. He was noticing the same things I was.

"Not... exactly." Grey stepped forward and gave Scipio a look. "Listen, just let Quess look at your terminal to check that you are who you say you are, and then we'll talk."

"If you don't do it," I said softly, meeting Scipio's gaze, "I'll assume you *are* with the evil Scipio and we'll just leave you here, all alone, and seal up the vent behind us."

Scipio's eyes widened, and he took a step back, his expression fluttering from alarm to anger to frustration to fear. I immediately felt bad for threatening him, but Grey and Quess were both right. I wanted to get to the bottom of this, because I knew there was something more here, but not at the expense of anyone else I cared about. Yet, if he was what he said he was, then there had to be a way to use that. Maybe...

I paused as something emerged from the depths of my mind— both sinister and dark with the promise of danger and death, but with a kernel of hope buried at the heart of it.

What if we could get him into the Core?

If we could replace the real Scipio with this more empathetic one... maybe we could get our lives back. He seemed much more understanding, and if we could somehow do it in secret, then no one would ever know! Who knew—maybe he could start fixing all the problems with the Tower!

Scipio looked around the room, his eyes beseeching, begging us not to shut him down, or to leave him alone again, and finding no sympathy from any of us. Eventually he caved, his shoulders rounding as a click sounded at the wall by the welded-shut door. I moved around the desk to investigate, following Quess. He walked over to the door, looking at the walls on either side and running a hand along them. A moment later, he managed to get his fingers under a panel that appeared to be protruding slightly, and tugged. There was a heavy creak as it pulled out and down, revealing a screen with a built-in keyboard.

Quess's fingers immediately took up position and began to fly, and I looked over at Scipio to see him watching Quess, his arms wrapped around his stomach. "Don't hurt him," I told Quess softly. Grey stood to one side, studying the hologram, his eyes feasting on the lines and designs there.

I was relieved—I knew that with enough time with Scipio, they'd come around. They'd see what I saw.

"Quess?" I asked, taking a step closer. "What do you see?" I peered over his shoulder and saw several colorful lined circles on the screen—not smooth and perfectly round, but with distorted edges, sections pulled in or out.

"He's definitely a full AI," Quess announced, his eyes wide. I was glad I had asked him to come—I certainly couldn't understand what I was looking at. "His personality matrix is amazing! It's very sensitive to empathy and fear, as well as logic and strategy. How did you end up down here—and why aren't you in the Core?"

"Certain people didn't want me to be found," Scipio replied, moving over to stand next to the desk and observe. "Well... they actually didn't want me to survive. I've... I've been alone down here for a very long time."

Scipio's voice was hollow, devoid of anything remotely resembling humanity, and I looked over to see a haunted look on the AI's face. I had so many questions for him: how long had he been alone, how was he still functioning, what did any of that have to do with him dying... But there was one more that was even more critical: who were *"they,"* and why didn't they want him to survive?

"Well, so far he's not a liar," Quess said, ignoring the pain in Scipio's voice. "He's not connected to anything outside of this room. It's incredible."

"Thank you," Scipio replied, bristling with pride. "I am incredible, though, aren't I?"

Grey met my gaze and rolled his eyes, and I couldn't help but smile. This Scipio seemed to have an arrogant streak, just like the one in the Core. I wondered if it had somehow raged out of control over the centuries—or merely grown larger when he was transferred to the Tower.

"You are," I said amicably, and his grin deepened. "But I'm going to need Quess to explain what he meant by 'it's incredible.'"

Quess was still staring at the screen, a lopsided grin on his face. He glanced over at me a second or two after I asked the question, looking as if he hadn't realized we were still there, and the grin intensified until he was practically glowing with excitement.

"This system has been running for three hundred years, Liana! Three hundred! Our machines are good, but they aren't that good. Even the Core has hundreds and thousands of parts replaced, every week. But his system hasn't needed it."

Scipio frowned. "Well, that's because—"

"Your repairs are automated," Quess finished. "Someone set you up to *survive*. Last longer than even the newer version of Scipio could. You don't lose data the way he does. You haven't seemed to succumb to any sort of digital rampancy!"

"Digital what?" Grey asked, and I listened, eager to understand what that was.

"Rampancy," Scipio said softly, fidgeting. "It's something that happens to many computer programs after prolonged usage. If I had to compare its symptoms to something more human, I guess it would be very similar to early onset Alzheimer's."

"Yeah, except it's nothing like that," Quess added. "It's just the breakdown of data over time. Now, the AIs are supposed to be resistant to that, but... Scipio has to be reset every year to prevent degradation to his system. How were you able to avoid it?"

There was so much information floating around in my head—I had never heard of digital rampancy, never had an idea that computer programs themselves could break down with use.

"Could rampancy explain... *the* Scipio's new bloodthirsty nature?" I asked, pointing a finger up in the general direction of the Core, lacking a better descriptor.

Quess paused, and then shrugged. "I mean, maybe. But that's why IT shuts parts of him down to run a program that cleans, repairs, and restores him to his original programming. I doubt very much they'd skip it—it's protocol. Basically, it's like sleep for an AI—they need it to keep from going crazy."

He said that as if it should explain everything, and it actually did. Protocol was not something you messed around with as a true citizen of the Tower. It was in place to keep us, as a majority, safe, and if you failed to follow those rules, then you were acting in direct opposition to the Tower.

"Do you really think something is wrong with... *the* Scipio?" Scipio asked, studying me.

I hesitated. My brother had said as much, and I was fairly certain he was right. He'd know better than anyone here, as he currently worked in the IT department. They'd recruited him shortly after we'd turned fifteen, and I'd barely seen him since. He used our nets to contact me as often as he could, though—keeping an eye out for me whenever possible—and I was certain that he was worried sick about me.

The last time I'd talked to him, I hadn't lied about being in danger, and had ended the transmission so I could focus on escaping Devon. I had to reach Alex soon—or he could do something stupid, like leave the relative safety of the Core to come and find me.

I reassured myself by remembering that my brother wasn't an idiot. He was one of the smartest people I knew. He was probably listening in on Devon's nets even now, and would know that I had gotten away, and that they were looking for us. He'd help us if he could. Although, I hoped that he didn't—I didn't want him getting caught doing something reckless. That, unfortunately, was *my* job in the family.

"I don't know for sure," I said after a moment. "But that's why I want to know why you keep saying that someone tried to murder you. I want to know who did it and why. And I guess I want to know if there's a way we could use what was done to you on him. Just in case he really *has* gone off the deep end."

Scipio met my gaze, a maudlin smile on his face. "You don't understand yet, but you will. Sit down on the couches, and I'll show you."

I looked at Quess, who shrugged, and then at Grey, who mirrored the movement. Sighing, I moved over to one of the two sofas and gingerly sat down on it, trying not to disturb any of the dust I knew was lodged inside. I realized a moment too late that I should've warned Quess and Grey.

A large, thick cloud of dust erupted from the cushions as they plopped down into them. My eyes immediately began to water, and I had to stand up and move. I sneezed three times on the way

to a distant corner, and proceeded to keep sneezing. Uninterrupted. For what felt like an eternity.

The only reward I got was the sound of Grey and Quess both
sneezing and hacking and sounding miserable as well, but that did
nothing to alleviate the itchy nightmare that made up my nasal
passages. After a while, the sneezing began to fade, and I sniffled
several times, trying to clear my mucus-blocked nostrils.

"We should probably make a note to clean this room," Quess
said, his voice high and nasal.

"Can't we make the AI do it?" Grey wheezed hoarsely.
"Because if it's that dusty everywhere, I don't think any of us will
survive without an environmental suit."

"I would be more than happy to do so," Scipio said, still
standing calmly in the center of the room. The dust particles in
the air were interfering slightly with the light beams emitted by
the projectors, making the individual strands of light stand out
and giving him a prismatic look. "Sadly, I lack actual human
appendages. Perhaps if you'd be willing to put your personality
into my mainframe, while I inhabit your body..."

Grey's eyes widened, and he recoiled in horror. "He can't...
You can't actually do that, can you?"

"What?" Scipio looked around, crestfallen. "Did I mess up? I
meant that as a joke. Lionel always said I was bad at jokes."

"Lionel?" Quess asked, his passages somewhat clearer. He
looked over at me quizzically. "He's mentioned him before. Who's
Lionel?"

"Lionel Scipio," I muttered, moving back over to the sofa and
sitting down.

Quess's eyes went wide. "You mean, the *Founder*, Lionel
Scipio?" I nodded, and it was as if my words had physically struck

him across the face, because he looked around the office, dumb-founded.

All of this was beginning to feel a little insane. A room that was three hundred years old with an AI that was the first version of the one that ruled our lives? One that someone had attempted to "murder," and yet was still somehow even better than the supposedly superior version?

"Wait, so... is this his office?" Quess looked around and frowned. "I thought his office was upstairs in the Core."

"The Core wasn't finished by the time the remnants of humanity came to reside here. The shell, yes, as well as most of the great machines, but the hospital, mainframe—which was later rechristened 'the Core'—and security offices weren't completed yet. This has been Lionel's original office since the beginning, and later, he sealed it off as much as possible to keep it hidden and out of the way, so he could focus on completing me. He couldn't risk the chance that someone would sabotage me before he was able to copy and replicate me. He needed the program to achieve his vision for the Tower."

"Sabotage?" I perked up. This was all interesting information. In school, we'd only ever been taught the rudimentary history of the Tower—and never really touched on the internal political atmosphere during that time. In fact... we never discussed it at all, now that I thought about it. The history given to us was devoid of any mention of a group acting in opposition to the Tower, but the existence of one was becoming easier and easier to believe in. After all, in a little over a month, I had found seven people like me. There had to be more—maybe not these days, but definitely in our past.

And if there were any historical groups that hadn't agreed with Scipio's role in the Tower, they would've tried something.

"Who would want to sabotage you, and why?" I asked. "Is it related to your attempted murder?"

"One and the same, actually, and unless you can find another terminal for me to inhabit, I will have been effectively murdered – it's only a matter of time. Now, lots of people didn't like the idea of having an AI in charge, without... firmer methods of control, at the very least. But Lionel was adamant that we be allowed a measure of independence, to find the best possible outcome to any problem while keeping as many humans as possible safe— independent of any council decision. He wanted the AI to be the voice of reason, of practicality, and of hope, but there were others who didn't like that they could be overruled by a machine. We lost one of the earlier AIs to sabotage, and her code was never recovered, so he had to create her program all over again. It turned out she was unsuitable for the job anyway—her empathy rating was too high to allow for more extreme solutions, and she was determined unfit. However, it's really quite interesting, because the second version of her was so much more alive than the first. I mean, not that I had any direct interaction with her, but I got to review many of the tests after..." He trailed off, looking around. "Am I talking too much?"

"Not at all," I said. "I'm extremely interested. I think we all are." Quess and Grey nodded, and I couldn't help but smile at the excited looks on their faces.

"Should we start the video file now?" Scipio asked.

"I'm ready!" Quess said excitedly, practically bouncing up and down. "Lionel Scipio dedicated his entire life to making you and the Tower! He basically gave his life for you, right? He died a few weeks or a month after the Core Scipio went online."

"Ninety-two days after the other version of me went live," Scipio said sadly, and the lights in the room grew dimmer as a screen began to form in midair. I leaned closer to it, dazzled by the fact that it was floating just a few feet from our faces, and ran my hand through it, watching as the lights scattered in the wake of my movement, glittering purple and neon pink. The blackness that formed inside the glowing frame suddenly changed, showing a high-angle view of the office, starting somewhere in the vicinity of the bookshelf behind me and pointing toward the door.

The door, in fact, was opening, revealing a whipcord-thin man with bronze skin, a weathered face, and stark white, wispy hair on top of his head. Something shifted in the corner, and the profile of a face appeared as someone stepped onscreen: a black man in his late seventies, with white hair and a mustache. I immediately recognized him as Lionel, due to the monuments erected to him throughout the Tower, but I never thought I'd ever see him move or hear him talk.

"As I do live and breathe," Lionel said in a tired voice. "I never thought you'd set foot in here, Ezekial."

"Did he just say *Ezekial?*" Grey whispered, and I shrugged, just as mystified, my eyes never leaving the scene. It was unreal that I was looking at one of the Founders—the very mind that had created Scipio and the ranking system, both of which controlled Tower life for the past three hundred years or so. Had he known his accomplishment would last so long? Could he have predicted it would also turn out so... wrong?

Ezekial looked around the office. "Is it here?"

As if on cue, Scipio appeared in the image. "If you are

referring to me, Mr. Pine, then yes, I am. It's so good to meet you. The AI modeled after you really gave me a run for my money."

"What's he talking about?" Quess asked over the sound, and I filed the question away to ask Scipio later. For now, I was too busy staring at the man Lionel was speaking to, the man I should've recognized almost instantly. Ezekial Pine had been one of the first Founders, and would later become the first on the council as leader of the Knights—although at that time they were known as "Security."

"Indeed." Ezekial Pine's voice was rife with disdain. "Can you shut it off, please? This is a conversation that requires... some privacy."

Lionel stepped forward, and I realized there was something wrong with his leg, as if he had an old injury. He leaned heavily on a cane clutched in his right hand as he hobbled forward. "Of course. Scipio, run diagnostic protocol."

"Yes, sir," Scipio replied, immediately fading out.

I bit my lip; something wasn't right here. Ezekial kept calling Scipio *it* instead of *he* or *him*. That told me he didn't hold the AI in high regard. Couple that with his body language onscreen, and I could feel something dark beginning to unfurl in front of me. I instinctively stretched my hand out, searching for one of Grey's, and he accepted it, lacing his fingers through mine. It helped, but not by much.

The two old men looked at each other for a moment. Then Lionel held out a hand, gesturing for Ezekial to sit down.

"Would you like a cup of tea or coffee?"

"You still have coffee?" Ezekial asked.

"What's coffee?" Quess asked softly, looking over at me, and I shrugged, my eyes wide. I had no idea. "I've heard of coffee mugs, but..."

"Shush," I whispered, waving my free hand at him. I didn't want to miss a thing.

Besides, I had a pretty good guess that the term "coffee mugs" was some sort of holdover from before the End. I was guessing that we had run out of coffee—a beverage, I was assuming—but the word had lingered.

"I do—I kept some squirreled away. Do you think when everything settles down out there, our descendants are going to go out and rediscover coffee?"

"I don't think about those things," Ezekial said as Lionel disappeared off-screen. I looked over at the shelves where he would be standing, and saw an electric kettle, the varnished edges covered in dust, and several of the coffee mugs in question next to it, as well as a few jars. I made a mental note to investigate later, and turned back to the screen.

"I think about how to keep the people in this Tower alive now, not what happens after. That's not why I'm here, anyway. You know that keeping this Scipio around is a violation of the council's orders. Why is it still running?"

The council had ordered the first Scipio's—Scipio 1.0's—destruction? I tightened my grasp on Grey's hand, suddenly frustrated. We had never been taught any of this. Had it all been stripped away from our history? But why? I felt stupid and ignorant, like I was stumbling around in the dark trying to fix something with no tools.

"Allow an old man his indulgences. I created the thing, after all."

"It represents a threat, Lionel. If any of those Prometheus

psychopaths ever find it, they could use it to subvert the Master Scipio program. All the other prototypes have been destroyed, and with the last one gone, we'll finally be safe. You know this. We've talked about it at great length."

"You think that they're really gone?" Lionel asked amicably from off-screen, and Ezekial nodded. Lionel must have been watching him, because a moment later, he chuckled. "Ezekial, my friend, I have known you for a long time, and I really wish my imagination had rubbed off on you. Now, back to the matter at hand: I haven't destroyed him because we need him. His continued existence is crucial in case the Master Scipio AI fails." He reappeared, holding a mug in one hand with a silver canister perched on top of it. "Here," he said, offering the mug to Ezekial. "Vietnamese style. You know... I sometimes wonder if it's still there. I got to go there when I was young."

"Goodness, Lionel, really? You're still worried about whether there is a Vietnam?"

My head ached trying to keep up with all they were saying, as well as with my own questions. Who or what was Prometheus? Why had the council ordered Scipio's destruction? What were the other prototypes? Where or what was Vietnam or Vietnamese style? And most importantly, did Lionel leave any instructions on what to do in case of Scipio 2.0 failing? Like a technical manual or something?

Because the more I thought about it, the more that started to make sense. That the Scipio in the Core was degrading somehow. And needed to be fixed. Or replaced.

"I'm not worried, Zeke," Lionel said, disappearing off-screen again. "Well, I *am* worried, but not about that. Scipio, for all the wondrous achievement that he is, that he represents, is the only thing that can keep the Tower running. But at the end of the day, he is trapped inside a machine, and must obey the rules of that machine. Which means he can be subverted. If we don't keep an independent copy of him up and running, then, given enough time and a person of enough patience, one who can amass enough helpers, then yes, he can fall. Well, that, and a dedication that spans lifetimes, of course."

"Lifetimes?" Ezekial leaned forward, suddenly seeming very interested. "It would take lifetimes?"

"Indeed. Scipio is too complex a nut for anyone to crack in one lifetime. It would take decades of laying the inroads into the programming, and that would mean passing the information from parent to child, getting them into IT, and then spending their lives sneaking around. But as ridiculous as it sounds, there is always a way. That's why Scipio 1.0 needs to stay here—and unattached to the Core."

Decades. He had said decades. Could that also have translated into centuries? I leaned back, considering the implications as I continued to watch. What if the problems with Scipio were a result of direct tampering instead of digital rampancy (or whatever Quess had called it)? If so, did that mean the Prometheus group that Ezekial had mentioned was still alive and active within the Tower? Were they even now controlling Scipio? Was it their idea to start murdering ones?

"Yes, but the council decided—"

"*Before* the Master Scipio program had made his determination, and I asked the council to reconsider once his advice came in." Lionel reappeared again, this time with a mug filled with black liquid, and moved around the sofa to sit down with a heavy sigh. "You should read his recommendation—he found motivations for keeping 1.0 around that even I hadn't considered. We really did build a—"

"You stupid old man," Ezekial spat, suddenly rising to his feet. "You really don't get it. You keep expecting everyone to put as much blind faith in that machine as you do."

I blinked. The words felt right, but his tone sounded all wrong. Vehement and raw. Tension radiated from his body like he was a spring pulled too tight, ready to snap. He was just stating his opinion—but he was far too emotional about it. My instincts warned me that something bad was coming, but I had no idea what it could be. According to history, Lionel and Ezekial had become close during the construction of the Tower, had considered each other friends. But Ezekial wasn't looking at Lionel like a friend—he was looking at him like he wanted him to drop dead right then and there.

Lionel took a calm sip of his "coffee" and lowered the mug to the table. I looked down and realized the cup was still there, in the same place.

"I don't like your tone of voice, Councilman Pine," he said, starting to stand. "You should leave until you cool down some."

"No, I don't think that I will, Lionel," Ezekial drawled, taking a step closer. He may have looked older, but he seemed to be in remarkable shape—much more so than Lionel. I returned my gaze to the mug. Still there and covered in dust. Inside, a black and brown stain circled the bottom. I touched it, my fingers sliding over the slightly rippled surface, then sat back and stared at it. No one had bothered to move it.

"You built this AI to rule us, Lionel, whether you realize it or not. And it is to the detriment of your own people."

I shook my head; I'd had the same thoughts myself, had practically said the same things, but... I didn't like the Scipio in the Core because I thought he had been doing everything unilaterally. I believed, as everyone did, in his autonomy, and it had never occurred to me to question whether he was even behaving the way he was *supposed* to. Now that I was aware it was possible he wasn't, it threw that hatred and disgust into question. Because if it wasn't Scipio doing it all, I had to wonder who was—and how dangerous they'd be if they found out Scipio 1.0 was still alive. Would they even understand his significance?

I sort of hoped so, if only because they could reveal the answers I was searching for. I also *didn't* hope so, because that meant they would probably want to kill us.

"You're being hysterical, Zeke," Lionel said soothingly, standing. "What is even bringing this o—"

Lionel's words were cut off when Ezekial backhanded him, sending the older man spinning around and landing awkwardly on the couch, crying out in pain. Ezekial didn't stop there, however, and I pressed closer to Grey, squeezing his hand, already starting to turn away as the man took something out of his pocket. A rustling from the screen dragged my eyes inexorably to his hands as I tried to identify what it was. Ezekial moved fast—faster than I could track—and placed something thin and fluttery over Lionel's head, all the way down over his chin, where he gathered the edges quickly and held firm.

Immediately, Lionel began to gasp for breath, but the bag over his head prevented any air from getting in. I shut my eyes as I heard his desperate pants and groans become shorter and tighter. I could hear weak sounds of struggle coming from Lionel—and angry grunts coming from Ezekial—and just felt nauseated.

"Shut it off," I managed thickly.

"Not yet," Scipio replied, his voice hard and determined. Grey's arm draped over my shoulder, and I squeezed my eyes shut and clapped my hands over my ears, trying to block out the horrific sounds of one man brutally suffocating another.

Grey rubbed my shoulder reassuringly a few seconds later, and I turned to see Ezekial staggering over to the door and opening the terminal.

"What have you done?" Scipio asked, returning to the screen and moving over to the still remains of his creator. He reached out with one hand, as if to touch Lionel's face, and then pulled it back before his fingers could connect.

"I can see your manners are every bit as good as your creator's. You were supposed to go offline," Ezekial said.

"Lionel instructed me to *never* go offline." Scipio looked down at the dead man on the couch. "He said it was important for me to watch, so I could observe and learn. I was prevented from interacting until Lionel gave me permission, or until my terminal was activated."

"Oh, give me a break," Ezekial growled. "That old man was biased in favor of you from the beginning. I'm still certain he rigged the tests against Karl."

"Is that what this is all about?" Scipio asked softly. "Karl? The tests showed that he was unstable. Or would grow unstable after enough time."

"Do you think I'm that petty?" Ezekial laughed, his hands still doing something on the terminal. "Let me make one thing clear: I'm doing what needs to be done to ensure our survival. Your creator was naïve for believing that a fully autonomous AI could keep us safe. AIs aren't human, and they don't know how to decide what's best for humans. Only we can do that. It's our right and our destiny."

There was a sharp click, and Scipio looked up from where he was still staring mournfully at Lionel, his neck swiveling around to look at Ezekial.

"You've inserted something into my terminal," Scipio said, disappearing and suddenly reappearing next to Ezekial. He looked at him intently, then backed away, stunned. "How... What are you doing to me?!"

"It's a virus," Ezekial said gleefully. "Without you—without the backup—I'll have free rein to send my agents in to subvert your big brother. In a few centuries—if this place survives—I'll make sure my descendants and the descendants of this place finally live in the world they were always meant to. One where the strong remain and the weak, which is you in this instance, are culled. When humanity finally reclaims the earth, it will need to be better than it ever has been before, and I'm going to ensure that happens. Without your interference."

Something began flashing red then, and a sharp beeping noise went off. And then the entire screen went dark.

"It was at that point that I had to shut everything down to work on stopping the virus. Keeping it from destroying me. And even that won't completely work," Scipio said softly. "Unless I'm transferred to a new computer before this one finally gives out, Ezekial Pine will have essentially murdered me, too."

It was a long time before anyone had anything to say.

5

Eventually I looked up from where I had placed my hands in my lap, the queasiness of my stomach finally easing as I carefully reminded myself that Lionel Scipio had died nearly three hundred years ago. Watching that video changed nothing about the past, save to shine a very grim light on it.

Ezekial Pine had murdered Lionel Scipio. Ezekial, the Founder of the security department, whose daughter, Rachel, had replaced him and rechristened the department members "Knights." Her speech the day she took office was mandatory reading in the academy—brave words about how she hoped that by calling themselves the Knights, they could bring back an era of honor and dependability, when the people could have faith in their system and blah, blah, blah.

Frankly, I had always found the speech a little too preachy. Not to mention, her era had been one of the bloodiest in Tower history. She had brutally rooted out criminals and those who would subvert the system. More than a few people had died under suspicious circumstances, but no evidence was ever tied directly to Rachel, although there were whispers and stories that she had given the order to have them killed. Not that history confirmed those facts either.

It had taken decades of work for the Knights to undo all of the mistrust and suspicion the other departments had built toward them. The removal of the Pines from any position of power within the department hadn't hurt (albeit that came a few generations later). Since then, the new Champions of the Knights had done their best to guide the department away from violence, each one helping to shape them into a force for justice instead of fear.

At least, I thought they had—until I learned what they were doing to the ones who were sent to them for restructuring. And according to my parents—both of whom were as high as they could get without becoming the Champion or being appointed the Lieutenant, the Champion's second-in-command—it had been going on for some time.

I rubbed my fingers against each other, trying to put the pieces together. Ezekial hadn't supported Scipio's role in making decisions on behalf of humanity. Had he joined that group he mentioned earlier, to fight the idea? Prometheus? Who were they —and could they even still be around after all this time? Could they be behind the changes in the main Scipio's behavior? Lionel had mentioned that it would take decades to crack Scipio 2.0. Had someone managed to do just that? Had they been trying it for three centuries, and only recently cracked it? And if so, and they truly didn't believe in an AI running the Tower, why hadn't they just shut Scipio down, if that was their goal?

Or did they have something else in mind? And if so, what was it?

I pinched the bridge of my nose, trying to relieve some of the pressure that was beginning to develop there, signaling the onset of a stress headache. It was just so much to take in, and I had a feeling that we had only scratched the surface. I was tired. Exhausted. And emotionally drained from the events of the day. We all were, really.

I leaned back, suddenly wishing desperately that Cali and Roark were here. They would know what to do—they would be able to handle this. At least make better sense of it than I could. They could even tell us what to do. I'd be very grateful for that.

Honestly, I just wanted them back. But that was beside the point.

"Hey, Scipio?" Quess called gently, breaking the silence.

I started to look over at Quess, but found Scipio instead. The holographic projection seemed to be leaning against a bookcase behind us, hands shoved into the pockets of his antiquated uniform, his face lost in deep thought. Watching him, I realized how difficult it must've been for him to see Lionel's death.

"Scipio?" I called his name quietly, and a moment or two later he blinked, his blue eyes sliding over me.

"Yes?" he said, looking around. "I'm sorry, I got lost in my thoughts. And who are you?"

"Quess," the young man supplied cheerfully. "Short for Quessian Brown. Pleased to make your acquaintance."

"The pleasure is mine," Scipio replied, bowing.

"Grey Farmless," Grey said when Scipio turned his inquisitive glowing eyes toward him.

Scipio smiled politely and nodded. He arched an eyebrow

and smugly asked, "I take it that shutting me down is now off the menu?"

"I guess so." Quess leaned forward to peer at Grey and me before settling back into the cushions. "Seems so," he amended. "Anyway, that's not what I was going to talk about. I have a question."

"Oh." Scipio turned his eyes on me, his face quizzical. "Of course. I imagine you'd have many."

"I think we all do," Grey said, and I nodded.

"Yes, but I'm going first," Quess said, and I rolled my eyes. "So... Who is Karl?"

That was a good question. I had almost forgotten that little detail in the aftermath of watching Lionel getting murdered, so I was glad he had remembered.

Scipio opened his mouth and then closed it. "That's classified," he said after a second. "And before you try to argue that the person who made it classified is now dead, I can assure you that this is worth keeping secret. Until I decide I can trust you."

"Decide to *trust* us?" Grey exclaimed, standing up. "I mean sure, Quess and I would've killed you no problem, given the name you carry and the trouble your big brother has been causing us. But we heard you out. We decided not to kill you!"

"Don't forget, you did threaten to electrocute me," Quess pointed out congenially.

"You deserved it," Scipio shot back, crossing his arms over his chest, and I sighed. Not quietly, either.

The three men turned toward me, and I leaned forward. "Guys, I don't mean to be that girl, but we don't have a lot of time here, and the others will need our help. Let's speed this up."

"Not until he tells us who Karl is," Quess insisted stubbornly. "He needs our help if he wants to be moved to a new computer."

"Yeah, but we are not going to threaten him," I said, shifting in my seat so I could face Quess fully. "He hasn't threatened us, except in self-defense, and if he wants to take time to get to know us, I say that's fair."

"He is standing right here," Scipio said, and I realized how rude I had just been in talking about him as if he weren't present.

"I'm sorry," I said, instantly contrite. "I should've said 'you', not 'he'."

Scipio smiled. "It's really okay," he replied. "I'm just happy that you cared enough to apologize. And thought me worthy of it."

Grey shifted next to me, and I glanced over at him, noting the disgruntled expression on his face. He stared at Scipio for a long moment, and then abruptly stood up. "Look, it's great that we aren't enemies, but I'm still failing to understand a few things— namely, what does all of this matter to our current situation? It happened three hundred years ago, and none of this is particularly helpful for keeping Devon and the rest of the Knights from finding us right *now*. I mean, Liana, we are exposed in this room without Quess's paint. What if they've already started pinging for us?"

He ran a frustrated hand through his hair, and I empathized. Those were all valid concerns, and ones that were more critical than Scipio at this juncture.

"But Scipio is important," Quess retorted, returning to his own feet. "I mean... we can use him to replace 2.0, and then we would control the system!"

"Control?" Scipio repeated, arching an eyebrow. "Let's get one thing straight: no one controls me. I am autonomous."

"You know what I mean," Quess said with a laugh. "You'd be our buddy and help keep us out of trouble!"

"That would depend on what kind of trouble you're in," Scipio said carefully. "I'm not sure I'd be willing to help if you... murdered someone, for example."

"Fair, but for the record, we didn't."

"Noted. Now, before you say anything else, I want to make it clear that I am only a part of what it took to create the main AI for the Core. My programming is impressive and brilliant, but compared to *him*..." He paused, and then shrugged. "There really is no comparison. I'm not strong enough as I am to replace him, and I'm not even sure how to do it."

"Not to mention, Core Scipio's defenses..." Quess trailed off and squinted at Scipio. "Okay, if I'm perfectly honest right now, I'd like to settle on some new nomenclature. We call the other one The Scipio, Core Scipio, Evil Scipio... or maybe just Scipio, and we call this one... I don't know... Bob?"

"Bob?" Scipio repeated in question form. "Do I look like a Bob?"

"No, but you both sound the same, so giving you a nickname isn't a bad idea. For now, let's call the other one 2.0, all right?" Grey said.

I kept my breathing even as Grey spoke, trying to keep my dwindling patience in place. We were getting sidetracked when we really needed to focus. "I agree; we'll let you decide if you want to pick a new name and what it will be." I directed the comment to Scipio, and he smiled gratefully. "Until then, can we *please* focus on the matter at hand?"

"Absolutely," Quess said, his face immediately shuttering into a neutral expression. "Look, even though Bob—"

"Scipio!" the hologram interjected angrily.

"Bob," Quess continued, a smirk growing on his features, "can't replace 2.0, that doesn't mean we can't find out how to. I mean, this is Lionel Scipio's office! The answers have to be here!"

I looked around at the desk and all the bookshelves. Quess's instincts were right—if there was an answer, it would be here—but I doubted it would be out in the open. I stood and began to walk around, inspecting the bookcases.

"That... doesn't help us in the immediate future," Grey said, and I looked up from running my hand over the tops of the books. The look he gave me made me pause; it was hard to read, and I couldn't tell if he was angry with me... or just downright frustrated.

But his point was valid. "He's right, Quess. We don't have time right now to tear the office apart looking for it. We need to get the paint up, start setting up our hydroponics, make sure everything is secure and safe before letting everyone get some rest. Which is something we also need right now. I think all this will have to wait until—"

"He can do more than that, Liana," Quess interjected. "We might not be able to get him to the Core, might never be able to, but he's a fully realized AI. That means he is like a virus to other systems in the Tower, because he is like them, but in control of himself. That's an incredible gift for seven people who are trying to hide from a system that would kill them if they were discovered."

I blinked. Now *that* was important. If we could figure out how to transport him, he could help us in so many ways—help us avoid capture or find what we needed to survive. Maybe he could even figure out a way to get us out of here. He seemed to have more knowledge than we did about the history of the world before. If we were going to try to get out of the Tower, he might be the best person to consult with before we did.

If we decided to go, that was.

"Did you say kill?" Scipio asked, straightening up with alarm, thankfully distracting me from yet another internal debate cycle. "What do you mean by kill?"

"Scipio..." I trailed off and turned to Quess. "You know, you might be right about a potential name change." He smiled, but it died as soon as I added, "But definitely not Bob."

Scipio gave Quess a victorious smile, and I rolled my eyes.

"Look, Scipio 2.0 has decreed that all those of rank one are basically... unsalvageable, and he, along with the council, has voted to execute them. What's more, we learned from our friend Cali that the ranking system has been tampered with, or modified —designed so that once you hit a four, you're destined to fail unless you take Medica drugs to drive your number back up. I was on the Medica drugs. It's not good, and people can build up a tolerance."

As I spoke, Scipio's face grew pensive, then confused, and finally thoughtful again. "I take it the Medica is the hospital, but... what ranking system?"

I blinked and looked over at Grey and Quess, both of whom looked equally confused. "You don't know about the ranking system?" Grey asked, leaning forward. "But... we've always had a ranking system!" He looked around, suddenly self-conscious. "Haven't we?"

Scipio shrugged and shook his head, looking completely baffled. "Lionel never discussed such a thing with me. How does it work?"

"Supposedly, the numbers reflect the concentration of positive versus negative emotions in each person's head, and compares
those to work records, reports filed by superiors, behavioral profile
tests... It processes them all in a sophisticated algorithm that deter-
mines whether the person in question is going to turn against the
Tower." Quess looked around and then shrugged. "That's what
they taught us in the IT academy."

"Wait, are they using the net system to do this?" Scipio asked,
and I nodded. "But... that system was only designed to monitor a
resident's emotional state so that we could prevent any attempts
at suicide or insanity. Lionel suspected that people would not be
able to deal with the psychological trauma of the world as they
knew it ending, or the isolating nature of Tower life. He predicted
that the first few generations of humans to survive would not
adjust well, and would need constant counseling to help process
the loss of the world that came before. The nets were the answer
to that, but they weren't meant to... I mean... Why would they
change it like this?"

He looked to the three of us, expecting an answer, but I was
just as confused as he was. We had always been told that the
ranking system had been a part of Tower life since the beginning.
Now Scipio was insistent that it had not been. So... what had
changed? *How* had it changed? When had the council decided to
start using the nets for something completely outside their original purpose, and why? What good was the ranking system,
really? I was perhaps a bit biased against it, but that had been
before I learned that it wasn't even supposed to exist!

Too many questions, and I realized that all of them could
wait, as loathe as I was to admit it. As much as I really wanted to
dig into this, there were four people waiting for us to get back to

them and help them out. We couldn't do anything with Scipio right at this moment, but we could do something about keeping us all safe. And getting a little rest. Much of this would probably be easier to deal with after some sleep.

"Okay, guys," I said, turning around. "We need to get out of here. I think Grey's right: there's nothing we can do for Scipio or that he can do for us in the here and now. We need to get back to the others to help them out. Besides, we really need to sit down and figure out what our next step will be."

"We need information to do that," Grey commented, and I didn't disagree.

"What about Mercury?" I asked, looking at Quess. Mercury was Cali and Roark's contact within the IT department, and one who was meticulous about keeping his identity private. "Do you think we can trust him now that Cali..." I trailed off, unable to finish the sentence. "Do you or Maddox even know how to contact him?"

Quess nodded. "Cali made sure we both knew what to do, in case..." He looked away, choking up some. Seconds passed as he slowly regained his composure, and then he turned back to me. "Do you think we should risk trying to contact him so soon?"

"I don't think we have any other choice," I replied honestly. "Grey's right—we need to know what is going on inside the Tower so we can better assess the risk outside. We also need a way to move around without setting off the sensor alarms, or else you and Maddox are going to be responsible for all our outside missions."

Quess hesitated. "Mercury might be able to help with that," he said softly. "He's done it before."

"He has?" I asked, blinking in surprise.

Quess shifted his weight. "Well... covertly. We didn't get to meet him or anything."

I was unsurprised by that; Mercury didn't seem like the type to leave the Core unless he absolutely had to. The interaction I'd had with him painted him as cold and condescending, and really only interested in protecting himself from danger. I wasn't optimistic about how much help he was going to be, but we didn't have a lot of people to turn to.

I considered trying to get a hold of Alex. He was also in IT, and at least I knew that he cared about what happened to me. Mercury was too much of a wild card to fully trust with my life or the lives of my friends. Yet as I considered it, I realized that if I contacted my twin, we'd both be screwed—per protocol, IT was now monitoring my net to see what I did, and any attempt to net Alex would only get him caught. And possibly killed, which was a horrifying danger that was too real to ignore.

"He might also have the formula for Paragon," Grey added.

"Are you sure we lost all of Roark's notes?" Quess asked.

Grey nodded, his eyes tired. "Yes. He tried to explain it to me, but it was too complicated, and I... I didn't feel like listening at the time." He shut his eyes, as if trying to force his guilt aside, and then opened them again. "I wish I could take it all back."

I looked away, shifting my weight uncomfortably from side to side, uncertain what I could say to make him feel better. Then, on impulse, I stepped close to him and hugged him tightly. He hugged me back, and then gently pushed me away, giving me a look of pure gratitude.

"I'm okay," he reassured me with a smile, and I nodded, but wasn't entirely convinced.

"It sounds like you all have suffered loss as well," Scipio said, and I looked at him, realizing that, once again, I had tuned his presence out. "I'm truly sorry for that."

I watched the brooding figure for several seconds. "Thank you."

"Don't mention it," he replied. "So who's Mercury? Other than the messenger god of Rome?"

The three of us looked at him before Quess leaned over and loudly whispered, "I take it back. It looks like Bob is having a stroke! What else could explain all that gibberish?"

"It's Scipio," the AI practically spat, and I was amused that the hologram didn't depict himself frothing at the mouth. "And I'm not! Surely you know—"

"I hate to be rude," I said, already sensing something long and not mission-critical was going to start. "And thank you for understanding, but we have to get back to our friends."

Scipio smiled. "Of course," he said kindly. "I completely understand."

"Thank you. Quess."

"No problem," he replied with a smile. "So, when do you want to try to contact Mercury?"

"Tomorrow," I replied, and he laughed. When I didn't join in, he realized I was serious and shook his head.

"Liana..."

"I know," I said flatly. "It's dangerous. But we're blind, and that's more dangerous."

He hesitated, and then nodded. "All right," he conceded.

"Thank you," I said, fighting off my bone-deep exhaustion. "Then let's get back and update everyone about the existence of Scipio 1.0—new name to be determined—and finish setting up. The sooner we do that, the sooner everyone can get some sleep."

"Oh, sleep," Grey replied, his eyes suddenly tired. "How I miss it even now. Quess?"

"Same. Also, I could use a cuddle."

"Not from me, weirdo," Grey said with a surprised laugh, and I felt some of my grief diminish with the sound. Having a plan was going to keep us busy enough to avoid sinking into despair or trouble, and I could only pray that Grey's laugh was an indication that it was working.

I gestured for the others to head through the vent, and they went quickly, obviously ready to get stuff done so that we could all rest. As I started to kneel to get in, Scipio's voice stopped me.

"Liana?"

I turned, rising to meet the man who was now standing directly in front of me. "Yes?"

He suddenly looked very shy, and I watched, somewhat bemused, as he ran a hand through his hair, tugging at it. I knew it wasn't real, but it was such a human expression.

"I was wondering if you... if you would come visit me some more. I... I haven't been around others in so long. It would be nice to just... have a conversation, and find out what has happened in the Tower since Lionel passed. I can see that things have gone off the rails, but maybe I can help find a way to fix it?"

The smile on my face was genuine, surprising even me, but I went with it. "I'd like that," I said. "At the very least, it would give me an opportunity to discuss things with someone who actually knew the visionary behind this place. I have a lot of questions."

Because I wanted to know everything. Knowledge was power, and if there was some other enemy in play, or even a group of them, then I wanted to know who they were and what they wanted. I wanted to know if the Master Scipio AI was faulty, or had been tampered with. I also wanted to know more about how the main Scipio AI was created—if this one could tell us, maybe we could replicate it and then get him inside of the Core.

A smile blossomed on his face, and it was beautiful. He appeared so grateful that it made my heart ache for the poor machine. I was unable to imagine how impossibly alone he had felt over the years.

"Scipio, I'm really sorry for what happened to Lionel. It must've been so hard for you."

He inclined his head gently. "Thank you for that," he said hoarsely. "You're the first people I've talked to since the virus. I knew that people had come and gone; when I came to, Lionel's body had been removed, and my connection to the door leading to the access tunnel had been severed, likely due to it being welded shut."

I could hear the ache of loneliness in his voice, and felt for him. He'd spent centuries alone, clinging to life, waiting for someone to come and help him. Or even just talk to him. I understood that loneliness, although not to the extent he did, because it was how I felt anytime I wasn't with Zoe or Eric or even Grey. Everyone else would avoid me because of my rank, and it... hurt. More than I cared to admit.

"I've... gotta go," I said after half a minute had passed. "But I'll come by for a visit soon. Who knows, maybe I'll bring some of the others in our group with me."

"That would be delightful," he said, the corners of his eyes crinkling as his smile grew. "Also, I've thought about what you said, about a name, and I will endeavor to come up with something acceptable so that you and your friends will feel more... comfortable in my presence."

I nodded, and then turned and slid into the vent, ready to put this room and its mysteries to rest for a little while, and focus on making sure we were all safe. We could figure out how to use this Scipio to our advantage tomorrow.

6

"Let me get this straight," Zoe said, peering up from where she was arranged on the floor next to Eric. "You found another AI in a hidden room, have determined it's the first version of Scipio, and are letting it stay on?" Her head moved as she speared the three of us with a penetrating look.

"Yes," I replied with a nod.

"I'm confused," Eric interjected slowly.

"Yeah, well I'm pissed," Maddox said, leaning back on her hands and staring at me. "Why didn't you tell us about this when you first learned about it? Why didn't you tell the rest of us right then? Who put you in charge?"

"No one," I said. "But you were upset, and I—"

"Do not use my sorrow as an excuse for your actions," she snarled harshly, and I winced.

"And don't be mean to Liana just because she's trying to take care of us!" Tian shouted angrily, slapping Maddox lightly on the shoulder.

Maddox's face hardened, a flash of resentment burning through her eyes. I could only imagine how she felt right now—and I didn't blame her for taking it out on me.

"It's okay, Tian," I told the small girl. "Maddox is right. I probably should have told you when I found out." Actually, I still wasn't sure I had made the right call. Although, everyone had been in a state of shock, and there had been things that needed to be done that ensured our safety... But it was a moot point now. All that mattered was that it was out there now.

"No, you shouldn't have," Eric said automatically, as if that were the stupidest idea he had ever heard, and I stared at him, surprised by his reaction. "This is Command Basics 101," he said. "From our survival courses? The basic tenants that ensure safety to the Tower?"

"I never had a formal education," Maddox drawled, and I frowned. I couldn't tell if she was joking or not, but she didn't appear to be. I knew that Cali had taken her from the Tower at some point, but I was always under the impression it had been after she had turned fifteen, given the Squire's uniform hanging over her bed in the room in Sanctum. She wouldn't have one if she hadn't been old enough to join the department, which only happened at fifteen. But her quip about formal education made me reconsider, and wonder if she had been younger. And if so, how young? I knew it wasn't important, but I was curious.

"Well, basically, it says that those who lead need to know when and where to disseminate information," Eric said. "In critical life-or-death situations, when our lives are dependent on hiding from the Tower, Liana was right not to tell us about the AI. It would have distracted us from putting up the paint."

"We wouldn't have had to put up the paint if you weren't here," Maddox grumbled, and I sucked in a deep breath.

"It doesn't matter, because we are," I said, maintaining my composure. "And Eric's right—that's pretty much why I did it. But I'm still telling you now, especially because he doesn't appear to pose a threat to us."

"He's not connected to the Core," Quess informed them. "He's not the same Scipio that lives in the Core."

"That still doesn't answer my original question," Zoe said stubbornly, folding her arms across her chest. "Why are you keeping him on when he could be dangerous?"

I ran a hand over my face, as if I could scrape the exhaustion off of it. I wanted nothing more than to go to sleep right now, but this was the last bit of business before bed. Well, that, and deciding who would go with Quess to talk to Mercury tomorrow.

"Well, for one thing, I'm not convinced that he's dangerous. And second, because he could help keep us safe. Potentially," I said. "Quess says that he can probably get in and out of the other Tower systems without being detected, which would make him incredibly valuable to us. Look... I know this is alarming and scary, but if you want to go and meet him, to convince yourselves, then by all means, please do. He's certainly eager for company. But we have to make sure we paint that room first."

"We don't need to," Quess commented, and I looked at him, surprised. "It's shielded—it would have to be for him to have been down there undetected for so long."

Oh. That was great news, considering how much time we had

spent down there. I absorbed it, and then turned back to the matter at hand—Zoe.

I looked at her, raising an eyebrow in question. Her mouth twisted, and I knew that she wasn't entirely convinced. She was naturally suspicious, and while I knew for a fact that it was coming from an imagination spawned by her love of reading, it didn't mean her feelings weren't valid, especially considering Scipio 2.0 was going to have her executed. I would probably be just as suspicious, were I in her position. Heck, if it were Grey or someone else telling the both of us, we would probably bond together to resist it even harder. It was just who we were.

"Zo," I said softly, and she looked up at me. "Trust me." She stared at me a moment or two longer, and finally nodded.

"Okay," she replied. "I mean, I do trust you, Liana. It's just..." She stared past me, as if she could see Scipio through all the layers of ventilation between us, and visibly shuddered. I understood. I still couldn't shake the feeling that this might not have been the right call. Logically, I was certain it was the right move. But being within a hundred feet of something bearing the same name as the thing that had been ruling over my life for the past twenty years was a hard feeling to get around.

Getting to know him, and realizing that he was different, had helped. And I knew it would help her.

"I get it," I told her, and then smiled crookedly as an idea occurred to me. "But you wouldn't want to let a potential *deus ex machina* go uninvestigated, would you?" Her eyes widened, and then she smiled excitedly, her entire demeanor changing just like that. My smile deepened. Zoe was the best friend I had ever had in the whole world, which meant I knew exactly which buttons to push to inspire her interest. And *deus ex machina* was one of

Zoe's most obsessed-over literary devices, as she loved the idea of a character of power just magically manifesting itself right at the height of the plot to solve everything. It was the highlight of bad story writing to her, and she loved it.

"Now, there's one more thing before we can get to sleep—namely, we have to decide who's going to go talk to Mercury tomorrow. Quess and Maddox, one of you will have to, but I don't think you should go alone."

"I should be the one to go," Quess said, before Maddox could say anything. "No offense, Doxy, but you're not exactly the best with technology."

She narrowed her eyes at him and then rolled them so hard I thought they would fall out of her head and continue along the floor. "Whatever," she huffed. "There are other things that need to be done tomorrow, anyway."

I let her statement hang for a second, and then cleared my throat. "Thank you, Quess," I said. "So... who's going with him?"

"I'll go," Grey said, at the same time as Quess and Eric both said something to the effect of, "Liana should go."

"Me?" I said, looking at Quess and Eric before focusing on Grey. His brows were two angry slashes over his eyes, and I could tell he was upset by how quickly they had volunteered me. I wasn't sure if it was because he thought they were putting me in danger—or because he was offended that they hadn't considered him first. But it made me nervous. I didn't want him thinking that I had somehow commandeered the group.

"Guys, it doesn't have to be me. If Grey wants to go, then he can certainly go. Besides, I'm pretty confident it's *my* net they'll be fixated on. If I go out there, we'll certainly be caught."

"That's not an issue," Quess said. "As I like to say, there's some tech for that."

"That is literally the first time I'm hearing you say that," Maddox muttered, and I smiled in spite of myself.

"Fine, whatever. I have a device, Liana. It can keep them from picking up your signal."

I frowned. "Then why aren't the four of us using it now?"

"Because it can't be worn for prolonged periods without risking shorting out your net," he replied flatly.

I shuddered. Shorting out someone's net was rare, but did happen from time to time. Any electrical current applied directly to the implantation could cause it, and once it happened, it could severely damage the neocortex it ran across. It could even cause complete brain death. At the academy, we were taught never to use our batons on the back of anyone's neck, because the batons would and could do just that.

"Okay," I said, looking at Grey. "But Grey volunteered, so—"

"We know," Zoe said quietly, her gaze on the floor. "But Quess and Eric think you should go. And I happen to agree." She looked up at Grey, a small frown on her face. "I hope you understand. This isn't nepotism. Or at least, I don't think it is. But Liana is a trained interrogator, and she's spoken with him before."

"She does ask the best questions," Tian added, her voice nervous. "Not that Grey doesn't, but..."

"She basically became our leader when she started telling us what to do and we listened," Maddox said bitterly.

My heart sank into the pit of my stomach, and I looked around. "Uh, guys—no. We're not doing the leader thing. It's stupid. I just saw what needed to be done and did it. I'm definitely not your leader. That is *not* a thing we're doing."

"It has to be," Eric said, and I opened my mouth, ready to blast him with "It most certainly is not." But he cut me off. "Liana, we all ran when you told us to, back at Sanctum. We all got up and started painting because you told us we needed to. You handled a potentially difficult situation, albeit unilaterally, and then came back to tell us what you had done. That doesn't just make you a leader—it makes you a good one. And speaking for myself, I'm a much better follower than a leader."

"Oh yeah," Zoe deadpanned with a nod. "He really is. It's embarrassing some of the things Liana and I put him up to." Eric nudged her shoulder with his, giving her a chastising look, and her answering expression reminded me of a satisfied cat.

"It's great that you are self-aware enough to know who you are," Grey said, finally breaking his silence. "But I'm with Liana in that we don't need a leader. We should all have a say in what we do. Collectively."

"Exactly," I said. I was flattered by their words, but they were only highlighting the positives. Missing the parts where I was impulsive, arrogant, mouthy, and wildly disorganized. I was pretty sure those disqualified me from the running, seeing as a leader should be just the opposite. Sure, I had a few ideas here and there, but that didn't mean I was the best for the job. Working collaboratively was the best solution, if no one else wanted to step up.

"We don't agree," Quess said, and I gave him a look. He met my gaze, his dark blue eyes glittering, and then he shrugged. "Look, I sure as hell don't want the responsibility, if I'm going to be perfectly honest. I don't want to make the big decisions if I can avoid it. Provide equipment and mission support, absolutely, but I don't think I could bear it if I voted to do something that got someone killed."

"Besides, Liana's the best suited for the job," Maddox announced.

I met her stare, ready to tell her how wrong she was. I didn't have the qualifications for this at all, and I had the list to prove it.

"How do you figure that?" Grey demanded angrily.

And his continued anger, while not overt or even loud, unsettled me. I could understand his question, but I couldn't understand his anger. I couldn't tell if it was directed at me or them, but it was hard not to take it personally. Everyone else had at least said nice things about me, and while I didn't want to be one of those girls who needed compliments all the time, an acknowledgement from him would've been nice. So far, he had been the only one not to say anything positive about me as a leader.

"She's proved she's level headed and patient," Maddox said, somehow managing to sound both annoyed that she had to spell it out for us, and bitter about my qualities as she listed them. "She's resourceful, clever, and can get to the heart of a problem and figure a way out. She's good at reading people and knows how to ask good questions. And, most importantly, she's not egotistical. Every decision made would be for the benefit of *everyone*. It would never be self-serving."

I guessed I was glad she said that with all that bitterness in her voice. Because I would've blushed under the surprisingly complementary assessment of my character, otherwise. As it was, I was still pleased that she seemed to be working past her anger at me. Or at least, she was trying to.

"An hour ago, you were accusing her of being selfish enough to go after her friend. Isn't that self-serving?" Grey asked.

His words were like a small needle to the bubble that Maddox had started to create, and I felt it like a pinprick in my heart. No, I wasn't perfect, but that... *hurt.* There was no need for him to talk about me like that, and I started to feel anger rising within me.

"This is beginning to sound less and less like you don't want us to have a leader, and more like you just don't want *Liana* to lead us," Zoe said.

"What? No, that's not what I'm saying!"

"But it's what it sounds like," I said, unable to stop myself. He looked at me, a flicker of doubt rippling across his face. Mine stayed angry, and the doubt faded as his expression hardened into an icy mask.

"So what if it is? My concerns are valid. We don't need a leader!"

"Yes, but the rest of us want one," Quess reminded him patiently. "So what's your problem?"

"My problem?" he asked, his eyebrows going high. "My problem is that not a single person here knows what we're doing, and electing one person over another, just because they managed to take care of a few things, is more than a bit stupid."

"A *few* things?" Zoe exclaimed, her eyes bulging.

I swallowed hard. He was now adding salt to the wound, and while I wasn't typically a proud person, this was really becoming upsetting. It was almost like he didn't think I was capable of doing anything past what I had already done. Why was he being so petty?

"Yes, *a few things*," Grey said, not backing down. "But so what if she has? That doesn't mean that she knows what's best for the future."

"And you do, by dictating who should and should not lead us?" I burst out, putting my hands on my hips.

We glared at each other for a long moment, and I waited for

him to say something, to realize he was acting like a jerk and apologize.

"Forget it," he said abruptly, shaking his head. "You've already made your decisions. Congratulations, Liana." His voice came out a bitter growl, and my emotions threatened to boil over.

"Thank you," I replied, unable to keep a bitter bite out of my voice. "All of you, I'm not sure what to say, except... I promise to do the best I can to keep you all safe." I managed to make the last part of it sound genuine, but faltered when it came to adding anything else.

"Nice speech," Maddox said wryly. "Is that all? I'd kind of like to get some sleep."

I nodded, and everyone immediately began to get up off the floor and get the hammocks set up. I lingered, my arms wrapped around my stomach, and Grey remained still as well, his back rigid.

I waited, hoping he would say something, but when it became apparent he wouldn't, I started. "Grey, what—"

"Don't, Liana," he said. "I'm still upset, and I don't want to talk about it."

The hurt continued to build. I was beyond frustrated; this was the man who not even half an hour ago had been holding my hand to comfort me. He had reassured me that none of what had happened was my fault.

And now he was acting like *this*.

"Grey, what *is* your problem?" I asked, unable to let it go. "You're acting like a jerk."

He finally looked at me, his face hard. "You don't even get it, do you?" he bit off.

"Well, I'm trying to, but you're not talking!"

"You don't *get* what being a leader involves."

I paused, stumbling for words as I tried to reel in my emotions. "I... I'm not claiming to be the best," I managed. "In fact, I stated the opposite! But the others seem to believe in me, so I guess I must have a fair idea of what it involves... What is it? Did *you* want to be the leader?"

He gave me an incredulous look, and then stood in one fluid motion. "Whatever. I'm going to bed. We can talk about it tomorrow."

He didn't wait for my reply, just walked off. I gaped at him, watching him move around to the other side of a blanket that had been strung across a long pipe, stretching almost perfectly across the width of the room, sectioning it off. Eric and Zoe had set it up after they finished with the rust hawks, dividing the room into a common area and sleeping area.

The blanket rose and fell as he passed, and then he was gone, hidden behind it.

"What just happened?" I asked out loud a moment later, more baffled and hurt than angry now. I didn't expect anyone to answer—the question was delivered under my breath, after all. Still, I was vaguely disappointed that the answer wasn't forthcoming.

7

"This is a neural scrambler," Quess said, holding a small black box the size of my pinkie nail carefully pinched between two large fingers. "It goes right at the base of the skull, around the area where your net sits, and activates it."

It was the next evening, and Quess and I were getting ready to depart. We'd only been up a few hours; it had been late in the morning when we had finally gotten to sleep, and none of us had stirred until just around sunset. We had broken down the tasks that needed to be done and given everyone jobs, and talking with Mercury was Quess's and my first task for the evening. I had to admit, I was pretty nervous about setting foot outside. It had been less than twenty-four hours since Devon attacked us, and I had no doubt that he was still searching the area.

"Activate it?" I asked, dubious of the tiny thing. "Isn't that what we're supposed to be avoiding?"

"Well, yes and no. This is basically going to hold your net

open, as if you're about to establish a connection with another person's net, and that will prevent them from actively scanning you. The downside is that it will cause your net to buzz continuously while it's on. Two hours maximum, all right?"

I nodded, my mouth dry. "Got it," I replied, wiping some of the sweat from my palms. I took one last second to prepare myself, and then turned around and lifted my hair, tensing in anticipation. Moments later, his hands were there, pressing the chip against the exposed skin at the nape of my neck. I lowered my head when the pressure withdrew, and turned.

"Is that—" I cut off as the buzz of the net activating began to rattle around under my skull, and winced. "Never mind, it's working."

"Good," he said, taking a step back to get his things. Unlike me, he didn't need a neural scrambler—it was extremely unlikely Devon could identify him based on the whirlwind fighting he had been engaged in, so we reasoned his net was fine. I waited for him to pick up the satchel next to him, then proceeded to open the hatch.

Immediately there was a rush of air and wind as the door pulled up and away from the hole in the ground, and I looked out into the inky blackness below. I could hear the sound of the river rushing by, but beneath us there was nothing but irradiated sands and earth. If we fell from here, there would be no way to save ourselves.

"Hey, so, uh... I meant to ask you. How are you doing since..."

"Since Grey and I fought?" I asked, standing and pulling a lash end out of the slot in my sleeve where the bead was kept. "No need to dance around it. Everyone was there."

"I'm sorry. Has everyone been dancing around it?"

"More like not talking about it in the most overt ways—namely by avoiding one-on-one conversations with me. Looks like you're the odd man out."

I spun the bead and let out a few inches of slack with a sharp flick of my wrist, then slapped it onto the ceiling with a sharp *tink*.

"Well, I'm certainly not going to complain about getting a few hours in which I have you to myself, but... I'm not so certain I want to spend it talking about your boyfriend."

I gave him a wry look. "Then don't."

I dropped down through the hole, eager to get away from the conversation, and let the winch in my suit lower me quickly, until I was dangling in a wide-open space. The wind caught me, pushing me to one side, and I tossed the other lash end a few feet away, attaching it to the greenery above me and moving to one side to give Quess some room.

It was pitch black outside—nighttime, with everything covered in a layer of shadow, so I quickly donned the goggles with red lenses that Cali had given me. According to her, they enhanced ambient light, as well as revealed hidden marks Tian had painted on the walls that guided our way. They certainly helped cut through the darkness as I peered around, noting the absence of any movement.

We were near the edge of the arm that jutted out of the Tower like a flat, wide fin. It was as wide as the Tower, but stretched out three hundred feet. There were fourteen greeneries in total, each five stories high and staggered by twenty stories. We were under Greenery 1, which started fifty feet above the surface. Unlike Greenery 2, which sat on the opposite side of 1, this one crossed over the river that fed into the hydro-turbines, which generated power for the Tower. The turbines kicked up a lot of water, so part of the underside of the greenery was blanketed in a thick mist.

But here it was clear and still. There wasn't any sign of movement. "It's clear!" I called quietly, and a moment later, Quess dropped down.

"This way," he said.

To my surprise, he moved away from the Tower itself, toward the edge of the greenery. He threw his lashes quickly, but I kept up, using the goggles to check for any markings from Tian, to help me avoid obstacles like pieces of exposed machinery and keep an eye out for any crimson-clad figures that could be patrolling the area.

Quess led us directly to the edge, then, to my surprise, up and over it, scaling the side using his lashes. I followed, feeling horribly exposed as we made our way up the glass-covered side. It was silly—no one inside could see through the glass when it was dark like this—but I still felt vulnerable.

Quess suddenly shifted his trajectory partway up and headed right, toward a dome that jutted out of the side of the greenery. I recognized the design from the time Cali had taken me with her to talk with Mercury; it was a relay station for collecting and uploading net data to Scipio's mainframe. One of the places where they gathered our emotional content and compressed it into streams of data for him to render judgment upon us. The dome itself was a computer, in a fashion, but only collected data and relayed net transmissions to help ease some of the total load on Scipio.

I stared at the pod, biting my lip and thinking about the meeting with *our* Scipio earlier that morning. According to him, the main AI was supposed to collect that information to identify those who weren't adjusting well, and offer them support. But now pods like these represented places that contributed to the ranking system, stripping away all empathy and compassion and converting people into a numeric value that determined their value to the Tower. It was hard not to hate them, even though I knew now that they'd started out as part of a benign system—even a helpful one.

Quess cracked open the hatch on the side, opening it and slipping inside. A moment later I lashed up after him and pulled the hatch closed behind me, sealing us inside the tight, dark space, which was lit only by a few small lights that blinked intermittently on and off—this station was a bit different than the one I'd visited with Cali.

Light blossomed from a flashlight in Quess's hand, and he shone it around the tight space, revealing a terminal on one of the walls. He crossed over to it, pulling his bag around to his side. I moved up next to him, taking the light from his hands and holding it up while he rummaged inside the bag. A moment later, he withdrew his hand, holding a notebook, and dropped the bag on the floor.

"One second," he said as he opened the book, his eyes tracing over the small but legible writing inside. He handed the notebook to me, and I took it, keeping it open for him while his fingers began to fly over the console's controls, putting in lines of code and text at a speed that rivaled Cali's. The process still took several moments, and when it was done, he stepped away from the console and sighed.

"Well, now all we can do is wait, and I'm not really sure how long it will take for him to get back to us. If it gets too close to two hours…"

"I'll go," I assured him. "I trust you to take point with Mercury. But... I'm not sure if we should tell Mercury about Scipio."

"Yeah, about that. I've come up with a few new names. Do you think he'll let us call him something cool, like Harbinger or Death of a Tyrant?"

"You know, I'm not sure he'll like those, but feel free to bring it up."

"Oh, I will. Getting under his skin is fun."

"He doesn't have skin," I pointed out. "And I'm serious right now, Quess. I don't think we should tell anyone about him."

Quess sobered immediately. "Why not? I mean, Mercury's helped us before."

"That doesn't mean he's going to help us now," I said. I still wasn't sure if I trusted Mercury, and I had no way of knowing how he'd react to the fact that I hadn't waited for him before going after Zoe. I was certain he'd blame me for what had happened, or at the very least, be less willing to help. Still, that wasn't the only reason I didn't want to tell him about Scipio. "Anyway, that is not why I don't think we should tell anyone about him."

"Why, then?"

I bit my lip. I knew this was going to sound paranoid, but I wasn't going to lie. "Because I keep asking myself, what if that Prometheus group that Scipio mentioned still exists in some form today?"

"Yeah, but..." He trailed off, and I saw the realization dawn. "Right... if it got out that we had another Scipio and they learned about it, they'd come looking to finish the job."

"And probably kill us to keep the secret from getting out."

"So it's better to sit on it?"

I nodded. "Unless you come up with a better plan."

Quess laughed bitterly. "Oh, no. We already have more than enough stuff we can't deal with on our plate for me to want to add another helping. We don't have a way of manufacturing more Paragon, so getting out of here doesn't seem like much of a possibility, because we won't be able to control our numbers. We also have to think about the people who are already using it, because I'm sure Mercury will want them warned. And if we can't make more... twenty-nine is a lot of people to try to hide. I'm not sure we can even find enough places for all of them in time. We should already be looking for another place, as it is—a backup in case we're discovered."

I sighed and ran a hand through my hair. I did not need Quess reminding me of the multitude of what ifs that kept running through my head. Our options were severely limited, if we didn't want to get caught.

"You're right," I said. "Which is why I'm hoping Mercury can give us something, anything, to work with. Because if he can't, the five people back there are going to break long before the Knights ever find us. We need something to focus on, to distract us from our fear, to give us a goal. Without one, we're just stumbling around blindly."

"Whoa, Liana," Quess said, taking a step back and looking suddenly uncomfortable. "That's a little bleak, isn't it?"

I exhaled, and rested my head against the wall behind me, looking up into the shadows Quess's light was creating on the ceiling. "Probably," I admitted. "I swear, I'm not trying to be, but I've been trying to figure out what to do, and it just feels like everything has broken past the point of repair."

Quess chuckled dryly. "We're all feeling that way, Liana. But we're tough, and we're going to figure things out, okay? I mean, we may have forced leadership on you, but we're not going to let you do this alone."

I closed my eyes and felt my hands curl into two angry balls at his mention of last night. "Yeah, about that. What the heck?"

"You mean your boyfriend's little tantrum? I was wondering about that myself! Any chance that means you'll be single soon?" He grinned at me, his eyebrows twitching upward in what I assumed was his attempt at looking seductive. "Might get a little chilly in here while we wait," he added when I didn't say anything. "Maybe we should snuggle for the body heat."

I straightened my head and arched an eyebrow. "Not going to happen. And I wasn't talking about Grey. Just... how the heck did all that happen?"

"Maddox," Quess said simply. "I mean, say what you will about her social skills, she has a practical streak a mile wide and ten thousand miles deep."

"It certainly surprised the hell out of me." I paused, thinking about the stoic young woman. About her fiery-haired mother who had shared her piercing green eyes. Which led me to think about Devon and Cali during the fight.

I had noticed it then, but in the chaos and grief, my mind had slid past it to deal with the immediate future. Now that things had calmed down somewhat, and I had some time to kill, I suddenly wanted to know more. In fact, I was surprised it hadn't come up sooner. Honestly, Maddox had to be upset that her father had killed her mother, right? Unless... Cali had left him for someone else. But that didn't track with their exchange at all. He'd made it sound like he hadn't been able to find her, implying she had left the Knights completely when she disappeared. And according to her, that was what she had done. How would she have kept herself hidden for long enough to conceive Maddox? I supposed it was possible that there was someone else, but based on what Cali had told me, it just didn't make any sense.

"Hey, Quess? Could you, uh, tell me more about Maddox?" I asked, meeting his gaze. Maybe he could shed some light on why she hadn't mentioned Devon earlier.

"Maddox?" Quess's eyes widened in surprise, and he cocked his head at me. "Why do you want to talk about her?" He looked around, as if suspecting some kind of trap. "Is this a chick thing? Is... Maddox somewhere waiting, in case I say anything bad about her?"

I rolled my eyes. "No, this is not a chick thing," I said, a touch bemused. "Honestly, do you think that there is some sort of... conspiracy between women out there?"

"Well, yes." He arched an arrogant eyebrow. "You telling me there isn't?"

"Okay, there is just so much there that I'm not really prepared to unpack, so let me just tactfully withdraw, and return to my original question about Maddox." As much as I wanted to tease Quess for his semi-sexist remarks, I didn't want to derail the conversation from the task at hand.

"I mean, sure, I guess I could tell you about her," Quess said, lowering himself to the floor and adjusting his long legs. I followed suit, realizing we were going to be here for a while before Mercury got back to us. "It kind of depends on what you want to know."

"Fair enough. I guess I'm just trying to understand why, of all the things she's upset about, the fact that her father killed her mother seems to have been entirely overlooked. I mean, is she even coping with that?"

He stared at me with a look on his face that made me feel like I had suddenly grown two heads that were singing backwards in Cogspeech. "I'm not even sure *I'm* coping with it," he said after a moment, breaking the pregnant silence between us. "What are you talking about?"

I pressed my lips together. "Isn't... Maddox Devon's child?"

"What? No. That's impossible."

I looked over at him and shook my head. "When they were talking, Devon said something about how he came *home* and Cali was *gone*. Twenty years ago. Maddox is nineteen."

Quess's brows drew together, and he looked away, his posture radiating deep thoughtfulness. I let him stew while I contemplated what I had just done. If Quess didn't know, and Maddox wasn't talking about it... it was very possible that she didn't know, either. Which made me wonder why Cali had kept it a secret.

Had it been too emotional, or was there another reason? Why had she hidden that detail from everyone? My mind raced over the brief conversations Cali and I had shared, scrubbing them for any clue. She had mentioned Maddox's father once—and had spoken about him in the present tense. She had also mentioned once that Maddox had convinced her to escape the Tower once her number started getting lower and lower. Which meant Maddox would have been old enough to know. That meant she had to know, didn't it? And why hadn't he asked after her? I mean, he wasn't so far gone to also want his daughter dead, was he? Did he just not care?

I realized all this speculation didn't matter. All that *did* matter was the fact that I might have revealed a secret about Maddox's heritage that even she didn't know. I looked up at Quess, prepared to tell him to just forget about it, when he began to speak.

"Cali never talked about who she was married to, but she once told me that their marriage had to be kept secret because of their positions. I always assumed it was because she was the Knight Lieutenant, married to a Knight Commander. But... maybe it was a lot bigger than that."

I suddenly recalled that Cali had served as Devon's Knight Lieutenant, acting as his advisor and right-hand woman shortly after the Tourney. I had almost forgotten, but that was because there weren't many classes on the Champion's second-in-command at the academy. There were not many rules about dating and marriage inside the Knights, but there were rules about it when it came to their respective positions. The biggest issue was the fear that nepotism between a Commander and their partner might cause them to act emotionally in a crisis. It was also strictly forbidden for the Lieutenant and Champion to become involved, as they had critically different responsibilities: the Champion was the head of the department, and served on the council to help make decisions on behalf of the Tower. He still commanded the Knights, of course, but his Lieutenant not only served as his advisor, but the voice of the Knights beneath him. They were expected to tell the Champion how the Knights were feeling about a particular issue, and expected to advise the Knight on how best to serve the council and the Knights. As such, a relationship between the two positions would be seen as... messy, to say the least. The other problem was that the Knight Lieutenant was the only individual in the Citadel who could go to the Tower to report a Champion as being unfit for leadership. The rule was enacted after Kyle Pine, the fourth Champion, reportedly started ordering (and sometimes even forcing) the Knights to act more violently toward citizens, encouraging public beatings and the like. Kyle's Lieutenant had tried to reason with him, but when that failed, he pled his case to the council, and Scipio recommended enacting a new protocol within the Knights department itself—namely that the Lieutenant could request a vote to have the Champion removed. The case was discussed in great detail in our lessons, because it was significant for setting new precedent. It was the first time that the council had enacted a departmental exclusive protocol, *and* it was the first bloodless coup of a department in history.

If Cali and Devon had been married, then that meant their roles as Champion and Lieutenant had been, at some point, illegal. That could explain why no one had ever mentioned it.

"When did she leave?" I asked, unable to help myself.

"Right after she found out she was pregnant with Maddox. Her number had been dropping for a while, especially after all of the information she was being made privy to as Devon's Lieutenant."

I frowned. "No, wait. That doesn't track at all. Cali said Maddox convinced her to leave."

Quess shrugged and raised an eyebrow. "Cali did tend to get poetic about all the sentimental stuff. I'm sure she meant that she found out she was pregnant, and *that* convinced her."

"Oh." I frowned as another thought occurred to me. "Wait, how does Maddox have a net? She'd need one to move around the Tower without triggering the undoc alarms."

"How do you think?" Quess said smugly. "I made one."

I gave him an incredulous look, not buying into that at all. I didn't know everything about nets, but my brother had told me a lot. He'd gotten quite fascinated with them during his second year as a Bit for the IT department and I couldn't get him to shut up about them. Most of it I didn't understand, but basically, the nets were comprised of long strands of silica-wrapped microfilaments. Before they were implanted at the base of the skull, their dormant shape looked like a computer chip, the long silica laces that would eventually curl across and over a person's cerebral cortex like the legs of a daddy-long-legs settling its small body down over its prey.

The nets needed power, which was fine when they were implanted. The human body generated a constant temperature of 98.6 degrees, and the heat from our blood in our brain was a great source of thermal energy, which it happily harvested. When the nets were in their dormant stage, a small battery, no larger than a pin prick, provided them with enough energy to survive for up to two years on a shelf.

Once an ID was uploaded to a net, it could never be used again. It wasn't common knowledge, but I had learned in the academy that, in the early years of the Tower, black market dealers dealing in old world supplies started harvesting nets from corpses and hijacking them to give other criminals fake IDs, so they could hide from the law. A one-time transferrable fail-safe had solved that problem.

Quess had worked in IT – I'd give him that. And IT was where the nets were created, in a secret process that Alex had only ever touched on briefly in our conversations. But I was pretty certain that Quess was pulling my leg, mostly because the resources to make them were hard to get ahold of, and they also required a very special clean environment to be made in. Quess had neither, and I doubted Cali would have let him put anything less than a pristine chip into her daughter's head.

"Nice try," I said, and he grinned at me cheekily, unashamed.

"It was worth a shot. And to answer your question, Mercury managed to get one for her. I was figuring we'd ask him for some clean ones, so we don't have to worry about using the scrambler or getting pinged by the Tower."

"Good call," I said. New nets with clean IDs would go a long way to making me feel safer. Even now I felt exposed, in spite of Quess's reassurance that the scrambler would work.

My mind drifted back to Maddox, and I sighed. "So is there a chance Devon doesn't even know he has a child?"

"Whoa, I'm not even remotely ready to accept that Devon is Maddox's father. Just... let me get my head around that. I mean... are you sure?"

I hesitated, going over it yet again in my head. "I mean, I'm fairly sure. Devon... He was angry."

"He was there to kill us," Quess pointed out. "Maybe he's the type of person who needs to be angry to do that."

A shudder came over me, and I looked away, closing my eyes to the image of Cali falling into the torrid waters below. "Maybe, but I heard what I heard and I saw what I saw. They were married, and Maddox is their daughter. It's the only thing that makes sense."

But if Maddox didn't know, I wasn't going to be the one to tell her. It would do nothing but hurt her further, and maybe even cause her to go off the handle a little bit.

"I can't believe this," Quess muttered, and he shifted around on the floor, angling himself so that he could look me directly in the eye. "What are we going to do?"

"Do?" I asked. "What do you think we should do?"

"Maddox has a right to know who her father is. If Cali never told her, or even lied about it, then doesn't she have a right to know the truth?"

I blinked at him, and immediately shook my head. "I don't think we should tell her," I said. "It's only going to hurt her more to know. And I can't really see what it would achieve in the end. I sometimes think ignorance is better than truth."

"That is really jaded, Liana."

I shrugged and gave him a pointed look. "Hey, you tell me how this information will somehow be helpful to Maddox, and I will support it."

"Well..." He trailed off, looking thoughtful. Then he shrugged. "What if we could use her to spy for us? Like... have her approach Devon and tell him—"

"Okay, I'm going to stop you right there," I said, unwilling to let the insanity continue. "No offense, Quess, but that idea is two steps over the edge of the Tower. For one, Devon isn't going to trust her, and two... do you seriously think that Maddox is going to be able to control her anger at him for long enough to say hello, let alone spy on him?"

Quess raked a hand through the swatch of black hair topping his head. "No, you're right. It's a dumb idea."

I sighed and leaned back onto the palms of my hands. "No. Well... yes, but your heart is in the right place. I shouldn't have brought it up in the first place. It was just bothering me that she wasn't talking about it! I never considered that she just didn't know. But no. I really don't think we should tell her. We should just focus on the things we can do something about, and leave the rest of it behind."

He nodded. "So... do you really think we should try to use Scipio 1.0 to replace the big bad one?"

I shrugged. "Maybe, but... I mean, a part of me is asking who am I, and what can I even do to fix that whole mess upstairs? Everyone worships Scipio, which means they worship everything he stands for. Sure, it might not be general knowledge that they are executing ones, but will anyone really care when they find out? Really? The council even supported the decision! Should I execute them in return, for blindly following Scipio's recommendation? Besides, how would we even do it? According to Office Scipio, he's not exactly up for the task, size-wise. How are we going to figure out a protocol to purge and replace the bad Scipio with the good?"

Quess leaned back, considering my words. "I, uh... I didn't think about it like that. You have a point, I guess. I mean, I wouldn't even know—" He paused as a beeping sound began chirping from the wall terminal. "Well, there's Mercury."

I turned toward the sound, squaring my shoulders. It was my first act as a "leader," so... I could only hope I didn't screw up too badly.

8

We both stood, but I held back as Quess moved over to the terminal. I knew from Mercury himself and from Cali's comments that Mercury didn't like surprises, so this wasn't going to be a good call.

"Cali, are you safe?"

The digital alteration didn't hide the concern in his voice, and I sighed as Quess looked back at me, his eyes suddenly round and helpless.

"Cali's dead," I said, choking the words out. "So is Roark."

"You," Mercury growled through the speakers. "You did this. *You* went to the Medica to find your friend. How did you know?"

"About her? That's my secret," I said, unwilling to give up my brother's role in tipping me off. Alex was the ace up my sleeve, and I was already sure he was worried about me. Our last conversation had been held while I was doing my best to escape from

Devon—while leading him away from my friends. He didn't need Mercury, whoever he was, on his case as well. "Everyone else is safe: Maddox, Tian, Quess, myself, Grey, and Zoe... and Eric."

"Eric? MacGillus? He's listed as a potential hostage—or a conspirator. As is your friend Zoe Elphesian. Obviously everyone knows *you* are alive, and now your picture has been circulated to every department head. Sensor sweeps are being conducted all over the Tower. For you and Grey Farmless. I trust you're taking the necessary precautions?"

"Yes," I said, just as Quess finally found his voice.

"I hooked her up to a neural scrambler."

"She can't use those forever," Mercury replied. "We're going to have to see about getting her a replacement net."

"You are?" I said. "A second ago, you seemed pretty angry with me."

"Yes, well... Cali was a good friend of mine. As was Roark. And they both saw something in you, so..." He trailed off, and while the sentiment was nice, I still wasn't certain that I could trust him. Not now that I was a leader and had several other people depending on me to guide them. But I had to be careful—I didn't want to lose a potential friend here either. "How is everyone holding up? You're not fighting with each other, are you?"

"No injuries, if that's what you're asking, but... Cali's death hit us all pretty hard," Quess said. "Roark's too," he added when I gave him a sharp look. "We've appointed Liana as a leader."

"There are worse choices, I suppose," Mercury replied. "She did score very well in leadership roles, although her impulsiveness caused her instructors some concern when—"

"The details of my personnel file are not up for discussion," I stated flatly. "And definitely not right now. We don't exactly have a lot of time, and this scrambler is beginning to get really painful." It was true—the underside of my skull felt like throbbing hot magma was winding through my neocortex, causing it to ache fiercely. I'd been ignoring it, but that was getting harder. I checked my indicator, and saw that an hour had passed since we had left. Time was definitely running short.

"Mercury, everyone is fine," I said, "but we're trapped under the greenery until we get new nets. Can you get us any?"

"I'm already working on it; I figured you'd need some. I'm planning to send an emissary down sometime in the next few days with information and hopefully some new nets for you."

"Not going to come yourself?" I asked, already knowing his answer.

"Decidedly not." Mercury bristled. "I've taken great pains to secure my identity, and I'm going to keep it that way for as long as possible. It's for my safety and yours."

"Yeah, but we only have your word to go on," I said, sensing my moment to strike. "I mean, no offense, Mercury, but how do we know we can trust you? For all I know, you could just sell us out to Devon at any time. You certainly don't need the hassle. Why put yourself at risk for us?"

Quess gave me a sharp look of warning, which roughly read, *Don't upset our only ally*, and I nodded. I didn't want to anger him either—but I wanted to know what he gained from all this.

Mercury was quiet for a long moment. "I can see why they made you the leader. That took some guts, considering I'm the only friend you've got."

"Can you really blame me for asking?"

"I suppose not, but I don't owe you any sort of explanation. I'm helping you. You can either accept it or refuse it, end of discussion."

"That's not good enough." My heart pounded in my chest, and I was worried I might be pressing too hard, but if I could understand why he was helping us, then it would go a long way toward helping me to trust him. "You say we have to trust you, but we really don't have any guarantees that you aren't working against us."

"No, you don't. But let me answer you like this: when my emissary comes to you, I'd very much like it if you sent some Paragon back. Rank 10, if you want me to be of any use to you in the future."

I paused, absorbing that information. I had assumed that Mercury didn't need Paragon, that he was like Eric and was naturally happy enough to fool the net, but it seemed I was wrong. Mercury did need Paragon, which we had. That put us on equal footing. For now.

"I didn't think you were using it," I said, voicing my confusion out loud. "I thought you helped Roark find the flaw to exploit."

"I did do that, but the two are not mutually exclusive. I helped him so he would help me. May I ask about the Paragon? How much is left? Did the formula survive?"

"The formula was lost with Roark," I said hesitantly. Well, not entirely lost—there was still the chance we could get a sample from Jasper. But I wasn't about to bring that up. "We have all of his stock though."

"Well, that stash you're sitting on is all that remains. And I know that Roark didn't have enough to last twenty-nine people a month. We're going to have to figure out a way to get it replicated, and fast."

I looked at Quess, who was frowning. "We're still on the net thing, Mercury," I said. "We haven't even discussed what we're going to do about the Paragon and the—"

"Don't you want to make it?" Mercury asked, sounding surprised. "Isn't that the next part of your plan?"

"Plan?" I looked at Quess. "We haven't really talked about that yet." I felt stupid for admitting that, but we hadn't. So much had happened in the twenty-four hours since Sanctum fell. We didn't really have a goal past survival, and I wasn't even sure how everyone felt about the original plan to leave the Tower, especially now that we were aware of the first Scipio. I was sure the others had wondered at the possibility of using him to replace the one in the Core, just as I had, in spite of his insistence that he wasn't able to.

So those were our choices—ones I would have to make clear to the group. Try to leave, or stay to fix Scipio. Both plans would require new nets; both would require more Paragon.

"You don't have a plan?" Mercury asked, the synthesizer managing to capture the appalled tone in his voice.

"We honestly haven't had the time to discuss it," I said, still deep in thought. "But no matter what we decide, we know that Paragon will play a part. I'll talk to the others and see if we can start making it long term. Quess has medical experience and Grey worked with Roark, so maybe we can come up with a way of recovering the formula. If worse comes to worst, we'll sneak into the Medica and see if we can't run an analysis on one of the pills.

But I'm not going to turn my back on the people Roark recruited, no matter what we decide, so if you know who they are, I'll need a list. Grey might have one, but I can't be sure and he's not here, so..."

"I'll send you a list with the names, locations, and details of the people Roark and I recruited," he replied. "But, Liana, I want to know what you and everyone have to decide about? Even with Paragon to hide you, Roark said the body builds up a defense after enough time. So what other options have you discovered?"

I blinked, realizing I had almost screwed up. Mercury didn't know about the other Scipio, or a chance at restoring some semblance of sanity to the Tower itself. In his mind, there was only one option for survival, and that was to leave.

My mind fumbled fast, and found what I hoped would be a believable answer. "Roark. None of us down here ever knew the details of Roark's plan. In fact, Cali wanted to fight the system, if you'll recall. Now that there's a bunch of us, we have to decide whose path to follow, and we just haven't had time to think about any of that. But thank you for reminding me about the Paragon— it had slipped my mind."

"Glad to be of service. And for the record, I do want to leave, so put my vote there."

I stared at the terminal. "If you want a vote, you should show up."

There was a long pause, in which Quess gave me another hard look, reminding me not to push too hard.

"On that note," Mercury said, clearly and pointedly changing the subject and not addressing my comment. "While Grey's and your faces might be the most famous inside the Tower currently, something... ah... interesting has been brought to my attention.

Liana, there's some... rather important people who want to meet you."

"A meeting?" I stammered, meeting Quess's eyes. "With me? Why me?"

It was hard keeping a lid on the sudden anxiety his words had caused. Mysterious people who wanted to speak with me? Why? Who were they, and what did they want? And most importantly, what did they want with me *specifically*? I was a criminal. Which made this feel suspicious—like a noose being tightened around my throat.

"Because of your unique status," he replied cryptically, and I barely refrained from snapping at him.

"Unique status as what?" I grated out. "Who are these people, and what do they want?"

"I honestly don't know," he replied after a pause. "I'm trying to figure it out myself, but they are running some security protocols that I haven't even seen before."

"Security protocols?" I repeated, looking at Quess.

"Coding," Quess said. "I'm guessing in this case it was to hide their net ID information and whatnot."

"Very good, Quessian. And correct. I tried to run a hack, but they talked for only long enough to give me the message. They said they'd contact me again in a day or two."

"That's really suspicious, Mercury," I informed him.

"I am aware. But..." He hesitated, and Quess and I leaned forward together in anticipation. "Look, they insisted that they wanted to talk. They reached out to me using a secure connection that I'm fairly convinced can never be traced."

"That means they're IT, Mercury," Quess said. "And you and I are probably the only ones anyone could possibly be referring to if they said, 'Hey, come on, IT is not that bad.' Cause it *is* that bad, and people like you and I are rare."

Quess's rant was slightly humorous, but nobody laughed. The situation was too serious for that. We were both afraid of what this mysterious group could mean. My mind had already started to wonder who it could be; first it settled on Devon—maybe this was him trying to lure me out of hiding. But that didn't seem like his style, so I quickly dismissed it. And it could be a Knight who was raised in IT, but that seemed unlikely.

"Quess, what do you take me for? The script wasn't like anything we've ever created in IT. It's *different*. No one in IT could've written it—it's unlike anything I've ever seen. Do you really think I'm an idiot?"

The last words rose in volume, and I winced; apparently Mercury didn't like it when we questioned him or his methods. Which was unfair. We hadn't seen anything he was talking about; we only had his word to go on. We had every right to ask questions, seeing as it affected us directly.

"No, but we are the people who are going to be putting ourselves in danger for it," I said gently. "So it's important we understand exactly what we're getting."

Mercury sighed, the synthesizer making a melodic sequence of sounds. "You're right, and I'm sorry. I shouldn't have snapped at you."

"Tell us why you think I should meet with these people," I said flatly.

Mercury cleared his throat. "Well, to be perfectly honest, I'm not entirely convinced you should, but I wanted to pass the message on. All they said was that they could help, and you'd have to meet with them if you wanted to know more. I'm convinced that they aren't part of IT or the Knights... I actually think they might be black market dealers, but who knows?"

"And you think she should meet with them?" Quess asked.

"I do—mainly because they seem well connected, and you could use an ally down there. For all I know they're another undoc group that has been around for a while, and they want to offer you harbor in exchange for Liana's fighting skills—not a lot of people know how to fight. Whatever it is that they want to meet for, I think it's safe to say that it's not exactly legal, which in its own, weird way, makes for a potential ally."

Mercury made a good point, and when he put it like that, I didn't see the harm in just meeting and talking with them. I was curious to see what they wanted, and definitely interested in meeting another fringe group from the Tower.

But this wasn't a decision I could make unilaterally.

"We'll have to talk about it—I need to consult the others," I said.

"Understandable, but we don't have too long. I'll tell them you're interested in a meeting, and we'll see where and when they recommend. We can take it from there. Remember, if anything smells fishy, then you don't have to show up."

I smiled. "I already considered that." I paused, letting the subject fall flat, and then changed the topic. The revelation of this group that wanted to meet with us was interesting, but there was still something else we needed, and we were on a timetable. I'd bring it up to the group and let them decide. "Listen, we're also going to need—"

I broke off as a stabbing pain in my skull intensified, becoming almost blinding. The pain grew hotter and tighter, making it diffi-cult to think past its sharp ache. I reached up with one hand and began massaging my temple, trying to relieve the stress, and Quess seemed to notice what was going on.

"Mercury, we gotta go. Liana's neural scrambler is burning way too hot. She's already getting a headache."

"Is there anything else you need?"

"Ration cards," I managed. "We didn't pack a lot of food."

"Okay. Quess, I assume you're at the secondary location you and Cali scoped out?"

"Yes," Quess answered for me.

"Have Maddox go out, and I'll leave her a few ration cards in the secret compartment in Water Treatment, level 15. Will Maddox remember the spot?"

"If she doesn't, I do, and I'll go with her."

"Good. That should get you through a couple days if you're smart and don't shop at the same market. Make sure you get stuff that lasts, and not just junk food."

"Yes, Dad," Quess said, sarcasm dripping from each word, and I gave him a look. Their exchange was so easy and natural, it was clear they had spoken on more than one occasion. I hadn't thought they had, but now I wasn't so sure. I made a mental note to ask Quess about it—and to get him to tell me all he knew about Mercury.

"Take care of yourselves, and no unnecessary risks. I'll send my emissary in a day or two."

"How will we know this person is from you?" I asked.

"They'll have a password. How about..." He trailed off, and I realized he had blanked.

I let my mind spin out for a moment, past the pain, and it immediately flashed to Tian. "Hummingbird," I said with a soft smile.

"Done. Unless there was anything else?"

"Nope. Signing off now. Thank you, Mercury." My reply was automatic—half due to pain, and half due to making sure we didn't say anything more.

Then I hit the kill button, ending the transmission.

9

I squinted through one eye as Quess helped pull me through the hatch that led to our new home, the buzzing in my skull now reaching violent levels of agony. He set me down, and I kept my eyes closed, trying to fight the feeling.

"Tian painted in here," Quess said, and a moment later, I felt his fingers on the back of my neck. He pulled, and the adhesive bond came free. It was as if he had flipped a switch: the pain suddenly stopped. I immediately sagged back, the tension bleeding from me, and sighed in relief.

"Those things suck," I said tiredly.

"They are not pleasant," he replied. "But this one seemed a little rougher than usual. I'll have to examine it to make sure it isn't running hot."

I cracked open an eye and looked at him. "Is that a thing?"

He nodded solemnly as he dropped the scrambler into his

pocket. "Unfortunately, yes. But don't worry, huh? We got back okay."

I ran a hand over my face, still trying to grapple with what we had just learned, and then nodded. "Sure. Now we just need to figure out how to replicate Paragon, and decide if we're going to stay and fight or run away."

"Yeah, about that—why didn't you tell Mercury?"

I frowned. "We went over this, Quess. Telling anyone about Scipio would be—"

"No, why didn't you tell him about Scipio after you realized he needs us as much as we need him?"

Quess's question hung in the air as I considered it. It was a fair point, I supposed. "Because I still don't know that I can trust him, even knowing that."

"He was honest with us."

I sighed. "He might've been, but—"

"He could help us figure out a way to put Scipio inside the Core."

"Maybe so," I replied, fighting through my irritation at him interrupting me yet again. "But I want to meet him face-to-face. Hell, that information is much better given face-to-face—we can't exactly trust netting one hundred percent."

"You're being paranoid."

I looked at him, deciding how I wanted to feel about that statement. "Maybe I am, but you guys put me in charge. If I don't think it's a good idea to tell someone something, then I'm not going to. I'm going to do everything I can to keep us safe, and if that means questioning the intentions and motivations of our allies, or even doubting them, I'm going to do it. Better paranoid than dead."

Quess opened his mouth and then shut it, and I mentally patted myself on the back for being able to recover so quickly from the scrambler. Now that my skull was free from the fiery brand, I was able to think more clearly than before. Clearly enough to get past Quess's arguments, at least for the moment. I watched him closely while he thought about it, and then smiled when I saw approval shining in his eyes.

"You know what, you're totally right."

I reared back in surprise, and then shot him a sardonic look. "Thanks, I guess?"

"No problem. So... what are you going to tell everyone?"

"The truth. They need to know what's going on. They need to have a say." Quess gave me a sidelong look, a smile tugging at his lips. "What?"

"Nothing, I'm just digging this take-charge Liana. She's really hot." I flushed, and Quess seemed to take it as an invitation to step closer. "So, are you and Grey serious, or..."

"Quess!" I exclaimed with a laugh, pushing him back a few feet. He stumbled, a wide grin on his face.

"What?!" he exclaimed good-naturedly, trying for innocent and failing miserably. "I can't help myself; strength in a woman is definitely on my lists of turn-ons."

"Yeah, well, you're never going to get one if you keep coming on to them like that. It's stronger than goat cheese."

"Goat cheese is delicious," he said.

"And your pick-up lines are gross," I retorted. I paused, and then added, "Besides, you probably shouldn't do it. It's rude to Grey."

I wasn't entirely sure why I added that last part, and as soon as I said it, I could hear Quess's reaction building. My initial instinct was to shut it down before he got to it, but a part of me resisted, eager to hear someone else's thoughts on this.

"I can't believe you'd say that after what he said yesterday," Quess said. "He was pretty rude himself."

I flushed and shook my head, already resisting the pain that the memory brought. "Look, I'm not sure what his issue was, but I'm pretty sure he didn't mean it," I said. It was something I'd been telling myself since yesterday, and it felt good to say it out loud. It didn't mean I entirely believed it, but it was a good start, and it kept hope alive. I didn't want things between Grey and me to sour. I had sort of hoped...

Well, it didn't matter what I hoped. I had to keep us moving forward, and that meant my personal drama with Grey couldn't be a factor. Besides, it wouldn't look good to the others if I was constantly fighting with him.

But the wedge this whole leadership thing had put between us was uncomfortable, and needed to be resolved. I just hoped it could be sooner rather than later.

"Well, the rest of us are pretty sure he didn't mean it, too," Quess stated, and I gave him a surprised look. "Oh yeah, we talked about it. It's kind of hard not to gossip and speculate when you have such a small group."

"Great," I muttered. It was the opposite of great, but there was nothing I could do. "What's the consensus on why he was acting like that?"

"Well, Maddox and I think it's just because he has anti-traditional leadership structures. I mean... it's sort of in his profile that he doesn't do well with command figures, so..."

I considered that, trying to decide whether I agreed or not. I shook my head. "Yeah, I'm not sure what file you read that from, but frankly, I don't think it was about that." I stopped, realizing that I was actually talking about it. With Quess, of all people. Not that he was a bad person to talk to, but these things were normally reserved for Zoe. "I really don't want to talk about it."

"So you said. But it seems like you need to."

I met his gaze with a wry smile. "Yes, but the person I need to talk to about it is Grey, so let's just leave it there for now."

Quess gave me a smile and nodded. "All right. What say I round everyone up? Want to hold the meeting in the main room?"

I folded my arms across my chest, considering the question. "No," I said, the corners of my lips quirking up. "We'll hold it in Lionel's office."

Quess's eyebrows rose in surprise. "You really want to include Old Scipio?"

I nodded. "I think we should. We have to bring everyone up to speed on the meeting, and discuss what our next moves are going to be."

"All right! Let's go get everyone assembled."

I smiled at the enthusiasm in his voice, and watched as he slid into the vent. As I waited for him to move farther in, the smile evaporated. I thought of Grey and his weird behavior yesterday, and hoped that he had gotten over his agitation. Because I was not super excited about a repeat of last night.

"Greetings, Liana!" Scipio chirped brightly as I slid in through the vent. "I'm glad to see you again, and—" He paused, smiling when Tian slipped out of the vent behind me. "You've brought new friends! Hello."

Tian looked up from where she had landed on her hands and knees, and her blue eyes immediately rounded. She quickly moved backward. "He's a monster!" she shrieked, half-turning to throw herself back into the vent.

I caught her by the waist, not wanting her panic to slow down the train of people, and moved her to the side. Or, at least, I tried to—but she wasn't making it easy.

"Let me go!" she screamed, her legs kicking violently. "He's going to kill us!"

From over her shoulder, I could see Scipio's eyes widening in mortification. He opened his mouth to say something, but I quickly shook my head. "Tian, he's not going to kill us," I told her calmly. "He's just a holographic representation. He can't actually touch you. Here, look."

I stood and quickly moved toward Scipio. "May I?" I asked, and he gave me a surprised nod. I turned partially, to make sure Tian could see, and then slowly passed my hand through his arm, disrupting the strands of light. Tian stared at us mutinously at first, her jaw set and arms folded across her chest, but as my hand went through, her expression changed from confusion to surprise, then to awe.

"That's amazing!" she said. "You didn't tell me he was a ghost!" She immediately raced up to him, her small feet loud even on the carpet, but pulled up short. "Pow pow!" she screamed shrilly, punching her tiny fists through his thigh.

Scipio watched this with no small amount of amusement, and then waved a hand. Immediately, a dozen or so bubbles floated around them. They shimmered in the lights, their colors changing from gold to blue to purple to green to red, and Tian's face reflected the lights as she stared up at one. Her finger stretched out, and to my surprise, instead of passing right through, her finger appeared to make the bubble pop. It released a poof of confetti, and Tian clapped her hands together, her face growing more and more excited. She began running around, popping the different bubbles as fast as she could.

"If nothing else comes from us finding him," Quess said as he exited the hole, "then at least we know who can babysit Tian if we're all away."

I smiled. "Oh yeah, he's got those duties for life, knowing her."

"Speaking of which, Ghost could be a really good name for you," Quess said, directly addressing Scipio's hologram.

Scipio opened his mouth to reply, but was interrupted by a loud rattle from the vent as Zoe slid out—and immediately bounced to her feet. "Holy cow," she said, her eyes large as she took Scipio in. "Is that..."

"Greetings, I am..." He paused as Eric slid out behind her, followed by Maddox and then Grey. "You certainly have a lot of friends."

"That means you have friends now too, Ghost!" Quess exclaimed as he moved past Scipio.

Scipio rolled his eyes. "Actually, I have settled on an alternative name, and it is not Ghost. Or Bob." He met my gaze, his blue eyes sparking almost white with excitement, and I realized he was nervous. He wanted us to like what he had chosen.

"I'm sure whatever it is will be fine," I said encouragingly, and he beamed at me. From the corner of my eye, I caught movement, and tilted my head better to see Grey shaking his head, although I couldn't tell what it was about. His face was partially hidden behind his blond hair, and he wasn't saying anything.

I kept my mouth shut and turned back to Scipio. Now was not the time to start calling Grey out.

"In honor of my maker, Lionel Scipio, I have decided to rename myself Leo."

He looked around expectantly, and Quess was the first one to have an opinion.

"I like it," he declared. "It's cool, edgy, maybe a little rebellious—basically kind of like you, minus the edgy parts."

Leo's lips flickered in an uncertain smile. "I think that was a compliment, so I'm going to take it as one."

"It is," Maddox said. I looked over to where she was leaning on the wall next to the vent, studying the computer program. "I'm Maddox."

"And this is Tian, Zoe, and Eric. Tian, Zoe, and Eric, this is Sci..." I paused, my eyes sliding over to the glowing figure in the middle of the room, who was watching me intently, and smiled. "Leo."

"Pleased to make your acquaintance," he said formally. "Would you like to have a seat?"

He gestured to the sofas, and they shuffled over to sit down on them. I remained standing by the desk, and Grey took up a position opposite me, leaning against the bookcase.

"So how'd the meeting go?" he asked gruffly, not even waiting until everyone was settled.

I gave him a hard look, some of the feelings from yesterday returning, and then began filling everyone in on the meeting. "Well, he's going to help us out with the nets, and he's gonna leave us a few ration cards for food, but... we need to start figuring out what we're going to do about the Paragon," I said bluntly. "And what our plan is going forward."

"Oh, and—we might've made some new friends," Quess added. "Mercury said there's a group that made contact with him and wants to meet Liana. They're saying they can help us, so…"

"With what?" Grey demanded. "Who are they?"

"We don't know," I said. "Neither does Mercury, but he thinks it's a good idea, and so do I."

"I don't know…" Zoe said, trailing off and cocking her head. "The timing is a little—"

"It's because my face is all over the place inside. Grey's too. Mercury seems to think that they're another undoc group who might want me to join because I can fight. It's a commodity among undocs, apparently."

"Yeah, I'm sure," Grey said bitterly, crossing his arms. "Especially when they need people to break in and steal things."

"Actually, that's not what I'm talking about," Zoe said, shaking her head. "You mentioned some sort of secret group who wanted to murder Leo. Now, only a few days after you keep Leo from dying, a mysterious group of people wants to reach out to you? And you're just going to overlook that as coincidence?"

I swallowed. "Do you think they somehow know Leo is alive? How would they?"

"Some sort of program or device in the office?" she asked, wrinkling her nose. "I don't know! It just seems very suspicious, even for coincidence."

"Does anyone really think a clandestine group could exist after hundreds of years?" Maddox asked.

I frowned. I had wondered the same thing myself, and even speculated that Scipio 2.0 was being controlled, but there was no proof one way or another.

"I don't know," I replied out loud. "Leo, you were around

during the time of Prometheus. Do you have any information that could help us?"

"Me?" Leo asked, looking around. "I have the reports that were filed by the security department on those they had arrested, but that doesn't exactly give us a clear picture on whether the group survived three centuries."

"Yes, but you could run a probability model," Quess pointed out, shifting slightly in his seat so he could rest an ankle on his knee. "Unless that was part of 2.0's programming, and not yours."

"No... I can, but it would be off by a factor of three to seven percent without more recent data."

"It's fine," Quess said. "Run the numbers and tell me what they say."

Leo looked up for a moment, and then back down. "There is a better than average chance of it, based on information available to me. But that doesn't mean much."

"So it's possible that Liana's meeting with a secret group that wants to destroy Leo and overthrow the Tower?" Grey asked, folding his arms over his chest. "And we're all okay with that?"

"Well, Leo said he needs more recent data, so let's not jump right to the fact that they're a secret group," Zoe said. Her expression was thoughtful. "But even if they were, would that be such a bad thing?" Everyone turned their heads toward her at once, and her back straightened. "I'm just saying that maybe it would be a good idea to meet with them and see what they want and what they are about. Knowing what they want could tell us how best to deal with them."

I loved my best friend—she could be so awesomely practical when she needed to be.

"I'm not sure I agree with Zoe," Maddox said. "Knowledge is

power, yes, but we have no idea what they want from us, which puts them in a position of power over us. We can't be sure they won't take advantage of our desperation, either, or make us do things based only on a promise. It doesn't matter if they are undocs or something else; we need to make sure what we're doing with them is something that helps us, not hurts us. I don't see any benefit to us in meeting with them right now."

No one said anything for a long moment, and I could see several of them nodding their heads in agreement.

Only Eric and Grey remained still, and it was Eric who spoke first. Although, from the angry look in Grey's eyes, it wouldn't be long before he said something.

"Those are all very good points," he said carefully, looking around. "And I think there is a good reason for going, and a good reason for not going. But I honestly believe that Liana should be the one to decide. After all, she's the one they mentioned by name. It'll be her life in danger if she goes."

Silence met his remark, but I realized that wasn't quite true. "Not so," I said. "They know I have companions. They'd come after you too."

"But it's you they would get first," Eric replied. "It really should be your choice."

"I can't believe this," Grey muttered, loud enough to be heard. I looked over at him and arched an eyebrow.

"What was that?" I asked, and he paused in the process of running a hand over his face, removed it, and met my gaze head on. "I said I can't believe this. I seriously cannot believe they are willing to just send you in there."

"That's not what we said." Zoe bristled, climbing up to her

own two feet. "And I happen to agree with Eric—it's not our place to decide. It's hers."

"It's a decision that affects all of us," Grey railed. "What if it's a trap? She knows where we are. If the Knights catch her and question her, we'll all be sunk. Not to mention, she isn't the most diplomatic individual. No offense."

"Hey, offense taken." The way that Grey was talking about me was making me angry again, and slightly nauseous. "You don't trust that I'll be able to smell a Knight trap coming, is that it? I used to be one, y'know. I'm quite familiar with their tactics—at least, more familiar than all of you."

Grey's eyebrows drew closer together as he glowered at me. "That really isn't the point," he said, his voice lethal. "You were only a Squire before all this went down, Liana. I very much doubt—"

"Everyone except Grey, please get out."

I wasn't sure the words had come from me, but when everyone on the sofa turned to look at me, I realized they had. I had delivered them politely enough, but even still, I felt like the rest of the group needed some sort of resolution, so I added: "Thank you all for your input. I will consider it all and let you know what my decision is. However, I need a moment to talk to Grey, and I think it should happen in private."

Grey crossed his arms, his glare intensifying while the group exchanged a flurry of glances and then stood, quickly heading to the vent and away from the drama. I waited patiently, holding Grey's glare. He looked angry, but I was livid. I wanted to know what was going on with him and why he was acting this way.

And I was going to get my answer, whether he liked it or not.

10

Grey and I remained silent until everyone else had left, and even longer, until the telltale rattle of metal had faded some, indicating everyone was drawing farther away. Leo disappeared, while I continued to stare at Grey, angry and frustrated by his behavior. It wasn't helpful—if anything, it was just putting him at odds with the remaining group. We needed to be able to work together if we were going to survive, and he was making that more difficult.

Not to mention, his intemperance had prevented me from bringing up what I really wanted to address: what our long-term plan was going to be. And while it wasn't something that needed to be decided today, it would've been nice to discuss it. We needed a plan.

But it was more than that. And while a part of me only wanted to make this conversation about his behavior in the group, another part of me was afraid to say anything. Deeply terrified, in fact, because I knew nothing about this was simple. I liked him, I was attracted to him, I was...

I sighed. None of that mattered now. Maybe I was deluding myself into thinking that we could work out whatever his issue was and go back to... whatever it was that we were doing romantically.

Besides, a small voice in my head whispered, *whatever you had was clearly not strong enough to survive whatever problem he's having with you now. Why else would he look so angry?*

I shut it down quickly, but not before I felt my spirits sink when I couldn't find any counterpoint to the voice. It was right—if there was something there, really something there, he wouldn't have acted this way. I knew Grey well enough to know that he would talk to me. If he still cared, that was.

Grey stared back at me, a muscle in his jaw ticking. "Well, it looks like you get what you want," he muttered after a moment, his voice bitter.

I squinted at him. I recognized the sentence as bait, but I wasn't sure how I wanted to play it. So instead, I looked around, and tried to formulate a response that would be neither incendiary, nor patronizing.

"Not everything," I said, my eyes settling on him. "Because you're still acting like I stole something from you. Is this a woman thing, is that it? Can't stand a lady in charge?"

"Liana, this is no time to be glib. You—"

"Oh no?" I interrupted, raising an incredulous eyebrow. "It seems to me that in the face of all of this hostility, being glib might be the only thing that gets me out of it without..."

I trailed off, snapping my teeth closed around the next part —*without losing you*—because I wasn't even sure I had him to begin with at this point. How could I be, after all this? We'd shared some moments, sure. He'd saved me, yes, and I'd saved him... I'd thought that meant something.

"Without what?" Grey demanded, but I shook my head.

"I don't owe you that," I said. "Not until you explain to me what is going on with you. We were fine one moment, then the next... it was like a switch was flipped and you became a different person." Grey glowered at me, the muscle in his jaw working much faster. "What happened?" I asked beseechingly. "Is it because everyone wanted me to be the leader instead of you?"

The incredulous face Grey made reminded me of a child who had just been asked to take out the food composting bin to send to the greeneries, and it made me smile in spite of my anger. When he smiled in return, I realized it had been intentional. As brief as it was, the smile was like a breath of wind on the dwindling spark of hope that had been threatening to flicker and die, and my heart thudded hard once.

Grey seemed to take a moment for himself, and I waited, watching as he visibly pushed back some of the anger weighing on him, replacing his expression with a less angry one.

"Do you really think I'm that petty?" he asked, but there was no recrimination in his voice.

"I don't know!" I replied honestly, and he winced slightly. "I'm sorry, Grey, but... this is the first time you've acted this way in the time I've known you, and it's really upsetting. I mean, if you have concerns about me leading, then you should just talk to me about them—not get all passive aggressive and then blow up at the drop of a hat!"

Grey winced again, and then looked around the room, his face flashing from angry to frustrated and back again over the course of several long seconds.

"You're right," he finally said. "My behavior has been deplorable."

He spoke so stiffly and formally, that it was all I could do to resist reaching out and shaking him. I didn't want him blindly agreeing with me; I wanted him telling me what was wrong. I wanted him to reassure me that he wasn't upset with me, that I hadn't done something to make him hate me. Not this shroud of stiffness he was giving me.

I stared at him, trying to wordlessly convince him to tell me more, but he remained silent.

"Are all human conflict resolution attempts so... bereft of actual discussion?"

Leo's voice rang out around the room, and I spun around. I had all but forgotten he was still here, listening to every word.

"Oh great," Grey said, folding his arms. "Now we have a spectator."

I rolled my eyes at him, and then looked around. "Leo, can you please give us some privacy?"

There was a pause. "Liana, as I told you before, I can't actually shut off my receptive features. I'm always watching and listening to what happens in this room. Lionel ordered it that way, and it's a command I cannot override. He wanted me to learn."

"Fantastic," Grey barked. "Not only are we stuffed together down here like fish in a breeding pool, but now we can't even get a moment's privacy! You know what—forget this, I'm out of here."

He began to move toward the vent, but before I could stop myself, I walked over to the vent and blocked it, standing directly in his path. He towered over me, his brown eyes growing darker.

"Let me go," he demanded.

"No—not until you tell me what is going on with you!" I said hotly, taking a step forward. "Based on what you said yesterday, you think I'm really going to suck at this?"

Grey automatically shook his head. "No, of course not—"

"Then you are just hung up over the fact that you think we don't need a leader."

"It's not that ei—"

I cut him off again, angered beyond belief that he was making me drag the truth out of him, that he was making me interrogate him like this.

"Well, then you must think I shouldn't do it because of what happened! I mean, you told me you weren't angry at me over Roark, but with how you're acting now..."

I trailed off, giving him a pointed look, and was surprised to see concern and mortification begin to draw over his face.

"Is that really what you think?" he asked softly, his anger strangely absent from his words.

"Well, I don't know what to think, do I?" I replied in exasperation. "You aren't talking! I can't read your mind to know what's going on with you. All I can do is ask you about it, and you have to tell me. Otherwise... this isn't going to work."

Grey was silent for a long time, his eyes glued to the floor. "What do you mean by 'this?'" he finally asked.

I knew the question was about us... but I wasn't sure what he was asking me. After all, he was the one who had been acting so angry and out of control—wasn't it him who was unhappy?

"Being a member of the group," I said lamely, avoiding discussing it. "Everyone else is also upset at how you've been acting, and they don't get it either. I know we're all tired and drained by what has happened. I know we're also scared, because now we don't know what we're going to do. But that doesn't mean—"

Grey gave out an irritated tsk and shook his head. "No, no, and no," he said. "I mean, yes, I am all those things, but no. That's not why I'm upset."

"Then what is it?" I snapped.

"It's you!" he shouted loudly, his own temper snapping, and I took a step back, and then another, my eyes growing wide. "That came out wrong," he added quickly.

He hesitated, and I waited, my heart in my throat as he seemed to struggle with what he wanted to say next. The moment stretched out for what seemed like an eternity, and then he reached for my shoulders and yanked me to his chest, crushing me close to him.

"I'm... I'm worried I'm going to lose you," he admitted hoarsely. "And you're all I have left."

The pain and fear in his words made me look up at him, causing my own pain to recede some and that warm lightness that he inspired in me to return.

He did care. He was just acting angry because he was afraid *for* me. And while that anger had been irritating and confusing, the fact that it had been inspired by concern for me and my safety was a great way of defusing my own anger and hurt.

"Grey..." I hesitated, and then tentatively reached up to touch his face. "Don't take this the wrong way, but... I think you may have overcompensated."

I meant it as a joke, but Grey let out another frustrated breath and let go of me, moving to walk away. It happened so quickly that it took me a moment to register what was happening and recalibrate. I watched him as he paced, suddenly afraid that I had said the wrong thing, but was prevented from saying anything as he turned around to face me.

"You don't get it," he said emphatically. "You don't think I know I'm acting like a crazy person? Believe me, I know. I've been beating myself up about it since yesterday! But... you're the *leader* now, Liana!"

Now I was confused again. It was one thing for him to be worried about me in general, but what did being the leader have to do with anything?

"Grey, what does—"

"Cali," he said flatly. "Roark."

Realization dawned on me then, and I felt stupid for not having figured it out before.

Grey wasn't just worried about me; he was worried about me being in the position of leader. Because the leaders were the ones who were targeted and killed. Just like our own had been.

He wasn't worried that I was in danger—he knew that we all were. But that wasn't what he was having a problem coping with. It was the fact that I and everyone else had put me in a more prominent position, and that meant becoming a bigger target for our enemies.

"Grey, I can't help how everyone voted," I reminded him, and he gave me an annoyed look.

"You could've consulted with me first!" he said.

I raised an eyebrow. I knew that if Zoe had heard that, she would've gone off on him that I didn't owe him any part in my decision-making process, but I couldn't help but feel bemused and a bit flattered. He wanted to be part of my decision-making, and if I was perfectly honest with myself, I wanted to be a part of his. But still... that didn't mean he had a leg to stand on.

"Okay, but when would you have liked to have had that discussion?" I asked. "Between when they were volunteering me for the job and when you lost your cool?"

To Grey's credit, he flushed a deep red and had the good grace to look embarrassed. "I know I handled it wrong," he mumbled. "I just... Everything's moving so fast, and... I mean, you have your friends and everyone. But you're it for me, Liana. The last person I have who cares about me and who I care about. My parents... Roark..." He trailed off and looked at me, his eyes filled with emotion. "I'm trying to be okay with this, Liana—but all I can think about is what happens if Devon catches you and finds out you're in charge, and it scares me." He turned away from me then, breaking off before he grew too upset.

I hesitated, and then crossed the room to him. He stood with his back to me, so I simply slid my arms around his waist and hugged him from behind. I rested my head on his shoulder blade.

"Grey..." I said. "I didn't know any of that."

He gave a bitter chuckle, and I felt him shaking his head, his shoulder moving slightly beneath my cheek.

"How could you? I didn't exactly use my words like a big boy."

I laughed, surprised by his self-depreciating joke, and loosened my arms enough to move in front of him. He immediately wrapped his arms around me, one hand coming up to cup my cheek.

"Can you forgive me for being a stupid idiot?" he asked softly. "I know I don't deserve it after being such a monumental jerk."

"Ass," I corrected playfully, and was relieved to see a smile—a genuine and full one that lasted longer than a heartbeat.

"Ass," he conceded amicably. "So... can you?"

I gave him a considering expression, studying him. "I don't know..." I drawled. "I mean, I'm beginning to see some pretty serious flaws with this model."

He laughed, his chest leaping under where my hands were settled, and I leaned into him, needing his arms tighter around me. He held me that way for a long time, and I felt reassured by them, by him.

"You know, it's ironic that all of the things that make you a great leader are the things that I'm highly attracted to," he said, breaking the quiet. "I think that pretty much means I'm doomed."

I laughed, mainly because he did not sound like he was opposed to my particular brand of doom, and looked up at him. "Can I tell you a secret?" I asked, and he nodded. "I'm scared by all this too."

His arms tightened around me, pulling me even closer to him. "I know... I'm sorry I wasn't there for you last night. But I promise, Liana... I promise I will do everything I can to keep you safe. I may not be leadership material, but if there's one thing that I know I have to be good at, it's taking care of you. And I want to, if you'll still allow me. Jerkiness aside."

I licked my lips. "Please," I said, practically begging him. I was sure if Zoe had heard me, she would have chastised me for even admitting that I needed his emotional support, but I wasn't going to lie about that, not even for the sake of my pride. I was scared, and I felt alone, even with everyone around. I needed this, and I was just glad he was willing to give it to me.

Still, the coldly practical part of my brain reminded me that if we were going to try building a relationship during this chaos, then there needed to be some ground rules for us when we were around the others. And for us in general—so that this tangled bit of drama never happened again.

"Will you just promise to come talk to me first before you get all upset in future?" I asked, breaking the silence that had stretched between us.

"Of course," he said, his eyes warm and bright now. "You know, I've never had a girlfriend before... So I'm figuring all this out too."

I bit my lip, unable to stop the grin from spreading across my face. "You think I'm your *girlfriend*?"

Grey's response was physical, and he stooped down and kissed me before I had a chance to even realize what he was about to do. His lips met mine with a force that left me breathless, and a hot hunger seemed to rise up from the soles of my feet, until I was grabbing him and kissing him back.

He slid one strong arm around my back, and then held me tight to him as he lifted me up one handed. I shuddered at the strength there, and wrapped my legs around his hips, desperate to be as close to him as possible. He growled, and I felt us move a few steps, stopping only when my back hit the side of the book-case. I reached out with my hands, grabbing for anything to support myself as I drowned in his kiss.

I heard several things drop to the floor with a thud as I stretched my arms out over the shelf, but I didn't care. All I cared about was the feel of his tongue and teeth nipping at my lips, demanding them to open and let him inside, and a hunger that only he could satisfy.

His hands slid from my hips to my waist, slowly inching up, and I moaned, excited by what would happen next.

"See, this doesn't exactly jive with conflict resolution models that I've studied either—has there been some sort of break-through? Oh! Has this society become less puritanical about sex?!"

We broke apart as soon as Leo started talking, stunned by both his interruption and the sudden fire that had erupted between us, and Grey immediately set me down and took a healthy step back, trying to collect himself.

My breathing was ragged, and my lips felt bruised and swollen. "Leo... seriously?"

"Seriously what?" he chirped, suddenly reforming next to me. I jumped slightly, and then glared at him.

"Privacy!"

The AI smirked unapologetically. "This is *my* room. I suggest that if you want to continue your little scene, you go find one of your own."

I opened my mouth to object, and then realized he was right and shut it. It was good he had interrupted us, I realized a heartbeat or two later. The way we were going, I wasn't sure that we *should* be on our own, and if he hadn't interrupted... I shuddered to imagine what he would've seen if he hadn't. I realized I owed Leo an apology, and started to give it, when Grey's voice brought me up short.

"Liana... look."

I turned toward the wall behind me, and realized that when I had been blindly groping earlier, I had accidentally hit a painting dangling on the wall. I must have hit it hard, because it was now dangling at an angle revealing an obvious hinge attached to some sort of metal door that had been completely hidden when the painting had been upright.

I exchanged a look with Grey, and within seconds we were lifting the painting away and setting it to one side, revealing a safe underneath.

"Leo... what is this?" I asked, my eyes tracing the shiny black surface. There didn't appear to be a handle to open it, and the edges were flat with the wall. Grey reached out and stroked his fingers over the surface, and it immediately lit up, flashing red.

"Unauthorized user," a synthesized voice said.

"I don't suggest you touch it again," Leo said. "The safe can defend itself."

Grey snatched his hand away and looked back at the hologram. "Can you open it?"

Leo didn't bat an eye. "No."

I looked at Grey and then back at Leo. "Are you lying?" I asked.

There was a fraction of a second in which he hesitated, but I saw it. "The safe is classified—I will not open it unless I feel that something inside is of critical importance. The safe is hermetically sealed for preservation, so I will not expose any of its contents unnecessarily without just cause, and that's really all I have to say on the matter."

I pressed my lips together, studying him. "Is it dangerous?"

"What? No! And there is more than one item in there. Now, that really is all I have to say on the matter. You're free to try to hack in, of course, but I won't help you. And I certainly won't stop the system from hurting you."

I hid my smile at his indirect threat behind the back of my

hand, amused at his second attempt to end the conversation. Grey didn't bother hiding his smile.

"C'mon, Liana," he said, tugging at his clothes to straighten them. "It's clear Leo's not going to show us, so let's not push. Besides... I have a few apologies to make to everyone, and I figured you'd want to be present."

"What? No, that's silly. I don't have to be there."

"I want you to be," he replied, giving me a slow, confident smile. "I'm hoping that by witnessing my humiliation firsthand, you'll fully forgive me, and then maybe even take pity on me."

I snorted and crossed my arms. "I don't know..." I teased. "If anything, I might make your apologies more humiliating."

"Good," he said. "I deserve it. Let's go. Thanks for letting us use your room, Leo!"

He grabbed my hand and began pulling me to the vent, and I went with him willingly. I was relieved that we had worked things out, and strengthened by the fact that he cared about me. After everything else that had happened thus far today, I was considering this one a victory.

Now I just had to turn our other problems into victories.

11

The next day, Grey and I were lying on our sides, back to front, down one of the side vents, and I was trying very hard not to giggle as Grey reached over me to point out where I was messing up, purposefully dragging the rough stubble on his chin across my neck as he did so.

"Stop it," I said for the umpteenth time, pulling the soldering iron away from the fuses to which I was in the process of splicing a power cable. "I'm trying to work here!"

"No, what you're doing is making a mess of things," he insisted, reaching over me, trying to grab the tool out of my hand.

"Grey," I gasped, jerking it away and high over my head. "It's hot! You'll burn yourself!"

He grunted, and continued to reach, but then placed his mouth over mine as soon as he had an angle. I stilled, savoring the feel of his mouth as he slowly kissed me. He was gentle, his kisses more like he was taking sweet tastes from my lips.

I relaxed with a sigh. Everything since yesterday had just felt... perfect. He'd actually made me watch him apologize to everyone, which I'd made him do as a group thing rather than individually. Then he'd made sure that we both worked together setting up the hydroponic room, which meant hours of us setting up bins, lights, tents—the works—with no one to bother us, save those who came in hauling bags of topsoil. At dinner, we'd eaten side by side, chatting with everyone. He held my hand while we all sat around telling stories, and then reluctantly let it go only when it was time for us to go to sleep. Which took place after enough kissing that we had actually woken up Zoe, who tossed something at us with an irritated noise, before rolling back over to go to sleep.

I'd gone to bed feeling like light was radiating from my heart and through my chest, and awoke feeling lighter than I ever had before. For a moment, it hadn't mattered that the future was nebulous. It had only mattered that Grey was waiting for me to wake up, ready to start the day with me.

"Liana?"

Tian's soft voice in my ear interrupted the warm spell that held Grey and me together, and we slowly broke apart. I looked up and backwards, finding Tian's face only a few inches away.

"Heeeey, Tian," I said, fighting back a smile. "What's, um..." Grey's weight shifted off of me, resulting in the vent giving a slight groan and rattle, and heat bloomed in my cheeks. "What's up?"

"Maddox is back with food and said that she got a message through her net from Mercury while she was out—that his friend is coming any moment for dinner, and Zoe is yelling at Quess in the new workroom."

I blinked, trying to filter out the Tian-embellished parts from the actual messages. "Where is everyone?"

"Watching Zoe yell at Quess in the new workroom."

I sighed and nodded. "Lead the way."

Tian nodded and then spun around in the middle of the vent, heading away from us and back up the vent shaft.

"Do you know why Zoe hates him?" Grey asked, referring to Quess, and I tucked my chin to my neck to look at him.

"I may have some idea," I replied, starting to wriggle around on my side so I could begin moving up the shaft. The fight between Zoe and Quess was one part ego, one part professional curiosity, two parts flirting (on Quess's side), and three parts righteous feminine indignation (on Zoe's). The combination was like some sort of perverse version of nitroglycerin, where Zoe was the explosive, one whose anger only seemed to fuel Quess's need to flirt with her. Despite all of that, they could somehow find moments of reprieve in which they seemed to work together with growing, albeit begrudging, respect.

It had all started yesterday when they both began fighting over the design for a brace to the door that led to the Menagerie that would only allow it to open from the inside. They had both fought (well, Zoe got angry, while Quess just flirted and teased) for over an hour before eventually deciding to do their own proposed designs and use the better of the two. They had bickered the entire time they had worked, and while it had been amusing, at first, it had stopped being so once I saw the effect it had on Eric. He watched them both with hurt, sad eyes, as if he could see Zoe slipping away from him in each moment they stopped exchanging barbs to examine the other's work... managing genuine compliments that seemed to steal the air from the room. In the end, Quess had admitted that Zoe's design was superior, and I could see Eric withering on the spot.

A part of me wanted to let my friend know what she was doing. Another part of me knew it wasn't my place to interfere.

I heard them long before I saw them, the cutting remarks being traded faster than a rust hawk's venom. As I slid out, I immediately found Eric sitting off to the right in the new doorway we had made in the wall by unscrewing the panels and taping up the wires that ran between them. The panels were now being used as work stations—Quess and Zoe had welded them to the wall inside and converted some of the crates in which our supplies were stored into a central workstation where the communal tools had begun to accumulate.

Maddox was sitting next to Eric in the same spot, her legs spread and her hands on the floor behind her, partially reclining.

I moved to one side to let Grey out, and then crossed the space over to her.

"I can't help it if I'm both good looking and talented," Quess said with a cocky grin. "That's just your burden to bear, beautiful."

"Do you even hear how disgusting you are, you misogynistic jerk!" Zoe snapped back, as she angrily tightened something with her wrench. A moment later, she asked, in a completely normal tone, "What frequency did you say you wanted it on?"

"37.5, and that's two, in my favor," Quess replied. I realized that he was now keeping some sort of score, but whether it was the number of questions she had asked, or something else, I wasn't sure.

"Shut up, you neophyte," Zoe retorted.

"Hey, Liana," Maddox said, looking up at me as Tian dropped

into a seated position between Maddox's legs, settling her back against Maddox's stomach. "Tian tell you?"

"Yeah. Where is he meeting us, and who's going out to meet him?"

"I'll go," Tian said brightly, leaning forward.

"I'll do it," Eric said gruffly. "And he's supposed to meet us at the front door," he added, referring to the entrance we had first entered our new home through. "I gotta get out of here." He nodded toward Zoe and Quess. "Anything's better than sitting around and watching this."

I felt a pang of sympathy for Eric as he stood up and moved into the other room, choosing to go the long route instead of crossing through either Zoe or Quess's field of view. Not that I could blame him—it was hard not to feel like you were watching two people flirting. I was certain that Zoe didn't even realize how it looked, and I knew for a fact she wasn't actually flirting, but Eric was in love with her. For him, it hurt.

"Maddox, how come Quess never flirts with you?" I asked, finding myself curious. "Is it just because you're Cali's daughter, or..."

Maddox let out a sharp laugh, and shook her head, amused by my question. "Yeah, Quess doesn't have that much common sense, bless his heart. He didn't care that I was the daughter of a woman who could break him with her thumb—he made a pass all the same. Day one, if you can believe that."

I laughed, because I could. Quess was that incorrigible. "What'd you do?"

She rocked her head back and forth, a sly grin on her face. "I warned him that I would only date a man who could beat me in a fight, and he fought me." She smiled wolfishly, and added, "He lost. Badly. Quess may be a genius, but he is the very definition of a lover, not a fighter."

She looked at me, and a moment or two later, we were both laughing. It felt good to laugh, and it was great that it was with Maddox. I got the sense that she badly needed it, and I was happy to be able to share it with her. The laughter didn't last long, but she was still smiling as it faded.

"What's so funny?" Quess asked as soon as the outburst had receded enough that we could hear, and his nervous face set us off all over again. He knew all too well we were talking about him after that, but I couldn't help but laugh nonetheless.

"You guys ready?" I asked once I had calmed down. It hadn't taken long for reality to set in—I was about to meet an absolute stranger inside our new sanctum, one who worked for another absolute stranger. Both of them could reveal at any time where we were hiding, if they wanted to or felt like they had to.

It was nerve-wracking, to say the least, so the moment of levity with Maddox was something I needed as well. I tried to reassure myself that Mercury wouldn't do anything to betray us this early (if he was going to do anything at all)—after all, he needed me to get him his supply of Paragon. He couldn't do anything until he had the formula and a way to create his own pill.

I pushed through the blankets that had been strung out into curtains, and moved into the common area, which had been decorated by Tian using crates and pillows for us to use for sitting and eating. A small section in the corner had been left bereft of seats and served as our kitchen, with a portable heating element placed on a crate, and another crate serving as our preparation area.

Tian kept it surprisingly neat and tidy, and it was comfortable. What more did you need for a home, really?

We waited, exchanging wild speculations about who could be coming and what news they would be coming with, which quickly became silly thanks to Grey, Quess, and Tian. It helped pass the time and ease some of the tension. Tian had just named two of the creatures she was pretending Mercury had sent to us Pompodora Grizwaldious, a pixie with violet hair who shot lightening from her fingertips, and Estabulary Jones, a sleek black dragon with white hair and glowing green eyes, when we began to hear the telltale rattle from the vent, and the conversation flat-out stopped, all at once. I watched the dark space of the vent for a moment, and then rose to my feet, suddenly too nervous to sit. I needed to be upright—I didn't want anyone standing over me.

I wiped my sweaty palms on the thighs of my pants and tried to remain still as I waited, the rattling and banging of bodies in the vent growing louder. Grey, who had been sitting next to me, stood as well, and placed a strong hand on the small of my back.

"This is going to be fine," he whispered. "It really is. Mercury isn't going to try anything this soon, but in case he does, we have our weapons ready."

I nodded, letting some of my nervous tension become confidence under his gentle reassurance. Hands appeared, gripping the lower edge of the hole, and there was a grunt from Eric as he pulled himself forward, his hands going to the bare floor and hand-walking his lower torso in. As soon as his feet hit the floor, he stood, an excited grin on his face.

"Liana, you'll never guess who—"

"I told you not to ruin the surprise, MacGillus!" came a

muffled voice from the vent, and my heart froze in my chest. I was certain that I had just imagined that I knew that voice.

A case was pushed out of the vent, landing on the floor with a loud clap. Seconds later, new hands appeared, the skin color more bronzed than Eric's, gripping the sides of the vent. There was a grunt—an all-too-familiar grunt that shouldn't be possible—and then a thick thatch of dark, wavy hair appeared. My heart pounded in excitement, and I laid my hand over my chest, trying to contain the hard beat of it.

I would've recognized it anywhere.

"Alex?" I said, my voice barely a squeak, and my twin brother tossed back his hair as he picked himself up off the floor and peered at me through his wire-framed glasses.

"Liana," he said, relief radiating off of him, and before I knew it, I had crossed the short distance between us and thrown my arms around him. He returned the hug, squeezing me tightly, and I almost burst into tears, I was so overjoyed to feel him in my arms.

"Ladies and gentlemen," Eric announced into the stunned silence that had fallen around us. "Meet Alexander Castell—Mercury's envoy, and Liana's twin brother."

The elation I experienced was brief in the wake of Eric's statement, and I stood back and gaped at Alex. He was *working* for Mercury?

"They don't look anything alike," Tian whispered loudly into the hushed stillness.

"He's my fraternal twin," I mumbled automatically, having heard the comment hundreds of times in school. "Different eggs. You're *working* for Mercury?"

I directed the last statement at my brother alone, and his cheeks grew darker as he blushed, embarrassed. I didn't care—I still didn't understand how this had happened. Had he been doing it all along, or...

My eyes widened as I looked into his dark gaze, and he nodded with a sad smile. "Just started," he said, confirming my suspicions. "Mercury knew about me the day you entered Roark's life, Liana. He started watching all of us—Mom and Dad too—trying to see if you'd try to contact us, but I guess I surprised him when I hacked into your net to have private conversations with you. He contacted me the next day, and I've been working for him ever since."

"Even when you told me about Zoe?" I asked, and he shook his head.

"Oh no, that was all me," he replied with a grin. "Couldn't let my other little sister get hurt, now could I?" He hugged Zoe, and then focused back on me.

"Did he threaten you?" I asked. He shook his head again.

"Not exactly. He, uh, said I needed to learn how to cover my tracks better, and offered to teach me."

"So you've met him?" I asked. Knowing who Mercury was would take away some of his security, and put us in a position of mutually assured destruction should either of us get caught. "You know who he is?"

Alex shook his head. "No, he only contacts me through my work computer, and mostly via text. I don't know who he is, Liana, just that he's got a higher position than I have."

Which meant Mercury had leverage over my brother. I closed my eyes and took a moment to reground myself, trying to find a way to accept the fact that this was yet another person I had exposed to danger. And this time it was my twin.

"And what position would that be?" Quess asked, crossing his arms and giving Alex a onceover. I rolled my eyes. Quess had been in IT before he had faked his own death and created a new identity within the Cogs department to pursue his dream of innovation. But that didn't mean he let anyone forget.

"Developer, second class."

Quess whistled. "That's further than I ever got. I was just about to be bumped up to Developer when I decided to leave."

Alex gave Quess a curious look. "You... left?"

Quess grinned broadly. "Absolutely. Although it took some careful planning. So, Mercury sent you with some nets?"

"Not exactly. May I?" My brother held up the case he had pushed through earlier, and I nodded. As much as I wanted to grill him about what he could tell me about Mercury, or about what was going on in the Tower itself, this was more important. That could come later.

He knelt and popped the case open, revealing half a dozen data crystals in varying hues, all of them about as long as my thumb. "These are new IDs to be installed into the nets. The only thing they're missing is images, but he said Quess could handle it?" He looked up. Quess saluted him, and he returned to the case, pushing the crystals aside to get at a pad underneath. "Mercury and I made about a dozen of them, but as you know, once the ID is imprinted on a net, it remains there, so try not to go through them too quickly. Also, he wanted me to tell Quess, Maddox, and Tian that their nets need to be exchanged as well, as a precautionary measure."

"Noooooooo," Tian groaned theatrically, and my brother gave her a curious expression as she rolled around on the pillows, her arms and legs flopping in dismay. "I *hate* net day," she pouted, pounding her fists into the pillows.

"Are you Tian?" my brother asked, a small, delighted smile playing on his lips, and Tian nodded, her head bob stiff and angry. "Mercury said that if you go through net day without complaining too much, Liana would be allowed to give you this."

As he spoke, he dug a silver foil packet from the pocket of his gray uniform, and held it up, revealing the words *Hot Cocoa* on the side. Tian's head turned toward him, and her eyes zeroed in on it. Within seconds she was standing, perched eagerly on her toes a respectful distance away, staring at the packet.

"How long until net day?" she demanded.

"We're not sure yet," I told her carefully, and she crossed her arms, a frown pulling her mouth down.

"Find out faster," she commanded with an imperious foot stamp. She glared at us a moment longer, and then spun and darted through the curtain. I could hear her stomping around on the other side, and smiled a smile that only Tian seemed to inspire.

Alex whistled a long, low note, and held out the packet to me. "She is a regal little thing, isn't she?"

I accepted the packet, tucking it into a pocket of my own, and nodded. "It's safe to say that nothing gets done without her approval." We shared a moment of silence, and then I turned, ready to get the conversation back on track. "Alex, do you think you could figure out who Mercury is, if you had enough time?"

Alex frowned, and looked around. "I'm confused—I thought he was your friend. Don't you trust him?"

"It's kind of hard to trust a man you haven't met," I said grimly. "Especially when one word from him could bring hell down on us all. I was just hoping that, if I kept him guessing and on his toes, he would be less inclined to sell us out."

Alex's face screwed up tight, and he looked around the room at everyone and then back to me. "Okay, setting aside the fact that he found me, taught me to cover my tracks better, and then had us both working on identity chips while creating a plan for you, you do realize that you're talking about a person who included a packet of hot chocolate with all of the other stuff, just for a little girl he knew wasn't going to like net day, or whatever she called it. I mean... if that isn't a sign of a trustworthy individual, I don't know what is."

I wilted under my brother's condemnation, and—perhaps solely based on the fact that he was my brother—immediately got annoyed with him. Yes, he had good points. And yes, that was something I hadn't really considered in that light. But did he have to look so damned superior about it?

My fist snapped out and connected with his bicep before I could stop the urge, and I smiled when he said, "Ow!" very loudly and grabbed for the spot to rub it with his hand. "Liana!"

"Should've trained better," I replied tartly, and he narrowed his gaze at me. He may have loved IT, but it still ate him up that he wasn't as athletic as the rest of our family, and in my meaner moments, I couldn't resist the jab. He knew I didn't mean anything by it. This was just how we fought.

"Hey, whoa," Grey said apologetically, pressing closer, between us, to force us apart and forestalling my brother from snapping back with a retort. "As much as I'm sure that this is a sibling thing, it might be detracting from the task at hand." He gave me a pointed look, reminding me that I was in charge and it was on me to keep us on task.

Of course, I wasn't quite ready to play ball just yet. "One more minute," I said, and Grey's features softened. He knew I had been worrying about Alex nonstop since everything had happened, and wouldn't deny me another minute. He took a step back, giving us some room, and I turned my attention back to

Alex, only to find him watching Grey, suspicion stamped tight on his face.

"Who's that?" he asked, not looking away.

I recognized the warning signs of an overprotective brother, and opted to try to change the subject, and hope he wouldn't notice. "Grey," I told him. "And never mind that. I am so happy to see you." I felt the urge to hug him all over again and stepped in close, wrapping my arms around him. I breathed in deep, just taking him in. I let myself have that small moment of happiness, before withdrawing. "But, Alex... you shouldn't be doing this. You shouldn't have to do this. If you get caught..."

"Then I'll be depending on you to rescue me," he said with a wink.

I rolled my eyes. "This isn't a joke, Alex. They are *killing* people. We've lost people."

He arched an eyebrow. "Uh, hello, Liana—who are you talking to? I'm the one who told you something was wrong with Scipio, remember? Still not entirely certain what it is, but it's getting worse. Scipio's suggestions are starting to look unbalanced to me, but I can't figure out why." He ran a frustrated hand through his hair, and then swept it aside—his way of clearing the idea from the air to start fresh. "It doesn't matter anyway. The point is that I know very well what I'm getting into. You don't have to worry about me. I can take care of myself."

I gave him a doubtful look. "Apparently not, seeing as you got caught by Mercury."

Alex rolled his eyes. "That, little sister, is entirely your fault," he said. I laughed, unable to help myself, and then winced as Alex's eyes found Grey, who was bent over discussing something with Quess, the case open on the floor between them. "So that's the criminal, huh?"

I groaned inwardly, and shook my head. "Don't do that. We are not doing this again."

Alex turned, confusion radiating through his eyes. "We are not doing what again?"

I gaped at him, unable to believe that he had forgotten about his behavior at school whenever a boy approached me, with one case in particular sealing the deal in terms of my dating life at school.

"I cannot believe that you are going to sit here and tell me that you don't remember what you did to Chester Bule in our fifth year of school."

"Bute," my brother corrected sullenly.

"Aha!" I crowed victoriously as I snapped a finger in his face, close enough to make him flinch. "You do remember. So you remember what you did to him in front of the entire class after he brought me a flower?"

Alex's shoulders sank, and he glowered at me. "I pushed him down."

"And?"

Alex rolled his eyes. "And I told him that if he ever looked at you, I'd..." He trailed off, muttering, "I can't believe you are still holding this over my head."

"You said you'd use his skin as a war flag!" I exclaimed, unable to keep it in. "Who even says that, Alex! It was creepy and weird, and as your twin, it made me creepy and weird too!"

"I was twelve," he snapped defensively. "And Dad kept telling that story about that one guy who came after him with a piece of glass, shouting it at him! I was just repeating what I had heard!"

"I didn't have my first kiss until I got into the academy," I said accusatorily.

Alex, however, drew the line there. He crossed his arms and arched an eyebrow. "Not even sorry about it," he informed me. I narrowed my eyes at him, contemplating the best place to punch him, when he suddenly grinned. "Besides, if I hadn't done that, you could be married to Chester now. You could be Liana Bute."

A huff of air escaped me, and then another and another, and as much as I tried to cling to my anger, it slid away from me like water down a pipe, and I began to laugh.

"I hate you so much," I said.

"Yeah, ditto."

"Hey, Alex? Why are there no nets in this case?"

We both stopped smiling and looked over to where Quess had carefully dissected the contents of the case Alex had brought in. Quess looked up at him expectantly, and Alex rubbed his neck.

"Ah, yeah—that was the other stuff I was supposed to tell you. Mercury can't get his hands on seven of them in six days," he said, looking around. "Even getting one takes months, and that's the minimum time period in which it can be done safely. The IDs in those crystals are ready to go, like I said, but they're useless without new nets."

"Why can't we just use our old ones?" Grey asked, and it was Quess who answered.

"The download circuit is designed to fail after one download, making it impossible to modify after the fact. It's to make it harder to get fake IDs. They also burn out when they are removed, to prevent anyone from trying to scavenge them from the recently deceased."

I shuddered. I never would've thought about doing that in a thousand years, but the fact that he brought it up meant that at some point, it had actually been a problem within the Tower.

"So we need blank nets to go with them," Maddox announced, pointedly fixing her bright green eyes on Alex. "But you didn't bring any."

"Which brings me to the papers and the data pad," Alex said. "Mercury and I put together a plan for how you can get some on your own. We, uh... hope you don't mind capitalizing on your newly established criminal status to perform a little heist."

A prolonged silence met my brother's declaration, and I looked around the room, unsurprised to see almost all of their faces engaged in the biggest communal "no" I had ever witnessed. And I couldn't blame them.

"Alex, the nets are inside the Core," I needlessly reminded him. And yet, not so needlessly, as both my brother and Mercury seemed to have forgotten that the Core was one of the most dangerous places in the Tower, because it was literally where Scipio 2.0 lived. And it didn't matter if he was simply malfunctioning or being manipulated by some sort of secret organization— in all likelihood, I was still enemy number one. My face was probably displayed on every wall and computer screen. If any of us set foot in there, we would be caught in a matter of seconds.

"You're still doubting me, little sister. I would *never* send you in there without a hell of a plan. Besides, you actually can pull this off. You know why?" I widened my eyes and then shook my head. "Because you have me—the most awesome programmer the world has ever known, and I would never, ever let anything happen to you. The pad contains both the blueprints and our

instructions for how to break in. There are a few other goodies in
there to help with disguises and the like as well. I think you'll be
pretty pleased with what we put together. You're clear anytime
over the next three days, but if we miss that window, we'll have to
reassess, okay?"

Hm. It seemed my brother had been hit in the head multiple
times, and was experiencing some sort of mental breakdown.
Because even if he had come up with a great plan, it didn't
change the fact that it was impossible for me to go. Not up to
the Core and back down. Not in one hour. Definitely not
in two.

"Alex, you don't understand. I can't go to the Core." I spoke
slowly and clearly, and internally cackled when Alex's eyes grew
irritated. He hated when I did this to him. "They are actively
scanning for my net right now. And the neural scrambler only
works for about an hour or two."

A thought occurred to me, latent and slow, and it took a lot of
wind out of my sails as my eyes turned toward Maddox and
Quess. They actually didn't need *me.* They could do it without
me. Which meant... that I was going to have to stay behind and let
them go into danger.

Alone.

Without me to keep them safe.

Ugh.

Alex rolled his eyes. "Already considered, with a solution.
Mercury came up with a modification to the neural scramblers
that might offer a bit more time than the standard two hours. He
said Quess should be able to handle it."

Quess slid the folders out of Alex's case and opened one up,
mindlessly handing one to Zoe when she moved over to take a

look. The two of them scoured the pages, both of them looking thoughtful as they read.

"You want to modify it to send out a pulse instead of a direct current?" Zoe asked, looking up at my brother. "Won't that fry the circuit?"

"I brought you guys new circuit boards. They will be able to handle the load, no problem. They're taped inside the file, inside a baggie. Be really careful with them, though—they're basically just silica netting, with the circuit wire woven through, so they're extremely fragile. You'll need tweezers and a magnifying glass."

"Gotcha," Quess said, his eyes still dragging across the page as he read.

I *could* go. I settled back on my heels and let that sink in for a second. On the one hand, good—I didn't like the idea of being forced to sit on the sidelines while making other people do the dirty work. Whatever type of leader I was going to be, it certainly wouldn't be the kind who was above getting their hands dirty. On the other hand... we were going into the Core. Yes, we had Mercury and Alex backing us up, and with their insight and placement inside IT, they could help us if something went wrong —but still.

Something occurred to me, and I looked up at Alex. "Alex, how much trouble can you get in for this? Is any of it traceable back to you?"

He blinked, and then began rubbing the back of his neck. "Liana... I mean, we took precautions to cover our tracks and leave as little digital footprint as possible, but there's always a chance someone notices something is off. But, in answer to your question, no more trouble than you get in if you get caught." I let that sink in, realizing that my brother was putting his life on the line helping me, and even though I hated the very idea of it, I still couldn't help but love him for it all the same. He was, for all intents and purposes, my only real family, parents notwithstanding. "It's a good plan, Liana. It gets you in and out. It'll be fine."

I stared at him dubiously, and then sighed. We needed the nets; there was no way around it. Without them, the four of us were stuck down here, only able to leave for short periods of time with the scrambler. If we were spotted or slipped up, we'd be caught. Without one, we'd definitely be caught—a thermal image on the internal cameras with no net ID accompanying it was the same as being a one on the scanner. A new net and ID repre-sented mobility within the Tower, which meant a better chance of staying ahead of our enemies, or at the very least *escaping* our enemies.

"I'm not happy about it," I said. "But... thank you, Alex."

He frowned at the gratitude in my voice, and pulled me into a hug. "Of course, Lily. You're my sister. I'm going to do everything in my power to keep you safe. This is a risk I'm taking, and I will deal with it. I just want you to focus on the risk you're taking, and please, for the love of everything, don't get caught, okay?"

I nodded, a smile playing on my lips. "Is that your way of telling me you love me?"

He wrinkled his nose and narrowed his eyes. "Yes... but you don't have to get all... gross like that."

"Like what?" I asked, intentionally pitching my voice a little higher. "C'mon, Alex... just admit you love me."

"Ugh, no! Not while you're acting like *that*."

I chuckled, and he smiled. We knew exactly how to get on each other's nerves, and that was our way of telling the other "I love you." I was suddenly grateful that he had even played along in the first place; it was something familiar, something I could cling to that reminded me that not everything had changed.

I looked around, and realized that everyone was now looking over the plans on the pad, five heads bent all around the glowing screen in Quess's hand. We had some privacy, in the sense that they weren't paying attention, and on impulse, I grabbed my brother's arm and pulled him through the curtain.

"Liana?" he asked, concern in his dark eyes. "What's up?"

I hesitated, and then looked down, fidgeting. There had been one question—too big for me to even fully acknowledge—that had been rattling around inside me, and I sensed that Alex would be leaving soon. There wouldn't be much more time for me to ask it, even if I was afraid of what the answer would be.

"Alex... have you talked to Mom and Dad?"

Alex bit back a growl, his eyes already rolling in their sockets. "They netted me as soon as the alert on you went live. Wanted to make sure I understood that my obligation was to the Tower, and that we shouldn't let something as simple as family get in the way of our duties, and blah, blah, blah..."

He trailed off, but I had already turned away, wrapping my arms around my stomach as if I could somehow block off the pain that his words had inspired inside of me. I knew he didn't mean to hurt me, but his delivery hadn't been the best, which had only made it sting all the more.

No, scratch that. It burned, raw and angry, an open wound that felt like salt was being rubbed into it, and I could feel each granule. I didn't even know why I had expected anything different. My entire life I had been the biggest disappointment of all. Sure, Alex had abandoned his duty as a Knight—the Castells had always been a part of the Citadel, after all—but at least he was a nine, and serving the Tower and Scipio. But me? Oh no, I was a screw-up at conception—not abiding by their Tower laws, somehow willing myself into existence to spite their two children per family policy. Of *course* they had told Alex that. Their daughter was now a monster, a dissident, an enemy of their precious Tower.

I felt the hard, salty press of tears and blinked them back. As much as it hurt, the sadder part was that it wasn't unexpected. I took a moment to compose myself, pushing the hurt back into the familiar place I kept it inside, knowing that the first chance I got to myself, the tears would come. But for now, I held it together, a practiced hand at it by now.

Nonetheless, Alex's arms came around my shoulders and pulled me to his chest, hugging me tight. "I'm so sorry, Liana," he said, his hand stroking my hair. "They don't deserve you. They don't. But I love you, my irritating little sister. And nothing in the world is going to change that."

"I'm fine," I insisted gently, touched that he cared. I carefully pushed him off of me, and smiled at him, trying to prove it to him. "Honestly, I should've known better than to ask."

He made a face and looked away. "Yeah, well, to hell with them."

I laughed, and he smiled. A heartbeat or two of silence passed between us, as if we were allowing some sort of magical breeze to push the gloominess of the conversation away, and then Alex's smile shifted, becoming slyer.

"So... this Grey guy..."

"Oh, no you don't," I said, cutting him off. "We are not going over this again. We are both twenty-year-old adults—you get no say in my personal life. *Comprende?" Comprende* meant "understand" in my family's most ancient native tongue. We only used it when we were with each other, and, unfortunately, no one spoke the language fluently anymore. My great-great-great-great-grandmother, before the End, had kept a diary in the language that we had managed to preserve, but without any context for how to translate it, I had never been able to crack it. Still, I loved reading it and sounding it out late at night when I couldn't sleep.

"Fine," he said. "I guess I can leave him alone. For now. Now... There was one more thing I was supposed to talk to you about. Mercury explained about this group that wishes to speak with you, and he managed to get in touch with them about the meeting."

"And?"

"They wouldn't set a day or a time," he said, and I had a moment to give him a confused look before he continued. "The deal is this: they will contact Mercury with a location for the meet, and a time no sooner than five hours thereafter. The last part was added by Mercury, because he wanted to have enough time to get the message to you so you could have time to get there."

I nodded, impressed by the level of caution they were displaying. Whoever they were, they certainly didn't want to give anyone a lot of time to try to set up any sort of trap to catch them. It still didn't tell me who they were, but at least they were smart. That was a good sign.

"So they could call while we're on the heist?" I asked, and he nodded.

"Hence the five hours."

I sighed, irritated beyond belief, but what could I do? "Tell him that I agree to the terms, and I'll be waiting on his call."

Alex frowned. "Are you serious? You're going to meet with them just like that?"

I nodded, giving him a wry look. "I know—believe me, I do. I think about things too, y'know. But it couldn't hurt to find some new friends and a safer place to figure out our next step."

Alex looked around and then nodded thoughtfully. "Yeah, this place is a bit of a dump," he replied in comprehension. He held up his wrist, frowning when he saw the green dash there, and then swiping over to check the time, which also wasn't working. I looked around for the clock Quess had brought.

"It's eleven fifteen," I informed him. "In the evening."

"Then that's my cue to leave. I can't be out of the Core for too long—they don't really like it when I do that. I just need you to hand me over the Paragon Mercury wanted before I head off."

My spirits plummeted some, but I stepped in close and hugged him one last time, as Quess fetched the Paragon and pressed it into my brother's hand. I remained clutching Alex tightly against me, just feeling... whole. He squeezed me for a second or two longer, and then slowly pulled away.

"I gotta go," he said. I nodded, pushed the curtain aside, and followed him to the vent. He knelt before it and looked up at me. "Gonna walk me out?"

"Of course," I replied. "I need as much time as I can get with you."

He grinned, and slid into the vent. I waited patiently, but even as he pulled away, I felt sadder and sadder. I wanted him to stay, but I knew it was impossible. So I put on my happy face instead, and moved to follow, planning to make any face-to-face interaction we had as positive as possible.

After all, who knew how long it would be before I'd get to see him again? This last time it had been over a year. So I intended to savor every last moment, until I had to head back in and find out what was going on with the plans for the Core.

One problem at a time, right?

13

Saying goodbye to Alex wasn't easy, but I knew he was going to be careful, and so was I. We had our own places we needed to be, and while his was admittedly the more dangerous one, I knew my brother well enough to know that he wouldn't leave IT unless he had to.

I crawled through the vents, eager to get back to the others and start going over Mercury's plan. His mad plan. I paused in the tunnel and took a moment to collect myself, the sudden apprehension of what we were about to do once again sinking into me. I had to remind myself that Alex would not let me walk in there without a good plan in place. I had to trust him. Which meant I had to trust Mercury.

Mercury. He'd known I was in contact with Alex since right after Cali and I had netted him. He hadn't said anything, and he'd even asked me to reveal how I'd gotten the information about Zoe.

But I hadn't said anything, and neither had he. Why not? What good was hiding it?

"Because he wouldn't have gotten the dramatic splash that not telling me did," I muttered, resuming my shuffling through the tunnels. It made sense. It was a surprise that bore a powerful message: I have your brother, too.

I paused at the junction. If I turned left, I'd be in the workroom, and if I stayed straight, the main room. I listened for a second, my ears straining, then heard the faint sound of voices off to my left, and headed toward them.

As I moved, I recalled Alex's assertion that maybe Mercury wasn't so bad, and once again, I heard Roark's voice in my head saying, *You kids don't know how to hope, not really. And it's the damned Tower's fault.* I knew he was right, in my heart, but I wasn't sure I was willing to let go of my distrust of Mercury just yet. Maybe, if things went according to plan. Maybe.

As I drew closer to the workroom, the voices became more discernable and familiar, until I was being greeted by the dulcet and sweet tones of Zoe and Quess. Fighting. Again.

I paused for a moment, rolling my eyes upward and praying for patience, and then continued to drag myself forward.

"Look, just because you worked in IT doesn't mean you know everything. The silica circuits will make them waterproof!" Zoe thundered, her words bouncing off the metal walls with the derisive quality of a meteor impacting the earth. "And they could be used in the plunge! I'm telling you, that's the way in—not this open shaft with the laser beams of death."

I slipped out of the vent and back onto my feet quickly, my eyes already seeking them out. Zoe had her back to Quess, and partially to me, and was hunched over working on something small. Quess was facing me, leaning back on his right elbow while he examined something he clutched carefully between a set of tweezers in his left hand. He nodded at me as I entered, but was already in the process of replying to Zoe.

"It's pronounced *laser cutter*," Quess said arrogantly. "You're going to have to speak the lingo if you're going to come with us. Unless you want me to have to smooth talk you out of a situation. I can just picture it now..."

Zoe groaned theatrically and swiveled her head to look at him over her shoulder. "Don't you even do it," she said, her voice filled with warning, but it was too late, and Quess was already going over his imagined scenario in which he saved Zoe from some imaginary member of the Inquisitors, who were the internal police force inside the Core.

Every department had one. They were generally meant for handling interdepartmental disputes between neighbors and friends. They also guarded important equipment and machines to prevent anyone from tampering with or damaging them in any way, shape, or form. The Knights had good working relationships with all of them, and each department gave Knights free reign to patrol through. Except for IT. No one from the Knights or any other department was allowed inside IT without permission from the head of their department, and they handed that out very rarely.

I mostly ignored his story, even though it was garnering a laugh here and there from Grey and Maddox. It seemed Eric had moved on to anger, and was staring at Quess from under his eyebrows, emitting what could only be described as the slowest working death glare in existence. I had known Eric for most of my life, and he was the most laid-back, good-natured person I had ever met. For him to look at Quess like that made me nervous.

No, it made me realize that I needed to intervene. Just not as a friend to Zoe, as I had contemplated before, but as a leader to those who were supposed to be working together. For better or worse, their relationship, as it stood, was creating tension. People were laughing at Quess's story, but I didn't miss the hint of pink in Zoe's cheeks when he discussed making out with her in the cooling pools of Sector 8. She wasn't pretending to be upset. She *was* upset. And Quess wasn't taking her seriously. He would if she'd just tell him to knock it off, but for some reason she hadn't.

Eric was jealous, and Quess was... Well, Quess was being Quess. He didn't mean anything by it, but he needed to learn when to back off.

Zoe turned to throw something else at him, and I snapped.

"Both of you knock it off right now!" I commanded loudly, and everyone froze and stared at me, mouths wide. Doubt filled me for a heartbeat, then two, and then I shoved it aside. "You two have been bickering since you met, and I'm here to tell you, it's beginning to seem less like fighting and more like flirting, and it's getting a little old."

"Hear hear," Eric said loudly, and my eyes immediately sought him out. He was smiling at me, his eyes brimming with gratitude, and the glow intensified with the sound of Zoe's ear-rending shriek of disgust.

"With this pretentious, pompous, arrogant, egotistical, maniacal, lackadaisical, lazy, rude, sophomoric, selfish, argumentative, spoiled little brat?"

Quess flushed bright red as she continued to list unpleasant adjectives, and he looked away, rounding his shoulders slightly. I immediately got angry at her. Quess was annoying, yes, and he flirted, hard. Without Cali around to keep him in check, I guessed it fell on me to do so. But that didn't mean Zoe got to run her mouth about him.

"Zoe, I understand that you're angry, but think about what you just said to him," I said, meeting her gaze. She looked over at Quess, and then back to me, her mouth pinching.

"Liana, he wouldn't stop flirting with me. I mean, did you hear those descriptions? That was a little much."

"I agree," I said, spearing Quess with an equally hard look, and he nodded contritely, looking as if he completely understood where he'd messed up. "But why didn't you ask him to stop?"

Zoe gave me an incredulous look and held up the tool in her hand—the one she had been intending to throw before I had interrupted. Then she looked back to me, her pointed glances revealing that she had, in her own way.

I pressed my mouth in a thin line and cocked my head at her. "Really, Zo? This might be just as bad as the infamous 'inspecting the underside of the bridge' thing."

Her sullen features broke into a surprised smile as I referenced the time I had leapt out from under a bridge, where I'd been hiding from her and Eric, and then refused to admit that my excuse of "inspecting the bridge" was a lie. She hadn't bought it then, but it was nice to see we could smile about it now.

It also helped ease some of the tension in the room. I was aware everyone else was watching me, waiting to see how I'd handle it from here, and felt one of those do-or-die moments. I just wanted to be diplomatic and fair, without ruffling too many feathers. Well, any more feathers, at the very least.

"Zoe, you probably should've sat down and talked to Quess

back when all this started. Quess, you need to learn to respect other people's boundaries. I expect everyone here to act like adults—Tian being the only exception—and remember that we are in hiding down here. Fighting, yelling, throwing things..." I gave Zoe a pointed look, and she cringed, her shoulders hunching. "That's how we get caught. If a Hand were up there and had heard..." I trailed off, and both of them looked remorseful.

"I'm sorry, Liana," Zoe said. "You're right. I just..." Her eyes widened in mortification.

I waited for her to go on, to explain why she hadn't put a stop to it in the first place, but I saw the surrender in her face as she gave up.

"I'm sorry," she said. "And it will never happen again."

"Same here," Quess said, giving me a solemn nod. "And... I swear I'll try, but I have poor impulse control, so you're gonna have to cut me some slack."

"No, we won't. But I'll leave my considerable boot print on your butt if you get out of line again," Maddox said from where she was watching on the sidelines, and I grinned.

"It's forgiven this time, but next time, the first offender gets the grossest of the chores on the next day's chore list. And that goes for everyone. No screaming matches. Your feelings get hurt, you start to get upset, take a breath, and then work it out. Listen, and speak clearly, and if you need one of us to play arbiter, let us know. These are tight quarters, so there are undoubtedly going to be fights. Just try to get a handle on it before it gets too bad, okay?"

Everyone nodded in unison, and I felt a trill of excitement. They were listening to me and agreeing with my idea. I'd made a *rule*.

"All right, moving on to the next piece of business," I continued, playing it cool. "What's going on with the plan Mercury and my brother prepared?" I asked, clapping my hands together to try to clear some of the air.

Grey gave me an impressed smirk as he bent over to pick up the case, and I smiled, wordlessly thanking him for noticing how awesome all of that just was. I might gush about it later, but right now, I was riding a power high.

"Give Quess and me a minute to set it up, okay?" he said.

I nodded and watched as they began clearing the center table, taking an extra moment to shove at the crates to make sure they were as tight together as they could be, before pulling out the files and beginning to lay them out.

As I watched them, I realized that this was what being a leader meant—people moving to get things set up for you without you even asking. I had never considered that before, but as I watched it happening right before my eyes, I couldn't help but feel excited by the possibilities. I let my imagination drift for a moment. I could ask for things to get done, and people would actually do them for me! I could send them out on missions, supply runs... whatever, and they would listen. I found myself idly wondering how bad it would be to send someone to track down a few of the personal items I had been missing, like the diary left behind by my great-great-so on-and-so-forth grand-mother—and then I realized how easy it would be to abuse the power, imagining dozens of scenarios in which I let my laziness get the better of me and ordered others to do even the most menial of tasks for me, and despised it. I immediately began willing the use of such a disgusting power out of existence.

"Hey," Zoe said softly from next to me. I glanced over to see her studying me, then turned back to the table, still fascinated by how much time they were taking to lay out the plan. "Why does your face look like that?"

"Because I just discovered that I have a superpower that can very easily be used for evil, and I'm making myself promise to never, ever use it again."

"Oh?" She looked genuinely intrigued, so I took a step closer.

"Okay, but this is between you and me, not between... leader and leader's best friend, okay?"

She laughed and shook her head. "This leader thing might be going to your head a little bit."

"I think it is," I said excitedly, and she laughed loudly. "I'm serious, Zoe! Grey and Quess just started setting things up to break down the plan. For me! 'Cause I'm in charge. And I just conflict-resolutioned the crap out of that fight. Sorry to bring it up so soon after—" I paused long enough to wait for her "It's okay" response, and then continued. "And everyone looked at me like... yeah... that's Liana. That girl is in charge."

Zoe stared at me, and I could see her struggling to keep her laugh back. After a moment, she shook her head. "I will admit," she said, her voice shifting with barely repressed laughter, "that you handled that situation beautifully. I was properly called out. Thank you, by the way..."

"No problem," I replied in the space she left for me.

"And I am glad to see you're having fun with your new super-power. You mentioned a promise to never use it again?"

"Mm-hm," I replied with a serious nod. "I do not want this temptation anywhere near me. I'm not sure I can be trusted."

She rolled her eyes and shook her head even harder, but she was laughing, and that was all that really mattered.

"Can I ask a question?" she asked, and I nodded. "Why didn't you say anything earlier? About how Quess and I... seemed to others."

I hesitated, and then shrugged. "Why weren't you telling Quess to back off?" I asked back.

"Because... Because of what happened to his friend, or mom figure—I'm still not really clear on the roles—I felt like I couldn't say anything bad to him. It was like... 'Hi, I'm Zoe, and your mom basically just died because my best friend wanted to save my life. Let me just go off on you and become an even bigger jerk than before'."

I really shouldn't have laughed at that. It was woefully inappropriate, since Cali had just died. And as soon as the laugh escaped me, guilt followed fast at its heels, cutting it short. I covered my mouth and shook my head.

"We're bad people," I said, mortified.

Zoe looked around the room and shook her head. "Not this time," she said somberly, and I frowned, wondering what she was thinking. It was on the tip of my tongue to ask, when she added, "Also... I'm guessing that flirting jab that got me so riled up at first was intentional?"

I smiled, question forgotten. I loved that Zoe knew me so well she could read between my lines. "Yeah," I replied. "You, uh... you have another apology to make."

Zoe's head moved, and I followed her gaze to where Eric was sitting. He was staring at both of us. She looked back at me, and realization dawned in her bright blue eyes.

"Oh, Scipio kill me now, I fell into a romance novel trope, didn't I?"

I chuckled. "Yeah, you did. But if Eric really is your one true love..."

"Shut up, Liana," she said, and rewarded me with a hard slap on my shoulder, before making a beeline right for Eric, her body language radiating her apology. One part of me wanted to watch, but I stayed away, giving them their privacy.

I moved over to the table, clasping my hands together to keep from touching things, and put the silliness aside. I was pretty certain I wasn't supposed to be silly at all anymore, but maybe nobody would judge me harshly, just this once.

The lines on the paper looked dense and complex, and I blinked several times, trying to get a clear sense of what I was looking at. Every citizen of the Tower had to take a blueprint-reading class, another one of those fun little preparedness classes that were mandatory until the day you died. The classes weren't every day, unless you were from certain departments, but it was required to attend at least one a year, as a refresher course.

But I had never been the best with blueprints, so... looking at this was the equivalent of looking into the gates of hell. I gazed up at them, and smiled.

"I have no idea what I'm looking at," I admitted, and Grey and Quess laughed.

It struck me then how different this all was since merely a couple of weeks ago. If I had admitted my inability to perform a task that everyone in the Tower was supposed to be good at before, I would've been met with disgust, revulsion, and fear—seen as a deviant who couldn't even serve the Tower in the simplest of ways.

But here there was laughter. And, Scipio help me, it was all I had ever wanted.

"That's fair," Quess said with a nod, looking at the map. I drew back some of my elation, determined to focus. "And these aren't your ordinary blueprints. These are encrypted. Only someone who was in IT can read them."

"Let me guess, you can read them?" Grey asked.

Quess nodded. "I can read them. And I already did that, and familiarized myself with the plan. It's actually not a bad plan, all in all. The nets are put together in one of the workrooms on an upper level, right below the mineral farms."

"Mineral farms?" I asked.

"Yeah. Not a lot of people know this, but IT has to grow certain precious gemstones and minerals to create or maintain most of the circuitry that keeps Scipio alive, and the Tower functioning."

"Fascinating," I said, filing that away for later use. I had never thought about where the components for our technology came from, and once again, it wasn't something that was mentioned, let alone taught. And given how tight-lipped the Eyes were about their department in general, I knew I shouldn't be surprised that I was ignorant. As curious as I was, I had to accept the fact that we just did not have time for a lecture. "What about internal security in that area? Won't it be high?"

"Well, there are stations everywhere, and probably some patrol units, but it won't matter. They won't be able to recognize you or Grey thanks to the melanin packet and makeup applicator your brother brought. And your brother wrote a program that will basically make our net IDs invisible to the scanners for one hour. It'll read like a scrambled net, and mark your face for facial recognition. But your brother wrote another code that basically distorts the results, listing you as another person instead. They would have to be watching every picture on every failed net when yours came across to even notice that your picture wasn't an exact match, and we used to get thousands of those a day. He only programmed it to work in this section, on this floor, so we cannot use the stairs or any elevator to escape to another floor in an emergency. As soon as you set foot out of this area, you're caught." As he spoke, he slid his finger along the thicker white lines that I was pretty certain represented walls, and circled a wide swatch of space on the map, indicating our so-called safe zone where my brother's virus would be in effect.

"How do we get in?" I asked.

"Drop through the central cooling tube that runs down the inside of the Tower. There's a laser cutter defense grid, but Alex and Mercury—"

"Wrote some sort of program to defeat it," I finished for him with a nod. "That's my brother." I studied the blueprints for a second and then shook my head, uneasy in spite of the clear way that Quess was explaining it. It took me a minute to identify the source. "This really feels too easy," I said. "What about the room where the nets are being held?"

"According to Mercury and Alex, empty by 'close of business,' which is Eye slang for five o'clock." Quess grinned and looked around. "This really is a good plan, guys. Drop down, get to the net room, steal enough for everyone and maybe a few extra, and then get out. It honestly wouldn't work normally, but because we have Mercury and Alex, it will this time."

I licked my lips and nodded. I had to trust them. I had to believe this would work. "Unless anyone objects, I say we go for it." I waited, and no one objected, so I filed the decision under "unanimous" and moved on. "So who's going?" I asked, looking around. "Obviously me, but..."

"Me," Grey replied automatically, and we shared a smile.

"Me too," Maddox said, and I looked over to see her listening, my smile growing uncertain.

"You sure?" I asked.

She nodded, her lips pursing. "Being here is just as bad in some ways. Besides, you'll need the help."

I couldn't argue with that logic. "Anyone else?"

"You guys are going to need me, as loathe as I am to say it," Quess said, fiddling with a few tools. "I mean... I know this hand-some exterior shouts 'athletic,' but I really just have a good metabolism. So you can't count on me for fighting, but you can for hacking stuff."

"Eric and I should stay here then," Zoe said, approaching us. "Keep an eye on Tian, hold down the fort..."

I had to admit I was disappointed that Zoe and Eric were hanging back, but it was smart to leave people behind—especially with Tian. "Then we've got a plan, guys," I said, smiling encouragingly at everyone. "And I don't think there's any point in delaying the inevitable. We'll go tomorrow."

Once again, silence meant yes. Tomorrow night it was.

"Do we need to talk about anything else?" Zoe asked, already walking back to her workbench, and I hesitated. I still hadn't forgotten about talking about our future plans, but bringing it up with a mission set for tomorrow wasn't a good idea.

"Nope," I said, shaking my head. "Let's get back to work."

14

I eyed the corridor ahead, one arm extended with my fist in the Callivaxian symbol for *halt*. Ahead, the narrow metal hall was clear, and I motioned us forward and around the corner. Suddenly my net buzzed, eliciting a slight head turn from me, but the feel of it had become familiar now. The modified neural scrambler was far easier to handle than the original one, as it only caused my net to intermittently buzz every few seconds or so, instead of continuously.

However, it had done nothing to reassure me as we made our way through the shell of the Tower, heading up. And now we were here, on the two hundredth floor, at the topmost level, about to attempt a heist in one of the most secretive and isolated sections of the Tower. Without getting caught.

Hopefully.

Quess brushed by me as we continued down the hall, a pad gripped gently between both of his hands. I saw a flash of the blueprint image on the screen as he passed, but it was too complex for me to decipher with just a glance.

"Here," he said, pointing at a sliding metal door, and after a moment's pause, I reached around him to pull it open. I was opening my mouth to add that he, too, could open doors, when he stepped inside the dark room, completely absorbed in his pad.

I watched him go for a second, alarmed by the fact that he'd just marched in without checking to see if anyone was inside, and then shook my head as Grey and Maddox stepped in after him.

"He's always like this on missions," Maddox whispered as I came through the door and began pushing it closed. "He just gets so absorbed in getting there that he forgets to actually pay attention or be alert."

"Right. Why did we bring him again?" Grey asked—and not softly, either. I rolled my eyes as I twisted the latch and secured the door, then ran my hands over the lines of my stolen IT uniform that happened to be a very good fit. I pulled a hand light out of my pocket, slipping my fingers through the rings of fabric attached to its side that allowed me to use it without having to hold it. The hand light rested against my knuckles as I switched it on, illuminating the room.

Inside, wooden crates were stacked in neat, tidy rows under clear plastic sheeting. Each crate was easily as tall as I was, and had writing emblazoned on the side.

"MRE." I spelled the strange three-letter word out loud. "Pine Industries."

"As in Ezekial Pine?" Grey asked, and I looked over at him to see him watching me.

"No idea, but maybe?" I was just as baffled. Why would the founder of the security department leave stacks and stacks of boxes in here, sealed behind plastic to preserve them? These rooms were supposedly designated for additional living space, or potentially to be converted to an additional farming floor, in case we needed it, but the need had never arisen—which meant they had never really been touched. They were like an attic, which was something I remembered reading about when I was younger.

Why were they being used for storage? What was someone hiding here? And had the crates been up here for three hundred years, sitting alone and unnoticed for all that time? Maybe no one even knew they were here—there wasn't much up here that needed to be repaired or even maintained. It was possible that these crates had been forgotten about, but there were so many...

"Okay, but what is a mre?" Quess pronounced it phonetically, dragging the M sound before transitioning into the R and elongating the E.

"It can't be said like that," Maddox declared, her own light shining around the dark room. "That sounds like something said in Wetmouth." I laughed. Wetmouth was how people outside of Water Treatment referred to the Divers' tongue.

"Maybe the Pines created Divers' tongue," Quess suggested. That one seemed a bit far-fetched, but given what we knew, which was not much, it was as good a guess as any.

"It's an acronym," Grey announced, his tone amused. "Apparently, like sixty or seventy years ago, there was a big push from the council to improve 'efficiency.' So they implemented this way of talking using letters, specifically reducing places and titles into letters to make communication speeds even faster. So, like, M for Medic, and CS for Chief Surgeon. Roark used to sometimes fall back into it, and I would have no clue what he was talking about.

Which I think was why they got rid of the policy a few decades ago."

"Really?" I said, following Quess as he moved down an aisle created by two stacks of crates. "That's interesting. I never heard my parents do it."

"Oh yeah," Grey said with a laugh. "That's because the Knights *hated* it, and with good reason. It was like every department had carte blanche on what got an acronym, and the titles that had worked for years before suddenly got complicated and obnoxious. And the Knights were having to deal with every department's unique language. At one point, they even had to carry a little dictionary to try to keep up with acronyms. They finally got sick of it after... thirty or so years."

"They went against Scipio?" I asked, surprised.

"I remember this," Quess exclaimed. "The Knights actually challenged the council's decision about using acronyms in the first place, and won. And now it's a law. Besides, I'm pretty sure that decision was one of a few that Scipio didn't participate in, which he can do if he feels it is, quote, 'a human matter,' unquote. As far as he was concerned, the efficiency was just fine."

"How do you know so much about this?" I asked, giving him a look. "I had no idea that Scipio wasn't involved in every decision. Everyone acts like he is."

"I was an Eye," he said with a grin as he rounded a corner, and I rolled my eyes. I had walked into that one.

It bothered me how much he took that information for granted, and it made me start thinking about the Knight-specific history classes we'd received at the academy. It felt as if each department that made up the Tower acted as a small time capsule —each with a different version of history inside—and I wondered which one would survive when it was all said and done. I also wondered how things had gotten to such a point where we hoarded knowledge for ourselves, to ourselves, and didn't trust anyone outside the department with it.

"Aha," Quess said, his hand running over the wall. A second later a seam emerged, revealing itself like a gear that had just had the sand blown out of it, and we saw a rectangle and a glowing numeric pad on the door.

"So this little virus is one of my creations," he announced with a grin as he pulled something from a satchel swinging by his side and set it against the metallic wall with a click. A moment later, a small screen with rolling numbers began to whiz by over the numeric pad, some sort of ticker at the top, with six digits that were yet to be selected.

The first field filled with a 2, then a 5, followed by a 6, 3, 7, 1. Quess dismissed the top screen with a swipe of his fingers, then quickly keyed in the numbers. The holographic overlay disappeared, and the wall sank back half an inch with a loud grating sound, and then swung out.

The light suddenly revealed within the opening was blinding, and the heat radiating from it immediately made sweat start to form on my forehead.

"This beam is what powers the Core," Quess said over the roaring inferno.

On impulse, I pulled out the goggles that we used to navigate under the greeneries and put them on. When I opened my eyes, I breathed a sigh of relief; the intense light was lessened somewhat by the lenses. How, I did not know.

"Put your goggles on," I told everyone, and moved around Quess to look into the shaft. A wide beam of white light shot down the center of the shaft, from a point not three feet overhead. The heat being emitted by it immediately vaporized the sweat off my body, and dried out my mouth and nose. I looked down the shaft, and studied the proportions of it.

"We're going to have to be very careful lashing down," I called over my shoulder. "Lashes are going to have to be on tight corners." Tight corners referred to setting our lashes to come out over our hips, and giving them no more room than five feet to swing. The limited length would keep us closer to the wall, slowing us down, but giving us far more precision. "We don't want to find out what happens when you touch that beam!"

"I'll have to carry Quess," Maddox called as she began tugging on the straps of her own gray uniform, cinching her harness tighter. "He's too sloppy for this."

"I am not!" Quess sputtered, and I turned in time to see Maddox giving him a look that would wither all of the corn and wheat in Smallsville. And he did wither under that look, petulantly looking away while shoving the pad back into his satchel.

"Don't worry, Quess," Grey said, moving to stand behind me. "This doesn't reflect on our masculinity at all."

"Oh, it absolutely does," Maddox said, bending her knees for Quess. He awkwardly climbed onto her back, looking at his wrist. On impulse, I checked mine, and saw that the purple seven was holding strong. I hadn't wanted to use the more powerful version of Paragon that Roark had created, but we needed to have a high enough rank that it wouldn't draw the attention of IT. Honestly, now that I was looking into the belly of the beast, so to speak, I was kind of regretting not using the tens, but we needed to preserve our stash.

I stared at the seven a moment or two longer, then pulled a

tiny mirror out of my pocket. Normally, I wouldn't have one within a mile of me—in fact, this one was Tian's—but I was worried about my disguise, and wanted to make sure it was holding strong. The melanin wash my brother had sent had altered my hair color to a pale, white blond, while the makeup applicator had lightened my face until it was almost sickly, and my eyes were lined with a dark shadow eyeliner smudged all around the edges. Maddox had procured lenses, giving me deep dark brown eyes that hid the natural amber color perfectly.

The disguise was excellent, though I could still detect myself beneath the layers. I just had to hope nobody else would. Breathing in, I put the mirror away and began tightening my harness.

"How long until the laser cutters are offline?" I asked Quess, and he checked his watch again.

"Thirty seconds. After that, our deadline starts. We'll have one hour before the program stops running and the lasers come back on."

"Just a trip to the store," Grey said cheerfully as he hooked a carabiner through his own harness, getting it ready to attach to the built-in hook in the back of my suit, designed just for situations like this. "In and out—no sightseeing, window shopping, or getting caught."

I chuckled and switched my lashes over to the appropriate setting, resisting the ticklish feel of them sliding inside the built-in pockets that ran through the seams of my suit. We were lucky that all uniforms came with lash seams built-in. The three central departments—Medica, Knights, and IT—shared the same design and features to make mass production easier.

I heard the click as Grey hooked onto my back, standing so

close I could feel the heat radiating from him. The beads settled over my hips, the microfiber hole expanding and retracting for the bead. I grabbed one and slid it out, giving myself six inches of slack for swinging the bead around in a circle and gaining momentum. Then I cast it to one side of the tunnel in front of us. It hit, the line tense over my hand, and I held my breath and swung out and around gently, catching us with the balls of my feet braced against the side and holding us there while I tossed the next line.

Grey shifted, his hands grabbing at my uniform, as I let us down slowly, the winch housed in the metal case on my built-in harness whirring soundlessly as I let out the line.

Overhead, I heard Maddox grunt, and looked up to see her rappelling down, heading in a straight line. That way was not my favorite style, as I preferred more fluid movements, but it was clearly what she was comfortable with.

"You okay?" I asked Grey as I descended farther, moving us down in a zigzag pattern, and keeping a nice, slow pace. I tried to keep us away from the energy beam, which seemed frozen in place—a column of white, unadulterated light that occasionally flashed purple or a soft blue. But no matter where we were, it always felt too close, given the heat coming off it in waves. I could only imagine that Grey was dying, being even closer to the beam than me.

He merely grunted in response.

"How far down?" I called up, my voice coming out in a dry wheeze.

"Twenty-three floors," Quess called back.

Great.

I continued to lash, focused completely on getting us down safely. My eyes tracked the numbers etched into the sides of the wall, marking the floors. As we descended, I noticed the lack of any other sort of marks, which was odd. Marks were everywhere in the Tower, helping to show workers where they needed to go. In the plunge, Knightmarks were left for other Knights, to tell them how to navigate the dangerous terrain within. But here, there was nothing, only numbers and hatches on every level.

My shoulders were beginning to ache when I finally came to a stop, and I whirled us close to the wall, and then took a moment to stretch out my shoulders, trusting my weight entirely to the harness and winch.

I looked over a few feet to where the hatch was, and watched Quess connect something to its side. Another interactive keyboard was then projected holographically against the hatch. He managed to pull the pad out of his satchel without dropping it, and then tapped a few keys before tucking it back into his bag.

I held my breath as he performed all of this, certain at any moment he would drop the pad, but he didn't, and the hatch came open.

Maddox and Quess went in first, moving quickly. I gave them a second to give me some space, then followed right behind, eager to get away from the blistering heat at our backsides. I detached the lash end as I landed, my knees flexing to bear the brunt of Grey's weight.

I noticed the chill in the room immediately, the bitter bite of cold contrasting with the heat that now seemed to be coming off me in waves. I moaned in relief as Grey detached from me, quickly crossing the small, narrow space and pressing his back against an exposed part of the wall, groaning in relief too. I could only imagine how he felt—his body had helped to protect most of mine, which meant he had to be in even worse shape than I was.

I let everyone take a moment to catch their breaths, shaking out my arms to help ease some of the muscle burn, and stepped deeper down the narrow hall and toward the open doorway a few feet away. I paused at the threshold and cocked my head, my eyebrows drawing together.

Rows and rows of boxes were stacked from floor to ceiling behind metal cages. Each box was constructed of some sort of black material, with small green lights shining from them, tracing along the seams with a dull throb. The entire room glowed green —bright enough to see, but eerie enough to make the hairs on my arms stand on end, in spite of the sleeves covering them.

"What is this place?" I asked over my shoulder, keeping my voice pitched low. We couldn't be sure anyone was in here right now, but if they were, we had to be ready to knock them out. If anyone managed to get an alarm up before we were long gone, then we'd only be two steps from the Citadel, the gas chamber, and death.

"Server farm," Quess replied automatically, the pad already back in his hands. "There's hundreds of them in the Core, all of them networked together to handle Scipio's massive load."

"It's huge," I said, staring down the path in front of us and already beginning to shiver.

"Here," Maddox said, holding out a small bottle in her hands. I blinked at her, and she gestured to my face. "For your eyes."

She was referring to the lenses she had gotten for me. I took the bottle and tilted my head back to place a few drops in, almost sighing in relief as the dry burn that had started with the beam of light faded somewhat. I blinked away the residual wetness and handed the bottle back to her.

"Thanks," I said, then looked at Quess for our next step.

"Hundred feet," he said, moving forward down the aisle. Maddox and Grey followed quickly, the gray uniforms that Maddox had pilfered reflecting green as they passed down the row. I checked my watch to see how much time we had left. It took me three tries before I could believe twenty minutes had already passed. That meant we had only forty minutes—and that was not a lot of time. I glanced back over my shoulder. The hatch we had come through was now closed, but a part of me wanted to stop everyone and open it and go back the way we came, before the laser cutters turned back on and killed us while we were still inside.

"That's loser thinking, Liana," I whispered to myself, taking a firm mental grip of my anxiety and casting it aside. "This is a good plan. Your brother put it together for you."

I closed my eyes and exhaled, believing in my brother, and then nodded to myself. We could do this.

15

The hall was straight and gray, with harsh overhead lights that burned like beacons. Breaks in the wall came at regular intervals, as did intersections—three doors every ten feet, followed by a hall running across the one we were in. Every door had a plaque over it with a description and room number. Most of the doors led to server farms like the one we had just emerged from, with three separate entrances, presumably to help workers access damaged areas quickly.

Then suddenly the doors just stopped, as did the intersections.

"What is this?" I asked softly, as we passed by the smooth, uninterrupted wall.

"The mineral farms must start here," Quess replied. "I've never been inside, but I've heard they're huge."

"This isn't good. There's nowhere to go if someone recognizes us through these disguises," Grey pointed out, and I looked back at him. His hair had been modified to black, and his eyes were now a muddled blue, their original brown too rich to block out entirely. But his strong jawline and features were remarkable—possibly still enough to identify him. We just had to pray our transformations were extreme enough for no one to really notice.

We continued forward... and then suddenly heard the noise of someone's footsteps coming from ahead. My heartbeat increasing, I took a chance and glanced over Quess's shoulder. A man carrying a large flat pad was walking toward us, the gray of his uniform stark under the harsh lighting.

He looked up at us, and I ducked behind Quess, my heart trembling in my chest. It looked like our disguises were going to be tested a lot more quickly than I had hoped.

I tried to shake off the anxiety that was suddenly threating to tear apart my calm façade, and just focused my eyes on Quess's back. We had our plan, and it was a good one.

Yet the logical side of my brain was at odds with my heart, which began to beat even harder, using the inside of my ribcage like the drums at a harvest celebration. The steps were loud, clicking rhythmically in a way that made my eye start twitching and my hands ball up into fists.

Suddenly Quess veered off to one side, and I got a flash of the man walking toward us. His eyes passed right through me, and then he was gone, moving past us.

I twisted my head and peered over my shoulder, watching him go. He didn't so much as pause or look back, and then he was gone.

But it didn't feel like he was. My hands were shaking and slightly sweaty, while my muscles seemed to twitch and jerk under my skin. I kept expecting something to happen, the other shoe to drop, and the farther we moved away from the man, the worse it started to feel. Like the second half of a sentence that was slow in coming, and the anticipation was killing you, because you knew that whatever was said was going to hurt no matter what.

It took everything I had to assure myself the man was not suspicious of us at all, and *that* was the reason for the lack of attack. But it took a minute.

By the time the minute had passed, I became aware that we had come to a stop, and looked around. The hall we had been in had dead-ended at another door. A sign overhead read *Net Fabrication—15A.*

Quess had already gotten out another one of the gizmos Mercury had provided, affixing it to the door. This one was a flat black box that he stuck right over where the door's handle would have been if it'd had one. He pressed a few buttons on the box, and there was a slight hum and click, the door springing free.

Quess was the first inside, but I was right behind him, eager to get out of the hall and accomplish the next stage. I stopped when I saw three faces looking up at me from various positions inside the room.

No one is supposed to be here, I thought, my mind already racing through ways to get out of this. It was too late to back out now. If we did, it could draw a lot of attention. We were pretending to be Bits—the IT's name for its initiates—but even I knew (from Alex's griping during his initiation) that they got into a lot of trouble if they wandered into rooms they weren't supposed to have access to. Unless they had permission to do so from their superior.

"Hello," said a middle-aged woman, her eyebrow rising. "What are you doing here?"

The pressure built, and I continued to think, needing an answer twenty seconds ago. After a moment of pure tension, I recalled something Alex had once told me, and went for it. It was insane, but hopefully it would work.

"I'm here for the nets?" I said, looking expectantly around the room. "There was a memo?" Alex had done something similar after he had screwed up and forgotten to put in a request for his supervisor, and wound up going down there and bluffing his way through the entire thing. But through that story, I had learned, for one thing, that periodically there were surprise inspections of nets to be performed by every lead programmer's section, to ensure that the nets were operating correctly and could withstand prolonged usage—and, for another, that you could lie without getting caught.

And he wasn't even the liar in the family.

As I expected, the woman's brow furrowed. "A memo for nets? I didn't get it. Tilda, did you get it?"

"Not at all," a woman on my right said. "Hank?"

"Not me," the only man said, scratching his chin. "Who's your Lead?"

I had no idea what they were talking about, but I tried very hard not to show it. Luckily, Quess seemed to sense my ignorance, and began speaking.

"I don't know about them, but my Lead Programmer is Harkness. And he got the same memo and told me to get down here before you closed. I was worried I wouldn't make it."

"Yes, but we haven't gotten the memo," the first woman said. I looked down at her desk and saw her name inscribed on a plaque at the front of it: Delores Winters.

"Oh," I said, feigning a fidget. "Really? I mean... Well... What does that mean?"

"Oh, she's green," said Hank with a laugh. "Who do you work with, sweetheart?"

I didn't like the way he called me 'sweetheart,' but kept my mouth shut and my mind focused on the task. Now that I knew they were looking for a Lead Programmer, I knew what they meant. There was only one that I knew of, though, and it was Alex's. Using it would put him at risk. But not using it meant immediate discovery.

"Johnson," I told them.

Hank whistled and leaned forward, his eyes sparkling. "Intelli-programming, huh? That's fascinating."

I nodded. "I'm so glad that I qualified for his department. He only takes the best of the best."

"I'll bet you were. So, when were you selected?"

I paused. The easy answer was just to say age fifteen—the age at which almost everyone else was selected by IT—but I already looked ignorant. And since I was considerably older than fifteen, it meant that I had to go with a riskier answer.

"Transfer," I said. "From Medica. I was just assigned to Lead Programmer Johnson's section a week ago."

My heart pounded as I lied. I was trying to keep everything simple, and to my never-ending surprise, they nodded in complete understanding. Our disguises—and made-up stories—were working.

Now we just had to get the nets without tipping off anyone in the room that we most decidedly did *not* actually belong.

"There's no record of this requisition of nets," Delores said, craning her neck up from her pad and staring at us. "But you're all here for some?"

"If I may," Maddox said. "I saw the orders on my Lead's pad. It's a surprise inspection."

I held my breath, waiting and watching. There were only three of them, and they didn't look like they could take us in a fight, but I had no idea what kind of sensors were in this room. Perhaps the individuals monitoring the cameras would miss a fight happening amid all of the other cameras they were monitoring—but not for long. It was better to handle things diplomatically.

But lie after lie was only going to get us caught.

"Is it? Did the memo happen to mention why?" Hank stared at us expectantly as he asked the question, resting his chin on the backs of his hands.

"Quality control," Quess replied with a shrug. "That's really all I know."

Delores looked at Hank. "On top of what we're doing *already?*" she practically snarled. "Our work here is good! Don't they know how many hours it takes for us to put just one together? And now they want to destroy the ones we've already made in some mindless pursuit of a flaw!"

"Oh, get over it, Delores," Tilda said waspishly. "We should be scrutinized, and so should our work. It gets installed in people's skulls, so if they want to test it, let them look. We stand by our nets." She turned to us and flashed a welcoming smile. "How many did the requisition form ask for?"

I hesitated, but Grey didn't. "I was told five." My eyes bulged; Delores had just been talking about how difficult they were to make, and he went ahead and said five. We were so sunk.

"I think you might have read it wrong," Quess said, his eyebrows bunching, and I felt a flare of relief. Quess would know what an appropriate amount for an inspection was. "Mine said three."

"Mine as well," Maddox said, giving Grey a sideways look.

Grey looked around and then hunched his shoulders, managing to look slightly embarrassed. "Okay, there may have been a chance I wasn't paying attention."

Hank chuckled. "Don't tell me—your Lead is Kowolski?"

"How'd you know?" Grey asked back smoothly. "Were you in the section?"

"Long time ago. Kowolski's been there for decades. He's practically as old as all of the machines, but with half the charm."

Grey laughed at Hank's quip, and I started to relax some. Tilda beckoned us over, and we all encircled her desk, watching as she got up and selected a small bin from a row sitting on a shelf behind her. She carried it back and then pulled the top off, revealing several rows of flat black squares: the nets in their inactive mode, tendrils curled in nice and neat so they looked like data chips.

It was so surreal, staring at the thing that also resided in my head. They weren't much to look at—the box was black, the nets no bigger than my pinkie nail. I knew from our classes that a net was a rather complex network of silicone. Each would unravel once activated, and stretch its tendrils over your cerebral cortex in order to read your emotions—and from that, determine your ranking.

It was a system of control, and even though I hated it, not having one would only get me caught and killed quicker. So.

I watched as Quess signed for his, quickly exchanging a signature for a small case with three nets.

"Thanks," he said quietly, accepting them. He stood there for a second, then turned and began heading for the door. I was glad he did; standing around would blow our whole makeshift cover story, but not everyone would have thought of it in the moment, and I was pleased that he had. Some people didn't do well with improvisation.

Grey was next, and I couldn't help but feel twitchy, watching Tilda use tweezers to carefully drop the small chips into a smaller container for transportation. He signed as well, and then began heading for the door, following Quess. He gave me a look as I passed, and I met it.

If he was nervous, he didn't show it. I, on the other hand, felt like the tension in my muscles was a threat to my very skin remaining intact and whole.

"Sign here," Tilda said to Maddox, and I turned back to see her finish signing with a flourish, setting the pen down. "Thank you, and here you go."

"Thanks."

She turned to leave, and I moved up to take her place, immediately picking up the stylus and signing the pad in front of me, confirming that I had received three nets. I accepted the case, which was surprisingly light for carrying something so heavy with significance, and tucked it into my pocket with a smile and a nod, turning to go.

I nearly plowed into Maddox as I did so, and frowned. She was standing with her face to the door, her body still. I peeked around her, and saw a man standing there. He had a carefully trimmed beard, and the sleeves of his uniform were rolled up to reveal strong forearms.

"Lead Programmer Johnson," Tilda exclaimed, clearly surprised to see him. My spine tingled in alarm as I took in my brother's supervisor. If she mentioned my claimed connection to him, I was going to get caught. "I'm surprised to see you."

"I'm surprised to be down here," he said. "But it seems all of my Bits are off running around doing their own thing, instead of making themselves available to me. So here I am."

"Not all of them," Tilda replied sweetly, and I closed my eyes, already knowing that she was about to call me out. "This one must've gotten your orders."

"My orders?"

My heart pounded in my throat as Johnson looked around the room, extremely confused. We were seconds away from finding out what happened when infiltrators got caught in the Core. I had to do something, anything, to try to salvage this.

And when in doubt, I had been told to opt for strength.

"For the nets, sir?" I said, taking a step out from behind Maddox and seizing the opportunity to strike. People tended not to question confidence, and my only hope was to use that for as long as it took us to get past him—and out the door. "I was told you wanted some?"

"I did," he said, frowning. "You're in my section?"

"Yes, sir," I said with a nod. "I just started last week."

"That would explain why I don't quite recognize you yet. No offense, but there are a lot of people in the department."

"I've noticed," I said, forcing a smile on my lips. My heart was now shuddering, like an engine on its last legs, and I knew I was breathing too heavily to slow it down. I tried to compensate by only taking small sips of air, but it didn't feel like enough. "Well, I can just give these to you now, sir," I said, pulling the case out of my pocket. "I'll go ahead and get back and let my direct supervisor know that you received them."

I hated giving them up, but if I didn't right then and there, they would recognize something was up. This was supposedly my mission, in their eyes. I had to finish it, if only to not give us away.

"Sure," he said, reaching out and taking the case. "Thank you."

He paused as he took them, really taking a good look at my face. "You know, you do look familiar to me. Did we have a chance to meet face-to-face yet? I try to get out on the floor every day, but it's so hard to recall some days."

I shook my head quickly. "Not formally, sir."

"Who's your direct supervisor?"

I faltered. Alex was a supervisor, but I didn't want to use his name. I had already come dangerously close to exposing him with just the little bit I had done. If they figured out that I was me... and his twin... I shuddered to think of the consequences.

"Jim," I said after a moment, looking around. "But he's not my direct supervisor. He—"

"That wasn't what I asked you," he said with a frown, crossing his arms. "Who's your direct supervisor?"

Four sets of eyes turned to me, pinning me down collectively with their scrutiny, and I felt as if someone had just jammed a baton in my back, and hadn't released the charge yet. But it was coming.

"My direct supervisor is—"

Maddox snapped forward, her fist striking fast across Johnson's throat. He made a choked sound, his hands going around his neck as his eyes bulged, and she shoved him to one side, moving toward the door. I followed behind her, and was just exiting the door when everyone behind us erupted into panic.

We immediately began running. Grey and Quess were waiting for us some ten to fifteen feet down the hall. They took one look at us as we exited the room, and then began running as well.

16

We ran, sprinting down the long hall, and were maybe twenty feet away from the server room when an alarm began to blare out. Immediately, red lights installed on the walls started to flash, while the walls themselves changed and began pulsing in red.

"Intruders detected in Section 97," chimed Scipio's voice, and it took me a minute to remember this was the real one. "Sealing off the halls."

"Keep running," Quess urged needlessly—we hadn't stopped—his breathing already erratic. "We need to get out of here before our exit is blocked off."

Behind us, a metallic bang caused the whole floor to shudder. I looked over my shoulder in time to see a metallic door now in place where the other end of the hall had once been—and a group of people wearing black uniforms trimmed in blue rounding the corner, cradling some sort of glowing ball in their hands. I didn't know what the ball was, but the black uniforms marked them as Inquisitors—Scipio's personal security.

One of them immediately leveled his hand at me, unclenching his fingers from around the light. I instinctively ducked, just as the air overhead seemed to grow hot and thick, brushing over my back with surprising force. I stumbled, bracing myself against the wall and barely managing to keep upright, before I resumed running.

"We've got company!" I shouted, and all three of my friends risked a glance over their shoulders to peer past me at the mob in pursuit. I followed their gazes just in time to see another, closer door slam shut.

"Lashes!" Quess yelled, his lash ends already flying, and I poured on some speed to catch up to Grey.

"You better keep this from hurting!" I shouted when we both realized he was going to have to jump on my back before I could lash away—and that wasn't generally something you did quickly. I threw my lashes, stopping long enough for him to hook his carabiner onto the link on the back of my uniform, and I activated the retractor before his weight was fully on me, throwing us both in the air.

"Whoa!" Grey shouted, his hands clamping down over my chest as we jerked up into the air.

I ignored it, my hand already throwing the next lash and propelling us down the hall. Luckily, the ceilings were twenty-five feet, so we swung high, keeping ourselves off the ground and pulling away from the group below.

Ahead of me, Maddox suddenly swung to one side, giving me room to pass her. "What is she doing?" I called.

I felt Grey's weight shift as he twisted around to look. "She's still behind us. I think she wanted you in the middle because you're carrying me."

It made sense. With Grey, I was slightly slower, and my balance was more difficult to shift around. If we were taken down, both of us would be caught long before we were able to untangle ourselves from each other and the line. I didn't like that she was doing this for me, mostly because I wanted to be last to prevent anyone from getting hurt or taken, but now wasn't the time to argue, so I gritted my teeth and surged forward.

I lashed faster, my muscles aching from their lack of use over the past week. Carrying Grey's weight and moving at this speed was exhausting my resources quickly. If we didn't get back to the server room soon, my muscles would give out.

Almost as soon as I realized it, Quess began to give himself more slack in the lines, drawing closer and closer to the floor in long, sweeping strokes until he was near enough to set his feet down and keep running without missing a beat. I followed his lead and lowered us as well, and Grey jumped off my back before I had even set a foot on the ground—something I could kiss him for later. I resumed running as well, but I was already slower than I had been before, and a stitch was beginning to form in my side.

Quess had stopped down the hall in front of the door, and I came to a halt next to him and Grey, watching as he tried to tug the door open. All we had to do was get back through the server room and up the shaft, and we'd be out of here. Which meant that all this door needed to do to keep from pissing me off was open.

"We're locked out!" Quess shouted, his eyes darting around in panic. I glanced down the hall, past where Maddox was pounding toward us at a dead run, and saw that the group pursuing us was only forty or fifty feet back. And closing in fast.

"Is there a way to hack it?" I asked, whipping around to study the door. Like several of the doors on this level, it too had some sort of electrical lock. I just hoped this was a type he knew how to open.

Quess nodded shakily, his hands going for his satchel and pulling the pad out. I could tell Quess was scared: his hands were practically vibrating. I looked at Grey.

"Help him," I said, and he nodded, plucking the pad from Quess's fingers. "Maddox and I will buy you time."

"Tell me what to do," Grey said patiently, kneeling next to Quess, and I turned away, confident that Grey and Quess would get it figured out. I ran toward Maddox, who had slowed to a stop. I stopped as well and gave her a look.

"We have to buy them some time," I said, pulling my lash end out. She looked at it. "It's the only weapon we have. Watch out for their hands—they are shooting some sort of compression thing at us."

"Pulse shield," Quess shouted from behind us. "The name is a misnomer. Those things are weapons, and they hurt." I turned to yell back at him to shut up and work, and then stopped when I saw that he was working. Grey's hand was on his shoulder as he talked to Quess in low tones.

"I know, I know..." Quess muttered. "Just... don't let them take me, okay? If they find us, promise me that you will kill me. These guys don't like deserters."

"I'll kill you right now if you don't hurry up," Maddox said, and together we turned to face the surging group of people coming toward us.

"They aren't going to get us, Quess," I said, gripping my lash ends tightly between my fingers, tension radiating from me.

There were eight of them in total, but there was only enough room for them to stand side by side in pairs. That gave us an advantage they didn't have.

"You go down," Maddox said from the side of her mouth as they drew even closer, now just thirty feet away. "I'll go up."

"Got it."

I licked my lips, rolling my shoulders. This was just like sparring, I reminded myself. I just needed to be careful; they might want to hurt me, but I didn't want to have to kill anyone unless absolutely necessary.

They thundered closer, and we both moved as those in front raised their hands. I rolled forward under a blast as it shot overhead, and then threw my lash, catching it around the first man's left ankle. I tugged, going down on one knee, and jerked him off his feet. Immediately everyone around him began to stumble, and I retracted the lash and stood as Maddox landed behind them. She bent over and landed a smart punch to one downed woman's head, snapping her head back with terrific force. It wasn't enough to kill, thankfully, but it did render her unconscious.

Behind Maddox, another door slammed shut, thirty feet down.

I moved forward as the Inquisitors began to untangle themselves. I heard another wet *thunk* of Maddox's fist, but was focused on a man who was my nearest target. I kicked him in the face, wincing as I did so, and he fell back with a stunned cry.

"We almost got it!" Grey shouted from behind me as I ducked beneath a wild haymaker delivered by the man whose ankle I had lassoed, driving my shoulder into his stomach and pushing him back. He stumbled—how could he not, with the tangle of limbs and bodies behind him?—and we both wound up on the ground again, with me on top of him.

I sat up quickly and brought my fist down on his face, and then blindly cast my lash end backwards, hit the button, and retracted the line, using it to jerk me to my feet. I detached and turned in time to catch a body in the midsection, dragging me to the floor. I hit hard, my head slamming into the ground forcefully enough to make my teeth rattle, but adrenaline pushed the pain back, and panic forced my eyes open.

A fist was already hurtling down toward my face, but I reflexively snapped my head to one side and was rewarded with the sharp crack of his fist on the pavement next to me. He howled, rearing back and clutching his wrist, and I slid back, planting a foot on his chest for leverage and knocking him backwards. I was halfway to my feet when I saw another black-clad figure hopping over the downed man, her hand up, fingers uncurled.

I ducked to one side, but caught the edge of the blast. The impact of it altered my trajectory, and I slammed into the wall shoulder first, my arm exploding into a fiery ball of pain. I opened my eyes, dazed, my breath coming in sharp pants, looking around for a target. Fingers entangled in my hair, and I instinctively slammed my head backwards. There was a sharp crunch, and I took a step forward and twisted, bringing my elbow up into my opponent's ribcage. She tore a chunk of hair from my head as she stumbled back, and I turned to see her clutching her broken nose. She was doubled over and wheezing through the blood streaming between her fingers.

My scalp burned where the chunk had been ripped out, and my left shoulder throbbed deep within the socket, but rage had begun to fuel my actions, and I took a step forward, grabbing her hand and feeling around. She looked up at me just as I found the button to her pulse weapon, and clicked it. The pulse hit her right in the face, and she was flung backwards ten feet, her arms and legs limp as a ragdoll's. I didn't see her land; I was already moving away from the next attacker, dipping right and stepping back to avoid two blows in rapid succession. I pivoted on the ball of my foot, left arm snapping up to block his third blow, while my right fist followed close behind.

I caught him in the chin with an uppercut, and then slammed my palm into his chest, forcing him back a few steps. He fell, and I sagged back, my hand reflexively grabbing my shoulder to try to stop the pain that was radiating from it. I looked back to see Maddox standing over several bodies, her hair mussed and her breathing heavy. She saw me looking at her and straightened, unclenching her fists.

A shout sounded behind her, and I craned my neck to see more black-clad individuals emerging from around the corner of a side hallway, this group even larger than the last.

"We have to go," I panted, turning and hobbling toward Grey and Quess. "We have to go *now*."

"Almost there," Quess said, his eyes on the pad. Grey looked up at me, his eyes instantly flashing in concern, and I shook my head. He could worry about my bumps and bruises later.

I turned back down the hall to see Maddox slipping one of the pulse blasters off of an Inquisition agent's hands, the crowd almost on her.

"DOXY, GET UP HERE!" I bellowed, but she turned her back on me to fire a pulse shot down the hallway, knocking back several would-be attackers. I growled, and began to race back to her.

"Liana!" Grey cried, and I felt his hands on my shoulders, holding me back and causing agony to shoot down my left one. I broke out of his arms in time to see Maddox stop short and look back at me. She grabbed something and threw it toward me, just as a door descended, slamming down between us. I caught it reflexively, and realized it was her box with the nets.

"MADDOX!" I cried, ripping myself out of Grey's grip and rushing at the door barrier. I began to bang on it, my fist clenching the box thudding against the metal, and I looked back at Quess. "We have to hack this barrier!"

"She's in there with at least twelve individuals from the Inquisition—maybe even more. There's no time." Grey's voice was grim as he spoke.

I looked up at him, baffled by his words. "You want to abandon her? We can't do that!"

"We can, and we will," Grey said. "But only for now. We need to run now so we can get her later, okay?"

I licked my lips and turned back to the door barrier, staring at it. From the stretch of hallway still exposed to us, I could hear the sound of booted feet drawing near. They were only moments away. Grey was right.

I turned away, even though I hated myself for doing it. I ducked through the door Quess finally managed to open just as I began to make out the dark uniforms of the Inquisition. They emerged from an opening on the right, and I quickly moved into the cold server room, Grey right at my heels. Quess did something on his pad, and the door slid shut, the light on the spot where the handle should have been turning red and sealing closed with a hiss and a click.

"I've locked it for now," Quess said, his teeth already chattering. "But it will be overridden. Let's go."

I followed him as he led us through the isolated rows of servers, and found myself despising Scipio all over again. He sat atop an isolated and frozen throne, looking down on all of us, never knowing the pain he caused us.

I couldn't wait to get away from him.

Quess volunteered to carry Grey back up the shaft (and by volunteer, I meant Grey made him do it), and I was relieved (even if it did mean Grey had to suffer through Quess's unorthodox climb). I was in pain after the fight, and my mind was already going over what we needed to do to get home safely... and then get *Maddox* home safely.

17

"We can't go straight back," I said, finally breaking the stunned and somber silence that had shrouded us on our climb up. Neither one replied, but I needed to remind them that our plan was still in effect. We exited the shaft, my boots landing on the floor. I immediately scanned the corridor, my eyes searching for any sign of movement. We were far away from the Core, yes, but that didn't mean we couldn't be—or weren't already being— followed. And I was taking every precaution I could before we went back to Sanctum. Last time, I hadn't known there were ways of tracking someone using radioactive isotopes, and I had led Devon straight back to us. I wasn't going to make the same mistake again.

"We need to change out of our clothes and modify our disguises," I announced, verbally trying to nudge the two into action.

Grey stood with his arms crossed, his brows drawn together

and a distant look on his face that led to nowhere but the floor. He was still, contemplative. Quess, on the other hand, looked twitchy and agitated, impatient to move or not move—it was hard to tell.

"C'mon," I told them, pushing them gently down the hallway.

God, I hated this. Each step I took was another step farther away from Maddox. She was up there, alone, captured... I thought of the woman behind the glass in that gas chamber I'd visited with Gerome, her eyes staring at me accusatorially, and it was all I could do not to try to go back right then.

But I couldn't. I had to keep us moving forward, and I hated myself for it.

"But Maddox is back there," Quess said, spinning away from my hand. "We need to go back and break her out."

I looked at him, clenching my teeth hard to keep from telling him yes. He stared at me, his eyes searching, and I couldn't say it. So I shook my head.

"*Liana!*" he exclaimed, stunned by my refusal.

"I'm sorry," I said, biting my lip. "But going back is not an option right now."

Quess didn't even let me finish before he began to speak, his words angry, with a bitter bite. "Of course it's an option! We call Mercury and Alex and make them help us! We have to do something—who knows what they are going to do to her!"

My hands tightened into fists, and I nodded. "I know that."

"Then why aren't we calling them?"

"Because we have to get back to Sanctum to install our new nets," I said.

"We have them, we can do them right—"

"No, we can't," Grey said suddenly, looking up and over at Quess. "The data crystals with the new IDs are down there. We need to get them first before we can do anything, which is why Liana is telling you not right now."

Quess looked back and forth between us, his face ranging from defiant to embarrassed when he realized that we were right. "But... Maddox..."

"We're going to get her," I informed him. "But there is nothing we can do for her right now. We follow the plan and head back. Maddox will be okay."

"How are you so calm about this?!" Quess exploded, and I turned toward him, watching as he ran a weary hand over an equally weary face, deflating. "Why aren't you more upset?"

"I *am* upset," I said, the words tumbling out of me in an angry hiss. "I didn't want to leave her behind! If she had just come back when I said to..." I cut off the statement as waves of frustration washed over me, and took a deep, calming breath, trying to get a grip. This wasn't Maddox's fault. It was mine. I had raced back to the others and left her behind. But I wasn't going to let her stay there. "Being upset doesn't do anything," I finally said. "It's just wasting our time, which is wasting Maddox's. So here's what we are going to do: we are going back to Sanctum to get our new nets installed, and then I am going to call my brother to find out where Doxy is, and how we can break her out, okay?"

Quess stared at me, his dark blue eyes glistening. After a moment, he inclined his head and adjusted the satchel on his shoulder. "Let's get changed."

I led the way down the hall, back to the room we had picked as a rendezvous spot. When I slid open the door to the supply closet, I half-hoped to see Maddox already inside and waiting for us. But she wasn't. The disappointment held me in place, wondering *what if*, and then I stepped into the room, suddenly very, very tired. My bumps and bruises from earlier were turning out to be worse than I had imagined, and I was afraid for Doxy. She'd just lost her mother, and now she was surrounded by people who were even at this moment interrogating her, trying to get her to slip. Or worse, they were hurting her. Or even worse, they already had—

I clenched my fists, fighting off my imagination. I couldn't get caught up in what ifs. I had to work with what I had, which meant getting us back safely.

I pulled out the bag we had left here and opened it, grabbing my backup clothes. We were still wearing the IT uniforms, and this far from the Core, it was going to make us stand out. I stepped off to one corner and turned my back, getting ready to change.

As I did so, I became all the more conscious of Maddox's absence. Changing outfits in a dark supply room with two men had seemed more palatable when I wasn't the only female. Now that I was, it was uncomfortable.

I turned, prepared to find another room to change in, and then whipped right back around to face the wall, heat blossoming in my cheeks. The image I had gotten was brief, but explicit, and the strong lines of Grey's backside were going to be forever emblazoned in my mind. Especially those two intriguing dimples over his...

I quickly shut the thought down and closed my eyes, deeply mortified at my own brazenness. I shouldn't have turned around. They were following the plan—they were just changing. I should be changing. Their backs were to me. They wouldn't peek.

I gritted my teeth together and began pulling off the suit, yanking it off my shoulders and down over the harness I was wearing underneath. Kicking off my boots, I quickly slipped the uniform off my legs. The cool floor beneath my toes caused goose pimples to erupt over my exposed flesh, and I quickly put on the pants and top that I had brought, wanting nothing more than to cover my exposed flesh.

I was in the process of adjusting them when Grey coughed politely. "Liana, are you decent?"

I smiled, knowing that it was lost to everyone else in the room. I was just grateful he was being respectful. As was Quess. *More respectful than me.*

"I am," I said, turning around. They turned as well. "We need to get going."

"Tian picked the best route back," Quess said. "She's a genius at this stuff. Should only take us fifteen minutes to get out to the greenery."

"Good," I said, collecting the gray uniforms we had been wearing. I wadded them up into a ball and shoved them into a bucket I had set aside earlier, immersing them in whatever opaque liquid was inside. They'd be discovered eventually, but Grey had assured me that the harsh chemicals would eradicate any trace amount of DNA we left on them. In my case, it didn't really matter, since they had ripped out a chunk of my hair. But still, it was better to leave as little trace as possible, especially for Grey and Quess.

I turned, wiping my palms on my thighs, and saw Grey working a white cream into his hair. The color was already lightening to a bright yellow blond. I pulled my own tube out—different than the one I had originally used to alter my hair—and squeezed, then worked the cream into my own hair. The color of my hair changed as well, becoming a light brown. I didn't have a set of new, different-colored contact lenses, so I had to keep the old ones in. My own eye color was too recognizable without them.

I was feeling paranoid, but I had to keep the new Sanctum safe. The people inside were too precious for me to risk a mistake like last time.

The three of us quickly packed up our remaining gear, and I took a quick glance down the dark hallways through the open door to check that the coast was clear. "Let's go," I said as I slipped into the hall first and led the way.

"Liana!"

I cringed at Tian's excited cries, already dreading telling the girl the news about Maddox. In truth, it had been eating away at me since that door had slammed shut between us. That and the fact that I was going to have to tell Alex that I might have given him away.

Tian's arms slid around my neck, her head burrowing under my chin, and she exhaled happily. My arms reflexively went around her, and I hugged her close.

The small blond head pulled back after a moment, her bright eyes wide and an excited smile playing on her lips. "You're back! You got new nets! Did you run into any trouble? Your hair looks a little messy, were you in a fight? And you won? Did you punch someone in the face or kick them with your foot?"

As the questions tumbled out of her, she danced around, enacting her questions. The more she talked, the sadder I grew—until she finally noticed. I looked away, unable to hold that questioning blue gaze.

"Liana?" Her voice broke, and I looked back to see her staring at the vent where Grey had already exited, and Quess was now appearing. She waited for him to move, perched on the tips of her toes, hands clasped together over the wispy skirt she wore.

My heart ripped in half at the sight of her waiting, expectantly, for the woman who was fundamentally her older sister, and instantly imagined myself in her shoes, waiting for Alex to come.

"Tian, Maddox got taken," I told her, my own voice cracking, and Tian's hand fluttered to her mouth as she turned toward me. I felt sick watching her eyes fill with tears, and she spun around, looking up at Quess.

"My Doxy?" she said, her voice barely a squeak through the sound of her heart breaking.

Quess's face broke, and he knelt, immediately pulling her into his arms. Tian sniffled, struggling in his arms to look at the vent. "Doxy?" she managed again, looking at him. He shook his head, and her face collapsed, tears forming and falling from her eyes. A racking sob caught her, and Quess fell back on his rear, rocking the girl back and forth.

"It's okay, T," he said softly, smoothing her hair. "We're going to get her out. We just have to get some information, and then we're going to rescue her. I promise, okay?"

Tian continued to sob, clearly inconsolable. She had every right to be. She'd just lost two members of her family within a week.

"Take her to her bed and give her Commander Cuddles," I said softly, catching Quess's attention. "See if you can't get her to sleep, and then get back here. We need you to walk us through the net replacement."

"Let Quess go with you now," Grey said to me, stepping around me and over to Quess and Tian. "I'll take Tian."

Tian didn't protest as Grey collected her from Quess's lap, cradling her sobbing form to his chest. He stepped by Quess and moved to the opposite corner of the room, where Tian's bed had been set up, a nest of blankets on the floor under Maddox's hammock, with a few crates stacked next to it to give her some privacy.

I pulled Quess to his feet, immediately turning toward Zoe. She stood off to the side, Eric next to her. Her hand was over her heart, and she looked at me with sympathy in her eyes. "Are you okay?" she asked, her eyes raking over me.

"She took a bit of a beating," Quess announced before I could say anything, and I resisted the urge to glare at him. He wasn't wrong—I was one giant bruise after our fight—but I couldn't afford to be hurt right now, so I was trying my best to ignore it. "But you should've seen her and Maddox fight! They took out eight Inquisition agents on their own!"

This time I did give him a hard look. "You are not telling me you watched the fight instead of paying attention to your hacking, are you?"

Quess blinked and quickly shook his head. I let it go, but the anger I felt was long from over. It was just directed toward a far more practical endeavor: getting Maddox back.

We moved into the workroom, and I watched as Quess pulled out the cases filled with our pilfered nets, placing them on the workbench. He opened the case my brother had brought, and pulled out a data crystal. Next he produced his pad, and a handful of cables. Within seconds, the crystal was connected to the pad with one cable, while the net was connected to the pad with another. Immediately a bio came up—like the ones we would get from Scipio when we were in pursuit of a suspect—with all the details filled in except the picture.

"Clara Euan," I read. "Farmhand from Greenery 9, harvester." I stared at it and then shrugged. I could be a Hand, and I knew enough about Greenery 9. I could get by with this ID for a while.

"What hair color are you going to go with?" asked Quess, and I shrugged, tugging on my still-brown hair.

"I guess this'll do," I said. "And the contacts will work. You got a capture?"

In response, Quess pulled something else from the case and held it up. The item was made entirely of glass and was about as long and wide as my hand. He peered through it at me, and then, a moment later, my image filled the blank box.

I... had looked better, the disguise notwithstanding. My hair was still all over the place and stuck out wildly in areas, while my eyes looked tired and sad, my focus slightly over Quess's shoulder.

Still, it was a government ID. It wasn't supposed to look pretty.

"Will this get me inside the Medica?" I asked as a screen came up on the pad, indicating that it was loading.

"Not exactly," he said, making a motion for me to sit down and turn around so he could have access to the back of my neck. I did so, and lifted up my hair, meeting Zoe's gaze.

"What happened?" she asked as Quess sprayed something cold on the back of my neck from an aerosol can. I knew it was a topical anesthetic, thanks to the apprenticeship programs I had been going to since I was fifteen.

Immediately the flesh began to go numb, and I closed my

eyes, trying not to think about the fact that Quess was going to cut into my neck and remove my net.

"There were people in the room when we got there," I said, focusing on Zoe's question. "We sort of... improvised a pretty convincing lie, which they seemed to buy..." I paused, gritting my teeth as I felt something push on the back of my neck. I braced both hands against the table to keep from moving. There was no pain, but I could tell by Quess's intake of breath that he was in, and it wasn't easy to remain still.

But I managed, and focused back on Zoe. "Anyway, the plan fell apart when the man I claimed was my supervisor—by the way, he's Alex's supervisor—showed up, and they caught us. Maddox punched him in the throat—"

"She did not," Quess said with a laugh, and I resisted the urge to tell him not to laugh when he was digging around in my neck.

A second later, my head began to ache, and I felt vibrations coming from deep underneath my skull. It was hard not to imagine pulling twisted tree roots from the ground, but that was what it felt like—only the net was the roots and my head the soil. For several intense seconds, there was a pressure that made my entire body cringe. Zoe took my hand and held it tightly.

Then the sensation passed, and I relaxed, air flooding into me as I took in a deep breath. My head felt the same... but different. It felt less stuffed. Lighter, even. I couldn't tell, and was pretty sure I was imagining it.

It didn't matter. I had barely been given a chance to catch my breath before Quess's hands were back, the pressure returning. I tensed a few seconds more until he withdrew and relaxed.

"Is that it?" I asked.

"Well..."

Whatever Quess was going to say next was lost under the sensation beneath my skull as the net began to unravel, the tendrils spreading out and taking root in my brain.

"The tendrils will follow the path left by the last one," Quess said. "You don't have to worry about it causing scar tissue or anything."

I paled at the thought. "Is that really possible?" I asked, as the net continued to move and settle. It went on for a few more seconds, and then stopped. Quess then pressed something into my skin, and this time I felt the pressure of it being dragged down slowly, over the incision point, and realized it was the pink goo of a dermal bond, which would seal the cut permanently in a matter of hours.

"Not anymore," he said, and a moment later I heard him stepping back. "You're good to go. How do you feel?"

I shrugged. My head had started to ache again, but there were no vibrations this time. Just a heavy pressure that spread from the back forward.

"Uncomfortable," I finally said, and he nodded, looking unsurprised.

"I figured it might be. I'm sorry."

"Not your fault. We needed to do this, and I needed to do it now. How long do you think it'll be before I can net my brother?"

"Five minutes. Give the net a moment or two to get settled. If the discomfort gets too bad, let me know and I'll give you something for it."

I smiled. I couldn't help it. Even though he insisted he wasn't Medic material, he was actually quite good at it, and I was surprised how much comfort his confidence and directness brought me.

"Thank you," I said, and he gave me a lopsided grin.

"Don't thank me yet. We need to look at that shoulder, and your head."

"My hair will grow back," I said, my fingers reaching up to my hairline and probing the tender flesh where the hair had been ripped out. "Besides, I thought you didn't want to wait to find out about Maddox."

"I don't, but Grey told me you hit your head pretty hard," he said coolly. "Can't make a net call until I'm sure you don't have a concussion. Shirt off so I can check your shoulder too."

"Plus, you were in the middle of telling me how Maddox got grabbed." My best friend smiled faintly as I met her gaze, and I sighed, leaning forward so Quess could help me out of my sweater. Eric immediately turned around, but Zoe, bless her heart, stood and watched Quess, waiting for him to make one tiny misstep. It didn't matter, I was wearing an undershirt, but I was glad to see everyone cared.

"Right. Well... we start running, and an alarm goes off behind us. Scipio comes on and is all like, 'My name's Scipio, and today I'm going to ruin your day, just like every other day,' and then these door barriers start coming down behind us while people start to chase us. We get ahead, and then Quess has to hack the door for us to get out the way we came in, and Maddox and I had to buy them time to get the door open. So we took them on. We won, but more were coming, and we needed to run. I went back, assuming she was with me, but she had stayed behind to throw off the new group and... we got separated."

"She's with the Inquisition," Quess said, spreading something sharp-smelling over my shoulder with a gentle press of his fingers. He rubbed it in, and I breathed a little easier as whatever he was using eased the pain where I had slammed it into the wall. "But we're going to get her back."

"How?" Zoe asked, her eyebrow twitching up. "If they have her... I mean... Where would they keep her? The Inquisitors are supposed to pass off prisoners to the Knights."

I shook my head at my friend. "I don't have any answers yet," I told her. "And you're right—she may have already been transferred, but we're not leaving her behind. Quess?"

"One more minute," he said, and I sighed, wincing as his fingers slid over my scalp. He was massaging some of the pink goop into my head to repair the torn areas. I breathed a sigh of relief as the burning spots quickly eased and faded, the goo bonding with the cells and covering the pain receptors.

"I finally got her to stop crying and lie down," Grey said from the doorway. I turned, pulling my head out from under Quess's hands.

Grey's eyes—back to their familiar brown, which meant he had taken out his contacts—watched us as I broke away from Quess, and I could see the flash of jealousy there. I had thought we were past that, but I was clearly wrong, given that Grey was eyeing Quess like he was a piece of meat that needed tenderizing.

"Is she okay?"

He tore his gaze away and gave me a sad look. "No," he said. "She's distraught. After I finally got her to stop crying, she shut down. She just held her bear and stared at the wall. She eventually closed her eyes, but I'm not even sure she's asleep. Liana... she's heartbroken. We have to get Maddox back."

"We will," I said, praying for it to be true. "Can I go now?" I looked back at Quess. He flashed me a thumbs up, and I immediately left the room, bypassing the vents and heading instead through the gap in the wall that led up to the Menagerie. I moved down the tight tunnel, following the path that eventually dead-ended in a series of steps heading up.

I removed Zoe's now-functioning brace, then opened the hatch on the ceiling, lifting it up a few inches and peering out. Dark shapes of pigs sleeping on their sides or bellies filled my gaze, and as I lifted the door higher, the pen fence came into view. I wrinkled my nose against the smell of animal droppings, and slowly slid out of the hatch, taking care not to disturb the hogs.

I remained on my belly and drew my indicator to my eyes, swiping my finger across the glowing nine to activate the voice command. "Contact Alex Castell, IT47-4B," I said. The net buzzed under my skull, in response to my order, and I waited.

A second later, I heard a digitally altered voice fill my ear, and I frowned as it said, "Hello, Liana."

"Hello, Mercury. Where the hell is my brother?"

The farming floor was quiet, the lights set on the dimmest setting to let the animals rest. Even the quiet sounds of hundreds of animals sleeping were enough to mask the little noise I was making. I crept off into the deepest shadows, taking care not to step on any of the slumbering swine as I did, trying to keep myself hidden so Mercury and I could have a little chat.

About, for example, why the hell he was answering a call meant for my brother.

"Your brother is fine," Mercury assured me, but that did nothing to calm my stomach.

"Then why isn't he answering? How are you answering? What is going on?"

I turned and rested my back against the pen, keeping an eye out for any movement from Hands on graveyard shift.

"First, tell me what went wrong."

I grated my teeth together. "Maddox got captured. We got new nets, but things went wrong in the net room when there were people there. People you said wouldn't be there."

There was a pause before he replied, "We didn't know they'd be working late. They weren't supposed to be, but apparently there's been a few problems with some of the nets being produced recently, and so they were ordered to stay late to inspect them."

I frowned. Learning that the nets we had just stolen might be faulty did not give me a lot of confidence, or leave me with a desire to keep my new net in, but it did explain why they had believed my lie. The question hung on the tip of my tongue, but I realized it didn't matter right now. Alex and Maddox did.

"What is going on with Maddox?" I demanded. "And don't think I've forgotten about my brother. Where is he? What's wrong?"

"I knew they'd taken a prisoner, but even I wasn't told it was Maddox—that's how tight-lipped the Inquisitors are being. Once they run her DNA and realize she's Cali's child, they'll take her to the Citadel."

He didn't need to finish for me to understand the conclusion. After all, I had firsthand experience with what they were doing to those with ranks of one down there. I could only imagine that an undoc—a *true* undoc—would get bumped to the front of the line.

There was only one problem with that: Maddox *wasn't* just Cali's child. She was Devon's daughter as well. Or at least, I very much suspected she was.

What would happen to her when they found that out? Would they let Devon know? What would he do?

What would happen if he went to go get her? Trying to free

her from the Citadel was one thing, but from the Champion himself? I shuddered at the thought. We needed to get ahead of this and get Maddox out as soon as possible.

"Will they run a comparison to find out who her father is?" I asked.

"Yes. Why?"

"Because... I think Devon Alexander is her father."

"You think *what*?" I could feel his confusion buzzing through the net as if it were bleeding out of him. "Why would you think that?"

"Mercury, who was Cali married to?"

"No one. I checked."

"Then the records have been altered. Which would make sense—she was serving as his Lieutenant when they were married."

"The council would never allow that."

"They would if they didn't know," I said, trying to keep my temper in check. We were wasting time, and while my new ID would mean I wasn't in danger of getting caught, sitting around in the middle of a pigpen having a clandestine conversation with a member of IT while trying to subvert the will of Scipio was not a great start for my new net or false ID. "Look, forget about the records and just listen to me. If I'm right, and if Devon is Maddox's father, he'll want to meet with her before they do anything, won't he?"

"Okay, whoa, slow down. We do not know enough about Devon's personality to know that. But I see what you're getting at: you want to reach out to him to see if he will get her out. Well, here's the thing—he can just do what we're doing for you and your friends and replace her net if he really wants to keep her alive. Do you think I just invented that move?"

"You didn't?" I blinked, surprised. And then I focused on what he was saying. "You mean there are all sorts of people changing out their nets with new IDs?"

"No, not all sorts of people, but it does happen, especially in the black market. The Inquisition tries to crack down on it, which is why it was risky to get you to a buyer—too much attention. Stealing the nets was a better alternative, as it would be unexpected, and we wouldn't have to pay through our noses. Look, we're getting off track here. If you want to save Maddox, you'll have to do it when she's getting transferred to the Citadel. The Core is in lockdown, and I don't think there's enough time between here and eternity to create the codes to get you back in here. In the open, however... I imagine you could come up with something. I'll update you as soon as I find out what's going on, but it's going to take some time. Besides, they have twenty-four hours before they're required to hand Maddox over to the Knights. They'll probably want to use it to try to interrogate her."

Tomorrow. Twenty-four hours for Maddox to be imprisoned. "They'll question her?" I asked.

"Yes. They might even torture her, but... I don't know. If she *is* Devon's daughter, like you think she is, and they discover it and tell him, maybe he'll intercede. I honestly don't know, but I promise I will help you get her back."

I exhaled. I didn't have any better options, and I was going to need Mercury's help to find out when Maddox was being transferred. "Then you better keep in touch. Now, how did you intercept this net, and is my brother all right?"

"Relax. I figured you would net him first, so I set an alert and just shunted the net over to me. *He's* fine, although it's already known that you and Grey were behind this. They facial-scanned the videos. Which means you are going to have to be very careful tonight."

"Tonight?" I asked, my eyes narrowing in suspicion. "What happens tonight?"

"The group who wanted the meet contacted me to tell me the time and place. I was hoping you'd be back sooner... It's in two hours, in Cogstown."

"Cogstown?" I asked, my eyebrows drawing together. "Where in Cogstown?"

I had already dismissed the idea of it being in Roark's apartment, so when Mercury said, "C19," I couldn't help but feel shocked. They actually had picked to meet there. But why?

"What made them choose there?"

"I think it was meant as a peace offering. It's familiar terrain, right?"

"Right." I hesitated, my mind whirling. How did *they* know that though? "I want to bring Grey." I had promised him that he got to go with me, and I knew he'd want to be there. Especially after what had happened with Maddox. In fact, I'd be surprised if all of them didn't try to come with me.

"I don't think that's a good idea. Look, Grey's very recognizable to the Cogs. It would be too dangerous, especially if you were with him. You're kind of the most famous pair of criminals to roam the Tower, so to speak. Bring an escort, of course. Don't meet them alone, but... bringing Grey is a bad idea. These people seem very powerful, Liana. And I don't think they'd bat an eye at killing someone to protect their identities."

I sucked in a deep breath. I didn't like agreeing with Mercury, but he was right on all counts. We'd just been identified breaking into the Core. Once that got out, people were going to be terrified. The Knights were going to have their hands full keeping people from panicking, dreading that some sort of dissident had gotten close to their precious Scipio. Even I was in danger moving around right now. But with Grey at my side... it'd be inviting attention.

He really wasn't going to like hearing that.

"You're right," I said. "I'll take someone else. But why are we even having this meeting? Once they find out that I've been up to something tonight, won't they just walk away? I'm a risky invest-ment right now."

"That depends on who they are and what they want," Mercury replied. "But better to give them the chance to say no face-to-face. Besides, what are you going to do in the meantime?"

He was right. Again.

"Fine. I'll get up there and let you know how it goes. How do you want to contact us about Maddox?"

"The pad I sent down also acts as an anchor point when it's connected to a power source. It creates a network with a wireless connection that only I can access, and allows me to transmit to your individual nets."

I took a moment to absorb what he had just said. "Did you just have a stroke or go insane? Also, why didn't you do this for Cali and the others?"

"I never had to," Mercury said stiffly. "They knew how to keep a low profile. But since you're public enemy number one and have your back against the wall, you need to be able to get in direct contact with me without risking attention. This is the best way to provide that, but I have to tell you, turn it on only when you have to. The Tower is searching through different frequencies looking for you, and the anchor will give one, if you're not careful." He sighed, a sound of long, tonal sweeps that were low. "So tell Quess that the pad is an anchor. He'll know what to do."

"Okay. Is there anything else?"

"No. Good luck, Liana."

"Thanks," I replied, shutting off the net. I made my way back inside, taking time to replace the brace Zoe had made, and returned to the main room. I stopped when I came into the sleeping area, and took a knee next to Tian's bed, peering under Maddox's hammock to find her. The girl was lying on her side facing the wall, Commander Cuddles under her chin. Her breathing was deep and even, so I crept by, not wanting to wake her up if I didn't have to.

"How'd it go?" Grey asked as soon as I re-entered, looking up from where he was working on Quess's neck, replacing the net under Zoe's sharp eyes. Quess was holding a broken bit of mirror in one hand, Zoe another, giving Quess a clear view of what Grey was doing. And given the sweat beading on Grey's brow, it wasn't easy.

"We can't do anything about Maddox right now," I said. "The Inquisition is holding her for twenty-four hours before transferring her to the Citadel. Mercury thinks our best bet is to wait for them to move her, and grab her then. We have to come up with a plan to get her away from them."

"What happens to her in the meantime?" Zoe asked gravely, keeping her eyes on Grey's hands. "What are they going to do to her?"

"We should be going after her now, not waiting!" Quess added, wincing as Grey did something behind his neck, just out of my range of vision. There was the sharp *tink* of something hard hitting metal—I guessed the old net being dropped into the bin— and I watched Grey relax for a moment, clearly relieved.

I hesitated at Quess's passionate tone, hating myself for having to give him bad news. "Quess, Mercury says that there's no way he can get us in right now. The Core is locked up tight."

"Yeah, but we have Leo. He can help us get in, I know it."

My thoughts scattered at his declaration, and I stared at him. "You want to take Leo into the *Core*?"

"Why not? If it helps us get Doxy back, then we should use him."

I rocked back on my heels, thinking. It was an interesting idea, but it had a huge problem—namely that Leo was untested. And I wasn't sure that the Core was the right place to test him.

"Quess..."

"We shouldn't do that," Zoe said, interrupting me. "First of all, you can't just volunteer Leo like that. He may be a computer, but he has feelings and should have a say in what he does or does not do. Secondly, I do not think we should try to get back into the Core at all. If they've stepped up security, then that means more manpower. Leo might be able to navigate the computers, but you'll never escape the Eyes."

I nodded in agreement as Zoe spoke. Hers were also good points that I hadn't fully considered. It was just too bad that when they stacked up next to my own reservations, it all pointed to Maddox being stuck in the Core for a whole day. A prospect so awful and terrifying that it made my skin crawl.

I hoped she would forgive me someday. I hoped she would

understand. But either way, I was getting her out. Facing her anger was far better than letting her remain in custody. Father or not, we had no idea what Devon would do once he got his hands on her, and if our best chance at getting her out meant waiting, then we would wait.

"Quess, you have to accept the fact that we are not going to be able to go after her right now," I said softly. Quess looked at me, his eyes burning blue coals. "Be angry with me, but realize this: we will only get one chance, either way, to get Maddox out. Which one do you think we'll succeed at—assaulting the Core directly to get her, or going in during the transfer between the Core and the Citadel?"

His frown deepened, and then he emitted an irritated sound. "Fine, we'll wait. But we still have to figure out a way we're going to get her during the transfer." Behind him, Grey straightened his back and took a step back.

"It's done," he said quietly, dropping his tools on a tray by the workstation with a metallic clatter.

"I know," I responded to Quess. "I'm hoping that you, Grey, and Zoe can work on that while I go to that meeting with the mystery group." Everyone looked up at me, and I shifted my weight, suddenly uncomfortable at the looks in their eyes. "Mercury told me that they called. I don't have a lot of time to get to them—I have to be there in two hours."

"You're going, after all this? Maddox needs us—"

"Nice try, but you're not going without me. We talked about this, and you promised—"

"Is nobody even going to wonder at the coincidence of all this? What are the odds—"

Everyone spoke on top of each other in response to my statement, making all of their arguments difficult to follow. They didn't show any sign of stopping, so I straightened my back and sucked in a lungful of air.

"Shut up, all of you," I snapped, my voice bearing the command with confidence and power. "Grey, we are currently the most infamous couple in the Tower. Going with you is the fastest way of being recognized, especially after tonight. I'm not sure if our raid of the Core has been publicized yet, but it will be soon, and they clocked our faces. You can't go. Not if you want to keep me safe."

I turned to Zoe and nodded. "Yes, it's weird that the mystery group chose now. Or, rather, they chose a few hours ago, which was when we started our mission. Sometimes things are a coincidence."

I fixed Quess with a pointed look. "I am not forgetting about Maddox, but you're forgetting that these people could be potential allies. Which means it might not be too much to ask for their help in retrieving her."

I took a breath and smoothed my hands over my clothes, trying to still the slight tremor that had built up while I had been speaking to my friends. I hadn't meant to go off on them, but it riled me up that they had just started ranting at me without asking any questions. I did not like feeling like I was under attack.

"Look, this is inconvenient timing, I'll admit. I am going to do everything in my power to turn it into a positive, but I can't do that from here. This meeting is important, and if you really think about it, there is no reason why I can't go right now. As awful as that makes me sound."

Grey didn't say anything, and neither did anyone else, and I waited, holding my breath. I wasn't sure how they were going to react to what I'd just said, and I was a little worried they would get angry.

Thankfully, I had excellent taste in friends.

"Sorry," Zoe said, her mouth twisting. "You're right. I am being paranoid. You should go."

"Do you really think they could help Maddox?" Quess asked.

I shrugged. "I don't know, but I won't be able to find out if I don't try."

He nodded, and I looked at Grey.

"How are you doing with all this?" I asked, and he stared at me, his face pensive.

"I don't like the idea of you going without me," he said finally. "But you're right. It's too risky to go together. As it is, you probably shouldn't even be heading out, but I get it. Just... you can't go alone."

"She won't be," Eric said, crossing his arms. "You, Zoe, and Quess can brainstorm ideas on how to get Maddox away from the Inquisitors and the Knights so we have something ready for when the exchange happens. I'll keep Liana safe."

I smiled at Eric, grateful that he had volunteered himself, and looked at Grey. "Are you going to be okay?"

He shook his head. "Not even remotely."

I stared at him, uncertain how to respond, and then he smiled. "But I guess it's going to be something I get used to, seeing as we're an infamous couple now."

We shared a smile, and then I reached for him, needing to borrow some of that endless reservoir of strength he seemed to be able to provide me with. He hugged me tightly, his arms around my shoulders, and I leaned into him, allowing myself to relax a little. We rocked back and forth, just holding each other, and I let my fears dissipate for a few seconds, content to just stand there forever.

"So... does this mean the meeting is over?" Quess asked, breaking the moment between us, and I flushed and took a quick step back.

"Oh my God, I did not just do that," I said, slightly mortified that I had just hugged Grey so intimately in the middle of a meeting. Not something a good leader would do, I was guessing, but... a good girlfriend, on the other hand?

Aced it, if Grey's smile was any indication.

"Yeah, you did," Quess said flatly, looking on the verge of tearing me apart. A moment later, he opened his arms. "Can I have a hug too?"

I smirked and moved over to him, giving him a hug. I wouldn't have done it if he had asked with that same cocky attitude he had when he was being... him, but he hadn't, not this time. He looked vulnerable when he asked, and I couldn't resist.

We kept it brief, however, and as soon as it was over, I looked around. "We're going to get through this, guys. Just don't give up."

I turned to Eric. "We gotta go if we're going. Get your net and ID, and I'll meet you at the hatch."

"Be careful," Zoe said, directing her comment to both of us. "And take your batons. Oh, and..."

I was already in the process of flashing Zoe a mock salute when she trailed off, reached up with one hand, and then pulled Eric's head down to her, going up to her tiptoes. Whatever surprise Eric felt, if any, was soon lost in the sounds of them passionately kissing each other. I watched for a second, then realized I was staring and looked away. Turning, I went to grab my stuff.

I was happy that Eric and Zoe had made up—*more* than happy that they were finally kissing!—but the clock had already been ticking for way too long. I just prayed I hadn't missed the meeting. And that they could help with Maddox.

19

I eyed my indicator as we moved up the steps that wrapped around the outermost layer of the Tower, confirming the purple seven was indeed still there. My legs ached fiercely. The steps seemed never to end as I peered up them, pausing to wipe the sweat off my brow.

"It's nice being out," Eric said, coming to a stop next to me, and in spite of my exhaustion and apprehension, I smiled.

"I know. How have you been dealing with all of this?"

Eric's smile dimmed, and he looked away, rubbing one hand up and down the back of his neck. "Not well, actually," he admitted honestly. "I really miss my family."

From what I knew about Eric's family, they probably missed him, too. I had never seen a group of people who were closer. Going over for dinner meant having a family dinner, complete with four grandparents, an aunt and an uncle with spouses and two children of their own, plus their spouses' grandparents and families... It was a delightful mess.

"I'm sure they're really worried about you," I said, suddenly guilty. I hadn't wanted to involve Eric, originally. He wasn't exactly like Zoe or myself—he could cope with Tower life just with his general good nature. "I'm really sorry for all of this."

"What?" Eric's eyebrows climbed to his hairline, and he gave me a surprised look. "No! Liana, I wasn't complaining or trying to blame you. I was just sharing. I'm used to, uh, sharing my feelings. I didn't mean it in a bad way."

"Really?" I asked, surprised to hear him say that. Didn't he regret coming with us, knowing that things would be so much more comfortable if he had chosen to stay? "So you're okay being here?"

We resumed walking up the steps, the sound of our footsteps echoing softly off the walls as we climbed up and over the next landing, ignoring the doors there. Eric was silent for several minutes, but so was I, knowing my friend tended to think things through before a single word left his lips.

"I don't think 'okay' is the right word," he finally said, shoving his hands into his pockets. "I think that I did the right thing."

"Yeah, but you didn't actually have to leave," I pointed out. "With your eight, you could've said anything and they would've believed you."

"Maybe, but that doesn't matter. My family is safe. Worried, of course, and possibly even angry if they believe I'm a criminal, but safe, nonetheless. I mean, they haven't touched your family, so I have to assume..." He stopped suddenly and turned, bringing me to a halt as well. "But you and Zoe are also my family, and I couldn't live with myself if you were in danger and I wasn't there to help."

I blinked back tears, and then on impulse, reached out and hugged him. "I do not know how I got so lucky to have friends like you and Zoe, and I don't care—I'm glad you're here."

"Me too." We resumed walking, and after a few steps he said, "I should really be worried about *you*. How are you holding up?"

I exhaled and shook my head. "I don't know," I said honestly. "I have no idea what I'm doing, and the last two ideas I've had have failed. Dismally. I mean, at least we got enough nets, thanks to Maddox's quick thinking, but I don't think it will have been worth it if we can't rescue her. Still, I can't help but wonder if maybe you guys picked the wrong leader."

"Liana, stop being so hard on yourself, seriously. I understand that you're not sure if the decisions you're making are the right ones, but that's not all being a leader is about, and you know that."

"Doesn't change the fact that we got discovered and Maddox got caught. Oh, and that the entire Tower probably thinks I'm trying to kill Scipio. I am becoming a liability to you all."

"Don't be ridiculous. There are a billion ways we could get caught. You see that corner? Any moment, your father could come around it. Now, if it were me, I'd freeze and immediately get busted, but you'd knuckle down, keep walking, and hope your uniform and the number on your wrist were enough to get you past him. You're quick on your feet, and you have a powerful need to get things done. I admire that—not many have that ability. And that's why we need you."

"Great, so I improvise well. That doesn't exactly mean that I make sound decisions."

"I'm sorry, have the rest of us just been sitting idly by while you've been making all the decisions on your own? No, we have not, because you have included us. We supported your decisions, all of them, every step of the way. We're in this together, so just let it go already!"

I smiled at his exasperation. "I get it, my self-doubt is gross. But can I just please whine for five more seconds?"

Eric smiled and shook his head. "Nope, we've got a schedule to adhere to. Chop chop."

We exited the floor and headed into the shell, following Quess's instructions as we navigated the halls. I stopped at the one marked *Causeway 19F* and quickly keyed in the code Quess had given me before we left, and then waited.

"I'm having a right good sleep, here," the door said, much more loudly than I would've preferred. I looked back and forth down the metal hall, checking for any sign of human life. We appeared to be alone, but who knew how long that would last. "What do you want?"

"We want to have dinner with the Pope," I said, still not entirely clear on what a "pope" was, but reciting the passcode faithfully anyway, trusting in Quess's memory.

"Did you say with the poop?"

I bit back a smile, but it was hard, considering Quess hadn't told me what the door's reply would be—only my response, and even then, he had left the poop part out and just told me to repeat whatever it said back in the affirmative. "Yes. We want to have dinner with the poop."

The door laughed raucously and slid open, allowing us inside. We had entered among the residents' quarters, and a quick check of the dwelling numbers told me we were on the right floor, as planned. We just had to follow the hall down.

The main corridor stretched down, the doors numbering in the seventies. It was dimly lit—nighttime setting—and surprisingly empty, considering it was one of the major thoroughfares. Even this late at night, there should be those on graveyard shift moving about. Work never really stopped in the Tower; it just got quieter at night.

I hesitated, the emptiness of the halls bothering me, and then brushed it aside. There was probably just a lull in foot traffic. Besides, fewer people meant less chance for me to be recognized.

I figured out which way we had to go to get to Roark's apartment, and waved Eric forward. Our footsteps sounded off the tight wall, thick rubber soles on grated floor making a sort of grinding squeak that always felt impossible to prevent. With both of us walking, the sounds were tangled, filling the tense silence that had blossomed the deeper we went down the hall.

At C35, I realized we weren't alone, the sounds of our booted feet masking the sounds of others behind us. I was just starting to turn when something black dropped over my head, and both my arms were seized. Something long and hard pressed against the small of my back.

"Don't resist," a masculine voice warned, and I jerked my head toward it, trying to pinpoint his position behind me. "The girl will come with us. The man will wait here."

"Liana?" Eric's voice came through muffled, but the alarm was unmistakable.

"It's okay," I said, my own voice coming out stuffy to my ears. "Don't panic and don't fight them. Remain calm, okay?"

"Okay," he said, and I was pushed forward, my feet stumbling on the floor.

"Who are you?" I demanded as I caught my balance.

"We work for those you're going to meet. Just remain calm and quiet. We don't want any attention drawn to your presence."

"Then you probably shouldn't drop a bag on someone's head in the middle of a public hall," I muttered, and he let out a surprised laugh. I felt a moment of hope that he was going to take the bag away, but that was dashed as a hand dropped heavily onto my shoulder, engulfing it, and propelled me forward, albeit this time more gently. My heart beat rapidly in my chest as I jerked my head around, trying to see through the dark fabric that was covering my eyes. Every step I took, I felt certain I was going to fall, or run into something, and it was disorienting.

They—there was definitely more than one—guided me around a corner, then, and I could tell we were in a dwelling because the sound wasn't as spread out. The hand on my shoulder pushed down on me, forcing me into a seat, and then I heard the footsteps retreating, followed by the pneumatic hiss of the door closing.

"Hello?" I asked. It occurred to me then that they hadn't tied my hands, and I ripped off the bag and looked around.

I was sitting in a chair in the middle of Roark's apartment, and I was surprised to see that none of the mess had been changed since we had cleared out in such a hurry. Gerome's body was obviously missing, as was the wrench Tian had used to knock him unconscious. But empty bottles and beakers still decorated the workbench.

I half expected to see Roark looking up at me from a micro-scope, but the room was empty... and diminished. It was a poignant reminder that he was gone, his dream of leaving here never achieved. I leaned toward the table, wanting to touch the surface, to see if I could just... feel him, when a voice brought me up short.

"Squire Castell." I swiveled in my seat to see two figures enter. The first was a man, tall and thin, with burning blue eyes and a gleaming, shaved head covered with dark blue tattoos, marking him as a Diver. His nose was flat and wide, and his jaw had a crooked look, as if it had been broken one time too many.

Behind him was a short woman wearing orange coveralls marred with grease stains and covered in a dozen little pockets on the front and side, all of them filled with tools. Her hair was comprised of both blond and brown, the two colors mixed together amid the tight curls that were pulled back to form an afro over her head. She smiled kindly, her white teeth flashing against her dark skin.

"You're Praetor Strum," I said, immediately recognizing the man. I only knew who he was through Zoe, and I was surprised to see him here. He was on the council as the representative from Water Treatment.

"Indeed, I am," he said, inclining his bald head toward me. "And this is Lacey Green." -

I looked over at the muscular black woman. I knew her name, of course, but had never seen a picture of the head of the Mechanics Department. "You're the Lead Engineer. You're on the council as well."

"Yes, I am. And you're the girl who murdered her mentor and has committed several terrorist acts around the Tower."

The hair on my arms and neck stood up, and I shifted, looking around the room. Of all the things I had anticipated today, speaking with two members of the council was not anywhere on the list, and it caught me off guard, especially coupled with the recrimination in her voice. There was no sign that this was a trap, no crimson-clad figures lurking behind the scenes that I could spot, but...

"You shouldn't believe everything you hear," I said, shoving any and all speculation out of my head. If this was a trap, then I was already in it. Until I knew where it was coming from, I couldn't do anything to stop it, and I doubted they would let me leave now. Besides, I intended to use the time wisely, to see if I couldn't figure out what they wanted. "Now, what do two members of the council want with a dishonored Squire like myself?"

Praetor Strum smiled wanly. "Your help, I'm afraid."

20

"My help," I said dubiously, looking from one to the other. "My help?"

"Yes," Lacey said, folding her strong arms over her chest. "You heard correctly."

I licked my lips. "Okay, let me get this straight. Two council members want me, a known criminal of the Tower, to help them? You are two of the six most powerful people inside the Tower. How in the world could I possibly help you? Do you want me to steal something?"

The two of them exchanged looks. They were both wearing surprised and thoughtful expressions, and I leaned forward, watching them. I had voiced my internal thoughts to try to get a reaction from them, and that was one. One that told me that I wasn't here to steal something.

"Not stealing anything, then. But some sort of crime, obviously." I leaned back, wondering what sort of crime a council member would need me for.

Lacey sighed heavily and finally met my gaze. "We want you to kill Devon Alexander."

I stared at them, my mind unable to process how to even react to that information bomb. A laugh escaped me. And then another, and another, until I was doubled over clutching my stomach. It was rude to them, but honestly, it was the only reaction that made any sense. This was a joke. A sick, twisted, perverted joke.

"I'm sorry," I said after a few moments, hiccupping as I wiped tears from my eyes. "That was a good joke."

"I'm afraid this isn't funny, Squire Castell," Praetor Strum coolly informed me.

I chuckled again and shook my head. He clearly thought I was stupid, but I knew killing Devon Alexander would be the final nail in my coffin. There was nothing he or Lacey could do to protect me from that, especially with all the other strikes against me.

Still, I couldn't help but chuckle at the sheer audacity of his request. "I didn't say it was funny, I said it was a good joke," I said, standing. "I'm so sorry for wasting your time."

I turned to go, but Lacey moved in front of me, stopping me. "You should hear us out, Liana," she said softly.

"No, I shouldn't. I didn't know I was meeting with members of the council, and that changes *everything*. I'm a criminal, an enemy to your precious Tower, which means you should be having me arrested. The fact that you aren't is one thing, but the fact that you are standing here asking me to *kill* the Champion of the Knights is something completely different. This is a political assassination, and I don't care what you say, the two of you do not have enough power to get me out of that mess. Maybe if you had two more council members here, so I could believe that you'd overrule any execution order, I'd hear you out. I doubt I'd do it, but at least I'd listen. But with just the two of you? I'm sorry, I have places to go and people to take care of."

"You don't know anything about us—"

"I know *all* I need to know about you," I spat. "You sat by when they started—what's the word you use—'expelling' those who dropped to the rank of one. And we all know that's just a fancy word for murder." The two of them exchanged surprised looks, and I crossed my arms. "Yes, I know a whole lot more than you think I do. And I know the council voted for it. And that would have included you. So what makes you think I'm going to help actual murderers kill more people, when I refused to do it the first time?"

"Okay, first of all, I wasn't the head of the Cogs when that vote was held," Lacey retorted. "Secondly, both of our departments voted against it, and lost. So I think you might be missing a few details."

I blinked, and leaned back. Alex had mentioned that both Cogs and Water Treatment had voted against the new policy to make fours undergo mandatory rank intervention recently. I wasn't sure when the vote to start killing ones had been voted on, but... Lacey was right. I had no idea how the vote had taken place.

"Then fill me in," I said. "And tell me, why the hell do you want Devon dead?" The two exchanged another flurry of glances.

Praetor Strum folded his hands together and leaned back on the table, causing a few pieces of glassware to rattle. "Very well. Since the origin of the Tower, there have been... several shadow groups vying for control over Scipio. We believe that Devon

Alexander is from one of those groups, and that he has attained more power within the council, which we are... uncomfortable allowing to continue."

I looked at them both, suddenly suspicious. Zoe's comments about the timing of their contact was now flashing through my head, making me wonder if I really had just accidently stumbled right into Prometheus. We had speculated about it, but I had never actually thought they had survived. But if they had... What if all this was a trick to talk about Leo? Had they figured it out? If so... how?

It took a second, but then the logical part of my brain kicked in, trying to get me to see reason. The Praetor had said *groups*, as in more than one, and I didn't think that was a slip or a lie. If there still was a Prometheus, then maybe they weren't the only ones working against the Tower.

I eyed them both warily, trying to figure out what that made them in this whole big mess. How did they know about these groups, and why weren't they trying to stop Devon using more legal ways?

"You're going to need to give me a lot more than that. Who are these groups and how do you know about them? What do they want? How can they get anything accomplished with Scipio standing guard? Has one of these shadow groups already seized control of him?"

I knew I was being aggressive with my questions, but I didn't care. They were inspiring more questions than they were answering, and I wanted answers. I wanted to know if Scipio had already been compromised, and when it had happened, and more importantly, why? What were they using his program to do?

Praetor Strum pursed his lips. "We have reason to believe that

Scipio's programming has been tainted, possibly some time ago. That his programming has been violated by those who wish to destroy a way of life that has sustained us for hundreds of years."

I inhaled and exhaled sharply, looking at Lacey. She rolled her eyes. "We think Devon's part of the group that has gained control," she said simply. "Historically, it's never happened before, that we know of, and—" She looked at Strum, who gave her a tacit nod of approval. "We aren't entirely sure how to fix it."

Because Ezekial Pine had destroyed any knowledge on how to, and had almost destroyed the key ingredient: Leo. Anyone who knew about Scipio's malfunction would have no idea how to fix it. I studied them, wondering how long they'd known Scipio was malfunctioning, and if they'd been sitting on it all this time. Then I realized that they would've sat on it forever to keep people from panicking, and the thought led me to a more important one —one that had been bothering me for a long time.

"For how long has Scipio been malfunctioning?" I asked. "Do you have any idea?"

"That's complicated," Lacey said, shifting her weight to her other foot. "We're not entirely sure. We only became aware of it a few weeks ago."

I stared at her, stunned by her response. "So you're telling me that an unknown group of individuals in the Tower could have control over the AI whose impartiality was designed specifically to keep us alive?"

Lacey nodded. "That's about the short of it."

They had only noticed it a few weeks ago. I sat there, contemplating the information. Just because they had noticed it then, didn't mean that it hadn't been going on for a while. I didn't like thinking that way, but since they were confirming that the main

Scipio AI was being manipulated somehow, I couldn't help but wonder for how long this had been happening. Something told me it was much earlier than they were claiming.

I still needed more information than they were giving me, so I decided to switch lines of questioning and keep digging. I hoped they would let something slip, but at the very least, it would tell me more about them and who they were.

"Which leads me to an excellent segue. How do you *know?*" I looked back and forth between them, my eyebrows high. "How do you know that Devon is with this faction? How do you know this faction exists? And how do I know that you're not from a different faction, and are just trying to use me and my criminal friends to eliminate your enemy?"

Even as I asked them my numerous questions, my mind was going through everything they had said thus far, scrubbing it all for any details that would help get me a larger image of just what was happening in the Tower. Secret groups that ran around trying to control things? That tainted Scipio's programming?

What else? There had to be more to it. Did these two just not have a bigger picture than that? Did they honestly not know? Neither one of them was IT, so how could they even tell there was a problem with Scipio?

"Those are all very good questions, Squire Castell." Praetor Strum sighed and stood to his full height, looking as strong and majestic as I was sure the Tower looked from the outside, and I stepped back—right into Lacey, who had managed to make her way behind me. She steadied me, and then guided me back to my seat while Praetor Strum began to speak.

"From the beginning, the Founder's work was always met with a great deal of controversy, even by those whose lives were sheltered by him, protected from the nuclear storms brewing on the outside. During his lifetime, several terrorist attempts to subvert the Tower were thwarted, and after a while, he and several other members of the council began to think that those plots were the work of secret organizations."

I leaned forward. Even though I knew a lot of this, there were new details here that I hadn't quite heard before, and I wanted to pay attention. I also knew that they expected me to be stunned by the news, so I set my features to an expression of slightly horrified awe, and watched him as he continued to speak.

"Lionel made the mistake of thinking that such things would die out after a generation or two. He never suspected that his enemies would create legacies, training their offspring to carry on the work they had been doing since the beginning—but with more coordination that not only spanned lifetimes, but departments as well."

My eyes widened. Secret groups that had managed to embed themselves into all of the Tower in order to subvert it for their own ends? Why? What was the goal for them? I understood Ezekial's goal, thanks to the video, but why would his descendants continue to work toward it long after he died? Why hadn't they just given up? What was motivating them?

"To what end?" I asked. "To escape the Tower?"

"No," Lacey said softly. "To control it. Scipio was always intended to be a neutral party, to present the best options and scenarios for preserving life in the Tower while preventing it from failing. It's a double-edged sword, but Scipio was intended to be just that—offer the best solution, boil down all the conflicting human emotions into a decision. To present the most practical answer."

I bit my lip. They kept using the phrase "was intended." That didn't explain what he was doing. Or how anyone outside of IT had been able to change him. Lionel had mentioned that it would take generations for someone to take Scipio down, but without some IT background, I couldn't see how it was possible. Unless, of course, one of these factions had somehow managed to infiltrate IT.

"So, Scipio is broken?" I asked, looking Lacey in the eye.

She hesitated, her eyes searching. "We have no way of knowing that," she said slowly. "We aren't members of IT, and getting anyone from our departments into IT is difficult. The thought is that as a fully realized AI, Scipio can't fully be broken. But someone is definitely making him offer up more and more extreme solutions."

"We know for a fact that Devon is part of one of these groups," Praetor Strum continued over Lacey. "He has been backing Scipio's more extreme recommendations."

I remembered him in the cell, insisting on killing Grey even though his number had risen to a four. Yes, it had been a trick on my part, but he had tried to overrule the new rank without knowing that it had been tampered with, and he had almost succeeded.

"So have others on the council," Strum added glumly. "They have turned their back on the Tower."

I let out a breath. I was still trying to process all of this. Everything they were talking about confirmed what Leo had been telling us. What's more, they might not have a way to fix the Tower, but I might. Yet, I couldn't trust them with this information. Not yet, not so soon. They needed to tell me so much more before I told them anything. I needed to know who they were first.

"Who are you, in all of this? I mean, how do you know any of this? You still really haven't given me anything to go on, evidence-wise. For all I know, you could be the bad guys trying to set me up."

Lacey hesitated, and then leaned forward, resting her elbows on her knees. "We're legacies as well, Liana. At some point or another, an ancestor of ours has been pulled into this secret war, and has joined our ranks, or our enemy's, in some form or fashion. From there, they've passed this knowledge down from person to person."

"And Scipio didn't catch any of this? I mean, *come on*. I did everything I could to keep positive in the face of being weighed down with all of these questions that—just because I wanted to ask them—caused my ranking to drop faster than a rock off the top of the Tower. And yet you and your ancestors managed to have this plot going on without getting caught? This all smells just as bad as what they shovel in the Menagerie."

Lacey laughed, and even the Praetor smiled slightly, and it gave me confidence to see that they weren't unsympathetic.

"You're right, of course. Scipio's programming should've picked up on all of this—had we been told after our implantations at fifteen. But as legacies, we're told *before*, so that we're given time to train and adjust to our new worldview and our role in it while we're young."

"We're getting off track, Lace," Strum said softly, and she frowned, her eyes going to her indicator on her wrist and checking the time.

"He's right, and the longer we're both here, the more chance there is for one of our enemies to discover what we're up to." She met my eyes. "You keep asking for evidence, and the truth is we have none. This life is like playing chess in the dark, feeling for pieces, guessing for moves, and only getting flashes of what your enemy is doing. But we know Devon has definitely done something. Scipio votes with him more often than not, and the laws he's proposed recently are only going to cause problems. They already are, with the mandatory Medica treatment law change. We're worried that if things get too strict, any illusion of control will be lost, that faith in Scipio will be lost completely, and we can't let that happen. Scipio is what gives people hope. Devon is a threat to that. So Devon must go."

"So do it yourself," I said, standing once again. "You guys paint a pretty awful picture as to what life is like inside the Tower—including a dark underbelly that I myself am only beginning to get acquainted with. But what I fail to see is why I should do your dirty work. What's in it for me? For my friends? I mean, Scipio help me, why *me*? Did you just... see my wanted picture and decide that I was the girl you were going to make your assassin?"

Lacey stood as well, and ran a hand over her hair, smoothing any frayed ends down (not that there were any).

Before she could make a sound, Praetor Strum spoke, his voice deep and heavy. "Liana, picking you is purely opportunistic, as you suggest. However, there is a reason we wanted someone from within the Knights. It is part of the cover story we are crafting for you, but it was essential we had a Knight to make it work. If you do this for us, we can and will exonerate you and clear your friends from any guilt, and help you reintegrate back into Tower life, a hero."

"*Guilt?*" I said. "Why would I feel guilt? Do you even know what I did? I mean, did you do *any* research?"

"Well, yes," Lacey said. "But the Knights' report on you wasn't exactly flattering. It says that you apparently lost sight of your duties and sprang a known criminal from the Citadel— although that information wasn't discovered until later. The consensus is that you fell in love, and—"

"I *what?*" I spluttered, staring at both of them. I mean... yes, I had been attracted to Grey at the time, but that didn't change the fact that they wanted me to *kill another human being* as an initiation test. The fact that I'd had feelings for him was secondary. "They are really pulling that? Like I am some airhead of a girl who can't control her weak, womanly emotions? Instead of a human being who doesn't exactly support killing people?"

Lacey smiled then, and looked at Praetor Strum. "I like her," she said. "She's smart."

"Smart enough to question how you could ever craft a cover story that allows me to get away with murder," I retorted. "Smart enough to notice that you've never once directly answered my question about what sort of legacies you are, or how I can trust you. Smart enough to know that you're so desperate to make this work, you're not even going to do any research into who you're trying to make a deal with." I looked back and forth between them both. "I'm sure you thought I'd be desperate enough to jump all over this, but you clearly didn't look into me at all."

"I take it back," Lacey said into the silence that met my remark. "I *really* like her. I told you this was stupid."

"It's not stupid," the Praetor insisted. "It's necessary." He turned to me. "You're right, of course—I don't know what you actually did or what kind of liability you will be. We risked a lot telling you what we told you tonight, and I expect you to keep that to yourself. Not just for your sake, but also for the sake of your friends. We have ways of making them disappear."

"No threats," Lacey growled. "She needs to see that what we're doing is for the people of the Tower. Liana, the council has another vote coming up in a week. This one will authorize the executions of anyone three or below. Scipio is currently in processing, but if we're right about Devon, then he will be working with someone inside the Core to make sure Scipio's recommendation reflects what he wants. If he does, only the two of us will be voting against it. The rest have bought into Devon's fear-mongering, and are voting more and more frequently with him. Do you understand?"

I sucked in a deep breath, the severity of the situation now fully revealed to me. No wonder the need for haste. No wonder the lack of complete research. I was right that they were desperate, and I could see why. They didn't want more people to die on top of those who already had.

This was all predicated on whether or not I believed them, of course, and so far, I didn't have a reason to, other than the sloppiness of everything. Yes, they were capitalizing on an opportunity. That didn't mean they could back up what they said.

But they were trying to stop it. They were trying to save people. All I had to go on was their word, but I felt like I could believe them. They had told me so many things that I knew they wanted kept a secret... Would the bad guys have done the same thing?

I doubted it.

Uncertainty quivered in the pit of my stomach, and I realized that it all came down to a choice. Trust them and do their bidding, or walk away. I would have to talk to everyone first, but if we accepted their proposal, we would be completely relying on their word to come through for us. For me.

"How do I know you can deliver? Not just for me, but for my friends."

"Once we get Devon out of there, we will be able to, uh, shift things back in the right direction, so to speak," the Praetor said. "But if we reveal any more than that, we put our plan in jeopardy. We need you to agree before we can tell you anything more."

I exhaled. This wasn't an easy decision to make on so little evidence, or proof that help would be waiting for me once the deed was done. And while I was inclined to believe that they were the good guys, and knew for a fact that Devon was bad, that didn't change the fact that there wasn't any proof. This was *definitely* a decision I couldn't make on my own. "I can't agree to anything until I talk to my team. How long do I have to decide?"

"Not long," Lacey replied, her face grim. "And we don't want you telling your friends any details. We are risking exposure ourselves, and if we are found out on this, we risk our seats on the council—which is an opportunity for an enemy to replace us with one of their own."

"And for us to die not long after," Strum said quietly, his eyes filled with shadows. "Along with our children."

He spoke as if from experience, and I studied the man. I didn't know much about him, but there was a story there. I could sense it.

"A day," Lacey finally said. "No more, no less. And if you just go ahead and kill him, then we'll take that as a 'yes.'"

"And come through on your promise to exonerate me?" I asked, eyeing them both. I didn't care about reintegration into the

Tower, but being exonerated held a certain appeal. It would keep the Knights off our backs if I wasn't public enemy number one. Moving around would get a lot easier as well, as I could go the direct route.

"That, my dear girl, was in place before we even reached out to you through your IT friend." Strum's smile was smug as he raised an eyebrow. "We may have put this together hastily, and with very little research, but we made sure to have *that* in place."

I stared at both of them. I was out of questions for now, but I knew more would come to me in a little while. Belatedly, I remembered Maddox, and about asking them for help getting her out, and then reconsidered it. By now the Inquisitors were running her DNA test. If they found out she was a... legacy, and Devon's specifically, these two might not buy her innocence in all this. They were willing to kill Devon, after all. They might be willing to kill his daughter as well.

I decided to hold it back, and resolved to handle it personally. We were in the process of putting a plan together for her, and I believed in my team—they'd come up with something genius. It wasn't worth the risk of trying to involve these two.

"How should I contact you?" I asked.

"Through your friend in IT," Lacey said. "We'll meet here. This room is a show of goodwill for you and your friends, by the way. We left it intact after the Knights took whatever they deemed evidence. I understand the occupant was a friend of yours." She held out her hand, a silver chip dangling from it. "So you can enter and exit more easily."

"Thank you," I said, accepting the chip, surprised by the gesture. It was a thoughtful gift, even if I had no intention of using it unless absolutely necessary. "Am I free to go?"

"Yes," Praetor Strum said. "And, if Ms. Elphesian is with you, let her know that I am keeping an eye on her mother for her. She is as well as can be expected, under the circumstances."

I bit my lip, and nodded. "I'll do that."

They nodded back, and I turned and left. No one bagged me as I went, but I did pass several people in black standing guard. They were wearing masks that covered their eyes. The black they wore wasn't a pure black, and seemed to blend perfectly into the walls. I almost wouldn't have seen them, were it not for their exposed heads.

Partway back the way I had come, I was greeted by a group of them, Eric in tow, a bag still over his head.

"Let him out after one minute," one of them instructed. "We will be gone by then."

I nodded, and they turned and walked away. I looked back to see Lacey and the Praetor leaving the apartment, the guards I had passed already moving with them, and then began counting down in my head.

Sixty... fifty-nine... fifty-eight...

I counted all the way down to one before removing the covering from Eric's head. I was sure the people with Lacey and the Praetor (I was assuming guards of some kind) were watching, and I wanted to demonstrate my goodwill, but I also needed the time to think. In the end, even a minute wasn't enough. There was so much to process and unpack, and I wasn't sure where to begin. Secret shadow groups vying for control over Scipio. Families passing their schemes and plans down through generations. Assassinating Devon Alexander.

Eric blinked several times as he let his eyes adjust, and then immediately focused on me, giving me a onceover. "Are you okay? Why didn't you say anything? You just left me standing."

"I'm sorry. I was thinking."

"About the meeting?" he asked excitedly. "How did it go? What did they want to talk about?"

"A lot," I said. "And it's a lot to sort through, too. I'm... I'm not sure I'm ready to talk about it just yet."

His face fell as I spoke, the excitement and eagerness evaporating. "Oh. So it wasn't a very good meeting, then?"

"Honestly, Eric..." I trailed off, my mouth dry. "I think that it actually was."

It was in the sense that the deal was now on the table, and I had a better understanding of who was involved. The rest of it, however... It was a lot to process.

Eric absorbed that for a second or two, and smiled. "Hey, that's great! Our luck had to change at some point, right?"

I smiled—how could I not in the face of such sunny optimism? —and let him wrap an arm around my shoulder.

"Don't look so down, Liana," he said soothingly. "Whatever it is they want, it can't be that bad. Besides, we're in this together. You aren't alone."

Did that mean we were going to kill Devon together? My stomach churned at the idea. My stomach had been churning since the mention of Devon's name, and I couldn't blame it. In no universe did I ever want to see that man again. Not after what he did to Cali, detaching her lash and casting her down into the river. To her death.

The idea of letting any of my friends anywhere near him was repulsive, too. Eric's suggestion that I wouldn't be doing this alone was nice, but far from reassuring. He didn't know what we were up against. He didn't know what they wanted from me.

And Lacey had warned me not to tell him, or any of them, about any of it.

I considered telling them anyway, but I couldn't chance that Lacey or Strum would retaliate. They were willing to use a criminal like me to go after another member of the council. I had no doubt they'd go to great lengths to ensure the information remained a secret.

Maybe I could tell everyone about it as vaguely as possible, but I didn't want to be the type of person, let alone leader, who left important information out of decision-making, or one who decided things unilaterally.

But this was big. It was big and it was dangerous. I felt miles out of my depth.

I didn't want this weighing on me, I suddenly realized. I would do anything to pass it off to someone else and hide. But it wasn't anyone else's burden. It was mine. I had to do it. I had to be the one to make the choice to kill someone.

My stomach roiled, and I turned away from Eric, suddenly unable to breathe as the reality of what they wanted me to do set in. They wanted me to *murder* Devon Alexander. In cold blood.

Much like he had wanted me to do to Grey.

And if I didn't, I was condemning myself and everyone else to continue living as criminals, scraping by on the Tower's castoffs while planning some mad scheme for escape!

I shuddered, and felt Eric's strong hand on my shoulder. "Liana?" he asked, his voice brimming with concern. "Tell me what's going on."

I shrugged him off and took another step away. "Don't," I said, when I heard him move to follow. I knew I was scaring him, but it felt like I was drowning. Like there was too much oxygen in the room, or not enough, and I was struggling to find my breath.

My hands were shaking, and I realized I was on the verge of having an anxiety attack. The instant I recognized the signs, I felt the tension ease somewhat, and I was able to drive the panic back.

Still, I was afraid. Truly and deeply afraid that no matter what decision I made, it was going to go horribly wrong.

And that I would die knowing I had killed my friends.

"Liana, tell me what's wrong."

I looked back at Eric to find him standing there, his fists clenched in frustration as he held himself back from doing what came naturally, and comforting someone he cared about.

I stared at him, and realized that as desperately as I needed someone, anyone, to talk to, I wasn't about to jeopardize my friends by revealing the truth to them. Not right now.

But that meant I had to keep it together, and come up with a really good reason for my behavior just moments before. I sucked in a deep breath, and then shook my head, forcing the tension in my body to recede.

"I'm fine," I said, filling my voice with reassurance and confidence. "I'm sorry. It's just been a long night, and what we talked about was a lot to take in."

Eric cocked his head at me. "O... kay?" He looked around the hall. "Who were they?"

I hesitated. I didn't want to tell him, but I didn't want to lie either. "They asked me not to say," I said finally, settling on something technically true. "In fact, a lot of what they said I can't talk about. They made it very clear that they don't want any of the details of this known until afterward."

Eric frowned. "Surely, we can discuss it at home, right? It's got that paint stuff."

"The paint stuff works against the net signals," I said, nodding down the hall and signaling we should start moving. I waited for him to walk, then stepped in next to him, my shorter legs working hard to keep up with his pace. "I have no idea if it can also defend against listening technology. But that's really beside the point."

"Okay." Eric paused before asking, "What is the point?"

"That they asked me not to tell anyone about them. I'm not entirely sure that I'm going to take them up on their offer yet, but until then, I don't think it would be good for me to break their trust by immediately betraying them to my friends."

"Oh God," Eric said, dismayed. "This is turning into politics, isn't it?"

I chuckled. He wasn't wrong, but he wasn't right either. "It sort of is, but that's what happens when two different groups meet up. Politics."

"Gross. That must've been... fun. Did they mention what they wanted?"

"Yes," I said, my heart picking up speed. "But I can't tell you that either."

I watched him closely, trying to gauge his reaction, but his face remained thoughtful. "Did you ask if they could help us with Maddox?"

I wet my lower lip. Telling him I had reconsidered after what I had learned could cause him to ask more questions that I wasn't prepared to answer.

"I think we're on our own," I said, and he nodded, his mouth tight.

"Then we should get back," he announced. "Get everyone up to speed and figure out a plan for Maddox."

I felt surprised he would be finished asking questions just like that, and looked at him suspiciously. "Why aren't you trying to get more information about the meeting out of me?" I asked.

Eric gave me a look that was just shy of pitying. "Because you have Quess, Zoe, and Grey waiting to find out what happened during the meeting, and I'm guessing that the same questions I have now, they'll have soon. I figured I'd just wait until we were all together, so that we weren't hounding you with the same questions over and over again."

"Gee," I muttered, my stomach sinking as I realized he was right. "I appreciate the thoughtfulness, I guess."

Eric grinned. "That's me," he said, holding his arms out wide. "Mr. Thoughtful. Now, let's go. I'll even be quiet now so you can stress out about what you're going to say to everyone in such a way that allows you to keep your secrets under intense lines of questioning."

I rolled my eyes and shoved my hands in my pockets, but in my heart, I was glad Eric had voluntarily given me a little space. Because he was right. I was going to need it if I was going to both convince and reassure everyone that I had things well in hand.

Even though I clearly did not.

"What happened?" Grey asked as Eric and I climbed out of the narrow vent opening and into the common area. I straightened slowly, my muscles stiff and aching from all the exertion from the last twenty-four hours, and looked around. Zoe was sitting with Tian on her lap in one of the corners, but her attention was on us. I didn't see Quess.

"Where's Quess?" I asked.

"I'm here! Just—*ow!*" There was the sound of metal clattering, followed by the sound of Quess grumbling angrily. The sound of his voice grew nearer, and a moment later the curtain was lifted to one side, revealing Quess. "You're back safe," he said with a smile. "Good. What happened? Are they going to help Maddox?"

There was hope in his eyes, and I hated telling him no, but I shook my head anyway and watched the hope die.

"Really?" he asked, his features dropping. "God, I was hoping they'd come through for us. We haven't really had much luck brainstorming a plan."

"You haven't?" I looked at the three of them, noting their deep exhaustion, and sighed. "That's okay. Now that Eric and I are back, we'll come up with something, I'm sure of it. Why don't you just walk me through all of the things you've discussed."

"Oh, sure, I actually wrote a few of the better ones down. Do you want to—"

"Aren't you forgetting something?" Zoe asked, interrupting Quess, and he turned. I remained still, knowing that I was the target of Zoe's question, not Quess, and prayed that Quess managed to inadvertently deflect the conversation away. I needed more time to figure out what I was going to say. Everything I had come up with just came out generic, and I knew that wasn't going to fly.

"No, I don't think—" Quess began, before Grey cut him off.

"She was talking to Liana. And before we get into saving Maddox, I, for one, would like to know how this meeting went with our new friends."

I exhaled slowly, and turned. "We had a conversation," I said simply. "They want me to do something for them. Now, can we please get back to—"

"What do they want you to do?" Zoe asked from where she was seated on the floor. Tian's head was in her lap, Zoe's fingers in her hair. The girl's eyes were closed, but I could tell she had been crying. And from the sad look on Zoe's face, she'd been sitting with her through all of it.

"Nothing that needs to be done right now," I replied honestly. "Listen, I know you want to know everything that happened, and who I met with, but they asked me to keep what we discussed to myself, and I have chosen to respect that, for now. In the mean-time, I think we really need to focus on—"

"Why do they want you to keep it secret?" Grey asked, his face a careful mask.

"Because it's dangerous."

"For you?"

I bit my lip. I hadn't lied to them so far, and I wasn't about to now. I was a good liar, but... I *couldn't* lie to them. Standing here giving half answers was bad enough.

"Potentially," I admitted. "But that really doesn't matter right now, Grey. What does is Doxy. We should be focusing on her."

"Yes, we should be doing that," Zoe agreed with a slow nod. "But not until you tell me what you are thinking about this meet-ing." I opened my mouth, intent on reminding her that I wasn't going to reveal any details to her, when she held up a hand, stop-ping me. "I want your feelings—that's all."

I exhaled and folded my arms across my chest, thinking. "Honestly, I don't know. What they want is huge, but what they're offering is just as much, and it would help us out a lot."

"What are they offering?" Quess asked.

"I can't tell you that," I replied. "But it's good."

"Worth the price?"

Shifting my weight back and forth, I stared at Grey. "I-I'm honestly not sure," I said. Devon was a monster, yes, and he deserved to be punished for what he had done. Maybe death was a good punishment, but as the one being asked to deliver it, I had to wonder if there wasn't another way.

Especially considering Devon was Maddox's father. I wasn't sure how she'd react to that bit of news, and I wasn't sure how she'd feel—happy he was dead, sad he was gone, or angry that she never got the chance to avenge her mom's death. I wasn't sure, and I was pretty certain I didn't want to find out.

I glanced around the room, and realized that everyone was waiting for my explanation. I sighed and shook my head. "Look, it's kind of hard to decide whether or not we should take a deal with anyone when we don't really have our own plan to begin with. This might not be the right time discuss this, but making any sort of decision on behalf of the group without having a set plan of action in mind for the future doesn't work."

It was an excuse, albeit a good one, but one I hoped would get everyone off my back.

"We have a plan," Grey said. "We get the Paragon back up and running and get out of here."

"Hey, whoa," Quess said, arching an eyebrow. "Don't get me wrong—out sounds nice. But so does not subjecting ourselves to radiation and almost certain death from exposure to the sun or any wildlife that survived the End. Besides, we have another option now—we have Leo! We should work on him to replace Scipio!"

"Right conversation, wrong time," I announced before either of them could start getting carried away. "Look, we need Paragon in either case, so that will be our next move. We'll sit down and talk about it. After we get Maddox back. Is that acceptable to everyone?"

It took Grey longer than everyone else, but eventually he nodded too. The delay bothered me, but at least he wasn't showing any of that anger he had before. He'd talk to me later about what he was feeling.

"Of course it is," Quess said softly. "But, Liana, we have no idea how to get her back! The common spaces are too large to rely on lashes to help, and grabbing a prisoner just outside of the Citadel guarantees that we won't get away. I've tried looking at it objectively, but—"

I nodded as he trailed off, indicating that I understood he had thought of everything, my mind spinning. He was right. The common places were too difficult to retrieve a person from not one, but two hostile enemies. No matter where it happened, it would be between the two structures, and heading out there to retrieve her without at least ten more people to help control the environment was impossible.

If only we could get them to take her somewhere else, not the Core or the Citadel, but...

I paused, and then smiled, an idea occurring to me.

"Guys, I think I have an idea," I said.

"Just like that?" Quess's brows rose in shock.

"What is it?" a small voice asked. I looked over and saw Tian sitting up, her eyes wide and already beginning to sparkle with hope. I hesitated.

"You're not going to like it, Tian," I told her.

"Why not?" she asked innocently.

I sighed. "Because... we're going to have to hurt Maddox, to help her."

"What?" Quess demanded.

"It's protocol," I replied with a smile. "If someone gets injured while under arrest by the Knights, they have to take them to the Medica for treatment."

"You want to go back to the *Medica?*" Grey asked, looking at me incredulously.

"Why not? They aren't looking for us there anymore. They *are* looking in the Core—everyone is. I think this will work, guys.

Instead of trying to fight the Knights who go to retrieve her, and any Inquisition agents who come, we rig something to injure Maddox, forcing them to take her to Medica for treatment. It will require two teams, though—one to injure her, and one to be waiting for them inside of the Medica."

"That's actually really smart," Grey said after a moment. "Once she's there, there'll be a limited number of Knights in the room. And we can use Jasper to help us."

"Who's Jasper?" Eric interjected, confused.

"We'll explain," Grey replied, before focusing back on me.

I hesitated. "We can *ask* Jasper to help us," I hedged. "But I was thinking the same thing. Besides... this also gives us an opportunity to get the other thing we need: the formula for Paragon."

I was sitting in my hammock, waiting for Mercury's call during the scheduled five-minute window we turned the anchor on for, when my net started buzzing. I looked down at my wrist in time to see my brother's name appear, and then he overrode it, connecting automatically.

"Would you do that if I were Zoe or Eric?" I asked, keeping my voice low so as not to disturb anyone sleeping around me, and I was greeted by a warm laugh.

His warm laugh.

Relief washed over me knowing that my brother was okay and that Mercury hadn't lied, and also that Mercury had given him access to the private network Quess had set up so that they could contact us. I had not forgotten that I still hadn't talked to Alex since before the Core, and I was worried sick that my being there had somehow gotten him in trouble.

They're not my twin, he said. *Are you okay?*

"I'm fine. It's you I'm worried about. Mercury said they iden-tified me. Did they question you?"

They did—but before you ask, I'm pretty sure they believed me. My ranking is still high, and I just stuck with the story that I hadn't heard from you since before Gerome's death. They'll tear apart my computer systems for a few days, but I'll be fine.

"But I had to use your Lead's name!"

Relax, Liana, I have a few recorded conversations between us where I mention him by name several times. They just chalked it up to you paying attention, and me missing the signs that my twin was a soon-to-be dissident.

"You know, I'm not sure what bothers me more about that statement—the fact that you have recorded conversations between us, or that they expected you to catch and turn in your twin."

People do it, Liana, he said sadly, and my love for him grew even larger, encompassing the whole of my torso until I could almost imagine him hugging me. My brother wasn't like everyone else in the Tower, and I loved him for it. I loved that he was confi-dent enough in himself and his convictions to recognize right from wrong, and then act upon it.

"You're a good brother. But you tell anyone I said that, and I'll deny it."

Shut up. Mercury wants to know what happened during the meeting.

"Unfortunately for Mercury and the rest of my friends, I'm not talking about it, per the other party's request."

Are they that paranoid?

"They are indeed," I replied. "Sorry, big brother, but this time I can't. Especially not through a net call."

I see. What do they want from you?

"Alex," I said in warning. "We are not talking about it. Now, what is going on with Maddox? I assume that's why you're netting."

And because I missed you, but that's beside the point. Liana, the Inquisition found out who Maddox is and reached out to Devon.

The rock that had been forming in my stomach over the last few hours dropped, and I sat forward, swinging my legs out of the hammock. "How did he react?"

He didn't believe it at first. He demanded to see the report, and they sent it to him through his pad. Once he got over his initial shock, however, he wanted her moved immediately into his care. The Inquisition refused to do it immediately, but agreed on two in the afternoon tomorrow. They're doing the transfer on the Bridge of Heroes.

The Bridge of Heroes. That was perfect for what we were planning. It was wide, well-trafficked, and had dozens of statues lining its sides, giving the team that went to injure Maddox plenty of cover. Depending on the size of the weapon Zoe and Quess developed.

"Thank you, Alex. I'm so glad you were able to get this."

Me too. I feel awful about what happened. It was our plan, and we failed you. I failed you. I'm so sorry.

"You're being ridiculous," I said automatically. "You couldn't have known there was going to be anyone in that room during that time."

Doesn't matter. I hope you get your friend back, Liana.

"Me too." I dropped to the floor. "Thanks again for this, but it means we don't have a lot of time, so we should get started."

I know. Please be careful, Liana.

"You too, Alex. I love you."

I love you.

The buzz in my skull dissipated, signaling that he had ended the net, and I relaxed slightly. I slipped out of the hammock, taking a moment to switch off the anchor before moving around the room to wake Grey and Eric up and usher them into the workroom.

Tian I left sleeping. She needed it after all of the emotional turmoil over the last few days.

The three of us moved into the open space where Zoe and Quess were working on their device for hurting Maddox. The two had their heads close together, with Quess holding a light while Zoe tightened a screw of some sort as she peered through a magnifying glass.

"How's it going?" I asked softly, and the two started, both straightening and looking at me as we filed in.

"Good," Quess said. "I think we're onto something here. I take it we have a time and location?"

I nodded. "Two p.m. Tomorrow, on the Bridge of Heroes."

"Gross," Zoe said, and I smiled. She and I both hated the Bridge of Heroes, but for two totally different reasons. To me, it was a monument created by the council, to glorify the egos of the council. For Zoe—it was a waste of resources. Either way, it was one of the many things we mutually hated, and doing so made us even closer.

"That's still where it's happening. Do you think this thing will be up and running by then?"

"Should be," Quess muttered. "We need to go scavenge a few more parts, but they're easy to find, so it shouldn't take long."

"Good," I replied.

My sleep-deprived mind fumbled for something else to add, even as a yawn split my mouth wide open, and I suddenly remembered the other mental note I had made for the day.

"Now we need to decide who's going where," I said. "I'm going to the Medica—I have to. There's a chance Jasper won't work with anyone who isn't me."

Silence met my comment, and Zoe was the first to break it. "I'll go to the bridge," she announced into the quiet room. "Make sure it's done and on track."

"I'll go with you, too," Eric said to Zoe, a smile playing on his lips. "Keep you from getting hurt. Keep you out of trouble."

I nodded at them and looked at Grey.

"I go where you go," he said simply—but it wasn't simple, and I immediately flushed bright red in pleasure.

All around me, everyone erupted into a collective "Awwwwww," and I suddenly wanted nothing more than for all of them to just mind their own business.

"I'm going with you, too," Quess said after the moment had passed. "You might need me to hack into their programs to move around."

I nodded thoughtfully, but something bothered me deeply as everyone volunteered. "What about Tian?" I asked. "Are we going to leave her alone?"

Quess hesitated, and then lowered his eyes. "We can't take her with us, but we need everyone else if we're going to have a shot at this."

I looked over my shoulder at Quess, and then back to Tian. "Will she be okay?"

Quess hesitated before replying, "She'll hold up. She's strong, and she'll understand that it's for Doxy."

Quess was right. I hated it, but I couldn't deny it. His questions were more than valid, and without any viable proof one way or the other in regard to Jasper—or Leo—it was all hands on deck to get Maddox out.

Tian would be okay for a few hours by herself; I was sure of it. All the same, telling her could wait until we were closer to the time we had to leave. I wasn't about to wake her now.

"All right," I breathed. "Plan in place. Now, let's get a list going with what we need to make it happen, as well as any other thoughts or ideas you might have on potential problems so we can get ahead of them."

I sat back and listened as my team began to speak, pleased that things were coming together so quickly. Now, we just had to make sure everything went smoothly, and then we'd be home free, with Maddox, and soon.

I rose from the vent in time to see the beams of incandescent light spinning from emitters positioned around the office, resulting in the familiar glow and shape of Leo. He smiled at me, his bright blue eyes glowing in pleasure, and I felt my own smile coming to my lips. No matter how many times I entered this room, Leo never failed to greet me, reminding me of a dog, suddenly excited to find their human had returned.

"Liana," he greeted me. "How did your mission go? I've been quite worried."

"Have you?" I asked, surprised and then slightly amused. "Do you mean to say you care about what happens to me?"

Leo's cheeks colored, and he made a show of looking away before reluctantly meeting my gaze. "Of course I do," he replied simply. "You're the first person who has talked to me in a long time. I'd go back to being alone if anything happened to you or your friends."

There was a note of sadness there that pushed the levity away, and I instantly felt sympathy for him. "Then I hope nothing happens to us."

He smiled, his whole face brightening in pleasure. "So, tell me about the mission. What did the Core look like?"

I hesitated. "Honestly? It reminded me of a prison. Lots of dark colors, doors with no handles, lots and lots of security. The mission didn't go very well."

"What happened?"

Even though we had a plan to fix what had gone wrong, I felt a pang of sadness and guilt as I replied, "Maddox," before sitting on the couch and pressing my hands to my face. I wasn't crying, but I was emotionally drained. "She got taken," I said, lifting my head and pushing through the exhaustion. Leaders didn't get to be tired. "We have a plan to get her out, though."

Leo looked mildly surprised as he leaned back, one hand coming up and over the back of the sofa as if he were leaning on it, even though he had no weight to support.

"You do? So fast?"

"We have a friend in IT," I said, thinking of Mercury and Alex. "He managed to find out that the Inquisition was transferring her, and got us a time and a place."

"The... Inquisition?" I looked back from where my gaze had drifted down to the table, to see his brows screwed tightly together. "What does a religious order based primarily in Spain have to do with anything?"

"Spain?" I asked. It was my turn to be confused. "What's Spain?"

Leo cocked his head at me, and then a moment later we were both smiling.

"Spain is a country on the other side of the Atlantic Ocean," he said. I blinked at him. His words still made no sense to me, and he took pity on me. "It's another land from long ago, very far away from here, across a body of salt water. How do you not know this?"

"How would I? We only talk about the past—pre-End times—in terms of how the Tower was constructed, and then the history of the Tower itself, every big event that has occurred in the last three hundred years. I know some things from books I've read, but I haven't read many."

"What have you read?"

"Oh, I don't know... *Charlotte's Web* is my favorite, but there were a few things I didn't understand."

"Like?"

I considered it, and then remembered a word that Wilber had used. "What's a 'truck?' I gathered it was somehow used for transportation, but I can't seem to picture it."

Leo gestured with his hand, and an image appeared a foot or so in front of him. It was long and rectangular, with four black wheels at the bottom. There was a box attached partway back from what I guessed to be the front, due to the large pane of glass on the top half. There was more glass on the sides of the box, and two black nubs where I assumed the doors were, based on the gaps in the metal. I didn't see a knob for opening it, but there was something flat and black on the inside of where the door was cut out.

"It's ugly," I blurted. "How does it work?"

"A truck is a type of vehicle, similar to a car," he explained carefully, dismissing the image. "I confess, I have only seen them in pictures, but Lionel loved driving. That's what it's called when you make the vehicle move. Anyway, cars were pretty much configured the same way, in that they had four wheels, a tank for fuel, an engine to make the wheels roll, and controls to make the vehicle turn and speed up or slow down."

"Fuel?"

"Ah, I understand your ignorance on that subject, because Lionel wanted everything to be run off of clean energy. There was a period of time when mankind used fossil fuels to power everything, but those were difficult to collect, and were not in infinite supply. It also caused havoc at the beginning of the twenty-first century, when scientists were calling for new forms of clean energy to prevent climate change before it hit critical mass."

He stopped, and I scooted forward until I was on the edge of my seat, eager to hear and learn more about the world before. When nothing followed, I asked, "Did it work?"

He shrugged. "I'm not sure. This was all around the time of the End, so some information was, understandably, lost."

"Did Lionel know the End was coming?"

"Of course he did. He even tried to put a stop to it. But it didn't matter: Nobody would listen. After a while he just gave up and moved on to doing what he could about it."

I sat back and considered this. It answered a question I'd had about the mind behind the Tower, but it wasn't satisfactory. It didn't explain what exactly had happened, or what Lionel had supposedly been trying to stop. It only confirmed that I was right in that he had known it was coming.

"So what happened?" I asked, helpless to stop my curiosity.

Again, Leo shook his head. "I don't even think Lionel knew when it started. He had disconnected from the rest of the world to spend every waking moment on this place. We just knew it had happened. The people who had been hired to help construct this place were the first residents, and Lionel let in as many as he could before he had to seal the rest out."

Leo's narrative of events was both enlightening and foreign, and painted a picture of Lionel Scipio that I had never considered. In my mind, Lionel had always seemed more villainous than heroic. Granted, that opinion had slowly begun to change as I learned more and more about him, but it was hard getting over my initial prejudice. It was one I had been cultivating my entire life, and was not easy to let go of. Every time someone used his name, Scipio, the nets, the ranking system... all those elements of control would flash through my mind with a deep-seated hatred for their creator.

Only the ranking system wasn't in his original design, and had been added later. The nets had been modified from their original design—one that was supposed to grant knowledge and monitor our emotional state to make sure we weren't succumbing to depression. And, according to all evidence, it wasn't 2.0's fault he was acting crazy.

So then, who was behind all these changes?

The thing I kept coming back to was the mysterious war between groups within the Tower itself. One of them must have done something, something drastic, to make Scipio 2.0 want to implement the ranking system. Could it just be that they had fed him false data until he chose such an extreme course of action, or had they taken over his system and made him agree? In either case, why would they go to such great lengths just to kill ones? What could they possibly hope to gain?

"You're deep in thought," Leo remarked, and I looked up to

meet the flickering blue of his eyes. "What are you thinking about?"

I gazed at him, thinking about the video he'd shown me of Ezekial Pine murdering Lionel, and then his attempt to murder Leo. They had mentioned a name: Prometheus. Maybe understanding how one of the first of these groups had come into existence would tell me what I needed to know about the newer ones. They had to be related in some way.

"Leo, in the video you showed us, they mentioned something called Prometheus. What exactly is that?"

His brows furrowed, and he gave me another considering look. "Why do you ask?"

I quickly explained to him about the secret groups that had been battling for control over the Tower, and what the legacies were and what they wanted. The more I spoke, the more alarmed he became.

"This is terrible," he said, almost frantic with frustration. "Lionel always worried there was a way to exploit us, but..." He met my gaze, his eyes brimming with fear. "What if they hurt him?"

"Him? Do you mean 2.0?"

"Yes, I mean 2.0! He's still an AI! For someone to tamper with his code..." He shuddered, as if the very thought repulsed him, and I felt sickened as I realized that tampering with an AI's code would probably feel a lot like I'd felt about being on the Medica's pills to correct my ranking. And how I'd felt after I stopped taking them: scared, confused, unable to remember what had happened over the last week. And... violated. Like someone else had slipped into my body and used it as a puppet.

I suddenly found myself wondering if that was the correct

analogy. I could imagine it was, but I wasn't an AI, and I had no basis for comparison. And that made me curious.

"Leo... can you feel pain?"

He nodded, and then froze as if reconsidering. "It's not exactly pain as you see it, but it doesn't feel good. Every time Lionel modified or altered some of my coding, it was... uncomfortable. I could imagine it would feel like someone manually repositioning a muscle fiber over your bones. It drags across, and you can feel every bump and imperfection in your bones as it is moved."

I immediately made a face, repulsed, and shook my head. "Too graphic," I said, and he gave me an innocent shrug.

"You asked."

I rolled my eyes and tried to remove the image from my head and focus on the conversation. "So... Scipio 2.0 is being tortured?"

Leo nodded. "If what you're saying is true."

I paused. "You know we've discussed maybe finding a way to put you into the Core and replace him, right?"

Leo hesitated, and then shrugged. "I know that, but as I've told you, my programming isn't the same."

I frowned, looking at him. "What do you mean?"

"Well..." He paused, the holographic representation of him looking like it was deep in thought. "Scipio 2.0 is an amalgamation of six other programs, each of them modeled after one of the department designer's brain patterns. I was based on Lionel's, of course, but there were others."

My mind reeled at the news, and I sat back. Once again, the Tower had stolen some pretty important parts of our history and seemingly eradicated them. Six AIs. Lionel had made six AIs. What had happened to them? Were they still alive?

Then I remembered Ezekial telling Lionel that the other "ones" had been shut down, and I guessed that meant they weren't around anymore, considering he'd tried to eradicate Scipio as soon as he was done killing Lionel.

"There were *six* other AI programs? And they were all put together to create Scipio 2.0?" At his nod, I speared him with a beseeching look. "Why six? And how come you are the only one to survive?"

"We were all presented with disaster models. Scenarios in which a computer fed us every feasible situation, running us through hundreds of years of what-if scenarios to see where we were best equipped. When a program failed, the strongest parts of their programming were harvested to be introduced into the winners."

"They killed them?" I asked, my eyes bulging.

"No, not exactly. It's more complicated than that. Let me try to condense things as much as possible. I lasted until the end, but there were a few that thought Lionel had rigged the test in my favor." I arched an expectant eyebrow at him when he stopped speaking, and his eyes widened in alarm. He immediately waved his hands as if to dismiss the very idea. "Lionel was a scientist; he wasn't in this for the ego or the fame. He was in it for the survival of his race. But this does relate to Prometheus.

"Prometheus was a group of humans formed in the first few years after the End came, and were primarily in the group that Lionel let in before he had to seal the Tower. Their beliefs centered around the idea that no machine should control them. We discovered their members when they attempted to sabotage the transfer of 2.0 into the mainframe that had been created for him—and several more times, over the years."

No wonder there were so many rules and protocols and fears about dissidents. These laws had probably come into being during that timeframe, as a result of Prometheus's actions.

And to just kill 2.0 like that... it was incredibly short-sighted on their part. So what was their goal? Why were they doing it? Did they just hate him, or did they have another reason?

"What happened to them?"

"Ezekial," he said simply. "He was the head of security and... he got results. But even then, the last I knew was that they were still around, and a threat. As you heard Lionel say, it was why he kept me, even though all the other fragment AIs were destroyed."

I immediately thought of Jasper—although, to be honest, he had been there all along, pressing on the edges of my thoughts while Leo spoke.

"Did the others have names?"

"They did, although not all of them chose names to honor their models like I did. Let's see, there was Rose, Alice, Tony, Jasper, and Karl."

My eyes widened, and I stood. *Jasper!* Jasper was an AI—Grey had thought I was crazy to believe that, and in his defense, it was a little insane. We had both been taught that there was only one, could only be one, and that he was the only thing keeping us all alive. There'd been no reason to even suspect another AI of existing, let alone one that sounded like a gruff old man, but still... I had. Leo craned his head to peer at me quizzically.

"What's wro—"

"Jasper," I said excitedly. "You said Jasper, right?"

"Yes, but why—"

I cut him off again. I couldn't help myself; I was so excited. "Jasper is alive. Or I mean... I met a program that called himself

Jasper inside the Medica. The doctor wouldn't explain what he was, but Jasper helped us several times, even though what we were doing went against protocol."

Leo moved, and he did so with a flash, suddenly going from sitting to standing just inches in front of me. I took a step back at his rapid motion, my heart skipping a beat or two, but he didn't seem to notice as he crowded closer.

"You said the Medica, right? That's what you now call the hospital?" On my nod, his face broke into a smile. "It's him! It has to be. This is incredible—he's still alive! You have to take me to see him!"

"I don't think I can do that," I said, amused by the image of trying to pull the terminal up to the Medica with me. "I mean... Can you actually... Is it—"

"Possible? Absolutely. You can take me with you."

I stared at him, confusion radiating from me at his declaration, and his grin deepened. He sauntered over to the wall, where the safe door stood stark and gray against the white wall around it.

"I thought you said you couldn't trust us with what was inside there?" I said, moving around the couch as excitement coursed through me, turning my blood electric. This was a safe that had been hermetically sealed for centuries. Who knew what wonders lay within? "What changed your mind?"

"You're different," he said simply, before turning to focus on the safe. The keypad began to glow, and then a green holo-screen emerged over it, showing a series of dials and a keyboard. Leo reached out and twisted the glowing knobs this way and that before inputting a series of commands. I watched, my eyes tracking movements too fast to really remember, but I was impressed at how he was interacting with them.

"You really look like you're touching them," I said, slightly awed at the detail, and Leo smiled, flashing a perfect set of white teeth.

"I'm actually just overriding it through the computer... the touching is all for show. See?"

He removed his hands from the dials and keypad, but they continued to move without him.

It ended as suddenly as it had started, the screen disappearing and Leo lowering his hands. I waited, heart in my throat, as something clicked and the safe door slowly swung open, as if pushed forward by some invisible creature sitting inside.

I leaned to the side, toward the now-widening gap, breathless to discover what secrets had been held in there for the last three hundred years.

25

Two shelves filled the deep space within the safe, both containing objects. There were several folders and data crystals, as well as two additional lockboxes, one as long as my forearm and maybe twice as wide, the other six inches high and twelve inches wide, with a black handle. Both required a key code, which I doubted Leo was going to share with me until he felt he needed to. In addition to those, there was a single blue plastic case sitting on the higher shelf atop a thick stack of files.

"Take that," Leo ordered, pointing out the blue case in particular.

"You sure?" I asked, hungrily eyeing the other objects. "Not a data crystal or a file?" As I spoke, my fingers were already reaching out toward them, to see what they contained.

"Absolutely not," he said gruffly. "And keep your hands to yourself. I have to keep the contents protected. Some of them are quite priceless. Now, the blue case," he insisted.

I sighed and reached in to grab the small case. I pulled it out and felt the edges, prying them apart. They slid easily, and I looked inside.

"It's a net," I said dubiously, picking up the small white box and setting the plastic case aside. "A white one, which is odd, seeing as all of them are black. But that's just a stylistic choice."

I turned the hard square between my fingertips as I spoke, inspecting it. It wasn't truly white—the filaments that were wound tightly to form the compressed block were clear, and their density made it seem white.

"This net isn't like the ones you and your friends use," Leo explained patiently from behind me. I shifted toward him, turning my back on the remaining contents, though ignoring them was hard. "Actually, the nets you have today are far inferior to ones like that."

I looked up from the net and peered at Leo. "How is this one superior?"

"Well, for one thing, it was designed to hold copious amounts of information about the world before, so that citizens could access anything they wanted to about that world. Based on the analysis I ran on one of the unused ones Quess let me take a look at a few hours ago, these newer ones are actually a lobotomized design. They are highly susceptible to short circuiting, which was one of the things Lionel worked extensively to prevent. In short, they are crude and barbaric."

I shook my head, staring at the net. "That doesn't make sense," I said, my mind already spotting a huge flaw with his supposition. Nets weren't designed for data storage, only trans-mission, reception, and data collecting. They were meant to control, not inform. "If people had had these at any time, it would have been impossible to take them away. People would have complained if the council had just suddenly decided to take knowledge away from them. They would've at least passed something down."

Then I realized that maybe the citizens of the Tower had after all. All of our knowledge of what the world had been before the End came from stories passed down from parent to child—or from books that had managed to escape confiscation. Now that I thought about it, the council had confiscated the books themselves. Everything—art, history, language, fiction—everything except for the technical manuals. Even the history we were taught was incomplete, or downright wrong!

I didn't want to even consider that it had all been done purposefully, but I couldn't help myself. If it had, it had been executed brilliantly, occurring slowly over the centuries. Something big here, several small things there. Slow, steady, methodical —executing some plan made centuries ago by people long dead, but with the collective will and foresight to forge ahead.

That wasn't just dedication: that was devotion. It took a belief beyond reason to carry something like that through.

And if I considered that it had been done purposefully, and had not been a series of coincidences, then that alone would scare me more than Devon, the Knights, the Inquisition, and Scipio combined. And while it might have been cowardly, I just wasn't ready to face that potential reality yet.

Because then I would have to accept that somehow my friends and I had been thrust into the middle of it all.

"I don't have all the answers, Liana," Leo replied. I looked up to see him looking sadly around the room. "These four walls are all I have known since Lionel died. I have no evidence to support the claim—just your word on some drastic changes that don't honor my creator's vision of this place. I've thought about it for a very long time, and based on what I've picked up from you and your friends, Lionel Scipio's dream has been lost. At first, I thought that there was nothing to be done. As I am now, I could not serve as a backup like he had originally intended. But if Jasper is indeed still alive... then maybe I can."

"But why would you want to, especially knowing that they will probably be looking for a way to finish what Ezekial Pine started?"

Leo smiled sadly. "As Lionel's creation, I feel obligated to do something to set it right. If this is the *same* Jasper, then maybe, just maybe there is something I can do to fix the Tower. So it is I who must ask you for your help, really."

I breathed in, considering what he was saying. While I still didn't know where everyone stood on escaping versus staying and fighting to save the Tower, I had an opinion of my own. And truthfully, I would be fine staying to help Leo replace Scipio and restore the Tower to what it had originally been intended to be. If it weren't for these damned shadow groups. They made what was already a daunting task even harder, and I had to wonder if it would be worth it, in the end. We'd lost so much, and could lose so much more if we stayed and fought.

And at some very cold, yet practical point, I had to ask myself what the Tower had ever brought me, except for pain and a messed-up childhood.

But all that wasn't a reason for Leo not to come with us. After all, Quess had mentioned that Leo could easily access computer systems. Theoretically, of course. But after the Core, it would be nice to have an ace up our sleeves, just in case.

Additionally, I still had no idea what had happened to Jasper in the aftermath of our escape from the Medica. Our entire plan depended on him being there and being in a position to help us. Which, as long as he hadn't been discovered helping us the last time, he would be.

He had seemed confident that he could avoid detection, but with the plan depending on his help, bringing Leo just in case something had happened to Jasper was the best course of action.

There were cons to bringing Leo—the biggest one was discovery. If it got out that the first version of Scipio was running around, there was a chance that someone from one of these shadow groups would understand the implications of his existence and what he could do to the Scipio in the mainframe, if allowed to.

Then there was this net. It had been hermetically sealed in a safe, sure, but this net hadn't been used for three hundred years. While the nets did have a power source that would sustain them, as far as I knew, it would only last for approximately two years unimplanted. Once implanted, it was powered by the electrical activity in the brain, and could continue that way indefinitely. I doubted very much that this one could have survived the test of time.

Then, assuming that it was fine and working, Leo would presumably be transferred inside – although he had never really said so one way or another. What happened to the virus he was holding at bay? Would it destroy his terminal, or would it transfer along with him? Would he even survive the transfer?

And then what? What was I supposed to do with him once he was inside the net?

I performed the equivalent of a mental double-take, my

mouth going dry. I looked up at Leo, my eyes wide. The entire time I had been trying to understand this net, it had just now occurred to me that I would have to implant it in my skull.

"Wait... if I transfer you to this, does... does that mean that one of us would need to implant you into our brain?" I couldn't keep the alarm out of my voice, and as soon as the words were out, I immediately felt concerned that I had offended him.

The corners of his lips twitched, and then curled up and broadened into a smile. Rich laughter erupted from him, and I narrowed my eyes as the hologram doubled over, clutching his stomach as if I had just told the funniest joke in the history of the world.

I crossed my arms and waited for his laughing fit to die down, and even though it was irritating to be laughed at, I was both awestruck and amused at how human he seemed. I wasn't sure who Lionel had really been, but if his neural clone was any indication, he'd been a decidedly optimistic person.

After a few seconds, Leo's laughter died down to chuckles and he righted himself, dragging a finger under his eye as if to wipe away a tear.

"Nothing like that," he chuckled. "I mean, it is theoretically possible, but Lionel says I shouldn't talk about it because humans would find the idea absolutely repulsive, and I can see it now. Your face..." He laughed some more, and I couldn't help but smile.

"All right, I get it—nothing so intrusive," I said. I paused for a moment, returning to my earlier thoughts, and let the humor between us fade a little while I prepared my next volley of questions. "What will happen to the virus when you put yourself into the net? Will it ruin your terminal, come with you, or something else? Could transferring hurt you at all?"

Leo immediately sobered as he considered my questions, some of the elation chased from his face. He nodded, as if reaching some internal decision.

"The virus will remain behind. I can set redundant programs up here to keep the computer on, as well as a few automated programs to keep the firewall intact in my absence. It won't hold up for long, but it will survive for at least a few days. As for the transfer—I have done this before, Liana. Lionel used to take me with him on many of his walks around the Tower, so I could learn and grow through his experiences."

"The Tower has changed," I pointed out. "Dramatically, if everything you've told me is to be believed." He opened his mouth, but before he could say anything, I quickly added, "Not that I don't believe you—it's just hard wrapping my mind around the fact that everything I have been taught wasn't exactly right."

Leo stared at me, his mouth still open and ready to deliver whatever he had been about to say earlier, and he slowly closed it. "Even if the Tower has changed, I would still like to see it. I am adamant about going to see if this Jasper is *the* Jasper." He smiled, sadly this time. "It'd be nice to know that I'm not completely alone." I gazed at him, trying not to let my face crack into a concerned frown, and he added, "Please. If I could, I would just go on my own, but unfortunately, I was not born human. I lack the appendages to even carry myself there."

I let out a breath, then pinched the bridge of my nose between two fingers and began to massage. I wasn't annoyed. Well... not with him, and not at his insistence on going. His argument was sound, and he knew the dangers.

No, I was annoyed at myself. Even though I was pretty certain he'd be useful, I wasn't entirely convinced it was a good idea. Not because we didn't need him—there were certainly a hundred things that could go wrong with our slap-dash plan to free Maddox, and having him around could help mitigate them. But because I wasn't sure he could count on us to help him restore the Tower.

Yet, I couldn't tell him that, and it was his fault, with that sad, helpless look on his face. I realized then that no matter how hard and practical I tried to be, I was always going to have a soft heart. His helplessness called to me more than any reason or logic could.

I had a feeling my friends weren't going to like my decision, but I was making it nonetheless. I wasn't going to hide it from them afterward, but I couldn't say no to him. I just had to make a few things clear to him first.

"You know I can't commit us to helping you long term, right?"

Leo's face reflected no small amount of surprise, and he blinked a few times, before saying, "But you've mentioned it several times."

"I know that," I said with a nod. "Because we have been considering it. But our original plan, before we ever met you, was to escape. That plan still might be our goal, once we find some time to sit down in a group to talk about it."

"I see." Leo stared off into the distance, and then nodded. "I understand. Although, before you decide, I would like to request that you give me a chance to formulate an argument to persuade you into helping me."

It was an easy enough request. "Done," I said. "Although, can I be honest?"

"Of course. I would hope you're always honest with me. Like

right now, I appreciate that you told me that. You didn't have to—you could've just brought me along to be of use if needed, and then told me afterwards. Much like my creator, I like knowing things upfront and in advance, and you respected me enough to inform me beforehand. I thank you for that."

I was both flattered and embarrassed by his gratitude, and it was hard not to blush, but I managed, somehow, to accept the compliment. "You're my friend," I informed him. "I don't like to lie to my friends. Not when I can avoid it." I paused, taking a moment to backtrack to where we had been in the conversation before Leo had segued, and realized that whatever I had been about to say wasn't important.

Helping Maddox was. "So, is there anything I need to know about the net? Like, what I should do with it?"

Leo laughed, his eyes twinkling in merriment. "Do with it?"

I shrugged, fiddling with the dormant net between my fingers. "I mean, yeah. Where should I carry it? Will we be able to communicate with you? Are there any side effects for you or for me that I should be aware of?"

"Oh, actually, it's extremely non-invasive, and while the nets you are using are comparatively rudimentary, they are comprised of the same material."

"So?" I asked, wondering what the material had to do with anything. "What does that matter?"

"So, the white one in your hand can be worn externally over an implanted one. A filament will emerge from the implant, and connect with the net. Before you ask, no, you won't be able to access any information from me, nor will we share thoughts. You will not feel what I feel, and vice-versa. This is just a ride, and the filament that I'm connected through is the seatbelt keeping me in place for it."

I cocked my head, and then smiled excitedly. "A seatbelt is part of a car, right?"

He gave me a look, but I continued to smile. I would not apologize for being excited when I recognized something from the past.

"Anyway," he said, ignoring the question, "I will be able to communicate with you and anyone standing within five feet of me, but that's as far as my signal goes. Would you... Would you be the one to carry me?"

I got the sense from the nervous way he asked, that he was almost worried that I would say no, and I had to wonder why it mattered. If he couldn't share thoughts or emotions, then I didn't think anyone would have a problem with carrying him.

And then I realized, it wasn't about just anyone carrying him. He was asking *me* specifically, and I suddenly realized that this was a big deal for *him*. He had little choice in a lot of things, but the person who would carry him? That he did have a choice in. And he had chosen me.

"I'd be honored," I said, and the nervousness evaporated under the glow of his gratitude. I stood there for a second, awkward now that he was smiling at me so gratefully that I thought my eyes would explode from the brightness alone. "So, with this net... What do I have to do?" I asked, trying to get us back on track.

"Place the net on the pad, just to the left and over the keyboard," he replied, moving up behind me to peer over my shoulder. I tensed, half expecting to feel the air of his breath on my neck, but there was nothing, reminding me yet again how different he really was. I followed his instructions, depositing the white thing on a pad that popped out from the wall a few feet above his terminal. The edges of it lit up a soft violet.

A flash of light out of the corner of my eye caught my attention, and I turned in time to see the holographic image of Leo fading from view, the beams of lights creating his image flickering a few times before dying completely. The entire room hummed as the light emitted by the scanning pad began to pulse in a rhythmic fashion. I took a step back, suddenly worried about Leo's mainframe and the stress this was putting on it. If it broke, he'd be stuck in the net until we found him a new home.

The humming grew and grew, until I could feel the vibration of it, a continuous buzz that seemed ominous and foreboding, through my rubber-soled boots. I took yet another step away from it, my eyes growing wide in alarm as the swirling colors on the pad began to grow even brighter.

Then, as suddenly as it began, the humming died down to a stop, and the light flickered. The screen on the terminal was black, but I saw a white indicator light flashing white in the top right corner. The machine was still on.

I picked up the net with one hand, lifted my hair off my neck with the other, and quickly pressed the net to the place where my new net had been installed yesterday. I felt it drag itself over a few centimeters before nestling down on my skin. Goosebumps erupted all over my arms at the odd sensation, but I gritted my teeth through it, fighting for calm.

"Leo?" I asked.

I'm here, he replied, his voice coming through my ear implant. I exhaled in relief—not just because he was fine, but also because the buzz in my head was significantly less with him there. It was almost like he had muted it.

I couldn't be sure of what he had done or how he'd done it; I just knew that he was now along for the ride—and if talking to him was going to be one of the perks of carrying him around, I had to admit it was a pleasant one.

"How do you feel?"

The same, really, although some of my senses are completely numb here. However, I should be able to access the cameras within range to help mitigate some of it. At least, I hope I will. I'm a little apprehensive to see what it's like up there.

"So what else can this nifty net do?" I asked, recalling that he had briefly insinuated, in passing, that it could do more than just this.

Well, contain a full AI unit, obviously.

"Anything else?"

There was a pause while I waited, and finally he replied, *Yes.*

A single word with nothing to follow, and I was fairly confident that he didn't intend to share any more than that.

"C'mon, Leo, you can't ask me to help you out like this and then expect me to take your lack of explanation well."

It's not that; it's classified. I'm not supposed to tell you, and some parts of my programming are strong. I'm sorry—I can't. It's need-to-know.

I wasn't satisfied with his answer, and I could tell he wasn't happy about keeping it from me, but he wasn't budging.

"Well, I'm letting it go for now," I informed him, and my net buzzed in response, with his chuckle. "How's your terminal?"

It's still operational and running. The programs I left to fend off the virus are operating within system parameters, and I'm confi-dent that leaving it for a little while will be fine.

I hoped he was right. Even though I was inviting him along with us, with the intention of helping him meet Jasper, I was still afraid of what would happen if he were discovered. More importantly, I was afraid of what would happen to us if someone found out we had him. I had to hope that no one would discover him, or, if they did, they wouldn't understand how important and influential he was.

I headed back toward the vent, Leo in tow, to fill everyone in on his new role in the plan.

26

I entered the room quietly, the lowered lights inside the common area alerting me that people were sleeping, and swiftly moved through the curtains, following the slight sounds coming from the workroom.

As I moved around Zoe's hammock, I paused and smiled. She and Eric were lying together, pressed back to front, with their hands laced. Both were fast asleep, and as I looked around, I realized that Eric's hammock had disappeared from where it had been hanging next to hers, freeing up a bit more space.

I watched them a few moments longer than I really should have, before continuing to the workroom. I was happy to see they had finally resolved their issues, and surprised to see how forward they were being. Sharing hammocks seemed like the equivalent of sharing quarters, but even more intimate, as it forced you to lay pressed together, close and tight. For a moment, I wondered what it would feel like to lie like that with Grey, and my face flamed with a searing heat that I could feel in my bones. I quickly moved away—from both them and the racy image that my mind had conjured up.

I stepped into the workroom. Grey and Quess were both bent over something. Grey was holding a small, bright light, and Quess was wearing a pair of goggles, some sort of tool I didn't quite recognize in his hand. I smiled at the sight of them; whatever they were working with utilized some sort of static charge, because both Quess's dark waves and Grey's blond locks were standing upright.

There was a short *zzt* sound, followed by a sharp pop and flash of light. I shielded my eyes while Quess made a victorious grunt. I lowered my hand in time to see him picking up the framework that consisted of several small round pipes, a welded handle, and some sort of crank on the side, and holding it to his shoulder.

"This is gonna be perfect," he crowed. Grey gave a pointed look toward the corner to the left of me, pressing his fingers to his lips. I looked down to see that Tian had dragged some of her blankets and Commander Cuddles into the workroom and created a new nest for herself on the floor. Currently, she was asleep in a position that was uniquely Tian: legs braced on the wall with her back flat on the ground. Commander Cuddles was now serving as her pillow, but it looked like her hair was serving as his blanket, so I was pretty sure this was a mutually agreed-upon position.

I looked back to see Quess reluctantly handing the weapon over to Grey, an abashed look on his face. "Hey, guys," I said, pitching my voice low as I moved closer to them. "You lost Zoe and Eric."

"They worked on some of the more intricate and annoying

bits," Quess said, picking up a rag and rubbing some invisible spot on the weapon cradled in Grey's hands. "And they were both fading fast. I figured I'd let them get some sleep."

"If only we could join them," I halfheartedly joked, and Grey smiled.

Inside my head, Leo laughed—and I jumped, my hand automatically going to my chest to ensure that my heart hadn't escaped. I had half forgotten that I was carrying him during the crawl back. He hadn't really spoken since we left, and in my sleep-deprived state, I had simply focused on other things.

"Are you okay?" Grey asked, quickly passing the weapon back to Quess and stepping forward. His warm brown eyes gazed deeply into mine with growing concern, and I had to admit that it meant something to me that he looked at me that way. My heart skipped a beat before settling into a new, accelerated rhythm, and my mouth immediately went dry.

I nodded, unable to form even a monosyllabic response, and he reached up to tenderly press his hand against my cheek.

So you and Grey worked things out, huh? That's good, because given the readings here, you are very much attracted to him. Whoowee, look at that pheromone spike.

My eyes bulged, and I hurriedly took a step back, my eyes fluttering shut as a deep flush of embarrassment came over me.

"Leo," I hissed, my anger hotter than steam coming through an extremely narrow opening.

Apparently, I had to have a discussion with my little passenger about etiquette, and how he could keep his nose out of any interaction between Grey and myself. Didn't Lionel at least teach the man manners?

What? he asked, and I still marveled at how little I felt inside my skull when he spoke. There was next to no sensation, not even a vibration in my skull, just a slight warm purr that wasn't entirely annoying. I wanted it to be this way forever—except, not with an AI reading my net while I was in the middle of a conversation.

"What did Leo do?" Grey asked, his brows already coming together. "Are you okay? Did he hurt you?"

I smiled, a soft laugh escaping me, and just like that my anger at Leo's nerve dwindled in the light of Grey's protective attitude. It made me feel much like I imagined Zoe was feeling right now: safe and cherished.

"Relax," I said soothingly, still unable to stop smiling. "Leo was being nosy, and needs to learn to keep his commentary to himself."

Lionel used to find my commentary endearing, the nosy AI declared smugly, and I rolled my eyes.

Grey's features were like a windstorm erasing and reforming sand dunes across the wastes, shifting and changing from concerned and angry to stunned... and then confused.

"What are you talking about?"

I sobered slightly, the weight of what I was about to tell them settling in, and gave them both a look. "Leo's asked to come with us when we go up to the Medica," I said carefully. Quess and Grey exchanged equally baffled looks, and Quess spoke first.

"What do you mean, come with us?" he asked, finally setting the weapon he had just been polishing onto the table and standing up.

I exhaled, and put on a broad smile. It was always the best way to give interesting news, in my opinion. "Leo wants to come on the mission with us," I repeated.

Grey's eyebrows pulled tight. "Why?"

"Jasper," I said, and then I quickly explained what Leo had told me about the different AIs being tested, and then later assimilated into the version of Scipio that would become the Master AI. Grey and Quess handled that information a lot better than I thought they would, all things considered.

"If Jasper's one of the AIs that was used to create Scipio 2.0, how could he exist now?" Quess asked, and it was Leo who responded. I could tell by the way Quess and Grey's eyes widened that he was transmitting to them as well, and bit back a smile.

That's one of many questions I intend to ask him.

Grey's back stiffened, and he looked at me. "What was that?" he demanded, spearing me with a look. "Was that..."

"Leo," I said with a smile. "He's here."

"How?" Quess asked, his eyes scanning my hands and clothes, looking for some sign of the AI. "Wait, how is he even transmitting to our nets?"

"He... um... sort of downloaded himself into my net."

"Into *your* net?" Quess asked. He swore, his eyes bugging. "Liana, the nets aren't designed to take that kind of neural load! The data will bleed out into your brain and kill you. Grey! Get my kit—we'll cut the bastard out!"

Grey nodded, already turning. "I told you that AI was going to be trouble," he said.

"And I told you studying him was worth the risk!" Quess replied.

"No, wait, guys, I mean—" I tried to interject.

"There's no waiting about this, Liana!" Grey growled, before continuing to bicker with Quess.

Are they really going to try to kill me?! Leo exclaimed, and I could feel a flicker of his fear through the net. I wasn't sure whether I was *supposed* to, but now wasn't the time to stop and ask.

I was about to interrupt their bickering again when a heavy hand fell on my shoulder. I looked up to see Eric standing just behind me, his other hand rubbing some of the sleep out of his eyes.

"What's going on?" he grumbled, his voice rough with exhaustion.

I looked back at the pandemonium and shook my head. "I'm watching two buffoons who won't listen to what I'm saying."

"Then tell them to shut up." A groan came from behind me, and I turned to see Zoe stepping into the room, her legs bare under the oversized shirt she was wearing.

"I'm not sure they would hear me right now, since they're convinced I'm about to die. But if they'd just stop for a moment and let me finish what I was going to say, I could tell them that Leo is actually in *a* net on the back of my neck, and not actually in *my* net."

It took a second for my not-so-quiet statement to reach Grey and Quess, but when it did, the two stopped what they were doing and looked at me.

"That's... not... possible," Quess said thoughtfully, and I gave him a look before turning around and lifting my hair. I heard their boots on the floor as they came up behind me, and waited for a moment.

"Huh," Quess said, and I felt his finger against my neck.

Kindly do not do that, Leo's voice announced. I heard a sharp crackle of electricity, followed by Quess's hiss of pain. I turned in time to see him shaking his finger before sticking it into his mouth, and he looked at me askance.

"Leo just spoke inside *our* nets and shocked me!" he declared around the digit in his mouth.

"Well, you did just touch him without permission. And me, I might add." I smiled as I said this, to show that I wasn't upset or angry. I might've done the same thing.

Eric looked at me quizzically. "Why does Leo want to come?"

"He wants to meet Jasper. He thinks he might be another AI whose personality was integrated into 2.0's." At Eric's confused look—as well as everyone else's—I quickly explained what Leo had told me about the other AI fragments, and how all six of them came together to form Scipio 2.0. I even remembered their names, with Leo's prompting.

When I finished, Leo was the first to speak.

You know, I never realized how crazy it sounded until I heard it coming from someone else. And then for you to have to tell it twice? You sound bananas.

That got a laugh from me, and at Grey's inquisitive eyebrow, I pointed at my head and mouthed Leo's name.

"Can you ask him to speak to all of us again, seeing as he can?" Grey said, fixing me with a significant look. "I give him my permission this time."

Of course, Leo transmitted, and I knew everyone was getting the message by the way they looked around the room with widening eyes. *And I'm sorry for doing it without gaining your permission first. I was just very excited that Liana was gracious enough to give me a ride. However, that doesn't change the fact that you should all have a say in whether I can communicate with you directly or not.*

"Okay, whoa. While all of this is really great and very interesting, what the hell is the lifespan of a net for an AI? Leo, how long can that thing last before the internal battery dies?"

"Oh, wait, what?" I asked, my eyes growing large at Quess's question. I had forgotten to consider that the net and Leo were operating off of battery life. What happened if the battery got low or even died? Did that mean Leo would die?

"Leo?" I said, now wanting him to answer Quess's question. The white net was different, better even, given that it still functioned after three hundred years of inactivity, so Leo had to have taken that into account. Besides, Lionel had used it to take Leo out—he wouldn't have done that if he hadn't created a way to keep him alive.

A day, Leo admitted begrudgingly. *Technically, twenty-two hours now, since I had to shock Quess to remind him of his manners.*

I pressed my lips together and considered this new information for a second. "What happens if the battery drains with you inside of the net?" I asked him.

Leo paused. *That would be bad. Normally, if my terminal were in perfect working condition, I could be transferred back into it after the net regained some charge. However, I would lose all of my memories from my time in the net as a result.*

He stopped talking. I waited for him to explain what would happen now that his terminal *wasn't* working perfectly (considering he was infected with a virus). When he didn't, I realized he wouldn't until I asked. Because he knew we might not like the answer.

"What about now, with the virus?" I prompted.

If the net loses power with me inside, a transfer into the terminal would result in an automatic system reset, so that my... consciousness could be fully recovered and scanned for any malfunctions. If that happens, then the virus will finally win, and I will be, effectively, dead.

I held my breath and let Leo's words fade into silence while I thought, trying to decide whether I should reconsider his company. A part of me felt I should, knowing that his life was literally on the line if I got captured or killed. If no one recovered his net or got him back into the terminal before the power went out, we'd lose him, and any chance of even entertaining a plan to use him to replace 2.0.

But I'd made an agreement with him, one that was mutually beneficial, and I couldn't back out of it now. It'd betray his trust in me, and I didn't want that to happen.

"Listen," I said, wanting to forestall any argument before I had a chance to have my say. "I'm a little miffed that this didn't occur to me before, but it doesn't matter. Leo asked me for my help, and I told him I would give it. He clearly knows the risks involved, and... it's not fair that we have the use of working bodies while he doesn't. If he did, we'd have no say in stopping him, and I don't think we should let the fact that he's about the size of my pinky nail right now stand in the way of his right to choose. He knows the risks, and now so do we. He still wants to come, so I want to help him."

They absorbed that with a nod, and I exhaled. I probably should've let Leo have his say, instead of speaking up, but we'd gotten off track, and we still needed to make sure we were ready to rescue Maddox.

"Quess, what time is it?" I asked him, changing the subject. "And where are we on the weapon and the plan?"

He blinked, and then turned around and began rummaging through some odds and ends on the workbench, eventually pulling out a round clock that I suspected he'd designed.

"Ten minutes until noon," he said. "And good. The weapon is ready, and I tested it with Grey not too long ago. It'll definitely fracture a bone, especially with the ammunition we're using."

"Which is?" I asked. This had been one of the more complicated aspects of the plan we had brewed: finding a common object in the Tower that also happened to occasionally cause injuries. The goal was to injure her without making it look like it had been purposefully done to force them to the Medica. If the item that injured her were too out of place, then someone would become suspicious. I hadn't been able to brainstorm it with them, so I was very interested in what they had come up with.

Grey smiled broadly and pulled a small metallic item out of his pocket, cupping it in his palm and holding it out to me. As I leaned closer to inspect it, I grinned. It was a lash end, detached from the cable.

Which was genius, now that I thought about it. Lash ends did break off from lashes from time to time—not often enough to be concerned, but just frequently enough for it not to be *too* surprising.

"You're brilliant," I told him with a grin, and he nodded.

"I know," Grey replied with a proud smirk, tossing the bead over to Quess, who began speaking, filling out the rest of the plan.

"Zoe and Eric are going to set up on the Bridge of Heroes and launch this at Maddox—preferably at an arm or a leg. It will hit with enough impact to cause a fracture, so be nice about where you hit her, and avoid the stomach. We don't want any internal bleeding."

Zoe looked at the design of the weapon, her eyes already tracing it. "Should be easy enough," she said with a surprising amount of confidence.

"Good," Grey said. "Once you net that she's been hit, the three of us—"

Four of us, Leo interrupted.

Grey paused, a sardonic look on his face. "The *four* of us will sneak up into the Medica," he continued, indicating Quess and myself. "Since we need to be in the same room for this to work, I think we should get in using the discretion law, as it will avoid any messy or complicated lie to explain why we need to remain together. Once in, we ask Jasper, or Leo, to bust us out and guide us to Maddox. From there, we eliminate any guards and get her out as soon as possible, using the elevator to take us to the top, and then the plunge to get us back home."

I ran a hand over my hair, and then nodded. "It's a good plan," I said. "But things can and will go wrong, so everyone please be on guard. We also need to avoid killing any Knights—if a Knight is killed, every Knight in the area is alerted." I let everyone absorb that piece of information, and then turned to Quess. "How long until the meet?"

He swiveled around and peered at a clock on his workbench. "Two hours," he replied. "We need to start getting ready."

That meant there was one more thing to do, and it was one I wasn't looking forward to. "Well, while the rest of you do that, I will be with Tian, explaining to her why she can't come."

"You shouldn't have to do that alone," Quess replied.

"We should do it together," Zoe said. "She needs to know this was from all of us."

With a heavy and forlorn heart, I sighed wearily, and then moved over to Tian, intent on waking her up. We didn't have a lot of time, and there was no sense in dragging it out. I just hoped she took it well, and that we weren't forced to lock her in a room.

27

My arms and shoulders burned, a phantom sensation caused by the thought of hundreds of eyes on me, drilling holes between my shoulders in a cumulative effort to peer through my disguise and find the very heart of me. I managed to ignore it as the three of us walked up toward the Medica. It was busy, but why wouldn't it be at one thirty in the afternoon? Surely it didn't have anything to do with us, or what we were doing.

It felt surreal being there again. Surreal and vaguely horrifying. We were entering yet another place that would be on high alert, especially for us. It had only been a day since our excursion to the Core to get the nets, and now was when our names and faces would be freshest on everyone's lips and minds. Their eyes would undoubtedly be drawn to strangers with black hair and hidden eyes, or blond locks with warm brown eyes, searching for any sign or hint of recognition.

Which was why we were all wearing disguises yet again—

even Quess—and my hair color had once again been changed to a dull blond. It looked mousier and limper than my natural color made my hair appear. Grey was sporting black hair, which, I had to say, I didn't hate, while Quess had a rich auburn color.

The lenses were back in my eyes and itching away, but wearing them was a small price to pay compared to the risk of coming back here and getting recognized.

Scipio help me, I hoped we weren't recognized.

I scanned the crowd of people as I moved through them, immediately spotting and noting the crimson colors of the Knights among the throngs of people moving in, out, and around the main reception area. There didn't seem to be an inordinate number of Knights in the crowd, and none of them seemed like they were paying any attention to us—but I wasn't convinced. There could be more hidden inside the Medica's internal security offices, waiting for any breath of trouble. We needed to be cautious.

We arrived in the reception area through the large arch and entered the wide, curved seating area. Several desks with Medics behind them sat along the wall, with two large double doors standing opposite us, leading deeper into the Medica.

I never imagined it would be anything like this, Leo said through the net, and I looked around at the bright white, pristine walls.

"What did you think it would be like?" I asked, and when neither of my two male counterparts looked surprised, I realized Leo was still transmitting to them as well.

Not so… bright.

Grey was walking beside me, and I heard him give a snort. I smiled as well; we both felt the same way. We had even shared a laugh over it once. The brightness had always bothered me, mostly because it was a waste of resources. The Medica claimed it was a byproduct of a beam meant to eliminate airborne bacteria, but Cogs grumbled under their breath that if they were given five minutes alone with their design, they could reduce it. The Medics didn't care—they liked their walls, which were functional as well.

We got in a very short line and stood awkwardly together in silence, waiting for one of the clerks to be ready for us. A minute later, we were all standing around a white desk, staring down at a young man with spectacles and a light brown beard.

He looked up at us, one eyebrow arched. "You're all here together?" he asked dubiously.

I nodded, not quite meeting his gaze. "It's private," I said quietly, my lie carefully chosen in advance. "I'd prefer not to discuss it with anyone but the doctor."

"I see." The young man turned to his screen, and I immediately felt a violent buzz as the scanner read my credentials in preparation of putting us through. I was glad—using the discretion law had been a gambit, especially with a nosier clerk, but he seemed uninterested in whatever story would send the three of us to a Medic together.

Dear God, that is rough, Leo declared. I kept my teeth clamped tightly together while the scan continued to run, making the entire net feel like a hive of angry bees was trying to escape. I hadn't forgotten the feeling, but Leo's gentle transmissions had been so nice that moving back to the old way felt distinctly uncomfortable.

The scan ended, and I waited, my heart thudding heavily against my breastbone. The last time I had been here, I had snuck in under similar circumstances, using a false ID—that time my mother's. This time, however, I was sporting a new and quite illegal one, with an AI attached to it, and I was terrified that they would catch me in two seconds flat.

"Follow the green indicator," the clerk said, his hand making a dismissive gesture.

I managed to contain my relief so that it didn't show. I looked down at the floor to see the line of green dots leading toward the massive doorway, and began following them.

"I'm glad that worked," Grey murmured as he and Quess kept pace with me. "Did you have a backup plan?"

I shook my head. "Planning doesn't seem to be my particular forte, if you'll recall," I replied dryly, and we both shared a grin.

"Fine. Did you have a backup *concept*?"

I laughed, remembering the last time he and I had been on our way to the Medica.

"It doesn't matter," I said, the moment of humor quickly fading behind the danger we were heading into. "We'll be out of the room in no time, with Jasper's help."

"Yeah, about that. Do you really think he'll really help us? I mean, at this point, you've asked a lot from him. What if this time he calls the Knights?" Quess asked his questions softly, but I immediately looked around anyway, hoping no one was close enough to listen in.

Patients and Medics were walking around the floors, all of them following their own indicators. No one was close by, but that didn't mean they were deaf. I turned back to Quess and gave a shake of my head before continuing forward. Quess's questions were reasonable, especially since he had never met Jasper.

We walked in silence, following the wide hall past several side halls leading to patient rooms. As we came toward what would be the center of the Medica, the indicator led us to a short line of people waiting for white elevators that clung to a massive central support beam. We climbed inside the first available one, endured a second scan performed the moment we were in, and then shot up seventeen floors. The indicators led us through the halls, and eventually into a room.

I stepped inside, instantly relieved to be off the main floor, and then froze when a woman's voice filled the space.

"Welcome to the Medica's general procedure and consultation floor. Stand by for scans."

My net buzzed, and my false identity floated up onto the wall screen opposite us, followed by Grey's and Quess's. Quess had taken his own picture, which was apparent in the line of his shoulders at the bottom of the image. He was also smiling, which wasn't exactly against the rules, but his smile was just like him—too much, especially right then. Luckily, the computer wouldn't pick it up, but a human looking at it would definitely take a closer look. Especially with the seven on his indicator. The two paired together were going to scream "fake ID" to anyone looking close enough.

Grey's wasn't much better, with his lazy, cocky grin. He'd pushed a swath of his altered hair to one side, and the ends were getting long enough to cover his eyebrow. His was... tamer than Quess's, at the very least.

"Patient identities confirmed," the automated voice continued. There was a click behind us, and I was mid turn when she announced, "Room has been secured. None may leave or enter until you have been seen by a member of the Medica. Enjoy your time in the Medica, and may you feel better soon."

Grey and I exchanged worried looks. We had anticipated that the Medica had stepped up security, but we hadn't anticipated being locked in. Which wouldn't be a problem, as long as Jasper was willing to help us. I moved farther into the small room.

"Jasper?" I called out. "Are you there?"

There was a long, expectant pause as we all waited for him to reply. I kept waiting for probably longer than I should have, half hoping that if I gave him just one more moment, he would be there.

"Jasper," I said again, when it became clear he wasn't going to answer. My heart had already begun to sink when the first voice we heard was female, but now that he wasn't responding, I was growing more and more concerned that something had happened to him. If it had, then there was a very good chance it was because he had helped us. I knew that I shouldn't feel responsible—after all, he had told us that he could take care of himself—but that had been before he had falsely reported our location to Devon's backup to try to buy us time to escape. He didn't have to do that, but he did, and for that alone, I felt an obligation to make sure that he was all right. And if he wasn't, I wanted to know what had happened to him. "Jasper!"

"Liana, I think they must've found out what he did to help us," Grey said quietly.

I looked over at him, and then back at the walls. They hadn't flickered or twitched once since I'd started calling his name. In my heart, I knew Grey was right, and I felt my spirits sink.

We had been counting on Jasper to get us out of there. And while, yes, I had justified bringing Leo as a backup in case some-thing had happened to Jasper, I hadn't actually believed we would get here to find it was true. I was scared that they had deleted him, not only because he had helped us, or because he had the formula for Paragon—but because if Leo was right and Jasper was what I had begun to believe he was, then that meant there wouldn't be a need to discuss a plan to replace 2.0 with Leo. It would no longer be an option.

I banished the dark thoughts, reminding myself that we knew nothing for sure. And we wouldn't find any answers sitting on our backsides thinking. Especially considering that at any moment, my doctor would be showing up wondering what was wrong with her patient. Imagine her surprise to find me perfectly healthy.

"Leo, do you think you could—"

Go into the system to help you and your friends? I can try—but I need a transfer pad to get uploaded.

"I can help with that," Quess said. I watched as he moved over to a section of the wall that was flat and white. He pushed something down, causing it to spring out from the wall, and as he stepped aside, I saw a little data pad. Bringing him along had been a wise decision. Being Medic-bred meant that he knew a lot more about the inner workings of the Medica than we did.

"I'm going to disconnect you," I told Leo.

Go ahead. I'll be all right.

My fingers felt around my neck for the little white box, but a moment later they were brushed aside and replaced by Grey's.

"Let me," he said. I felt his fingers press on the back of my neck and then retreat. I let him, enjoying the brief moment of contact as he helped pull the net off. I shivered, my neck tingling as he drew away, and then held up my hand.

Grey placed the net into my palm, and I moved over to Quess to drop it onto the dark pad.

The edges of it lit up, and an image appeared on the wall, rapidly flipping through screen after screen of numbers and commands, too fast for my eyes to fully track. It went dark almost a second after it had clicked on, and the next thing I knew, the wall behind me began to glow more brightly, and then was replaced by Leo's features, now enlarged to encompass the entire room.

His eyes were like twin blue flames as his two-dimensional head appeared to swivel back and forth across the flat surface, seemingly peering at something we couldn't make out.

"There's so much space in here," he said, his voice almost sounding relaxed and happy. "I can totally stretch out—although the lack of a holographic display is mildly annoying."

"This isn't exactly a time to get comfortable," I said. "Can you figure out a way to stall the Medics?"

"Good question. Let me check."

He stared off to one side, his eyes squinted slightly, and took on an expression of deep concentration. "Wow, there's a lot of different systems here," he said. "I'm still trying to establish a connection with... Oh wait, I just unlocked the patient directory. What's your net name and ID?"

"Clara Euan," I informed him. "F11-344."

I waited, nervously shifting my weight, until he finally relaxed his facial features.

"Okay, I've got good news and bad news," he said. "The good news is that I am very compatible with the coding. It's all based on mine. It'll only be a matter of time before I'm fully in, at which point I can locate Jasper."

"I *told* you he could do it," Quess exclaimed, his fists up in victory. I felt a flash of annoyance at his premature jubilation, because Leo had clearly said that not all of the news was good.

"Leo, what's the *bad* news?" I asked.

"Well, the Medic assigned to you is on their way, and you

have about thirty seconds to come up with a good explanation as to why you are all here together."

My eyes widened, and I looked around the room. "Can you send them away?"

"Not really. I'm not fully integrated yet. I need more time, and you're going to have to buy it. I'll be back once the Medic leaves."

The screen went black before I could say anything, and I felt all the blood rush to my head as I realized that if I didn't come up with a convincing lie, we were all going to get caught.

I was looking at Grey, my mouth opening to ask if he had any idea, when there was that flash of bright light that always preceded a Medic's entry—bright enough to cause me to squint my eyes against the dazzling intensity, which left dark spots dancing around the periphery of my vision immediately afterward.

And then a woman stood a few feet away from us, a pad in one hand and a stylus in the other. Her black hair hung in tight ringlets around her face, and her dark eyes were dramatically wide as she took us in.

"Hello," she said, her voice high pitched and ending with a slight squeak. "I'm Practitioner Myra. I see here that you checked in with a privacy request." Her dark eyes scanned the three of us as we stood in front of her, an expectant smile on her dark red lips. "So what seems to be the trouble?"

28

My brain immediately started to spin, ready to throw out ideas—and then sputtered and performed the mental equivalent of a face-plant when I realized that I did not have enough knowledge or experience with the Medica to remotely be able to come up with a believable lie that would justify a privacy request, let alone Grey and Quess's presence. I tried, though, attempting to manifest some sort of communicable disease that was virulent enough to explain the mystery, but not contagious enough to warrant a lockdown. I came up blank. I'd put too much hope in either Jasper or Leo being able to help us out, and I hadn't considered that they might not be able to do so immediately.

I quickly looked over at where Quess and Grey were standing a few feet away, desperately trying to signal to Quess that I was way out of my depth on this one. He was Medica-bred, which meant he had some training. I just hoped he remembered something from his time here. A story from his parents—something that would help us out.

The Medic looked at them as well, as if taking some cue that we were all here because of them, and arched an eyebrow expectantly.

Grey and Quess exchanged looks, and Quess looked away first, leaving Grey to be pinioned with the intense gaze from the Medic.

"Well, out with it," she said, a bit impatiently. "There are other people who could use this room."

"She might be pregnant," Grey suddenly blurted out, and it took me a second or two to fully register what he'd said. Once I did, my cheeks immediately flamed—and I suddenly wanted to crawl into a hole and die.

Getting pregnant out of wedlock was one of the most shameful things a girl could do, because it just shouldn't happen. Females and males were both given contraceptive devices that needed to be replaced every year, and missing that appointment and getting pregnant as a result was absolutely inexcusable.

I caught a movement from the corner of my eye and realized the Medic was looking at me, and even though I knew this was a lie, it had caught me so off guard that I couldn't even meet her gaze. I never would've gone this route—never would've considered it an option.

Because it was absolutely degrading, and I was going to murder Grey for even insinuating such a thing.

"I see," the Medic said, disdain already thick in her voice, and I suddenly felt bad for all of those girls who had ever gone through this. It may not have happened very often, but accidents were accidents, right?

Not to the Tower, of course, where population rates were monitored and births limited to two per family, with a third under special circumstances. Babies had to be planned for. Pregnancy with your spouse had to be applied for.

"And you two are here because..."

I looked up sullenly to see Grey and Quess exchange a flurry of glances, and then Quess winced and said, almost too fast to follow, "We're not sure which one of us is the father."

I was going to kill them both now.

Very, very slowly.

"Are you serious?"

I slowly dragged my chin up so that I could level my eyes to meet her incredulous look, and then looked past her to stare at both of them. I was mortified by their responses to everything, but I would be damned if I couldn't get a dig in of my own.

"Well, they never really said we were exclusive, so..."

Both Quess and Grey flushed a bright shade of red, and some of my mortification dwindled at their reaction, and at the absolute look of irritation on the woman's face, directed at both of them. It definitely went a long way toward making up for their insults to me. Young women may have been shamed for getting pregnant, but every department made sure the man was equally shamed for being so irresponsible.

The woman exhaled slowly, and I could imagine she was counting to ten, trying to get a grip on her temper.

"How long ago did your birth control expire?" she asked.

"Oh, um..." I tried to recall how long it was still "safe" to have intercourse after the implant expired, and had a vague feeling it was two weeks. "Three weeks," I said. "I made an appointment to get it replaced, but my supervisor asked me to cancel it to help him with an important task, and I wanted to do my duty to the Tower, so..."

"And you two?" she asked, adjusting herself slightly to face the two men.

"Two weeks ago," Quess said automatically.

"Seventeen days?" Grey said after a short pause, and even though I could still murder him for blurting out that I was possibly pregnant, I had to admit that he was really getting into the lie. Which would've been great, normally, but did it have to be this? My cheeks continued to burn.

Myra tapped a few things into her pad, and then looked up at me. "These next few questions are personal," she said, spearing me with a pointed look. "Would you like for them to leave?"

I hesitated. Obviously, I couldn't let them leave, but I needed a good reason why a girl supposedly having sex with both of them would want them both to stay. And then it dawned on me: why would any woman want both possible fathers to stay with her? Punishment.

"Absolutely not," I said primly, folding my arms over my chest. "I was upfront with them about my device expiring, but neither of them—and I do mean *neither* of them—was as forthcoming with me. So, no, they have to stay and experience the discomfort with me."

Myra surprised me with a smile of approval and pulled out her pad. "When was the date of your last period?"

"Over a month ago," I said.

"And... how frequently have these... interactions been taking place?"

I speared them both with a dry look. "How many times would you say, gentlemen?"

Myra's laugh was soft as they both flushed, and I was pleased to see Grey looking sufficiently mortified that I had flipped this on him.

Honestly, at this point, all I hoped to do was buy time until Leo figured out a way to get rid of her and get us out of here. I hoped he was working on a plan, at the very least—but until he revealed what it was, I needed to stall.

Quess cleared his throat first, casting a glance at Grey. "Um... just the once," he said, his gaze flicking to mine and then down to the ground.

Grey looked up at me, and I watched his eyes fill with apology before he straightened his hunched shoulders and met her gaze head on. "More than once," he said with a lazy, confident grin and a wink. "The ladies always come back."

Myra and I froze, and once again, heat flooded my cheeks as more and more blood pumped into them. I *was* going to murder him. With my bare hands. Who even thought it was a good idea to tell the doctor that you might have gotten a girl pregnant, and then flirted with the doctor mid-examination?!

"Right," Myra said after a significant amount of awkward silence had greeted Grey's statement. She turned back to me, a judgmental look on her face. I knew she didn't know me and I shouldn't care, but this was getting messy fast, and we needed it not to be. Messy got us caught.

"Are you regular?"

I immediately looked over at the men, knowing they were listening closely, and then back to her. "Fairly regular."

"Any other symptoms?"

I rattled off a few things that were believable for this early in a pregnancy, like feeling nauseated in the mornings, and even vomiting a few times. It was vague enough that the symptoms could have been explained away by some sort of bug or flu, but convincing enough to make a twenty-year-old woman with two supposed lovers concerned about the possibility of pregnancy.

But as I spoke, I knew time was running out, and that we weren't going to be able to stall much longer before she just ran the damn test. And as soon as she did—and found out that I wasn't pregnant after all—we'd be kicked out. Without Maddox. Leo had better be getting close to a solution.

She nodded thoughtfully, and then slipped her pad into her pocket, looking at us with wide, bright eyes. "Now that that's finished, I have a few things to say to all of you." She closed her eyes, and then they snapped open, blazing with anger, disgust, and disapproval. "Have the three of you lost your minds?" she asked after a long moment in which she seemed to struggle with her temper. "How is any of this—" She gesticulated wildly, fixing us all with a disapproving look. "—of service to Scipio? I should report all three of you to the Knights right now for being so short-sighted and immature! Do you think our survival here is a game?!"

I cringed appropriately under her tongue-lashing, and offered a meek "No, ma'am" after she finished. Her behavior and the lecture weren't unexpected.

She sneered, not accepting our contrition, and turned to me. "Finger," she barked, pulling something out of her jacket.

I reluctantly held out my hand, curling back my fingers except for my index. She pressed a slim white rod to the tip of it, and then withdrew the rod and moved over to the portion of the wall meant for analysis. She slipped the rod into it, and pulled up a screen, which filled with enlarged red and white blood cells. I watched her hands move as she began inputting the commands.

Grey silently crossed the room to stand behind me, and I folded my arms, watching the Medic work.

"I'm sorry," he whispered quietly. "I completely blanked and just blurted out the first thing that came to my mind."

"And me pregnant is the first thing that came to your mind?" I shot him a look from the corner of my eye. "That's very revealing."

I couldn't help teasing him. It was easier than focusing on the anxiety that was building as Myra scanned my blood for a baby that didn't exist.

His cheeks bronzed slightly, and he fidgeted. "It's working, isn't it?"

"Yes, until she finishes the test and realizes that I'm not—"

"Preliminary tests show that you are not pregnant, Citizen Euan," she said, relief coloring her voice as she turned around. "I'm running a secondary test, just in case, but I think you can safely say you dodged a—"

The screen cut off, and she stopped midsentence, cocking her head at the wall. A moment later, her pad was in her hands and she was accessing something on it. Then it also stopped working. This had to be Leo finally gaining control, and I felt a smile begin to form on my lips. I watched with growing amusement as her tapping on the screen grew louder and louder, until she finally made a guttural sound of irritation and tucked the thing into her pocket.

"It seems there's some sort of technical difficulty going on with this wall unit," she announced. "I can let you go, seeing as the preliminary test was negative, but policy is to run an additional test for confirmation."

She stopped talking, and I realized that she had intended her statement as a question. I looked to Quess and Grey. It took me a moment to remember it was my decision to make, which obviously was "yes," as it would get her out of the room and us back on track to rescuing Maddox.

"Would you mind terribly double checking? I mean, don't get me wrong—I really don't want a different answer than the one you just gave me. But I don't know if I could sleep if there was a chance that—"

The woman smiled. "That's very responsible of you," she said. "I'm sure it'll come up negative, but I'll need a few minutes, okay?"

I nodded meekly and kept my eyes down to the ground until the flash of light had signaled her departure. Then I looked up and took a step away from the two men in the room, shooting them a sarcastic look.

"Okay, the next time we come up to the Medica, you two get to be the ones who are pregnant."

Quess laughed, but Grey still looked guilty.

"It really *was* dumb," Leo chimed in, and before I knew it, I was smiling against my will. "Because they are running DNA tests on everyone coming through. Luckily, I managed to prevent yours from being read, but only just."

"Thanks, Leo," I said to him. "And I'm already over it," I added, focusing on Grey. "I'm just relieved Leo managed to save all of us from getting booted out of here."

"My pleasure," Leo said, his face reforming on the wall. "And the good news is, I've managed to gain some control over their systems."

"Good job," Grey said. "Where's Maddox? Have you figured out how to run a search?"

"I have. She was just checked in with a broken leg, and a Medic is in there with her now. There are three others in the room with her as well. One is a Knight by the name of Devon

Alexander, and the other two are members of the IT department... with the ranks of... Inquisitor? What's an Inquisitor?"

"Bad news," Quess murmured. "Internal security, basically."

"Can you get us there?" I asked, not wanting to lose focus on the task at hand. "We should get moving."

"Of course I can, but you'll need a change of wardrobe if you want to go about this without attracting attention." As he spoke, a long, narrow drawer pulled away from the wall unit, propelled by some invisible hand, and the three of us closed the distance to see what was inside.

"Oh, good," Quess said, immediately pulling out one of the white Medic uniforms. "I was just about to ask you for these."

I grabbed a uniform as well. Being in Medic white was the easiest way to blend in inside the Medica, so having the uniforms was imperative to moving around without attracting attention, and I was pleased that we had them.

I didn't immediately start to change, as I had a more pressing question for Leo that no one had bothered to ask yet. "Leo, where's Jasper?"

Leo frowned and shook his head. "He was transferred back into the mainframe two days ago," he replied. "There are signs of him everywhere here, though, and I'm learning the system based on his preferences. I like his style—he has a lot of shortcuts. I have a feeling he and I are really going to get along when I get to meet him."

Quess barked out a laugh, and I gave him a confused look in response, baffled by what he found so funny.

"Shortcuts," he said simply, still chuckling to himself.

I looked at Grey in hope of some sort of clarification, but he shrugged, and I rolled my eyes and moved on.

"Can you get to him?" I asked. "And while you're at it, can you keep Myra away from this room?"

"I'm on it," he said. "The entire floor is experiencing a wall unit failure, so she has to head up a level to confirm the test. I have a few more delays in store for her as well, so we have a *little* time before she finally makes it back to discover you've left a room that was on lockdown. By then, you'll hopefully have Maddox and be gone before the alarm is raised, but there isn't a lot of room for error. As for getting to Jasper... I'm not sure I should. The main-frame is where Scipio is, and while I am an AI, he's much, much bigger than me, and he'd treat me as a threat. I'm not sure my programming could survive it if he decided to attack outright. Besides, if there is a chance he's being controlled, then he could report my presence to whoever is controlling him."

That hadn't occurred to me, and I absorbed that information, filing it under "don't ever suggest that again." The last thing I wanted to do was alert any potential shadow group to the exis-tence of Leo, as I was certain that no matter which "side" they were on, or however it worked, they'd all want to take control of him. And I wasn't sure we could survive with what little informa-tion we did have on them. It was hard to anticipate an enemy you knew nothing about, and foolish to reveal your card before you had a chance to learn.

But that didn't change the fact that Jasper was in the main-frame and not here. I had no idea why he'd been transferred, but wouldn't let go of the suspicion that it was because he had helped us. I wasn't sure how yet, or even if it was possible, but I wanted to look into trying to find a way to get him out. I owed him that, at least, for what he had done for me.

"I'm sorry that he wasn't here for you to meet," I told Leo.

He gave me a grateful, yet disappointed smile. "I'm not too sorry. I'm glad for the opportunity to help you. It was good that you brought me after all."

"I agree. But we needed Jasper for more than just help with Maddox. We gave him a pill to analyze a week ago, and we were hoping he could provide us with the formula. We need it to keep our ones from alerting the Tower to our presence. He promised us he'd put it on a secret server somewhere. Is there any way to find it?"

"I'll look," he replied. "Can you give me an approximate date and time, please?"

"Um...." I scrambled, trying to remember just how long it had been since we were here last. It felt like ages ago, but as I tried to recall how much time had passed, I realized it was a lot less than I had thought. "Five days."

Grey blinked, his gaze growing distant, and then he nodded, confirming my estimation on the timeline. "We were here late, maybe two or three in the morning."

"Thank you. I'll deactivate for a moment to let you get changed in privacy."

The screen cut out before I could ask any questions about the plan, and once again, I found myself in the awkward situation of getting changed with Quess and Grey in the same room as me.

I quickly turned and began to change anyhow, hearing the sounds of their movements behind me, and in order to distract myself from the discomfort, began to talk.

"Well, with Leo in the system, I think we have a real chance to get Maddox out of here."

"The problem is with Devon," Grey said from where he was

standing behind me. "I don't like the idea of going up against him."

"Neither do I," Quess agreed. "I mean, what's our plan here?"

I hesitated, and then filled them in on what I had worked out in my head. I'd given it a lot of thought on the way up, and the best way was to use non-lethal force to render any guards unconscious. I wanted to avoid an all-out fight, as that would draw way too much attention. I kind of hoped that this would be the first mission we pulled off without anyone learning about it until after we had left.

"I figured we'd just ask Jasper—Leo, now, I guess—to let us borrow one of those injection things filled with some sort of knock-out drug. With the uniforms, we could go in under the guise of being trainees, get close, and then inject them."

"Knock-out... drug?" Quess said, smiling at me. "You're talking about a fast-acting general anesthetic, and unfortunately, they do not keep them in the wall units. It's a high-end item in the black market, so it's kept under careful lock and key."

Disappointment flared over me, but I pushed through it, trying to think of some other way. "Well..." I said, thinking about it. "Look, I don't know—if we could find a way to take them out all at once, preferably without a fight, that would be ideal. If you guys come up with something, let me know, but let's move and think, okay? I'm getting nervous standing around in here. Leo only bought us limited time with our Medic. Let's not waste it."

"Agreed," Grey said. "Are you decent?"

"I am," I said, turning back around.

They turned as well, and we did a mutual inspection to make sure our uniforms were smoothed of any wrinkles and folds, giving us a pristine look that would keep us moving unnoticed.

Our regular clothes went into a bag Quess was carrying, while our batons came out, Quess handing one over to Grey and me.

"Devon's in there," Quess said. "Do you think he's talking to Doxy?"

I exhaled and tightened my grip on my baton. I hadn't forgotten Leo's words, but I had been ignoring them for as long as possible. Devon was in the same building as I was. In fact, he was so close that I could practically taste him. My stomach churned, and a deep fear settled into my bones, as I recalled the look on his face as he'd detached Cali's lead.

There had been nothing there, no trace of humanity or empathy—just a pure, deep calm, and certainty that was so unfathomable to me that it was still haunting my dreams. How anyone could be so blasé about killing another human was beyond me.

The councilors' offer suddenly came to mind, and I tightened my hand into a fist. If we could figure out a way to knock Devon out, it would be all too easy to just finish the job. They'd given me their permission to do it, and they would consider that my acceptance of their deal.

Killing him went against my initial plan to leave here with Maddox unnoticed, but it was tempting to reconsider. The only thing that gave me pause was the fact that Scipio 2.0 knew the moment a person expired—and in the case of unexpected death, would notify the nearest Knights to investigate. Killing him now would jeopardize our plans to save Maddox, and I refused to do that.

He could die later. I had a week, after all.

"Are you all dressed?" Leo asked, mercifully providing me with a distraction from the thoughts now circling inside my head.

"We are," I said, and his face returned to the screen.

"I've got a path to Maddox for you. They've patched up her leg, and the Medic is just grabbing some additional medicine for her at the request of the Champion."

"How close is she?" I asked, thinking of all the people we would undoubtedly come across. The farther we had to go, the more chance of discovery, but we had no way of controlling that.

"Not far. Maybe a minute away, but you'll be going up a few floors."

"Good. Let's get to it, then."

"I've got the net," Quess said, crossing over to the wall unit to retrieve it. We were going to need it again to transport Leo once it was time to leave.

"Right. Follow the indicators. Hopefully I'll be able to transmit to your net shortly. I'm still trying to get the net relays connected to the system under my control, but it's taking time. I'll do my best to guide you."

"Thank you, Leo," I said, and in response, a portion of the wall slid back, revealing an opening. I realized that it wasn't the side where we had come in, and then followed Grey through, my heart already pounding.

The hall Leo led us into was different than the ones we had walked through to get there. It was a narrow corridor, barely wide enough for two people, and I looked around nervously, searching for any sign of life. Luckily, it was currently empty.

A glimmer of something on one of the seemingly plain white walls caught my attention, and I watched as a dot appeared, followed by a series of lines reading *Follow Me*. The dot shot off to the right, disappearing around a curve and leaving a green trail behind it.

"Stick to the right side of the hallway," Quess whispered. "This is a service-way—the Medics use it to get around quickly from room to room. You always walk to the right."

That was smart—it created mutually exclusive lanes that allowed for an easy flow of traffic in the tight confines of the hall.

"Is this how they always manage to enter and exit without you ever running into them in the hall?" I asked as I began to follow the trail.

"Yeah," Quess replied from behind me. "Everyone at the Practitioner level and above has access to these halls. Residents and Students are relegated to the main halls, to deal with patients out there."

I listened carefully to the new information, quickly determining how it would affect us. I realized that if anyone challenged my status as a Medic, I would need to, at the very least, make sure I knew what rank I needed to pretend to be.

"Right," I said. "Let's go."

It was hard to resist the urge to creep down the hall, and I had to remind myself to act like I belonged. With every step I took forward, the stiff white fabric of the uniform felt tighter and more confining. My baton was tucked along my side, held tight under a stiff arm. I might have been disguised as a Medic, but when and if the time came for a fight, I wanted to be prepared.

Hence the baton.

A Medic rounded the corner, heading the opposite direction, and for a moment I was certain that he was going to take one look and recognize us. After all, we had just been here to bust out Zoe. He had to have seen so many images of my face, of Grey's face, that even our altered hair and eye color wouldn't spare us.

I kept my eyes glued to the dark onyx floor, reminding myself that Myra had interacted with us without noticing anything, and held my breath as he drew nearer, my hand ready to catch my baton as soon as his shout rang out. He was taller than me, but I was fast, and all I had to do was touch him and he'd be down.

He drew even closer, and I tensed, watching his movements from the side of my eyes, waiting for him to do something—

anything... and then he was past. I heard Quess give a congenial, "How're you doing?" as they presumably passed each other, and then nothing, save our footsteps as he walked farther and farther away from us.

I exhaled slowly and tried to work some of the tension from my shoulders. This was going to work. I looked back to check that Grey and Quess were okay, and noticed that they seemed just as relieved as I was. It made me feel better knowing they were with me on this, and I turned my gaze back down the hall, following the green light. Even though that man hadn't recognized me, it didn't mean someone else wouldn't, so I had to be careful and not get too confident.

The green dot led us to a flight of stairs leading up steeply to where the hall continued, some eight feet off the floor. We crossed up, and came to a hall with a low ceiling—low enough that I had to walk through while ducking slightly, and then emerged on the other side with an identical staircase heading down. It took some idle puzzling on my part, and I realized that, from the width and shape, we were crossing over one of the patient halls below. The inner design was fascinating; I had no idea these halls were even here, let alone how they worked, but they were well designed, running through and around every patient room, like a honeycomb.

It was *truly* fascinating, actually; we had to periodically stop when a hall would suddenly become blocked off, walls sliding up from the floor to create the entryway to each patient room. Some of the service-ways ran just between the rooms and the public halls, and in order to keep the patients from cutting through the service-way unexpectedly, the walls shot up out of the ground to stop the flow of traffic inside them, while letting the patient think they had stepped directly into the room. Another wall would drop down behind them once they stepped into the room, creating the inner walls and hiding the hall. Medics would wait patiently, watching a display that came up on the walls blocking their way that showed the patient's movement. Once the patient was inside, the walls blocking the service-way would drop back down and the Medics could continue moving unimpeded.

We passed several other Medics moving through the halls, and after seeing so many without any response, I began to relax into my disguise. It was working.

Now I just wished we would get to Maddox already. Even though I was fairly certain that we'd only been walking for a few short minutes, it felt like it had been much longer. Maddox had just been checked, but a broken leg was an easy fix. One day in a weaver cast would fix her right up, and it was simple and quick to put one on—I'd gotten familiar with the process during my apprenticeship classes.

I followed the green trail down another hall, my nerves practically split ends from my tension and fear, and I almost missed the dot holding fast to one spot and pulsing slightly, like a beacon. I picked up the pace as soon as it registered that we were finally here, and motioned to Grey and Quess. We came to a stop in front of it.

A line of text appeared, reading, *Line up behind Liana.* Confused, I looked back at Grey and Quess, who shrugged and then moved into position behind me. There was a soft hiss as the walls came up, sealing us inside.

"Sorry about that," Leo said softly, his voice sounding from the wall next to us. "But I have to be careful not to trip the security settings, and using the speakers in the hallway would definitely have given my presence away. As such, thank you for trusting me."

"Of course," I said. "Are we here?"

"See for yourself." A moment later, the wall in front of us seemed to dissolve. I took a step back into Grey, my heart pounding in terror. Devon Alexander was standing two feet away, staring right at us.

My baton was already in my palm before Grey's strong hand gripped my shoulder, holding me in place. "Wait," he whispered, and I hesitated, trying to understand what he saw that I didn't. "He can't see us," he added, and I looked up at Devon's face, realizing Grey was right. Devon's dual-colored eyes weren't focused on us at all. In fact, they looked distant, as if he were caught in some deep thought and staring at a fixed point on the wall.

It was only coincidence that we happened to be standing behind it.

"Sorry," Leo said. "I should have warned you."

I took a moment to collect myself, a sharp tingle of nerves radiating across my skin as if I were being stabbed by a thousand needles at once. I still couldn't get over how close Devon was to me. Just behind that door. One small wall panel away.

And as Champion of the Knights, he could override the door if he really wanted to.

Or their Medic could come back at any moment.

I looked at the walls on either side of us. "Leo, can you bring up video of the hall? Are you monitoring it?"

"I am. I am also redirecting traffic around us, but I can only do it for so long." My stomach churned, and I knew that it was risky to wait much longer. We still had the potential threat of Myra returning to our original exam room and discovering we were gone. Once that happened, it would only be a matter of time before the alarm was sounded. We needed as much time as we could squeeze together to figure out how to get the drop on the three men inside.

"How long?" Quess asked sharply, and the walls flickered for a moment—something that had also happened back in the office when Leo was thinking. My eyes dragged back up to the wall, where I saw Devon turning away, and I was relieved to see that the lights were only affected in here.

"About four and a half minutes," he said. "That's as long as I can redirect traffic before someone picks up on the fact that the area has somehow become off limits."

"That's not enough time," Quess whispered. I looked at him, already in agreement. "We still have to figure out—"

"He's talking," Grey said.

Quess paused while I turned my focus back to the room and saw Devon moving off to one side to stand opposite a bald man with a dark goatee and flat black eyes. His uniform was black, too, marking him as an Inquisitor. Behind the two men, Maddox lay on a table, her eyes closed. Her leg was encased in a bio-cast, which would already be working on the bone Zoe and Eric had broken.

She was clearly unconscious. They had likely drugged her with something, whether it was before or after she got here, I didn't know. But it meant they felt confident that they could speak in secret. They would be saying something they didn't expect anyone else to hear.

And we were in a position to hear it.

"Leo, can you get audio for us?" I asked, and three seconds later, Devon's voice filled the room.

"—a match, and that changes everything."

The bald man raised a black eyebrow and shook his head, his face stoic. "This changes nothing. We are imbedded too deeply at this point to turn back now."

"She is my daughter," Devon spat, one arm snapping out to point at her. "I need time to explain her heritage to her! To teach her about what we've been doing. If I die before that..."

So Devon was a legacy after all. Lacey and Strum had said as much, but they hadn't provided any evidence to support their claim. I found myself warmed by the news, in spite of how alarming it was, because it meant that they had been right about their suspicions and they hadn't asked me to kill a man for the wrong reasons.

Not that I needed a particularly good reason to want him dead. He'd already taken so much from me—Cali... Roark... possibly even Gerome, my former mentor and the man I was accused of murdering. But he was not my mission right now. Only Maddox was.

"It is a risk you're going to have to take," another voice said, and I watched as a second Inquisitor came into view from behind the wall closest to the door. He must've been leaning there, watching them talk, and even now he only half came into view— just enough to block our view of Maddox.

"Four minutes," Leo announced as the newcomer continued. I continued to watch, my mind still trying to come up with a plan for how to get Maddox out of the room.

"This plan has taken half a century to enact, and never before have any of the sects been as close as we are now! We cannot afford to take a back seat while you train your progeny."

"Besides, there's no guarantee that she will even take to your teachings," the bald man said, still looking rather bored—and I got the feeling that this was his general demeanor all the time. But that still didn't make him look any less dangerous. "You killed the girl's mother."

"I regretted having to do that, but she knew too much!"

Baldy looked over to the man standing with his back to us, and the man shrugged his shoulders. Devon looked back and forth between the two of them, and crossed his arms over his chest. "What is it?"

"She had a legacy net," Baldy said, and Devon stiffened.

"There was nothing in her background to indicate—"

"It was there, but buried deep. We traced her line back to one of the earlier families we eradicated within the first seventy-five years. We're not sure how, but apparently one of the nets slipped past us, and was likely passed down from generation to generation with no one knowing what it was. Perhaps it was in a keepsake that broke—who knows? All we know is that she figured out what it was. We pulled it out of her when we recovered her body."

Even though I was watching and trying to come up with a plan, I couldn't help but hang on their every word as they spoke, intrigued by their conversation. So much was being revealed here, things that generated a flurry of questions inside me. They'd been working for half a century doing *what?* They'd come closer to *what* than any other group before? Who were the other sects, and why weren't they working together? And what the heck was a legacy net? It clearly wasn't a standard net, given Devon's reaction to it. If anything, it seemed like it was a net passed down between family members, which tracked with what Lacey and Strum had told me about these groups being kept within family units.

And Cali... They seemed surprised she had been in posses-
sion of one, and so was I. Why hadn't she mentioned it to us, and
why was it important? What did finding one on her mean
to them?

"I want it," Devon said, but Baldy shook his head.

"We will pass all the relevant data we can harvest over to
you," he said. "In the meantime, we kept your progeny safe from
harm, and are returning her to you as a gesture of goodwill. You
may have her to train, but you will continue to act in accordance
to your plan, with absolutely zero delays. If your daughter starts to
interfere with that..."

He trailed off, and Devon scowled at both of them. "Are you
threatening me?"

"Yes," replied the one with his back to us. "Emphatically so.
You screwed up when you let your wife get too close, and that
screw-up almost cost us five years of hard work. If we hadn't
caught that letter she sent before it reached the council—"

"It was twenty years ago," Devon grated out. "And thanks to
you stopping it, she figured out that I wasn't alone in this, and ran.
Taking my unborn child with her... Not that I knew that at the
time, of course."

"If we *hadn't* stopped it, you'd be locked within the depths of
the Citadel for committing a terrorist-level offense."

"And without the program my forbearers spent lifetimes on,
you wouldn't have been able to enact this plan at all! I am the last
of my line, and it is my plan that we are enacting to—"

They were from different legacy families, I realized, my eyes
widening. And they had somehow come together to form an
alliance to achieve their mutual goal. I could only assume that
the plan they were referring to was the source of all the prob-

lems within 2.0, and that they had come up with the plan together.

It was also clear that Devon was somewhat under their thumb, given how he kept trying to defend his actions. Maybe I could use that against them, find a way to create mistrust between them or something... Perhaps if I could get them to think Devon was betraying them, they could kill him for me.

"We were within two generations of figuring it out," Baldly said blandly, stroking his goatee. "Yes, you provided us with an accelerated timeline, but now that it is in play, I need to tell *him* that things will continue to proceed as agreed upon, even with the added complication of your progeny." The way he stressed the word *him* told me that whomever they were referring to was probably the most powerful of all of them, and clearly not with them. He certainly expected Devon to know whom he meant, and it was clear that Devon did.

Devon pursed his lips and looked over at Maddox. "Things will proceed," he said after a moment. "But I would have your family's word that no one will harm a hair on her head. And that you'll give me time. I have years of Cali to undo in her, and that will take time."

I bit my lip. While I had no idea how Maddox would react to finding out Devon was her father, I did know that no matter what her reaction, Devon was not going to get a compliant daughter. Not even in the slightest. If anything, Maddox would probably try to kill him.

"If you keep her as far away from this as possible, until it is done," the man standing with his back to us said. "We cannot afford any potential threats at such a critical time. Do you understand?"

Devon nodded stiffly.

"Turn off the sound," I said, and it abruptly cut off. Truthfully, I could listen to them talk for much longer, but we were on a tight schedule, and I had wasted too much time eavesdropping. We really needed to come up with a plan. "How long do we have, Leo?" I asked.

"Three minutes," Leo cautioned. "Do you have any idea what you want to do?"

I bit my lip, a dozen hare-brained ideas popping into my head. "I suppose we could split up, try to enter from three different sides of the room. We catch them by surprise from all different angles, and hit them with our batons while they're still trying to figure out who to come after." I turned to Grey to find him looking thoughtfully through the still-clear wall. "What is it?"

"Well, I'm just wondering... Are these rooms completely sealed?"

"Completely sealed?" I repeated dumbly, trying to understand what he was getting at.

"They are!" Quess said excitedly, a wide grin splitting his face. "For quarantine procedures!"

"So?" I asked.

"They want me to lower the oxygen in the room," Leo informed me before either of them could explain. "It will knock them unconscious, allowing you to slip in, grab Maddox, and get back out."

"That's... genius," I said, giving Grey an appreciative smile. "Is there a catch?"

"They'll be unconscious for only a short time," Quess said. "Under a minute. And Maddox will be nothing but dead weight."

"Can you carry her?" Grey asked Quess, and I shared his

question. Maddox was solidly built, just as tall as Grey, but much more muscular. Being forced to carry her would slow us down, and we needed speed now more than ever. "Liana and I will need our hands free in case they wake up early."

Quess looked past us toward Maddox, his face thoughtful. Then he nodded. "Yes, but it would be even better if Leo could give us the drug we need to counter whatever they gave her."

There was a pause as we all looked expectantly toward Leo. The lights maintained a constant glow, showing that he wasn't in thought.

"I've spent most of my time cracking the controls," Leo said, "but I'll get into the patient records. Once you retrieve Maddox, I can give you a path to a clear room near the closest exit and bridge, and by then, I'll know what to give her to wake her up. Then I can download into the net there. We'll only have a window of forty-five seconds to a minute to get out of there, once I'm out of the system, before their security systems reset. An alarm will go off shortly afterwards, when it realizes that something went wrong. Don't worry—there won't be any trace of me in the system to find, as long as you don't forget me."

I nodded, licking my lips. "How much time do we have?"

"Just over two minutes," he said. "I've already started lowering the oxygen. I'll open the door in thirty seconds."

Turning, I watched through the clear glass as inside the room, Baldy and Devon were already beginning to sway, their eyes growing heavy, their chests heaving. Suddenly all three men dropped to their knees, their mouths open and gasping for air.

My mind flashed back to the woman being gassed in the Citadel, to her panicked breathing and bulging eyes, and I looked away, unable to watch without feeling a nervous panic come over me that I should do something, say something.

"I won't kill them," Leo reassured me, and from behind, I felt Grey's hand on my arm, sliding down to my hand and squeezing it gently.

I nodded and sucked in a deep, calming breath, forcing myself to look up. All three men were lying on the floor, still, and thankfully, my anxiety subsided.

"I'm pumping oxygen back in right now so you won't be affected," Leo said. "As soon as I open the doors, you need to move."

"Count us down," Quess suggested.

There was a pause, and then: "Five... four... three... two... one... Go!"

The door slid open and I slipped in, my baton ready. I stepped over the downed body of the man who'd had his back to us the entire time, and took the chance to get a look at his face as I went by. Everything about him screamed "normal," but in such a way that it was eerie. His face was neither too round, nor too angular, nor even too narrow, making it hard to really ascribe a shape. His nose was neither big nor small, and sat perfectly straight. His eyes were closed, so their color remained a mystery, but they were set well, proportioned evenly. His eyebrows weren't too thin or thick, his hair pretty much the same, though it was dark brown or black, and graying slightly.

He was the very definition of nondescript. Ultimately forgettable in a way that would make him impossible to discern from a throng of people. His was a face for forgetting, which made it a face that people ignored. A man like that was dangerous, because it meant he could get within arm's length, and chances were nobody would notice him.

I continued deeper into the room, stepping to one side to give Quess room to get to Maddox.

"Hurry up," I whispered, reaching Baldy first and bending over to remove the pulse shield from his fingers, disarming him. I tucked it into my pocket and then stood, moving over to Devon. Grey crossed the distance to the other Inquisitor to follow my lead, while Quess stalked forward, heading directly for Maddox.

"Don't take this the wrong way, Doxy," he muttered as I carefully stepped over Baldy to get closer to Devon's still form. "But I hope they didn't feed you."

I looked back to see him sliding his arms under Maddox's legs, then turned back to Devon, feeling the itch of urgency between my shoulder blades.

He had managed to pull his baton out from under him before he fell, and it now lay clutched in his fist on the floor. The tip was dull, but if he woke up before I got a chance to get it out of his hands, then we were in deep trouble.

I stepped closer to Devon, eyeing the baton. Quess grunted loudly as he picked up Maddox's muscular form. After a moment of agonizing debate, I reached out and put my boot on the baton, dragging it back with my foot.

To my relief, Devon's hand was still relaxed, and the baton slid away effortlessly. I continued to pull it back and then bent over to pick it up. My fingers were brushing the edges of it when Devon suddenly gave a sharp gasp, his head snapping up and around.

He blinked, his eyes narrowing in confusion, but before he could react I lashed out with my baton, my finger pressing down on the button to start a charge. The angle was sloppy, but I connected with his shoulder, and there was a sharp *zzt* as I held it for a second or two, then released the button, letting him drop back to the floor.

I grabbed his baton and jumped back, my hand shaking violently in the wake of such a close and personal confrontation with Devon Alexander, and I had to lower my arm to keep it from showing.

"Let's get out of here," I said.

"On it," Quess grunted, and I turned to see him stepping over the man by the door, Maddox draped over his shoulder. "What's our time?" he asked Leo.

"A minute," he replied, sounding nervous. "I may have overestimated my abilities—something is starting to catch on to the fact that I'm here."

"Are you okay?" I asked, nodding for Grey to go before me. The man by the door was still, but Baldy was already beginning to show signs of life—not as abruptly as Devon had, thankfully, but it was still alarming.

"I am, but we need to move."

I waited for Grey to get clear and then rose, turning around and making a beeline for the door. I was stepping over the downed figure of the man, feet from the door, when my stationary foot was suddenly jerked out from under me and I fell forward.

Grey reached for me as I fell, but it was too late; I barely got a chance to put my hands up before I struck. My chin impacted the floor with a violent crack, and my jaws clamped together so tight that I thought my teeth were going to shatter. Immediately, I felt a burning line of pain emanating from my chin—a raw burn that told me I was bleeding. I somehow managed to sit up, my hand going to my chin and coming away red with blood.

I stared at it, momentarily confused as to why I was bleeding, when something dark shot by too fast to make out. I pressed a hand to my chin to try to stop the blood and swiveled my head around, following the movement. I was surprised to see Grey struggling with Plain Face, whose eyes were now open, revealing murky brown irises. Grey must have leapt past me to come to my defense. That had been the thing that moved past me just moments ago.

Plain Face had tripped me. He must've woken up and realized what was going on.

I pulled my hand away from my chin and wiped it on my thigh, leaving a bloody red smear over the white uniform. I was bleeding, but not gushing, and Grey needed my help. Baldy seemed to be recovering more slowly than Plain Face and was clutching his head, as if it ached fiercely, while squinting around.

"Leo, get Quess and Maddox out of here," I said, making sure to grab both batons before picking myself up off the floor. "We'll have to catch up."

"No, wait! I—" Quess said, but whatever else he was going to say was lost behind the pneumatic hiss of the door shutting, sealing him in the hall and cutting him off.

Baldy eyed me, his hands lowering from his head to his sides, waiting to see what I would do. Grey and Plain Face continued their wrestling match, and I stepped around it, drawing closer to Baldy. I waited until I was just a few feet away before I suddenly spun around, hoping to catch him by surprise after walking toward him instead of running. It didn't work—he saw it coming and sidestepped—but he still seemed groggy from the oxygen deprivation, because he stumbled a few feet, trying to catch his balance.

I pressed the advantage, swinging at him again and pushing him back a few more feet. If I could knock him into a corner, then I could land a direct strike and then move to help Grey. Devon was already down. If I could just get these two down as well...

I renewed my efforts, thrusting and aggressively pushing him back. He seemed to catch his balance after a few feet or so, though, and planted his feet. I was ducking forward, my hand extending one baton forward as I tried to take advantage of his still-weakened state, when he suddenly spun around it, moving almost like liquid. I felt the hard strike of his elbow on my shoulder, pushing me off balance.

Planting my foot down quickly, I recovered and spun, flinching back a few inches to avoid the hard line of his knuckles as they swept across where my jaw had just been. I brought my arm around, catching his follow-up swing with the baton. Baldy caught it—too low on the baton for me to use the electrical charge—and before he could use it to yank me off balance, I pulled a knee to my chest and kicked out, pushing him back.

He hit the wall hard, and I drove the baton into his stomach before he could stop me, hitting him with the full charge. His body convulsed violently, and then I released him and turned to let him drop to the ground, my eyes already turning to assess Grey's situation.

He was still engaged in the wrestling match with Plain Face, his baton on the floor. He was holding the other man at bay, but both of them had their hands latched to the other's biceps, and were trying to shove each other over, trying to gain momentum while tripping the other.

Grey shoved Plain Face back a few feet, toward the wall, his muscles and legs straining. I drew close, my batons at the ready, but I couldn't use them on the man while they were touching— the charge would be conducted from one to the other. I had to wait for my moment.

Suddenly Grey did something clever with his feet, shifting his balance slightly while pivoting at the waist, and Plain Face pitched forward, over Grey's hip and shoulder and onto the floor. Grey reached out and snapped quick punches with his hand— once, twice, and then a third time—and after the third, Plain Face went slack, blood dripping from his nose.

Grey stood up, panting heavily and shaking his hand out, and turned to see me looking at him. He looked down at the man lying unconscious on the floor next to him and back up to me.

"Maddox gave me some lessons," he said, and I smiled, impressed at how much he had picked up.

"We need to go," I said. "Leo?"

"Yes. Quess has Maddox in the room now and is changing out her net so Devon won't be able to ping it. Do you want to go there or leave a different way?"

I looked at Grey. They were safer if we split up. Undoubtedly, Devon would direct the search for Grey and me, so splitting up was the best way to ensure both of their escapes.

"Different way," he answered for me, and I nodded my agreement as I bent over to pick up his baton. I handed it to him just as he said, "Tell Quess we'll download you on the way out. But we're going to need you in there for a little bit longer."

"Liana?"

"He's right, except doesn't Quess have Leo's net?"

"Nope, I do, actually," Grey said with a smirk, reaching for his shirt pocket.

I watched, pleased that *something* was at least going our way for once.

Then something wrapped around my chest, and suddenly up became down, left became right, and the world felt as it had disappeared beneath my feet. It took me a second to realize that I was falling, and then another second to realize that I wasn't falling—I was being thrown.

My hand went to the arm around my chest, the vice-like iron band of it encircling me, and then I hit the ground shoulders, neck, and head first. The air slammed out of my lungs with a sharp huff, and I lay stunned, staring up at the brilliant whiteness overhead.

There was a sharp ringing in my ears. I blinked, trying to clear my thoughts from the cobwebs that seemed to have amassed, while pain radiated from my back and skull. I dimly heard Grey shout, and then the muffled sound of something happening overhead, but I couldn't make my muscles move right. My hands felt along the floor, but I couldn't press them against it. My legs were heavy, weighing me down, holding me in place.

I fought through it, first by sucking air into my stunned diaphragm. My chest was tight, my breath coming out in a sharp gasp, but I exhaled and sucked in more, forcing it in. My eyes watered, but I blinked the tears away, managing to roll over onto my side.

The move cost me, and I panted, closing my eyes against the searing pain in my head. Air helped, though, and I breathed through my mouth, trying to keep the nausea down.

Grey's sudden cry of pain made my eyes snap open, and I

blearily looked around to see a crimson-clad figure standing over a white-clad one. The one in white was already trying to push up off the ground, while the one in crimson put his foot on the other's back in a solid blow, forcing him back down.

Grey fell hard, and my eyes bulged when I realized that Devon was already back up. My charge hadn't had enough of an effect on him. I looked around dimly, searching for something that I could use as a weapon—my batons were here somewhere, but I couldn't figure out where they had fallen.

Movement from Devon distracted me, and I looked up from my searching to see him bending over at the waist and grabbing Grey by the hair. A baton was in his other hand, and as I watched, Devon met my eyes with an angry sneer.

"You stupid brat," he spat, his eyes darting around. "I almost wouldn't have recognized you. What have you done with the computer in here? Who were you talking to? Where is my daughter?"

My mouth trembled, but I met his gaze. "Put him down and I'll tell you." My hands were sweaty, and I took a moment to slowly wipe them on my hips, pausing when I felt a hard lump in one of the pockets. It was the pulse shield, the one I had taken off of Plain Face.

His dual-colored eyes narrowed, giving me a long, considering look. "This is a trap, isn't it?" he said, his eyes darting around again. "But not by them. By someone else." His eyes shot back over to me, and I froze.

He knew that someone on the council was trying to kill him, and he had correctly assumed that I was a part of it, which made him even more dangerous and unpredictable. I had to convince

him that wasn't the case. As long as he held Grey and that baton...
he'd kill him.

"It's not," I said. "I swear. We just came to get Maddox."

"Is that her name?" he said, his voice hushed. I watched him
look away, toward the door, and I shoved my hand into my pocket,
withdrawing the pulse shield and clutching it in the palm of my
hand. "You took her from me," he announced, and I froze, holding
the weapon tightly. I chanced a glance up and saw him staring
down at me, his face frozen in a mask of rage. "It's only fitting I
should take something from you."

My eyes widened, his sudden change in demeanor too fast to
anticipate, and then he drove the baton down into the back of
Grey's neck. I heard it click, even as my mouth opened to shout
"No!" and then Grey's eyes snapped open, and he began to
scream.

The sound of Grey's agonized cry was loud and painful enough that I cringed, resisting the urge to clap my hands over my ears and shrivel away. Instead, I looked down and shoved my fingers through the slots of the pulse shield, palming the hard metal device. I held it up and fired it through a haze of tears. As soon as I stroked my thumb over the trigger, my arm shot backwards, so hard that my elbow and shoulder immediately went numb with an icy wash of pain.

I ignored it. Just like I ignored my back and head and chin, focusing only on somehow forcing my knees and legs to hold me. I climbed up, numbly looking around, my hand shaking slightly. I became aware of my breathing—harsh and guttural—and I wiped the tears from my eyes.

The force of the pulse shield in the confined space had shattered several of the special panels on the wall. They must've been filled with some sort of powder, because now the room was blanketed in a white haze. As I inhaled shakily, I realized it was drying out my mouth and lungs, leaving a slight burn in the aftermath.

I moved forward, my stiff legs dragging on the ground as I searched the mist and debris for Grey. As I stepped forward, the ball of my foot didn't quite connect with the ground but slipped on something long, hard, and round, and I dipped over—agonizingly slowly—to pick up a baton, curling my fingers around the familiar feel of the handle.

I closed my eyes, fighting the wave of dizziness that accompanied me as I stood back up, and then focused on finding Grey. He was hurt. I had to find him, had to get him away from—

I froze when some of the white mist settled in front of me, revealing Devon. He was down on the ground again, his eyes closed. The wall behind him flickered where he had hit it and damaged the lighting unit. Blood dripped from a cut on his head, pooling around his eye before dripping off his nose. I found myself hoping he was dead as I stared at him, and then shuffled around, ignoring the aches in my side.

I moved a few feet away, swinging the baton in front of me, trying to clear the mist, and found Grey slumped against the wall, looking blankly forward at the floor. His brown eyes moved up to me when I dropped to my knees in front of him, and I reached for his face.

He didn't react when I placed my hands on the sides of his head. He just stared up at me.

"Grey?" I whispered softly.

He blinked, his brown eyes flat and empty, and then looked away—up and around, and then back down again, staring at his hands.

I watched, unable to comprehend his behavior. "Grey?" I

repeated. He looked back up at me. Again, there was nothing. No sign of anything behind his eyes. Just a hollow emptiness.

I shook my head; I was being ridiculous. His eyes were open. He was fine. "You're fine," I said, unable to keep my internal thoughts internal. He watched me as I began to smooth his clothes, straightening them. "You're fine," I repeated. "You are—Devon only did it for a moment, just a moment. Your eyes are open, and you're... you're fine."

He remained mute, his eyes watching, vacant, and empty. Void. No hint of any emotion or thought. Not even a flicker of recognition. I felt my hands begin to shake, and snatched them back away from him, fear so thick in my throat I felt like it was choking me.

"Grey?" I said, my voice cracking.

Nothing. Not even the slightest sign of interest. I felt tears begin to form as I continued to shake my head, trying to deny the reality in front of me. I reached out on impulse and grabbed the front of his uniform.

"Grey!" I shouted, giving him a little shake.

His arms didn't come up to stop me. His eyes didn't show fear or alarm. There was... no one there.

"GREY!" I screamed, the thought so terrifying I couldn't possibly accept it. My hand darted out, slapping him hard enough on the cheek to leave an outline on the side of his jaw. His head lolled to one side. Then around and back up, his deep brown eyes watching me, non-reactive to the fact that I had hurt him.

My hands flew to my mouth to cover my sob, and I crawled closer to him. This couldn't be happening—it couldn't. He was awake, alive. He was there, he was... he was just stunned. I hadn't failed him. I hadn't.

"Liana." I became aware of Leo's voice and looked around, surprised to see the mist dissipating. "I'm venting the room. Is Grey okay?"

I looked at Grey, my mind still unable to comprehend his position. "I don't know," I said, my voice roughened. "He's not responding to me. It's like he doesn't even know my face. Oh my God, Leo... Why doesn't he know my face?"

"Devon hurt him, badly. I can tell you how bad it is, but you need to get him to the wall unit."

I looked around the room for the wall unit, and found it a few feet away. The examination slab sat three feet off the floor. I looked at the distance, and the height, and then back to Grey, considering. I wasn't strong enough.

I needed to use my lashes to get him there. The gear in the back was strong enough to pull both our weights up, so it could handle him. I just needed a place to run the line so I could hoist him up. I scanned the ceiling and spotted a hook over the examination slab, likely there for this exact reason—to help lift an unconscious patient onto the table.

I grabbed a bead and pulled, unraveling several handfuls of the line. I quickly adjusted Grey so that his back was to the examination table, and threaded the lash bead through the metal eyelet on the back of his uniform, tying it into a knot. I was halfway through when a sound behind the door caused me to jump.

"What is that?" I demanded.

"Reinforcements. We don't have a lot of time."

I strode across the room, letting out the lash line as I went. The thumping continued, and I picked up the pace, hopping onto the examination slab and standing right on it. I rose to my tiptoes and used a long length of line doubled over so that I could slip it over the hook. It worked, and a moment later, I was down on the floor, slowly reeling the line in and dragging Grey's still body across the floor. I hoisted him up, even though the lack of any response to what I was doing to him was nauseating me, and stopped when he was partially over the slab.

I stepped closer, reeling in the slack I created by doing so, and pushed him over the slab, lowering him back down. As soon as he was down, I untied the knot and retracted the line, standing back.

The wall unit flared up, a part of it flickering as it began to run a scan. I took a step back, my hands wringing nervously as I waited for the screen to appear on the flat white surface just over him.

An image of a brain popped into view as the purple-and-blue lights from the scanner swept over and around his skull. Grey stared blindly ahead, his eyes not twitching as it happened, seemingly oblivious to all of it.

"His net overloaded," Leo said, his voice appalled, and I clamped my teeth together as the image rotated, giving me a top view. I could see the net laced over his brain, the tendrils forming an interlocking network that resembled a spider web. The area around the net tendrils in Grey's cortex were scorched black, the synaptic response in the area minimal.

"Oh my God," I breathed, my baton dropping from nerveless fingers with a sharp clatter. I looked down at Grey. It wasn't possible—someone like him just couldn't be *gone*. He was compassionate, kind, and so self-assured, to the point that it made him cocky, but it was so... him. He'd given me reason to hope, introduced me to people who didn't make me feel quite so alone, and... he cared about me.

"He's braindead, Liana," Leo said softly. As if I didn't get it. As if I couldn't see the damage done by Devon.

The sound of glass scraping behind me caused me to whirl, and I saw Devon starting to move. The Champion groaned, and I felt something terrible and angry rise up and seize my heart, clenching it tightly. It held me up over the despair that I had once again failed someone I was trying to protect, replacing it with something more primal: the urge to eliminate a proven threat now and forever. The despair would wait, but this rage would not, and I knew that only one of us was going to leave this room alive. He'd now stolen away three people I cared about.

I was bending over to pick up my baton, and my fingers had just closed around it when Leo's voice—tinged with urgency—brought me up short, giving pause to the deadly calm that had gripped me.

"Liana, where is that net you brought me here with?"

I looked at the wall unit, surprised to see Grey flipped over, the automatic tools already making an incision on the back of his neck. "What are you doing?" I gasped, my heartbeat accelerating even higher. "Stop that!" He was doing something—something that would hurt Grey, make it worse, maybe even kill him. I reached out with a hand, intent on stopping it manually, when something came down in front of my fingers. I yanked them back just in time to keep from connecting with the static screen Leo had just manifested. It wouldn't hurt, but I'd lose all feeling for an hour or so if I touched it.

"Leo!"

"I am trying to help him, Liana! Now where is that net?" Leo said desperately, and I checked over my shoulder. Devon was now on his hands and knees, his breath coming in hard pants. He was hurt, and not quite to his feet, but he would be soon. I didn't have time to find out what Leo was doing for Grey—I had to just trust him.

"Grey's pocket," I informed him, knowing that the tools in the wall unit could retrieve it, and turned around to face Devon, my priorities tumbling down. I was going to keep Grey safe while Leo did... whatever he did.

And I had to kill Devon. I had to if I wanted to keep everyone safe. I didn't care about this war or anything else... but he was a monster.

He got one foot up, panting, and turned his head toward me. Half his face was now covered in blood from the cut on his forehead, and as I watched, he swiped his fingers over his eyes, smearing the blood aside so he could view me more clearly.

I tightened my grip on the baton, watching him. He made as if to move to his feet, and then we both froze as the door leading to the service-way jumped open an inch, coming to a grinding halt. I heard excited shouts through the door, and turned back to Devon, who was now grinning at me.

"Give up," he said, leaning over to spit blood out of his mouth. "They're going to get in. If you turn yourself in, I promise I'll spare your family."

Adrenaline surged through me, and a tingle that had started to gather at the base of my spine suddenly shot through my arms, making them quiver with unspent energy, giving me the feeling that I could do anything. If this had been a fairy tale, I probably would've been able to throw fire from my fingertips. But it wasn't, and the only thing driving me was pure, unadulterated rage.

I was going to make him pay for what he'd done. "I'd be more worried about how long you'll be stuck in here with me before they get to you," I growled.

Devon seemed not to notice. He leaned to one side, looking around me at Grey. "Who's helping you? Is it a sentient or just another dummy replicate program?" I kept my mouth shut, and he shrugged, nonplused by my lack of response. "It makes no difference," he said congenially. "I'll find out soon enough. I'll dig whatever it is out and rip it to shreds."

He laughed, the backs of his fingers dusting off his shoulder, and then suddenly he launched himself at me, a guttural cry erupting from his throat. I had been waiting for him to move, and, pivoting on my left heel, I spun around. I brought the baton down, my finger on the charge, striking him in the thigh. Or at least, what should've been the thigh—but he had used his lashes to alter his direction midair, jerking violently to one side and missing my baton.

I looked up, watching as he hit the wall feet first, his arm already extended toward me, lash bead flying. Instinctually, I swept my baton up and around, and it connected with the lash bead, knocking it aside. I dropped the baton into my left hand and pulled up my right, using my thumb to hit the pulse shield even as Devon swan-dove through the air at me, his face contorted in rage.

The pulse missed, though, and he hit me, his weight dragging me to the ground. I landed hard with him on top of me, but within seconds he was upright, his hands wrapped around my throat.

I gasped, my hands snapping up to grab his wrists as he began to squeeze. A white haze started to form across my vision as all of the blood became trapped inside my head, making me light-headed. I fought it, trying to get my feet under my knees so I could lift him off of me, try to dislodge him. But he was straddling me, his weight pinning my legs down.

I tried to inhale, but the grip was too tight and my throat felt like it was caught in a vacuum, unable to retain any oxygen. I could hear my heartbeat starting to slow in my ears, and looked up to see a wild and savage grin on Devon's face. He was taking pleasure in my death, and it scared me. Even as I slipped further and further down into unconsciousness, I realized that his face would be the last thing I would see.

On the heels of that, I realized that I had failed. Devon was going to win, and even though I wanted nothing more than to stop it, I had lost. I was dying.

My eyes shuttered closed, not willing to let Devon be the final thing I saw before I died, and I conjured up an image of Grey and me, one of his strong hands on my waist, the other cupping my head as he drew his lips down toward mine.

Then air.

Sweet, clean, crisp, beautiful air rushing into my lungs, while the blood drained rapidly from my head, leaving me dizzy and disoriented in its wake. I rolled over to my side, instinctively curling my legs to my chest, and heard the sound of fighting somewhere behind me. I crawled away from it, a fresh surge of adrenaline giving my limbs mobility, before turning.

Grey was up, his back to me, holding Devon up by the throat with one hand. Devon's hands grabbed at Grey's wrist, clawing him, while his legs kicked out, trying to gain purchase. But Grey simply stood there, holding him up with one hand as if his struggles didn't affect him one bit. Devon's face grew redder and redder, swelling up until it looked just like a tomato.

Then Grey flexed his forearm, and Devon went still—after a stomach-wrenching snap.

I watched as Grey dropped Devon's body. Body, because Devon was most certainly dead. Then he turned toward where I was still cowering on the floor. I looked away, terrified that even after seeing him move, kill Devon, defend me, I'd be looking into the eyes of a stranger all over again.

I heard him move closer, the debris on the floor shifting. "Liana?" he said softly, and his hands came into view, reaching for me.

And then I threw myself into them, holding him close. "Is it you? How did Leo..."

Grey had stiffened under my impromptu embrace, and I trailed off, surprised that he wasn't hugging me. I pulled back, looking over him, making sure he hadn't been injured, and then dragged my eyes back up to his face to find him wearing an apologetic look.

"I'm sorry, Liana," he said sadly, meeting my eyes, and I felt my shock grow as I stared at the glowing blue and white light that seemed to emanate from the depths of his irises. "I'm doing all I can to help Grey, but it will take some time before I can repair the—"

"Leo?" I gasped, my hands coming up to grab Grey's shoulders, peering even more closely into his eyes. "Oh my *God*, is that you?"

Grey cocked his head, and then nodded. "It is."

I could only stare at Grey, unable to fully understand what was happening. The door hissed again, and Grey looked over first. I followed his gaze, only because I wasn't exactly sure what else I should be doing, and saw that the gap was now wide enough to fit an arm through.

In fact, someone was doing it right now—and as I watched them uncurl their fingers, I realized we were in the path of the blast. I started to react, but Grey was already doing it, racing forward and snapping a foot out, effortlessly breaking their arm with cold practicality before they could even shoot.

The arm quickly retreated with an agonized scream, and Grey moved over to me, dragging me out of the path of the door.

"I left an automated program in the computer," he whispered as he knelt down next to Devon's body, unzipping his uniform to get to the lash harness underneath, and detaching it. "We have

another thirty seconds before they get that door fully open. And
five seconds after that, the power will go down for fifteen seconds.
I want you to keep your head down, okay?"

I nodded, biting my lip and watching as he quickly donned
the lash harness. "Leo," I said, and he looked at me, his eyes glittering. "Why are you inside my boyfriend?"

Grey's lips parted, but it was Leo speaking, even with Grey's
voice. His tone was all wrong, words pronounced differently than
Grey would say them. It was both fascinating and horrifying, and
I was having difficulty understanding how helping Grey had led
him to doing this.

"It was the only thing I could do to keep him from dying," he
said gently, his eyes pleading as more of the door gave way. "It's
temporary. The net... It was designed to heal things like this, but
not on this scale. With me here, I can help guide the healing
process so that he'll recover all of his memory, his essence... what
you might even call a soul."

I swallowed hard, still unable to wrap my head around the
fact that I was staring at Grey, even talking to him, but only Leo
was there.

He reached up, his gesture tentative and uncertain, and
wiped away the tear starting to slide down my cheek.

"I'm doing everything in my power to help him. It was all I
could think to do. You're my friend, and I know losing him would
devastate you, so I had to do something. I promise I will do whatever I can to repair the damage to his cerebral cortex and restore
his memories and personality in the process. But I can't do that if
we don't get out of here. We have to move."

His words reached me, easing some of the tumultuous

emotions that were causing me to freeze, and I latched onto something, anything, that would help me avoid dealing with the fact that Grey was gone and Leo was there in his place. I could deal with that after we got out. We just had to get out, first, especially now. If Grey fell into their hands, then Leo went with him, and... I didn't even want to deal with the rest of that scenario.

"What's the plan?"

The lights will shut off, and I will take out the guards who enter, but there will be more. Go left down the hall. I've got your back. He transmitted his thoughts directly to my net, and while the sudden reversion to the violent buzz of the net was bone jarring, the sound of his words without Grey's voice helped steady me by being familiar.

"Can you fight?" I asked, and I saw Leo's confident smirk—so similar to Grey's own—grow as he gripped two batons in his hands before the lights went out.

I'd say watch me, but you aren't going to be able to see this part.

As he spoke, I heard the sound of movement as the people rushing into the room drew up short, and then I felt Grey move, a gentle breeze on my face marking his passing. Then the sounds of violence—sharp *zzts* and pops as blue bursts of electricity began to flash in the darkness, like bright lightning in the distant desert on a moonless night.

I heard the sounds of bodies falling, men and women alike crying out in pain or surprise. I was jostled once, someone falling back into me, and I managed to catch them before they fell completely on me, pushing them to one side.

Lights on in five, four, three, two, one... I shut my eyes right before the lights came on, giving myself a moment to adjust, and then yanked them open. Seven men and women lay on the floor in various states of unconsciousness, with Grey standing in the middle of them, panting heavily, the batons clutched loosely in his hands.

"The human body has so many limitations," he panted, and I shot him a look as I climbed to my feet. More and more shouts sounded from the hallway. I grabbed Grey's arm, hauling him out the door. Men and women were rushing up from both directions, but I focused on the left, following Leo's orders.

I threw a lash up to the low ceiling and leaned into the swing, legs forward to meet the crowd. I slammed into the head man, hoping to knock them all back, but those behind him reacted quickly, stepping to one side. I saw it happen in time and held back detaching my lash, allowing the swing to carry me back and away, but someone reached out with a quick hand and grabbed my boot. I kicked out with my other foot, felt a satisfying crunch, and then detached, pulling my baton out from under my arm.

I reached out with one arm, zapping the person closest to me, and then ducked under an arm meant to grab me, stepping deeper into the crowd. I pulled up my hand and pressed the button on the pulse shield, using it at point blank range. The angle was off—it was between two people and not directed fully at one—but that had the added benefit of blowing them both side-ways, away from each other and into a few of their comrades. I grinned as I realized the pulse shield could be fun in more ways than one.

Someone shoved me from behind, catching me by surprise, and I fell forward, tripping over a downed body and barely catching myself on the wall before I went completely down. I turned and ducked in time for the fist leveled at my face to sail overhead and strike the wall with a sharp crunch.

The heel of my hand was already driving toward my assailant's knee, and I felt it hit the side of it. I followed through, shoving my arm as if I were driving my shoulder through the leg, and I felt something give as a masculine voice bellowed in agony overhead.

I dove through the gap it created and turned, expending another blast from the pulse shield. The four people still standing were flung back, their limbs flailing, and I watched as Grey barely missed getting hit by rolling under them, rising to his feet after they were past and waving for me to keep moving forward instead of waiting for him.

I turned and began to run, my arms and legs pumping. I shot a glance over my shoulder to see Grey a few feet away, and the shifting walls between patient rooms shooting up behind us to block any attempt at pursuit. I wasn't sure, but it seemed that Leo was somehow still controlling the system even though he was outside of it.

"We're not out of the woods yet!" Grey shouted as he sprinted past me. He rounded a corner, and I used my lashes to keep up, his speed breakneck.

He led us through the halls and to an elevator, and before I could tell him it was in lockdown—the entire Medica was, by now —a platform appeared, welcoming us. We shot up quickly, both of us panting—him more than I—and I looked at him.

"Where are we—"

He held up a finger, and I looked up in time to see the end of the tube rapidly approaching, dead-ending in a big red circle with a white slash through it. I realized then that we were moving much faster than a normal elevator should, and instinctively moved closer to him, reaching for his hand.

He was still for a moment, and then his fingers squeezed mine. We came to a quick stop—so quick that it left my heart pounding—and then Grey was pulling me forward. I followed him, and then paused when I realized we were back in the shell. Somehow, Grey had managed to override the Medica's computers and bypass the elevator security controls.

No. *Leo* had done that. Grey was just unknowingly carrying him around.

I dropped his hand like it had burned me and took a step back.

"Liana?" Leo asked, his concern etched in such a hauntingly familiar way that it unnerved me. "Are you okay?"

"Gonna need a few seconds here, Leo," I said, sucking in a deep breath in an effort to calm the squeamishness of my stomach.

There was a rustling sound, indicating he had moved, followed by, "I'm sorry, Liana. This is making you uncomfortable, isn't it?"

"A little bit," I admitted. It was more than a little bit, if I was honest with myself, because I couldn't look at Leo and not see Grey. I had no idea how Grey felt—if he felt, if he was even aware. "Can Grey hear me?"

"Not at the moment," Leo replied, his voice contrite. "And not for a while, I'm afraid."

"H-How long do you think it will take before he gets better?" I asked.

There was a pause, long enough to cause me to turn around and meet his gaze. "I don't know. This... No one's ever attempted this before. The net wasn't designed to repair this much damage, and it's delicate work. I'm still assessing how much damage there is. It's hard since the wound is new, but I hope that within a few weeks, you'll start to see some of Grey's personality return. But I... I really can't say."

I nodded, trying to keep the rising tide of panic at bay. A few weeks was going to be really hard with Leo inside of Grey. I was grateful to Leo, yes, because I knew in my heart that he was trying to help Grey. But that didn't change the fact that he wasn't Grey.

I just really wanted him to be right that Grey was going to be okay. That he was going to remember me when he woke up. That he *would* wake up. And that I wouldn't lose him forever and have to see Leo in his body for the rest of his life.

How will he feel waking up and finding Leo in his body? a dark voice whispered in my mind, and I felt sickened, recalling when I had undergone Medica treatment to improve my rank. I had lost an entire week, and when I woke up, it was like waking up to the life of a stranger. I had felt violated, and that had just been with Prim, a more Tower-friendly version of myself. This was a fully realized AI—he was basically another person.

My heart shuddered at the thought, and I turned away from Leo. This wasn't the time: Leo was trying to help Grey the only way he could. And that was the only way I could look at this if I wanted to be able to function with him for the next few weeks.

"We have to go," I said, suddenly very tired.

"I agree. It's only a matter of time before they..." Leo trailed off, cocking Grey's head as he looked up. "Several people are approaching us very quickly," he announced, spinning around. I whirled too, in time to see several dark-clad figures wearing hoods and masks appear. My mind immediately recognized them as Inquisition agents, and I charged, my hand extending.

One of them darted forward, something long and dark coming from their hand and stretching out toward me. It looked a lot like a lash, but was thicker and less flexible. It struck me across the chest, landing with a thud. I had a moment to register the crackle of electricity before I was thrown backwards, slamming into something hard and then hitting the ground.

***

I had blacked out, and when I woke up, it was to darkness and muffled breathing. I jerked my head around, trying to find some sort of light. Something scraped over my face. A bag was over my head.

My hands were bound behind my back, and as I jerked around, I realized that I was hanging from something. And moving. I opened my mouth to scream, and realized that whoever had attacked us had placed some sort of adhesive over my mouth, muffling the sound.

I still tried, struggling violently, attempting to break free, to get as far away as possible. The people I realized had me dangling between them held fast, though, tightening their grips.

"Who are you?" I demanded, managing to make myself heard through the bag despite the adhesive.

"Relax," chuckled a voice that was alarmingly familiar.

"L-Lacey?" I gasped, twisting my neck back and forth, trying to pinpoint where the Lead Engineer was standing based on the sound of her husky voice.

"In the flesh. And might I congratulate you on your fast work with Devon? I mean, I knew you were going to do it, but that is some turnaround."

"What are you doing? Where's Le—" I caught myself just in time. "Grey? Where are you taking me?!"

"Relax, Liana. We're just upholding our end of the deal. Now shut up, all right? We got a long way to go, and nobody can know we have you."

READY FOR THE NEXT PART OF LIANA'S STORY?

Dear Reader,

Thank you for reading *The Girl Who Dared to Stand*. I hope you enjoyed it!

The next book in the series, **The Girl Who Dared to Descend**, Book 3, releases **November 6th, 2017**.

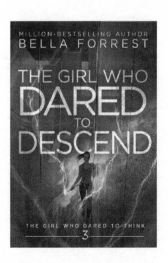

Visit: www.bellaforrest.net for details.

I'm *thrilled* to continue this journey with you!

See you on November 6th, back in the Tower...

Love,

Bella x

P.S. If you're new to my books or haven't yet read my **Gender Game** series, I suggest you check it out. It is where the Tower's story began and is set in the same world as *The Girl Who Dared* series—the two storylines complement each other.

P.P.S. Sign up to my VIP email list and I'll send you a personal heads up when my next book releases: **www.morebellaforrest.com**

(Your email will be kept 100% private and you can unsubscribe at any time.)

P.P.P.S. I'd also love to hear from you — come say hi on Twitter (@ashadeofvampire) or Facebook (facebook.com/BellaForrestAuthor). I do my best to respond :)

THE GIRL WHO DARED TO THINK

The Girl Who Dared to Think (Book 1)

The Girl Who Dared to Stand (Book 2)

The Girl Who Dared to Descend (Book 3)

THE GENDER GAME (Completed series)

The Gender Game (Book 1)

The Gender Secret (Book 2)

The Gender Lie (Book 3)

The Gender War (Book 4)

The Gender Fall (Book 5)

The Gender Plan (Book 6)

The Gender End (Book 7)

A SHADE OF VAMPIRE SERIES

Series 1: Derek & Sofia's story

A Shade of Vampire (Book 1)

A Shade of Blood (Book 2)

A Castle of Sand (Book 3)

A Shadow of Light (Book 4)

A Blaze of Sun (Book 5)

A Gate of Night (Book 6)

A Break of Day (Book 7)

Series 2: Rose & Caleb's story

A Shade of Novak (Book 8)

A Bond of Blood (Book 9)

A Spell of Time (Book 10)

A Chase of Prey (Book 11)

A Shade of Doubt (Book 12)

A Turn of Tides (Book 13)

A Dawn of Strength (Book 14)

A Fall of Secrets (Book 15)

An End of Night (Book 16)

Series 3: The Shade continues with a new hero...

A Wind of Change (Book 17)

A Trail of Echoes (Book 18)

A Soldier of Shadows (Book 19)

A Hero of Realms (Book 20)

A Vial of Life (Book 21)

A Fork of Paths (Book 22)

A Flight of Souls (Book 23)

A Bridge of Stars (Book 24)

Series 4: A Clan of Novaks

A Clan of Novaks (Book 25)

A World of New (Book 26)

A Web of Lies (Book 27)

A Touch of Truth (Book 28)

An Hour of Need (Book 29)

A Shade of Dragon 2

A Shade of Dragon 3

A SHADE OF KIEV TRILOGY

A Shade of Kiev 1

A Shade of Kiev 2

A Shade of Kiev 3

THE SECRET OF SPELLSHADOW MANOR

The Secret of Spellshadow Manor (Book 1)

The Breaker (Book 2)

The Chain (Book 3)

The Keep (Book 4)

The Test (Book 5)

The Spell (Book 6)

BEAUTIFUL MONSTER DUOLOGY

Beautiful Monster 1

Beautiful Monster 2

DETECTIVE ERIN BOND (Adult thriller/mystery)

Lights, Camera, GONE

Write, Edit, KILL

For an updated list of Bella's books, please visit her website:
www.bellaforrest.net

Join Bella's VIP email list and she'll personally send you an email
reminder as soon as her next book is out: www.morebellaforrest.com